The Day We Meet Again

Miranda Dickinson

ONE PLACE. MANY

D0260270

HQ
An imprint of HarperCollins*Publishers* Ltd
1 London Bridge Street
London SE1 9GF

This edition 2019

1
First published in Great Britain by
HQ, an imprint of HarperCollins*Publishers* Ltd 2019

Copyright © Miranda Dickinson 2019

Miranda Dickinson asserts the moral right to be identified as the author of this work.
A catalogue record for this book is available from the British Library.

ISBN: 9780008323219

MIX
Paper from
responsible sources
FSC™ C007454

This book is produced from independently certified FSC™ paper to ensure responsible forest management.

For more information visit: www.harpercollins.co.uk/green

This book is set in 10.7/15.5 pt. Caslon

Printed and bound in Great Britain by
CPI Group (UK) Ltd, Croydon, CR0 4YY

For Bob and Flo –
my two curly-headed serendipities and proof that
life is endlessly surprising. I love you to the moon
and back and twice around the stars xx

'Take chances, make mistakes.
That's how you grow.'
Mary Tyler Moore

THE DAY WE MET

14th June 2017

Chapter One

PHOEBE

ALL TRAINS DELAYED, the sign reads.

No, no, *no*! This can't be happening!

I stare up at the departure board in disbelief. Up until twenty minutes ago my train had been listed as ON TIME and I'd allowed myself a glass of champagne at St Pancras' Eurostar bar, a little treat to steady my nerves before the biggest adventure of my life begins.

'Looks like we aren't going anywhere soon,' the woman next to me says, gold chains tinkling on her wrist as she raises her hand for another glass. She doesn't look in a hurry to go anywhere.

But I am.

I arrived at St Pancras two hours early this morning. The guys driving the cleaning trucks were pretty much the only people here when I walked in. They performed a slow, elegant dance around me as I dragged my heavy bag across the shiny station floor. I probably should have had a last lie-in, but my stomach has been a knot of nerves since last night, robbing me of sleep.

I'm not always early, but I was determined to be today to make sure I actually get on the train. I want this adventure more than anything else in my life, but doubts have crept in over the last two weeks, ever since all the tickets were booked and my credit card had taken the strain. Even last night – frustratingly wide awake and watching a film I didn't really care about, after the farewell drinks in our favourite pub in Notting Hill when I was *so* certain I was doing the right thing – I found myself considering shelving the trip. Who jacks in everything and takes off for a year, anyway? Certainly not me: Phoebe Jones, 32 years old and most definitely *not* gap-year material.

It wasn't just *that thing* Gabe said, either. Although it threw me when it happened. After all his bravado inside the pub – the *You won't go through with it, Phoebs, I know you* speech that in his actor's voice rose above the noise and look-at-me-I'm-so-important laughter from the tables around us – the change in him when he found me on the street outside was a shock.

'I'll miss you.'

'You won't, but thanks.'

And then that look – the one that got us into trouble once before, the one that has kept me wondering if it might again. 'Then you don't know me, Phoebs. London won't be the same without you.'

Why did he have to launch that at me, the night before I leave for a whole year?

But the money is spent. The tickets are in my wallet. My bag is packed. And Gabe is *wrong* if he thinks I won't go through with it. I know my friends privately think I'll cave in and come home early. So I got up hours before I needed to this morning, took my bag, closed the door on my old life and posted my keys through the letterbox for my friends and former flatmates to find. And I'm *here*, where Gabe was so certain I wouldn't be.

But now there's a delay and that's dangerous for me. Too much time to think better of my plan. Why is the universe conspiring against me today?

'Having another?' the woman next to me asks. Her new glass of champagne is already half empty. Perhaps she has the right idea. Maybe drinking your way through a delay is the best option.

'I don't think so, thanks,' I reply. I can't stay here, not until I know exactly what kind of delay I'm facing. 'I'm going to find out what's happening.'

The woman shrugs as I leave.

The whole of St Pancras station seems to have darkened, as though a storm cloud has blown in from the entrance and settled in the arcing blue-girdered roof. Beyond the glass the sun shines as brightly as before, the sky a brave blue. But I feel the crackle of tension like approaching thunder.

At the end of the upper concourse near the huge statue of a man and woman embracing, a crowd has gathered. Somewhere in the middle, a harassed station employee in an orange hi-vis gilet is doing his best to fend off the angry mob's questions. And then, without warning, the crowd begins to move. I'm almost knocked over and stagger back to stop myself falling. Being trampled to death is definitely not in the plan today.

The mob swarms around the station employee as he makes for the stairs to the lower concourse. The forward motion of their bodies pushes me backwards until my spine meets something immovable. I gasp. Around me the angry commuters part, a splitting tide of bodies flooding either side of me, their feet stomping inches from mine. Once they pass me they continue their pursuit of their prey as the poor station official flees down the stairs.

I'm shaken, but then I remember: I hit something. *Someone*.

'I'm *so* sorry,' I rush, turning to see the poor unfortunate soul I've slammed into. But my eyes meet the kind, still expression of an iron man in trilby and suit, his billowing mackintosh frozen in time as he gazes up, as though checking the departure boards for his train.

The Betjeman statue.

I'd forgotten he was here. Compared with the huge iron lovers beneath the enormous station clock over the entrance, he's diminutive. I've seen visitors double take when they find him. He's just *there*, standing in the middle of the upper concourse, humble and friendly. The only thing marking him out as a statue and not another train passenger is the ring of slate around his feet, the words of one of his poems carved into it in beautifully elegant script. I've heard station announcements asking commuters to meet people *by the Betjeman statue* when I've been here before and thought nothing of it. But finding him here this morning, when everything has suddenly become so uncertain, is strangely comforting.

'I don't think he minds,' a voice says.

I jump and peer around the statue. 'Sorry?'

Over the statue's right shoulder, a face grins at me. 'Sir John. He won't mind you bumped into him. He's a pretty affable chap.'

Laughter dances in his voice, his green eyes sparkling beneath dark brows and a mess of dark curls. And I instantly feel I know him.

'I can't believe I just apologised to a statue.'

'Happens to us all, sooner or later.' His hand reaches around Sir John's arm. 'Hi, I'm Sam. Sam Mullins. Pleased to meet you.'

I hesitate. After all, this is London and my seven years in the city have taught me strangers are supposed to stay anonymous. But Sam's smile is as warm and inviting as a newly opened doorway on a winter's night and – suddenly – I'm accepting his handshake. His hand is warm around mine.

'Phoebe Jones. Pleased to meet you, too.'

The concourse is eerily empty now; the raging commuters all disappeared to the lower floor chasing the poor man from the train company. It's as if me and Sam-with-the-smiling-eyes-and-laugh-filled-voice are the only people in the world.

Apart from the statue, that is.

'Did you get to hear what the bloke from the station was saying?' I ask, suddenly aware I am still holding Sam's warm hand, and quickly pulling mine away.

'Most of it, before the mob closed in. They've stopped all trains in and out of the station. I haven't heard the Inspector Sands announcement, so I'm guessing it isn't a fire or a bomb threat.'

My stomach twists again. I've only heard the automated announcement used to alert station staff to a possible emergency like a fire or a bomb once before at Euston and I ran from the station like a startled hare then. Given my nerves about my journey, if I'd heard Inspector Sands being mentioned today I would already be halfway to Holborn. 'Did he say how long it was expected to last?'

'Well, I heard four hours, but there were so many people yelling around the chap by then I guess anyone could have said that.'

'*Four hours?*'

'Nightmare, huh? Trust me to pick today to make the longest train journey.'

I blink at him. 'Me too.'

'Oh? Where are you headed?' His eyes widen and he holds up a hand. 'Sorry, you don't have to answer. That was rude of me.'

It's sweet and it makes me smile. 'Paris, actually. To begin with. You?'

'Isle of Mull. Eventually.'

'Oh. Wow. That *is* a journey.'

He shrugs. 'Just a bit. Already had to change it because of the engineering works at Euston, so I'm going from here to Sheffield, then over to Manchester then changing again for Glasgow. Going to stay with two of my old university mates near there for a night or two, to break it up a bit. Then I'll catch a train to Oban, take the ferry to Craignure and then it's a long bus ride to Fionnphort, where I'm staying with a family friend.' He gives a self-conscious laugh. 'More than you wanted to know, probably.'

Although I'll move on from Paris later, Sam's journey sounds epic and exhausting by comparison. And it's strange, but I don't even consider that I've just met him, or question how he can share his entire travel itinerary with me when we don't know each other. Like the heat from his hand that is still tingling on my skin, it feels like the most natural thing. So I forget my nerves, my shock at finding myself here beside the statue, and the looming delay. And instead, I just see Sam.

'How long will all that take?'

'The whole journey? *Hours*. Days, even.' He laughs. 'It's okay. I have several books in my luggage and my music. I'll be fine.'

Novels are one thing I do have, although they are safely packed at the bottom of my bag. Books are the reason I'm here, after all. The Grand Tours across Europe inspired my PhD and have underpinned all my dreams of seeing the places the authors wrote about for myself. My much-loved copy of *A Room with a View* is in my hand luggage and I'm more than happy to hang out with Lucy Honeychurch and George Emerson for the thousandth time, but I'd much rather be on the train heading off already.

What if this delay is a sign? I hate the thought of Gabe being right, but the doubts from last night return, swirling around me, Sam and Sir John Betjeman like ragged ghosts. *There are other ways of pursuing a great adventure*, they call. *You don't have to spend a year away to prove you're spontaneous...* My room at the flat-share is already someone else's but I could persuade one of my friends to let me stay at theirs until I can sort out a new place. I don't really want to go home to Evesham, but I know my parents and brother Will would love having me to stay for a bit. Maybe I should be a bit less intrepid – Cornwall would be nice this time of year, or maybe the Cotswolds? Safer, closer, easier to come home from...

I don't want to doubt this now, not when I'm so close to boarding the train, but I can feel panic rising.

But then, Sam Mullins smiles – and the ground beneath me shifts.

'Look, if you're not going anywhere for a while and neither am I, how about we find a coffee shop to wait in?'

Did I just say that? But in that moment, it feels right. Who says my new, spontaneous self can't start until I board the train for France?

'Yes,' he says, so immediately that his answer dances with the end of my question. 'Great idea.'

As we walk away from the statue of Sir John Betjeman, Sam's fingers lightly brush against my back.

And *that's* when I fall in love.

Chapter Two

SAM

What am I doing?

I hate complications. As a musician I've done my level best over the years to avoid them wherever I can. When band politics have got too much, I've quit. When my brother stopped talking to me, I walked away. When relationships have become too demanding, I've backed out. Simple. Effective. Safe.

And I've been doing okay with that. Mostly. The last four years have been the happiest of my life professionally – playing my fiddle in studio sessions in the winter and spring and joining festival-bound bands in the summer; teaching where I've needed to make up shortfalls; even scoring studio time for my own new-folk project and producing a half-decent EP that, touch wood, will bring in a steady flow of cash on iTunes and Bandcamp. And my new studio venture with Chris that we launched last night finally gives us a chance to make real money. To be fair, I said I'd postpone this trip so close to the launch, but Chris said he wants to get it running smoothly and I'd just be getting in his way. So that complication has been ironed out, without me even trying. Why would I willingly volunteer for one to take its place?

She just looked so lost by the Betjeman statue.

And gorgeous…

I should have been annoyed by this unplanned delay to the journey I've promised myself for years. I've waited so long for the time to be right and then, suddenly, it was. Time to make the journey to find who I am. It was supposed to begin now, not in four hours, or whenever the train system deems it possible. Train delays are the worst, especially for a jobbing musician travelling to gigs across the country and particularly given the shenanigans I've already encountered changing stations for this journey. On any other day I would have been right in the thick of that angry commuter mob, baying for someone's blood.

But I'm not.

And it's all because of Phoebe Jones.

I glance at the large ironwork clock over the coffee concession counter and I'm surprised to see almost an hour has passed already. She was shy at first, but as soon as she suggested we come here she just – *blossomed*. Like watching a water lily unfurl on the other side of the bleached-wood table.

It's beautiful to witness.

'I know a year away is a big step. I mean *enormous* for me. But ever since I first read *A Room with a View* and Mark Twain's *A Tramp Abroad*, I've dreamed of doing this. Paris, Florence, Rome – seeing the places the authors and characters in their books saw. I've saved forever to do it. My parents gave me the last bit of the money I needed when I got my PhD last month.'

'So you're *Dr* Jones?'

I could bask in the way she beams for a long time.

'That sounds so funny, doesn't it? Dr Jones. I like it but it still feels like it should belong to somebody else.'

'A PhD is a huge amount of work, though. You've earned it.'

'I have.' There's a self-conscious laugh she does that's like a flash of sunlight. Blink and you'll miss it. 'I loved every minute of it, though. It was such a surprise to find that from a piece of work.'

'Maybe that's what you're supposed to be doing.'

'How do you mean?'

'Well, like for me, playing and gigging and the studio I've just set up with my friend – none of that's easy. It's all long hours and hard work' – I nod at the concourse beyond the coffee concession window which is packed with stranded passengers – 'and train delays… But I'm energised by it, you know? Because this is what I'm meant to do.'

Phoebe nods but she isn't smiling. 'I hear that all the time. My best friends all seem to have found what they're meant to be doing. Meg's the most amazing event organiser, Osh is a film director and Gabe is an actor. When they talk about what they do, it's like they are describing a piece of themselves; like if you put them under a microscope their job titles would be imprinted on every cell. I haven't found what I should be doing yet. But I think this year I might get closer to working out what I want.'

'Do you write?'

A patter of pink traverses her cheekbones. 'No – well, not unless you count my PhD dissertation. I mean, I love the idea of writing fiction, but I wouldn't know where to begin. Gabe says I'm not personally tormented enough to be a writer. I don't know if that's a good thing or not.'

She isn't wearing a ring – I mean, of course I've checked. But she's mentioned *Gabe* a few times already and I notice her right hand instinctively touches the finger on her left that would have worn one when she says his name. Who is he? A recent flame? An ex? An unrequited love?

'He thinks I can't do this. But I know I can.'

'Why do you care about what he thinks? He sounds like a knob.'

She laughs. The sound is joyous. It surges up from her core, like champagne bubbles. 'Maybe he is. But I've always talked to him about everything. We used to trade awful dating stories when both of us were between dates – it became a game we'd play to make ourselves feel better.' She toys with the teaspoon in the saucer of her almost empty cup. 'So, enough about me. What's taking you to Scotland? Work?'

'No. Well, maybe a little.' I see a fine line form between her brows. That's me sussed. 'I'm going for personal reasons,' I reply. And then, just because it feels like she's the person to say it to, I say more than I have to anyone else. 'I was born on the Island and then my father left home. He played fiddle, too, although he left before I discovered music for myself. I guess I've always wondered, you know? What happened to him.' Suddenly aware I've said too much to be comfortable, I pull back. 'But I plan to hook up with some friends from the circuit while I'm there, too. Relearn the trad stuff.'

'You're a folk musician?'

'New-folk, I guess you'd call it. But I want my next project to be the old tunes I vaguely remember from being a kid on the Island.'

'I thought you had a bit of a Scottish accent.' She blushed. 'I'm sorry, should that be *Hebridean*?'

It's the most hesitantly British thing to say and it's all I can do not to laugh out loud. 'Scottish is fine.'

'So you're going home?'

Home. That's a word I haven't used for a while. With Ma gone and my brother Callum as good as dead, I don't know what I call home any more. The flat I've been sharing with my drummer mate Syd is homely, but is it *home*? Is that what I'll discover in Mull when I return?

'I don't know. Maybe. You?'

I've asked it before I can think better, but here in the too-warm crush of the coffee concession, I realise I want to know the answer. I expect her to sidestep the question, but to my utter surprise, she doesn't.

'Not a home to live in. I want to find out how to be at home with myself.'

Until that moment, everything Phoebe Jones has told me could just have been polite conversation. But this is something else. It's a window, inviting me in. I lean closer, zoning out the clamour and conversation around our small table, not wanting to miss a thing.

'Me too.'

Her eyes hold mine.

'I haven't said that to anyone before.'

'Not even Gabe?'

'Especially not him. He thinks I'm too serious.'

'No!'

'I know, right? I mean, look at us, Sam. We met – what – an hour ago? And all we've done is laugh.'

'You're a very funny lady.'

'Well, thank you for noticing.' Her eyes sparkle as she mirrors my grin. There is so much more going on behind those eyes than she's allowing me to see. I sense it bubbling away, just out of view.

And *that's* when I realise.

Sam Mullins, your timing stinks.

The more we talk, as the minutes become an hour and head towards two, the more the feeling deep within me builds. Phoebe Jones is *perfect*. And I know my own battered heart. I'd sworn I wouldn't fall for anyone again, not after Laura. The pain and injustice I've battled most of the year and the bruises still stinging my soul have all been good enough reasons to avoid falling in love.

Could this be love?

No.

But what if it is?

By now we are wandering the concourse, passing crowds of stranded travellers. Every available bench has been commandeered and people are claiming the floor, too, perched on makeshift seats made from suitcases, holdalls and folded-up coats. It's like a scene from a disaster movie, displaced people caught in limbo, dazed by the experience. Some groups of travellers are even *talking to each other*. In London, that's pretty close to a miracle.

I have to step to the side to avoid a small child who's weaving in and out of the crowd – and when I do my hand brushes against Phoebe's. Startled, she looks up and our eyes meet. The noise around us seems to dim, the pushing bodies becoming a blur as I sink into the deep darkness of Phoebe's stare.

'Do you believe in fate, Phoebe?' The words tumble out before I can stop them.

'I think I do,' she breathes, as her fingers find mine. 'Do you?'

I gaze at her, a hundred thoughts sparkling around us like spinning stars. And suddenly, all that matters is the truth.

'I didn't before today.'

Chapter Three

PHOEBE

He feels it, too. Whatever is happening between us is real.

The moment Sam's fingers lace though mine, the air between us seems to shift. I don't even think about pulling away.

We move at glacial pace through the crowded concourse until Sam spots a gap for a service door between the glass-fronted concessions and we sneak into it.

Now we're standing within a breath of each other. It would be so easy to close the distance and kiss him...

What am I doing?

Twenty-four hours ago I wouldn't have considered kissing someone I hardly knew. But twenty-four hours ago I didn't know Sam existed. Our hands are joined between us and we both look down as if seeing them for the first time. When Sam laughs, I feel the buzz of it through his skin.

'Well, this is unexpected.'

'It is.'

This is where my apologies and caveats would normally begin, my usual rush to backtrack on an impulse. But instead, calmness fills the space where those words would be. They're not needed here.

I've only known Sam for a couple of hours. How can this be possible?

'Reckon they can delay our trains for another four months or so?' His whisper is warm velvet against my ear.

'Only four months?'

I love his laugh. It shudders up from his chest to his shoulders, throwing his head back as it escapes into the air around us. It's wild and unbridled, unconcerned by anyone else's opinion. His laugh is who he is, as if his spirit shimmers out of him in that moment.

His fingers squeeze mine. 'Oh well, excuse me. What I meant was four years. Forty-four years. Four *centuries*.'

'Steady on…'

'Even when we're wrinkly and incontinent and basically breathing dustbags our love will burn as bright…'

I don't know whether I'm breathless from laughter or just being here with Sam. He's talking as if we've been together for years, but it doesn't scare me like it should. I can imagine being loved by him, even though I've yet to kiss him. It's a game that feels so much more than make-believe. And I'm happy to play along. 'Thank you for your faith in us.'

'My pleasure. This is surreal, isn't it?'

'Completely.'

'There are a million things I want to ask you. I don't even know where to begin.'

'Then let's begin here…' I dare to flatten my palm against his chest, feeling the unfamiliar rhythm of his heart through the faded fabric of his T-shirt. This heart has been beating for years, I think, and I never knew.

For a while we stay like this, saying nothing, the only movement our breath and heartbeats, the familiar-unfamiliar sensation of closeness surrounding us.

Then without warning, I'm crying.

Mortified, I try to smother my sobs, jamming my eyelids shut to squeeze the tears back. But it's too late. Sam breaks the embrace and lifts my chin with his hand.

'Are you crying? Phoebe, why are you crying?'

'I'm sorry…' I rush, but speaking flicks a switch that releases more. I don't want Sam to see, don't want to break this perfect, wonderful moment. What will he think of me? I don't even know what to think of myself.

I don't cry much in front of other people – never in public and certainly not with someone I hardly know. But I *do* know Sam, crazy as it sounds. So despite every scrap of head-logic screaming at me to stop, my heart won't listen. It feels wrong but it seems like I don't have much choice.

'Hey, hey… Let's sit down, okay?'

'There isn't any room.'

'Then we make room.' He slips the strap of the violin case from his shoulder and places it on one side, his rucksack on the other. In the space between he concertinas his body down until he's sitting cross-legged, reaching up for me. 'Your seat, milady.'

I laugh despite the tears staining my cheeks. 'I can't sit on your lap.'

He shrugs and slides his rucksack beside one leg. 'An alternative, then. Although, you'll need somewhere to sit when we're 400-year-old, hot-lovin' dustbags. You could just get used to it now.'

That smile will be the death of every argument we ever have, I think.

'Your rucksack will be perfect, thank you.' I sit, my legs still shaking from my sudden tears.

'Glad to help. Now, what's happening?'

I've heard loved-up friends of mine say things like, 'I see myself in his eyes', and 'when he looks at me it's like he can see into my soul' and always thought them ridiculous. I mean, I've dated guys with nice eyes before and I'm a fan of meaningful looks as much as the next person. But until this moment I thought it was the kind of clever phrase dreamed up by authors and screenwriters. Not anything you'd ever experience in real life. But when I lock eyes with Sam, it's like nothing I've experienced before. And I *can* see my reflection in the moss green of his irises.

'I don't know,' I say, embarrassed by the tremor in my voice. 'It's just I wasn't expecting this. To be so sure. I feel like I've known you forever, but I know hardly anything about you, about your life.'

He nods and I wonder if he feels it too. 'Then we should start there. Even if there are other more interesting things we could be doing…'

He's cheeky but I can't help smiling. 'Be serious.'

'I'm trying. Believe it or not my friends think I'm the serious one. Okay. Best start with the basics, I guess. Full name: Samuel Hamish Mullins—'

'Hamish?'

'Mock that and you're mocking my heritage, lady.'

I stuff my giggles away behind my hand. 'Sorry. It's a lovely name.'

'Tsk, typical English sarcasm. I know your game.' He grins. 'So, what else? I'm thirty-two, although my ma always said I was born with an old soul so nobody ever believes me when I tell them my age. Like I said, I was born on Mull, but I grew up in Edinburgh and Carlisle and moved to London when I was eighteen. Been here for more years than I'm comfortable admitting and I play tunes for money. I'm just under six feet tall, but I'll usually add an inch to feel better about it. Oh and I'm allergic to early mornings, although I'm quite glad I got up before eleven today. Done. You?'

It's strange to be trading introductions now, after everything else we've shared, but I find it strangely comforting, too.

'Phoebe Eilidh Jones, also thirty-two.'

'Eilidh? That's not a very English name.'

'That's because my great-granny was an Erskine from Paisley.' I like this card when I play it. He clearly had me pegged as a dyed-in-the-wool Anglo Saxon. *Shows what you know, Samuel Hamish Mullins*. 'She moved with my great-grandad to Evesham to take over a fruit farm with six children in tow.'

'So, Caledonian heritage all round. Excellent. I don't know any Eilidhs but I have an Auntie Ailish – she's not a blood relation, but my ma's best friend. I'm going to see her when I get to Mull.' He chuckles. 'So in another life we might have been Hamish and Eilidh. It has a ring to it, don't you think?'

'It does.'

'Continue, Phoebe Eilidh Jones.'

I giggle. 'Okay – I'm five feet six inches exactly and I'm quite happy with that. And I love early mornings. And late nights, actually. I don't sleep much.'

'How come?'

The truth is, I don't know. I remember as a kid being concerned that I'd miss something important if I slept, although I don't know where that fear originated. 'I've just always been that way. Although every few weeks I'll have a day when I just sleep a lot. Maybe it all evens out in the end.' I grin at him. 'So we're the same age. When's your birthday?'

'March 2nd. You?'

'May 4th. My life, I'm lusting after an older woman!'

I cuff his arm. 'Oi, watch it!'

'Hey, I'm not complaining. So what do you do for work – or rather, what *did* you do, considering you're taking a year off?'

'Oh all kinds of things. Most recently I've worked in a publicity office for a large West End company. It's fun.'

'But it's not what you wanted to do?'

'I like every job I've done. For a long time I thought I'd end up working in horticulture – I trained as a horticulturalist at college. And then I came to London to see my friend Meg and ended up staying. Then I did my PhD while working for Ebert and Soames Theatre Productions. But I do know that books will always be my first love. That's why I'm going to Europe.'

The thought of the journey makes my heart drop to the floor. Because getting on that train, whenever the gods of Network Rail deign that to be, will mean leaving Sam. And *this*. And *us*.

Chapter Four

SAM

We talk. About everything.

Well, everything we can think of, which in the grand scheme of things probably isn't even scratching the surface. The urgency takes me by surprise. It's as if we're trying to conduct a whole relationship in a few hours. Packing everything in so we can justify what our hearts knew immediately.

She sparkles when she learns stuff about me; shines when she shares things about herself. Playing catch-up has never been so thrilling.

And she's so close to me. On her rucksack perch, the length of one thigh is against mine and although I'm no longer holding her hand she keeps touching my arm as she talks. I feel like a kiss is in the air between us. One move from either of us could bring it into being.

It would be so easy to kiss her.

But I can't let it happen yet.

When you're always on tour – or always on call for a gig – you tend to make decisions quickly and regret them at leisure, but it's like you're in this loop. More times than I'll admit, I've started a relationship, gone away and returned in time for us to both admit it wasn't working. A weird way to conduct relationships, but then nothing about being a gigging musician is ever regular.

So much of what I'm learning talking to Phoebe is about myself. I even tell her about Laura – and though it's been six months since she left me for an annoying Russian conductor and stamped all over my heart, I haven't wanted to talk about her to anyone before.

'I'm sorry to hear that,' Phoebe says and I'm struck by how genuine this is. Most people say sorry when what they really want you to do is change the subject.

'It's hard to make relationships work in my line of business. Always heading off in opposite directions, too many hours between meetings to stop doubts setting in.' I realise how close this might be to Phoebe and my current situation. I push the thought away. 'With Laura, I thought I could make it work. And it did. Until the other bloke appeared.'

'Was Laura a musician, too?'

I nod. 'She's a session singer who also plays cello, violin and viola – and when string sections cost the earth to hire, she's a good person to know. In a few hours she could record all the parts a string quartet would perform, for a fraction of the cost. Saving money appeals to studios and record companies, so she always had more than enough work to keep her in one place. And I liked that, in the beginning. It was good to know she was there, even if I was called away on tour for weeks at a time.' The rawness returns to my gut. Time to move on. 'Anyway, she chose someone else. I started working to make the studio happen with my mate Chris and here we are.' I decide to hedge my bets. 'So, Gabe. Is he an ex?'

Her eyes widen and for a moment I think she might be offended. Then her shoulders slump a little. 'No. Not really. *Once*. But it was a mistake and we're still friends.'

'How long?'

'One night.' She pulls a face. 'That sounds terrible out loud, but it's the truth. One night, after drinking too much beer and both of us being dumped at the same time. I hardly remember anything and he was drunker than I was. Anyway, it was a mistake.'

A mistake I can deal with. But it makes me realise how little I know about her and how much I *want* to know. Even though Phoebe and I are cramming as much information as we can into the time we have together, it still feels like nowhere near enough. When she cried earlier, it shocked me. If I'd known her for a while longer I would have known how to be, but I'm flying blind with so much of this. My head is still trying to make sense of it all. My heart has no such confusion, which is confusing in itself.

I can't think about this now. There will be plenty of time once I'm on the train.

But do I even want to get on the train any more?

I was serious when I mentioned a longer delay to Phoebe. What if meeting her was meant to stop me going back to Scotland? What if this is life dealing me a last-minute detour that I'm supposed to take?

It wouldn't be the first time I delayed this trip.

I was supposed to visit Mull the year I turned 30 and was all set to go, but then I met Laura and put it back. I haven't been able to escape the thought that maybe if I'd followed my heart instead of my – well, you know – I might have had an easier time.

Phoebe could be another Laura.

I don't think I could bear that.

I check myself, refocus on the beautiful woman beside me. She is *not* Laura. She could well be the love of my life. So what do I do?

Phoebe has changed subject and is now talking about her childhood, growing up on a fruit farm in the Vale of Evesham.

'That sounds idyllic.' I catch her expression and hold up my hand.

'I mean, I'm sure it was hard work. But working in fruit orchards, being surrounded by your family – that sounds great.'

'I guess. When you're a teenager dreaming of being anywhere else but Evesham it doesn't seem like that.'

'Sure. I mean my growing up was a world away. When we moved to the mainland we lived in a series of dreary council estates in Edinburgh and Carlisle. Not quite as picturesque as a Worcestershire fruit farm.' I'm pretty certain Phoebe's mother wasn't a functioning alcoholic like mine, either, but I don't say that. I loved my ma, but I know she was never happy after my father, Frank Mullins, disappeared. 'Mind you, I have one of the places we lived in Edinburgh to thank for this.' I pat my violin case.

'How did that happen?'

'We were living in Dumbiedykes and Ma was friendly with the landlord of our local pub. He'd put bottles by for her behind the bar and it was my job to go fetch them. So I was waiting by the bar one evening and there was a group of regulars who always sat in the corner nearest the fire with their instruments. While I was waiting they just started playing. The pub was practically empty, save for them and, I don't know, I found it magical. To be so unworried by what anyone else thought and just be able to start playing like that. I shifted around the bar so I could be closer to them and then one of the old guys saw me watching and invited me to sit with them.'

'And that made you want to play the violin?'

'Yeah. A Polish guy called Jonas played the fiddle and I fell in love with how he made it sing. The way he played – it was the most beautiful thing I'd ever heard. And I wanted to play like him. He offered to show me a few tunes and for the next two years he gave me free lessons after school in the pub. The landlord let me stay because he liked the music and I guess he worked out that life wasn't the easiest at home. Funny how little bits of kindness like that can change your life.'

'He sounds like an amazing man.'

'He was. And more of a dad to me than mine ever was. But then my ma's cousin offered us use of her tiny granny flat in Carlisle. I was distraught about leaving Jonas but on the day I said goodbye, he gave me his second-best fiddle to take to my new home. And he said, "You were born to play this. Promise me you'll play every day." So I did. Every day since.'

Phoebe's eyes light up when she hears this. 'And that's why you're a musician now?'

'It is. I wanted to make Jonas proud of me.'

'Did you keep in touch?'

'For a while. But you know how things are. He moved, didn't leave a forwarding address. Hopefully, he's found a nice warm corner in a pub somewhere to play out his jigs and reels with a bunch of regulars. That's how I'll always picture him.'

'I know what you mean about how people we meet can change our lives. I fell in love with words when a customer left their copy of *Jane Eyre* in my parents' farm shop. It was the first grown-up novel I'd ever read. And, coincidentally, it led to the first lie I'd ever told, when the old lady who'd left it came back and I hid it under a stack of apple boxes beneath the counter.'

'Phoebe Jones, master criminal! *Now* I'm learning the truth.'

She blushes – and it's the most glorious sight.

Glorious, Sam? I don't think I've ever used that word before. What is she doing to me?

And then, in the middle of her laughter, Phoebe's smile vanishes. 'I don't want to get on the train, Sam.'

'What?'

'I don't think I can. And I can't ask you to miss your train – that's not what I'm saying… But how can we leave when *this* is happening? I'm scared if I go I'll miss it.'

'Like you feel about sleeping?'

She shifts position until she's looking straight into my eyes. 'It's more than that. What if we were supposed to meet instead of getting on our trains today? Or what if we were meant to travel together? I—' She exhales a breath, looks down. 'Oh, stuff it. I am the most organised person but this is the most disorganised thing I've ever done in my life and it scares me. I've told everyone I'm totally fine with going away but the truth is I've been tempted to talk myself out of it so many times. What if I somehow knew this was going to happen? Meeting you. What if—?'

'Phoebe – wait – stop.'

She clamps a hand to her mouth and her eyes glisten. I see fear bloom there and am acutely aware of my own. Slowly, I coax her hand away.

'Right – just take a breath. And listen to me. This isn't a *no*, okay? It's not a no. I just think…'

But she's shaking her head and I feel like I'm losing her already. Before we even get on the train. 'It's okay. I'm sorry. Let's just forget it and…'

And then I'm kissing her. It happens so instinctively that we're halfway into the kiss before I realise what I've done. It's the wrong time and the perfect time at once; the most ill-advised act but the one thing our time together was missing.

Phoebe doesn't pull away. As our kiss rises and falls she slides onto my lap and her tears dance down where her face touches mine. It isn't an answer. But it's what we both want.

I could stay there forever but eventually I move my head back. 'I think we should test this.'

'You're right,' she says. And suddenly it makes sense. 'We have to make these journeys. I just wish we were going together.'

'Me too. Maybe we could…?'

'No, I think you're right, Sam. Unless we test it, how will we know if this is what we both hope it is? I don't want to get a year down the line and realise we rushed in too soon.'

I try to wrestle every racing thought to order in my mind. I want Phoebe in my life and I don't want to wait for her. But we both have things to do – promises we've made to ourselves – and I know from experience with Laura that resentment always builds if you've put your own promises on hold. I don't want to feel like that again. I don't ever want Phoebe to feel that way about me.

Suddenly, a huge round of applause breaks like a hailstorm across the concourse, as loud as a dozen trains thundering into the station at once. We stand, our muscles stiff from sitting. Phoebe steps into the concourse and looks up at the Departures board.

'The delay signs have gone,' she says – and I see a battle in her face as she turns back to me. 'My train leaves in forty minutes.'

I don't want to look now. Because as soon as I do, everything changes. I want us to stay here, in our little square of station floor, just Phoebe and I. But she has a departure time, which means I do, too. Heart heavy, I raise my eyes.

'Mine leaves in half an hour.'

Chapter Five

PHOEBE

It feels like the whole of London is queuing.

Gone is the bulldog spirit that brought so many stranded travellers together: abandoned like the takeaway-food wrappers and carrier bags littering the concourse floor like mounds of freshly fallen snow. Now it's every person for themselves. The London attitude is back and you can almost feel the station itself breathe a relieved sigh at the return to normality. All anyone wants to do now is get on their trains and leave.

Except Sam and me.

But we need to leave, don't we?

I hate the realisation that has hit us both, that this serendipitous magic we have discovered in St Pancras station is coming to a rapid end. In less than an hour we'll be speeding as fast as possible in opposite directions, our own plans pushing us forward while our hearts gaze back at the widening gap between us.

That kiss. That kiss changed everything.

As we stand at the back of the queue for Sam's train I risk a glance at him, jumping when I realise he's already looking at me. The now familiar touch of his hand on mine is at once comforting and heartbreaking.

'What are we going to do?' I hate the fear in my question.

His eyes hold mine. They smile even though his lips don't. Sam lifts his hand to stroke my cheek and I see the rise of his chest as he inhales.

'We'll meet back here – in a year. Exactly twelve months from now. When we've had our adventures and made our journeys. Come home and meet me by—'

'—Betjeman,' I say, as our words collide. 'Where we first met.'

'We are getting far too good at spooky,' he grins, his arm pulling me close to him. 'But we'll only do it if we still feel the same. Things change. People change. You might find your heart lies elsewhere.'

'I won't.' I mean it, too. But he's shaking his head and I know he's right. This can only work if we're both certain. And a year is a long time to think about what we really want.

'You might. I might. We have to be free to walk away if it isn't what we want. So here's the deal: if you feel the same about me in twelve months' time, meet me by Betjeman' – he checks his watch – 'at eleven a.m. I'd say seven, when we actually met, but you know about me and early mornings.'

'Can we keep in touch while we're away? I don't think I could go a year without hearing from you.'

Sam looks up as if he might find the answers pressed against the glass roof panels. 'Absolutely. I'd lose my mind if we were silent for twelve months. But we need rules. We can't work out how we feel if we're always in contact. So – one phone call a month? I'd say video call but it depends on where we are.'

'And email,' I add. 'But only in emergencies.'

'Noted. Anything else?'

My brain feels rushed in the fast dwindling time we have together. If this is what my heart believes it is, we are at the beginning of the greatest love story of our lives. Emails and phone calls don't seem significant enough. I imagine us telling the story when we're old to our wide-eyed grandchildren: *It was his emails that won my heart...* No, it needs to be something – timeless.

'Postcards,' I say. 'I won't be travelling all the time; it sounds like you won't be, either. So when we're in one place for a while, we can send postcards.'

He raises an eyebrow. 'I have rubbish handwriting.'

'Doesn't matter. It's powerful to write something down. It means more than typing. You have to think about it. And if your handwriting is *really* bad then deciphering it will keep me busy until the next one arrives.'

He considers this. Ahead of us the queue starts to move. The barriers are now open, slowly admitting impatient passengers.

'Okay, deal. But I can't promise to send you sonnets.'

I shrug. 'I don't expect Shakespeare. Just Sam.'

'I'm better with music than words.'

'So send me songs. Via email. In emergencies.'

We pull out phones, exchange numbers and email addresses and then Sam puts his arm around me, drawing me close as he takes a photo of us. He does the same with my phone. This will be my constant companion for the year ahead. I take another as he's looking over the heads of the queue – I want to remember Sam as I first saw him: an unguarded, non-posed moment that is just *him*. Secretly, I think I'll look at this image more. Without me in the frame, I can make sure all I see is Sam. That way my heart can be certain.

And then the people in front of us surge forward. Another barrier has been opened and a tide of bodies is rushing towards the gap. Sam's hand tightens around mine and my heartbeat quickens.

We've only just met. But time is running out on us already.

As we near the barrier, Sam steps to the side, gathering me into his arms. My lips find his first and our kiss says everything we no longer have time to express. I'm pulled tight against the warmth of his body, his jacket parting to let me lean against his chest. One arm holds me, the other hand brushes the side of my face. My fingers trace the line where his curls meet the soft skin at the back of his neck. It's startlingly new, but familiar all at once. I let myself melt into this moment, my thoughts of everything that lies ahead momentarily gone.

All that matters is *this*.

Us.

Sam and me.

And then we have no more time. The guy checking tickets at the barrier clears his throat and Sam takes one last look at me before shouldering his rucksack and swinging his violin case over the other shoulder.

'Phoebe, meet me by Betjeman, a year from today. If we're meant to be together, we'll both be there. If we're not, it was never meant to be.'

'I'll be there, Sam.'

He pauses for one moment longer, his smile sad and joyful, full of hope and promise.

Then he walks away.

I am on my own again. Lost in the sea of bodies dashing for their train. Except, as I hurry in the opposite direction to the upper concourse where my Eurostar train awaits me, I don't feel alone any more.

When I reach the top of the steps I see the statue of Sir John. As people jostle past me I pause beside him to pat the iron man's shoulder. His kind half-smile gives me hope, and his eyes are raised to the sky as if watching the future. *My* future.

No matter what happens this year, Sam, I will be waiting here for you.

I blow the statue a kiss and run for my train.

Chapter Six

SAM

I'm on the train.

I grab the things I need for the journey – the thick novel I probably won't read, my mobile, charger and the bag of fizzy cola bottle sweets my best friends DeeDee and Kim insisted on packing for me like I'm five years old. Then I stash my rucksack in the luggage section, place my violin case next to me and settle into my seat.

Who am I kidding? I can't settle.

I can't settle because of *you*.

That's another thing: why am I talking to you in my mind like you're still here? You're headed to a train that will be halfway under the Channel in less than an hour. Probably. Geography never was my strong point. Nor was timing.

I glance at my watch. Almost 1 p.m.

Six hours, Phoebe. Six hours since you changed my world.

And *now* I'm talking like a nutter on the night bus. Can today get any weirder?

The old mariner on the battered cover of my paperback eyes me suspiciously. I don't blame him. If I could have seen last night what six hours in the company of Phoebe Jones would do to me today, I would have been horrified.

Well, Sam Mullins, you are officially a sap. How does it feel?

I take a deep breath, stretch my hands across the table, blocking the old mariner's eyes, just in case he's in the mood for more judgement.

It feels…

… like my world just exploded into colour.

My heart is kicking out a double-time beat against my chest, a bass boom to my breath. My skin hums, like a low string section. I feel alive. Real. For the first time since I can't remember when. And it's because of you – *her*. I can't keep talking to you like it's *you*. That would just be weird.

My sigh fogs the window glass. I'm losing the plot.

I watch my fellow passengers hustling onto the train and notice how irritated they all look. That could have been me, if there'd been no delay this morning, no Phoebe Jones looking lost and wonderful by the Betjeman statue. I wouldn't trade places with them for anything.

She made me *feel*… Phoebe, *you* made me feel. Like I do when I play, only *you* made the music flooding my soul.

And now I'm *lyrical*. *Bloody hell, Sam*.

But maybe lyrical is who I want to be.

The glow inside remains as I take a breath and pick up my phone. My world might have altered but I still have a journey to make.

I wrote a list last night, at home, all packed with nothing else to occupy me. Laura had rocked up to the studio launch earlier, and though DeeDee and Kim saw her off, I was still rattled by it. The empty hours before bed were dangerous territory for my head. I know I don't love Laura any more but the bruise of her still remains on me. Even after meeting Phoebe.

I pull up the list on my phone now – names and telephone

numbers, half-recalled places, old friends I hope still remember me. First things first: uni friends.

I didn't attend university in Scotland, having moved to London the day I turned 18. But as my not-really-auntie Ailish says, Caledonian hearts find one another. My closest friends on my music degree course all hailed from north of the border. Maybe it was the comfort of finding people who spoke like me. I guess wherever we go in life we look for people who speak our language. It began with an accent; now music is the language I share with my closest friends.

We were a party of five Scots in a sea of southerners, and while now we mainly stay in touch via emails and Christmas cards, they are still closer than many of the people I see every day. Donal – forever known as D-Man because all of the other nicknames he accrued during our three years at King's College London aren't suitable for public utterance; Shona, religiously called *Shania* by every English student we encountered (but call her that at your peril); Kate – self-appointed agony aunt to us all and the loveliest person you could ever hope to have rooting for you; and Niven, fellow violinist and sadly destined to remain a frustrated musician working as a teacher on the island on which we were both born. I won't see Shona in Glasgow – last I heard she was touring Scottish schools with a Gaelic language show. Niven's on Mull, so I'll look him up when I get there. It will be good to hang out with him again.

Donal and Kate finally admitted what the rest of us had long known and are now happily married with three kids. It's their home I'm headed to first. Although I've already promised myself I won't tell anyone about Phoebe yet, I might make an exception if I get a moment alone with Kate. Of all my university pals I'm confident she'll understand. Depends on how much we drink, of course. Pretty sure Kate can still drink all of us under the table.

Thinking about my friends makes me feel better about pulling out of the station, knowing Phoebe will be boarding her train to Paris now. Maybe, if it all works out and she's waiting for me next year, I'll take her to meet the old crew. I think they'd like her.

Chapter Seven

PHOEBE

I'm going the wrong way.

I shouldn't be going to France. I should be going with you.

And I know we talked about it, and I accepted everything we said about being true to ourselves first, about testing how we feel to be sure. But I wish I hadn't agreed now.

I was so certain this was what I wanted, but… Then *you* happened.

Sam. *My* Sam.

I watch the blur of fields and green sidings passing the window and can't hide my smile. How did my life change in just one morning?

And that *kiss*. I don't think I've ever been floored by a kiss before.

I feel like we've shared an entire relationship in a few short hours. How is that even possible?

Last night, when my nerves were tumultuous as a storm, threatening to break over my head and sweep me away completely, I felt like I was teetering on the edge of the world. I don't think I've ever felt as alone as I did at 2 a.m. when I was close to calling the whole thing off.

I don't feel alone now.

Because even though we are fast moving away from one another in opposite directions, you're *with me*, Sam. I have the memory of you all over me. The whisper of your kiss still playing on my lips, the shiver of your touch still tingling on my skin. And this year will pass because every second is one closer to the day we meet again. When all our hurried promises will find space and time to be fulfilled. When I can feel your skin on mine and never let you go…

My phone buzzes on the table in front of me and I see my best friend Meg's grin illuminating the screen. Packing my thoughts of Sam away, I answer the call.

'Phee, hey! Are you okay? I just saw on the news about them closing St Pancras and King's Cross.'

'It's okay. I'm on the train. Not sure how good reception's going to be so don't worry if I disappear.'

'Do you have WiFi?'

'Yes.'

'Hang up and I'll call you back on Skype.'

Thirty seconds later her image appears again and I accept the call. 'So what happened?'

'I still don't know. But I'm moving now, so that's all that matters.' I suddenly remember the arrangement I'd made for the end of my journey today. In the whirlwind of Sam it was lost. 'Oh, Meg, Tobi doesn't know! I'm so sorry! In all the confusion I forgot to call him.' I didn't look at my phone, that is. Not once. Another startling change in my life I can thank Sam for.

'Relax, I just spoke to him. He says he'll come and meet you at Gare du Nord when you get in.'

'But the delay – he'll end up having wasted his entire day waiting for me. I can't ask him to do that. I'll just get a cab or walk when I get there.'

Meg's chuckle is bright and familiar and suddenly I'm homesick.

'Then you don't know him yet. He insisted. Luc might be with him, too.'

I first met Tobi when we hung out after one of Gabe's press screenings for *Southside*, the hit primetime crime drama he had a supporting role in. Tobi had the loudest laugh I've ever heard. He was sweet, though, and Meg adores him, which is the best recommendation you can get. He was the first to suggest I stay with him in Paris when Meg told him of my travel plan, which was the kindest gesture anyone's made for me. Meg visits him several times a year and was best woman when he and Luc married last spring at an achingly gorgeous turreted chateau in the Pyrenees. I haven't met Luc yet, but he sounds lovely, too.

'I'm due into Paris at three-twenty p.m., I think.'

'He'll be waiting for you by the barrier. He's making a sign, bless him, in case you don't remember what he looks like.'

'That's sweet.'

There's a pause, then: 'Phoebe, are you okay?'

'I'm fine.'

'Okay. It's just, you sound… *different*.'

Do I?

'I'm on a train, so…'

'It isn't that.'

'Oh.' Do I tell her about Sam? Meg is my closest, dearest friend and she would understand. No – it feels too soon. I like him being just mine for now. Maybe I'll tell her later.

'Don't worry. Probably just me being over-protective. We're all a bit lost without you here. Gabe found your key on the doormat this morning and went off in a total grump. He'll get over it, though. We all will. Have a safe journey and call me when you're settled in, okay?'

I sit back and gaze out of the window, waiting for the tunnel that will spirit me away from England for twelve months. Well, *good* if they're missing me. They didn't think I'd go through with this – and despite all the odds, here I am.

Chapter Eight

SAM

Settled onto the Glasgow train after two quick changes at Sheffield and Manchester, I must have dozed off because I jump when my mobile rings, cracking my forehead against the carriage window in the process. The woman in the seat opposite is kind enough to hide her amusement behind her magazine.

Smooth, Sam. Very smooth.

The sight of my two best friends pouting at me from the screen makes me smile regardless of the injury their call has caused.

'Hey,' I say, resting back into my seat. Beyond the window a landscape of purple-crowned Cumbrian peaks stretches out beneath lead grey clouds.

'What happened?' DeeDee demands. 'Kim and me saw the news. Was it a bomb?'

'No idea. Nobody seemed that bothered so I'm guessing not.'

I can hear Kim in the background and picture her, hands on hips, barking questions at DeeDee. 'I'm *asking* him… Kim wants to know if you got a train.'

'On it now. Just heading through the Lakes. Tell Kim it looks like rain here.'

Another off-speaker discussion ensues, followed by an

angst-heavy sigh. 'Okay, look, why don't you just tell him yourself, hmm? Sam, putting you on speaker so *Miss Kim* can yell at you instead.'

'Hi, Kim.' I can't hide my smile. They are such a double-act and always appear to be three words away from a row, but it's all love as far as they're concerned. They aren't related but they've sung together in bands for so long they might as well be family. It's spine-tingling stuff when DeeDee and Kim sing, like they've developed a magical symbiosis that they just couldn't recreate with anyone else. But not so much when they're arguing.

'Samuel. We heard it was a terror alert.'

'I don't think so. They would have evacuated the station if it had been. Anyway, I'm fine. I'm on the train now.'

'Do your friends know?'

'Not yet. I'll text them when I'm nearer Glasgow, just in case there are any other delays ahead. Anyway, they'll just expect me to rock up when I'm there, so it'll be no problem.'

There's a pause and I can hear another barked exchange, this time in urgent whispers because, of course, I'm on speakerphone and can't hear them.

'Something I should know?' I ask.

I hear a loud tut from DeeDee. 'We weren't going to tell you…'

'Laura came,' Kim finishes.

I stare out at the blur of moorland grass streaking past on the sidings. 'When?'

'About an hour after you left. She had a suitcase with her.'

'Kim!'

'What?'

'You didn't have to tell him that! I thought we discussed this…'

'Hang on, what?'

45

I wait for DeeDee and Kim's debate to stop, leaning my head back and closing my eyes. I don't feel angry, or hurt – just *weary*. I felt weary most of the time I was with Laura and during the six months since we broke up.

'The Russian kicked her scrawny butt out, didn't he? And who can blame him?' DeeDee's tone is heavy with disgust. Part of me would love to have been there to witness her reaction when Laura turned up. But mostly I'm just relieved I wasn't. 'She was all poor-little-rich-girl, with her red eyes and privileged whining. Like we'd just agree you should take her back. Like she was entitled to that.'

'Why did she come to yours?'

'She'd been to Syd's first and assumed you'd be here.'

'Was she trying to move in?'

'She wanted to go with you.' Kim's laugh is bitter. 'Can you believe it? Syd refused to tell her where you were going and what time your train was, so she came to us. Like *we* were ever going to help her!'

Well, today is certainly the day for revelations. It doesn't surprise me that Laura and Artem didn't last – especially as I know how many times she'd tried to get back with me (and the three times I'm ashamed to admit that I gave in). And yeah, maybe I'm a little bit glad. It feels like a justification for my mistrust. She *wasn't* worth the pain I've endured in her name. Not that I'm the kind of person who revels in someone else's misfortune, but Laura had it coming.

I thought last night's appearance at the studio launch was a one-off. More fool me, eh?

She'd managed to press so obviously against me as DeeDee took a photo of everyone in the studio. The designer off-the-shoulder sweater she wore pulled just a little too far down, the obvious lack of a bra. I knew exactly what she wanted me – and every other bloke in the room, available or otherwise – to be looking at. Subtlety is a foreign language to my ex. I'd walked away as soon as the photo was done, but in the crush of the studio with so many friends, colleagues and hangers-on gathered for the launch party, it was impossible to avoid her. Before I knew it, she was back – alone: her Russian boyfriend nowhere to be seen.

She'd performed one of her famous sighs, the kind that used to summon me to her side, desperate to make her happy. Only now it just made her look ridiculous. 'Oh Sam. Why can't you just be happy for me?'

'Why are you here?'

'Artem wanted to come.'

'Oh, *Artem* wanted to be in the same tiny room as your glowering ex? I'm sorry, I find that hard to believe.'

'Well, he did. Despite everything, he respects you.'

I didn't want to shout, or give her the satisfaction of making a scene at *my* launch party. I took a breath, hauling back my anger. 'Look, I didn't invite you.'

'I heard you were leaving,' she blurted out, casting a careful glance about her to make sure no one else heard. 'And I wanted to know why.'

'That's none of your business.'

'It's because of me, isn't it?' Her hand was on my arm and there were too many bodies around us for me to shake it off. I went cold at her touch.

'No. Because not everything in my life is about you.'

'Wait – Sam – this isn't over with us. I know you!' she'd called after me, but by then I was pushing through the studio party guests towards the exit. And I didn't look back.

'She honestly thought you'd want to be with her,' DeeDee continued. 'Honest, babes, we told her where to go.'

'Thanks. Sorry you both had to deal with that.'

'Don't worry. It was amusing. Kim tore a strip off the woman.'

I wince at that. I love my friends but I don't ever want to *not* be on their side. One is terrifying enough; having both of them taking issue with you could likely stop your heart. 'Ah. Thanks – I think.'

'We told her you were going to Aberdeen.' I can hear the smile in Kim's voice. 'So good luck to her if she thinks she can track you down.'

When the call is over, I take a deep breath and watch the world pass by. I never told Laura about my father, or where I grew up. She only met my university friends once when they came down to London for a gig I was playing at the Royal Albert Hall with a band of new-folk artists. Beyond that, she never asked about where I'd come from.

Which is odd, because Phoebe Jones asked within the first hour of meeting me.

I pull up the photo I took of us just before I left her at the barrier. She is beautiful, of course. But then my gaze slides to me. I look different. I think of all the selfies with me that Laura posted on Instagram – countless squares of a picture-perfect couple all taken at an identical angle for maximum effect. I never smiled in any of those images like I do in this single, hurriedly snapped photo with my arm around Phoebe.

Have I ever smiled like that before?

I stroke Phoebe's face on the screen, remembering the warmth of her against me, the scent of her perfume and the touch of her hand on my arm. *That's* what matters now. Not the past – or anyone from it trying to get back in. And I'm going to hold on to this feeling until I see Phoebe again.

Chapter Nine

PHOEBE

Paris Gare du Nord breaks through in an explosion of light and colour and noise as the train door opens. I take a breath.

Bonjour, Paris.

It's just a station platform: grey concrete, the smell of oil, pools of light filtering through the run of glass skylights high above. It could be anywhere. Except it *feels* different. Dad said that the first time he took Mum to Europe in their early twenties even the echo of his own footsteps sounded 'continental'. I don't have to see the platform signs and illuminated advertising boards to know I'm not in London any more.

Then I am through the barrier and looking around for a man I've only met once before who may or may not be holding a sign. It takes a minute to get my bearings, head dizzy with light and sound and movement. I make myself breathe, summoning up a memory of being in Sam's arms in our little space of concourse at St Pancras. It calms me.

I can do this.

Sam only just met me and he believes in me. I've known me for a lot longer, so maybe I should believe in myself more.

Sometimes the way to prove you're capable of something is just to do it.

'Phoebe!'

I follow the sound of the voice and a group of commuters disperses to my right revealing a face that's surprisingly familiar. Tobi is smiling and waving. And he has a sign with my name on it.

I'm going to be okay.

'Hi!' I grin, accepting a very French double-kiss and a very un-French bear hug from my host.

'The delay! The nightmare! My darling, are you okay? Meg told me they closed your station.'

'They did, but I'm here now.'

'Yes, you are. And now we celebrate your *grande aventure*.' He throws an arm around my shoulders and takes my bag despite my protests. 'First to home, then to wine!'

Twenty minutes later we're almost at his apartment in impossibly lovely Montmartre and my head is a tumble of streets and traffic, noise and colour. It's lovely to be in the company of someone who lives in the city. We skirt roads, pass through tiny back streets and lush green parks. Dad was right: even the everyday sounds of traffic and footsteps are unfamiliar here. Once I get my bearings it will all become second nature, I know. Like it did when I arrived in London, fresh out of horticultural college in Worcestershire and feeling as if I'd run away from the first twenty-five years of my life. London was a whim that became part of me. Maybe Paris and the countries beyond will become the same.

'Here we are!' Tobi exclaims, holding the apartment building door open for me to walk in first. We climb a narrow staircase with metal banisters to the second floor. Tobi opens the door and I walk into my home for the first part of my year in Europe.

It's perfect. White walls and long white gauze curtains at the floor-to-ceiling windows; warm parquet flooring in diagonal chevrons across the open plan living room and kitchen; three large, low couches draped in jewel-bright Moroccan throws with more cushions than even Meg has in her room (which is saying something); and greenery everywhere, from large potted palms standing sentry-like in the corners of the room to the impressionist wash of green in the window boxes on the small balcony the other side of the windows.

'It's beautiful,' I smile as Tobi takes my coat. '*C'est magnifique!*'

'Ah, *bon*. Don't worry. We speak English here as much as French,' he says, as if sensing the jolt of panic that hit me as soon as I tried out my rusty French. 'Luc is from Canada so we switch between the two all the time. Often, we argue in both.' I remember his smile now. It's the kind of smile that instantly puts you at ease. 'Let me show you your room and then we can relax.'

Tobi strides down the short corridor that leads off from the living room and kitchen. Tucked away, between a compact but stylish bathroom and a larger room I imagine is his and Luc's bedroom, is a smaller room with a futon and a large single window draped with soft yellow gauze. It's facing the rear of the building and when I peer out I can see it overlooks a tiny courtyard. Ivy spills down from the walls to a cluster of pots on the paved floor, so it looks like a secret garden. The faded blue and terracotta pots have been planted with red and white flowers.

'Who owns the courtyard?' I ask, as Tobi sets my bag beside the bed and hangs my coat on a hook on the back of the door.

'It belongs to the building and we all pay maintenance, so I guess we all own it. A few of the residents keep it looking good. Later I'll show you how to get down there, if you like. I don't use it much but Luc sometimes paints there in the summer.'

'I'd like that.'

It's such a luxury to have any kind of green space and to be honest it's the only thing I missed about home when I moved in with Meg, Osh and Gabe. There are parks everywhere in London, of course, but having a bit of green you can call your own is special. I think the courtyard and I might become well acquainted. I love the idea of snuggling up with a book in a little hidden square of Paris.

Turning back into the room I see that the entire wall behind the head of the bed is covered with white bookshelves. The spines provide a blast of higgledy-piggledy colour like the cushions on the living room couches and are lovely to look at. The sight of them makes me feel at home.

'Meg said you would be happy here,' Tobi grins, nodding at the wall of books. 'Many of them are in English – I rearranged them at the weekend so you have a whole section to choose from. I know you're a book lover.'

My heart swells. His thoughtfulness sends the last of my concerns about being in a new place floating away like dandelion seeds on a summer breeze. 'It's perfect. Thank you.'

'My pleasure. Now, make yourself at home and I will fetch the wine. Are you hungry?'

Right on cue, my stomach growls and we both laugh.

An hour later, Tobi and I are relaxing in the living room, a bottle of wine almost drunk between us, catching up on the gang's news. We've just started talking about Gabe's new play when the door swings open and Tobi's husband Luc strides in. His bag, coat and scarf are dropped in a pile in the middle of the parquet floor and I'm suddenly airborne, lifted into his hug.

'Phoebe! You made it! Welcome!'

Luc embraces me like a long-lost friend.

'Nice to meet you,' I laugh, as he sets me down.

'You too. And you're as gorgeous as Meg said.' His Canadian accent is unmistakable and his laugh rivals Tobi's for volume and enthusiasm.

'I rescued her from the station.' Tobi heads into the kitchen for more wine, pausing to kiss his husband. I see the sparkle between them and it's the loveliest sight.

My mum and dad sparkle like that, even now – almost forty years since they got married. My brother and I pretend we're embarrassed by their enthusiastic PDAs whenever we're out together, but really we're proud. Being as daft with each other as you were in the first flush of love is rare.

Will Sam and I still be as besotted forty years from now?

When we're basically four-hundred-year-old breathing dustbags…

'Tobi has been reviving me with wine,' I say.

'Excellent plan! I'll join you.' Luc kicks his things behind the largest couch and accepts a huge wine glass from Tobi. 'Sit, sit, Phoebe Jones! Tell me everything.'

So as Tobi makes dinner Luc and I talk about the journey here and the year ahead of me. Being in Paris, talking about my plans, makes them feel startlingly real. I'm *here* – and my adventure has already begun.

'Tomorrow I don't have work so I can take you on a tour, if you like? I mean, I know you know some of Paris, but I can show you all the cool bits we love.'

'That would be great, thanks. But I don't expect you both to take me everywhere. I know how busy you are.'

'Luc likes to think he's a Paris expert,' Tobi laughs in the kitchen, releasing a cloud of fragranced steam when he lifts the lid of the pan on the hob. 'Five years as a Parisian and he knows this place better than me.'

Seeing the city from a resident's perspective would be good, I think. I have a list of places I'd like to see – standard tourist stuff from the guidebook I've marked with so many sticky-note strips its pages resemble a rainbow. But I also want to experience life here as a local; I want to discover my own special place.

Meg believes that if a city wants you to love it, it will reveal a place that's special, just for you. In London I discovered mine in the heart of Notting Hill, in a small private park Gabe blagged us admittance into, late one night. Back then he was in a crime drama that had the nation gripped and was discovering all the good things that a single, well-placed mention of *Southside* could bring him. Sneaking around the darkened garden in the moonlight was when the city came alive for me and I've loved it ever since. Gabe's special place is just outside the Almeida Theatre, where he made his first professional stage debut; for Meg it's Golden Square in Soho; for Osh the centre of the Millennium Bridge at dusk, gazing out at the lights of London appearing either side of the Thames.

'All cities have the potential,' Meg assured me during one of my late-night wobbles in the weeks before I travelled. 'You just have to turn off the guidebook in your head and *feel* the city in your heart.' I hope she's right.

Tobi serves dinner and we work our way through two more bottles of wine. My head will hate me in the morning but tonight I don't care. I'm celebrating.

Chapter Ten

SAM

Ah Glasgow. Hello, old friend.

I'm aching and tired from the journey, but the sight of Glasgow Central's vast, glass vaulted ceiling fires my body back into action. I take my time collecting my things and stepping down from the train, the need to hurry gone. My fellow passengers have mellowed somewhat, too, many of them lulled to sleep for part of the journey creating a symphony of snores around me, which amused me no end. I swear a couple of them even managed harmony at one point. Even so, when they disembark I see their steps quicken as our merry company disbands to our own adventures once more.

I reckon I slept too, a few half-hour snoozes at most, although my memory of the journey has already passed into a sludge of sameness. One thing's for certain: I'll sleep tonight. Especially if there's alcohol involved.

I managed to get a message to Donal before reception deserted my phone completely and the reply I received was typical *him*:

Nae bother, pal. BEERS tonight!

Man, I've missed that guy.

I thought about Phoebe a lot, as the towns and cities passed into green and the hills rose to become mountains. It rained almost solidly from Lancashire onwards but as soon as we crossed the border the rainbows began. I can't remember the last time I saw a rainbow, but on this journey I've seen seven. I'd forgotten that about this train journey. But now I remember travelling south from Edinburgh to Carlisle as a kid: me and my brother with our snotty noses pressed against the train glass, spotting rainbow shards illuminating passing glens and moorland.

Does Phoebe like rainbows? I didn't ask, but I'm guessing she does. They're bright and unexpected, completely spontaneous and elusive, and I kind of think that would appeal to the woman who's just stolen my heart.

But a *year* apart from her…

I know what we said before we left London, but it struck me as I was travelling here just how much of a challenge we've set ourselves. Emails and postcards and once-monthly chats are all very well, but twelve months without her in my arms is suddenly a towering wall of a task. Can I do it? Can she?

I have stuff to do this year and I owe it to myself to focus on that as I planned. But I'm going to need strategies to keep perspective. At the end of this, I have to know for certain Phoebe is what I want. I owe it to both of us to be sure.

Leaving the station I ease back into Glasgow time like slipping on a favourite old pair of boots. It feels like home, even though I've never actually lived here. Weekends and Hogmanays and occasional weeks spent here with Donal and Kate over the years have endeared this city to my heart. As I walk its streets now, I don't feel like a visitor. The dry humour, the unapologetic moxie of the people around me and the rise and fall of the accent welcomes me like a long-lost son.

I've missed this.

Don't get me wrong, I love London. It's my home, my place of business: my stomping ground. But I miss the humanity sometimes. The humour. The way you're in the middle of a conversation before you know it; how every other person on the street beside you is one joke away from being a pal for life. It can be suffocating when you're in it, but when you're not it's the thing you miss.

Home. Phoebe asked if I was going home and it's only now, as I jump on a bus that will take me out north of the city to the town where my friends live, that I realise I already feel more at home in the forty minutes I've been here than I've done in London since Laura left me.

And when I get to Mull? Will that feel like home, too?

I push the concern away, along with the ghosts from my past, stuffing them all into a cupboard marked 'LATER'. That stuff can wait. I watch the city slouching past the window, not minding the slow progress of the traffic-slowed bus to Port Glasgow. At long last, I have time. To think or not. To just *be*. That's a luxury I haven't had for years.

My stop is at the bottom of a hill that overlooks the River Clyde, the road rising steeply ahead. Though the water is some distance away, the shimmer of early evening sun on the dark river framed by purple hills on its far shore seems close enough to touch as I walk up the hill to Donal and Kate's place. Their house is almost at the top, just where the road curves for its final ascent. The sight of Donal's ancient yellow Mini parked on the drive makes me smile. How it's still roadworthy is a mystery to everyone but he loves that rusting heap almost more than life itself. I have many fond and not-so-fond memories of cramming equipment into its interior and praying it up hills as we travelled to gigs across Scotland.

Donal misses the band and I get the impression he doesn't play as many gigs locally now as he'd like. He's one of the most gifted guitarists I know and it's a shame more people can't hear him play. But he's also Dad to three of the most awesome kids on the planet, so that audience rightly gets first dibs on his time.

The front door whips open before I even set foot on the drive and I'm almost knocked off my feet by an excited clan of Cattenachs. The last time I saw the kids they were tiny; now the twins Addie and Ivor are almost level with my shoulder, and their not-so-baby sister Lexie can reach my waist when she hugs me. I've seen the kids in our Skype chats a couple of times a year, but being with them in person brings home to me how much they've grown. Somewhere in the middle of the giggling horde is Donal; Kate follows behind, her smile as bright as the sunlight dancing on the Clyde.

'Let your poor uncle Sam get some air,' she laughs, giving in when she's ignored and joining the hug instead.

When they finally let me go, my sides are hurting from laughter and over-enthusiastic embraces. 'Where the heck did you lot come from? What's your mother been feeding you? Great big towering giants!'

'Maybe you've shrunk, Sam,' Lexie giggles, her father's wit clearly inherited.

'Aye, maybe I have. It'll be all that incessant English rain falling on me, eh? I've shrunk in the wash!' It's an old joke, but like the house and the kids and the sunshine yellow Mini beside us, it's familiar and warm and wonderful.

We pile inside the house, everyone talking at a million miles an hour, words and laughter crashing together, a joyous cacophony of noise that wraps around us. I've been here less than five minutes and it already feels like home. The last time I visited was almost six years ago and I'm shocked by how much has changed. I see it most in the kids, of course, but the house is different, too. Donal started the renovations they'd talked about for years just after he lost his mum eighteen months ago. His way of dealing with it, I think. When my ma passed, I wrote songs and jumped on any tour I could for a year. Syd spent six months in Ghana after his mum died, finally meeting the family she'd talked about but never visited. Losing someone puts brakes on everything else; changes how you see your priorities.

I only met Donal's mum a handful of times, but I think Taral Cattenach would have approved of her son's handiwork. She was an artist in India when Donal's dad met her on an exchange visit from the company he worked for in the early 1980s, and the home they made together back in Glasgow was filled with her vivid oil paintings.

A hand slaps my shoulder and Donal grins at me. He still looks as young as he did the first day of university, the only hint at the years that have passed the first peppering of silver in the splendid jet beard that's become his trademark.

'One of your ma's?' I nod at the painting above the fireplace. A white lotus flower, its petals edged with gold, on an azure blue pool, delicate Henna-style patterns picked out in bright ochre framing the canvas.

His blue eyes glisten. It was the first thing I noticed about him when we met in the registration line in Freshers' Week – that and the Glaswegian accent, which I'm ashamed now to say I didn't expect, either. 'Aye. I reckon she'd be happy to see it there.'

'Place looks great, man.'

Donal nods. 'Cheers. Didn't think we'd get there but the kids helped me finish it off.'

I glance at Addie, Ivor and Lexie, still giggling with their mum. 'I bet they're all artistic.'

'They're annoyingly talented at everything,' he chuckles. 'No idea where they get it from. Kate and I were lucky to graduate. Addie's taught himself so many instruments I've lost count, Ivor's studying piano at the conservatoire on Saturdays and Lexi's pretty much fluent in Gaelic, singing and playing guitar with a trad band at school.'

I love the pride with which Donal speaks about his kids, but I think he's selling himself short. 'I hope you're planning on getting that guitar of yours out while I'm here.'

'Show him the *lair*, Donal,' Kate grins, and instantly the clan are dragging their father out of the patio doors into the garden. He protests, but it's nowhere near convincing.

A large wooden building sits at the end of the garden, more a pine lodge than a shed. When we step inside, it's a tiny studio, complete with a square vocal booth and a rack of amps and processors my studio partner Chris would be envious of.

'Dad's doing an EP,' Lexie says, looping her arm through mine. 'Mum's singing on it, too.'

'You kept that quiet,' I smile at my friend who beams back.

'Well, it's only a bit of messing around, you know. I just figured it was time I sorted it out and rescued my guitars from the attic.'

Kate joins her daughter beside me. 'Don't believe him, Sam. He's been gigging most weekends this year and he's already working on album projects for a couple of local bands.'

'Then it's a business?'

Donal shrugs, but his eyes sparkle. 'Could be. Part-time for now, but if I can get a good number of clients, who knows?'

I'm proud of my friend but also sad that I've only learned this now. I retreated after Laura, more concerned with my own studio venture. This year will be different, I promise myself. This year my friends come first.

After dinner the kids are grudgingly coaxed up to bed and Donal and I finally collapse in the living room at 9 p.m. I have no idea how my friends function at their frenetic pace. Their kids rock but, *man*, they are full-on. Kate seems to thrive on it – a fact confirmed when she appears, fresh-faced and smiling, her arms laden with beer bottles and a large bowl of crisps.

'Right, lads. *Beers.*'

Those three words have heralded many an unwise imbibing of alcohol over the years and I know I'll regret it tomorrow. But I have been looking forward to this for weeks. We grab a bottle each and handfuls of crisps, which turn out to be teddy bear-shaped snacks.

'We ran out of the usual ones.' Kate shrugs. 'Don't tell Lexie but I raided her packed lunch crisps.'

'Very rock 'n' roll,' I laugh.

'Robert Plant is a Pom-Bears fan,' she says. I love the sparkle in her voice when she's joking. I've missed it – and Donal's hearty guffaw, too. 'Probably. Dave Grohl too, when he isn't drumming.'

'So tell us about your studio, Sam. Is it going to rival Abbey Road?'

I grin at Donal. 'One day maybe. It's all set up now and we have bookings for the first four months.'

'And Chris doesn't mind you leaving, just when it's all starting?'

'He's glad I'm not under his feet,' I admit. It's true: I was always going to be the one who funded things, while Chris was hands-on. 'Truth is, neither of us expected to find premises as quickly as we did and by then my year out was already arranged.'

'Like Kate and me,' Donal says, draining his beer bottle and reaching for another. 'She's the brains, I'm the brawn.'

Kate bats him with the back of her hand but the way they snuggle together on the sofa warms my heart. It took long enough to get them together, but they're inseparable now. Will Phoebe and I be like that?

My phone is on the coffee table where I left it and occasionally notifications illuminate the screen. I'm trying not to look, but each time it happens I wonder if it might be Phoebe. Is she thinking of me? I guess her first night with her hosts will call her attention from her phone more than mine. She mentioned she's only met one of them before. That makes me glad I know the people I'm staying with.

'Will you be seeing Niven while you're on Mull?' Donal asks.

'Hope so, as often as I can. Have either of you heard from him lately? I tried calling a couple of times before I left but I couldn't get hold of him.'

There's a very definite look that passes between my friends. 'He's on some kind of training course for work, I think. He'll be in touch soon as he's able. You know Niven.'

I smile back but it makes me wonder what they know about him that I don't. I know things have been up in the air since his fiancée moved out, but the last I heard he was dating again. Before I can ask any more, Kate pulls out a large bottle of single malt whisky from between the sagging sofa cushions.

'Time for *this* baby, I think.'

Donal and I protest, but it's useless. Kate only has to raise an eyebrow and suggest a *girl* might beat us in a drinking competition and we're both in. Years have not taught us wisdom on this. Donal fetches glasses from the sideboard while I clear a space between the empty beer bottles covering the coffee table. It's like being in our earliest days as friends: the whisky may be more expensive now, but the friendship is as strong as it's ever been.

We settle into an easy silence as we take our first sip of peaty liquor and I glance at the clock. Midnight already. Will Phoebe be asleep now? Kate's head is resting on Donal's shoulder, his eyes closed as he enjoys his dram. I sneak my phone from the coffee table and jump as the screen illuminates.

PHOEBE – 1 MESSAGE

I look up at my friends but they haven't moved. Heart racing, I open the message.

> Hi ☺ Arrived in Paris and in my new temporary home. Excuse the text but it's just this once because I miss you. Speak soon and sleep well xx

That's why she's no Laura, I tell myself. Laura would only text if she wanted something, or to have a go at me. Phoebe *misses* me. So much that she broke her own rule of limited contact less than twenty-four hours into our year apart.

Shielding my mobile from view of my friends, I reply:

> I miss you too. All good here apart from my arms being empty. Sweet dreams, beautiful xx

Kate raises her head and I pocket my phone before she notices. But I'm humming now. I can't tell if it's alcohol or lust… or love…? No, not love, not yet. But if I still feel like this in twelve months' time I'll fly faster than the train back to St Pancras and never let her go.

We talk, we laugh, we drink. My phone remains silent. But the thought that she might text again – the unpredictability of it – warms me more than any amount of single malt could.

I'll text her when I leave here for Mull, I decide. If Phoebe can bend the rules, so can I.

Chapter Eleven

PHOEBE

Daylight brings colour into my room, closely followed by a wall of pain crashing against my skull, so an equally delicate Luc suggests we ease as gently as possible into our tour of his favourite bits of Paris with a visit to his beloved local café.

Soon we're sitting by the window looking out across the street and it seems like the whole of Paris is parading past. Beyond the people with never-ending cigarettes and expertly folded copies of *Le Figaro* directly beyond the glass – who alone are fascinating enough – old and young pass by, a thousand different lives and stories walking along the street. I can see why writers have found inspiration here. You wouldn't even need a story idea: sit here for long enough and the city would write it for you.

I glance at Luc – or rather the enormous pair of dark sunglasses he's currently hiding behind. He picked up a newspaper from the seller on the corner of the street below the apartment but it's still where he put it when we first sat down, folded under his hand on the polished wood table. 'How's the head?'

'I think it hates me.' Behind the lenses his eyes crinkle into a smile, quickly followed by a grimace as his hangover protests.

'Listen, we don't have to do this today. I'm quite happy to wander around by myself…'

'No way! You are our guest and I promised you a tour of my neighbourhood. But every great tour of this city should begin with the best coffee. So,' he spreads his hands wide like a magician at the big reveal, '*voila!*'

I raise my cup to salute him and Luc nods at a passing waiter to order two more. At this rate I'll be carried around the streets of Paris by caffeine buzz alone. But at least my headache isn't stabbing quite so ferociously.

Another hour and a half later, helped by the pastries that finally tempted us and yet more coffee, Luc and I emerge squinting in the strengthening sunlight. The chill that whistled round the streets first thing has relented and I can see Parisians shrugging off coats and jackets to brave the walk without them.

The Sacré-Cœur Basilica is only a short walk from the café, so we head there first. It's set near parks, surrounded by cobbled streets and its white walls, tall towers and elegant domes are dazzling in the mid-morning sun. I've seen it in guidebooks and Meg's told me about it so many times – she loves it more than Notre Dame and reckons it's one of the most underrated buildings in Paris. But standing here is something else. The sounds of the city are a constant low hum but here birdsong joins the noise as their fleeting shapes pass between the ancient structures. We don't venture inside, but I intend to do that on a day when I don't have anywhere else to be. I plan to *reconnoitre* Paris landmarks and locations during my first week, and then return to the ones that I like best over the remainder of my stay.

The first time I visited Paris I was at primary school. We stayed in a grim bed and breakfast place in Normandy in November, and were granted one day in Paris, which wasn't enough time to see much of anything. We spent most of that day stuck on the coach in traffic around the Arc de Triomphe and on the most mind-numbing river cruise up and down the Seine (all the bridges from one side, then all the bridges from the other). My eleven-year-old heart sank as Notre Dame passed like a ghost, frustratingly out of reach. We did climb the Eiffel Tower, though – only to the second level, as it was a windy day, but climbing the steps instead of taking the lift – and standing on the famous tower gazing out across the neat squares of the city was the moment Paris stole my heart.

Despite his poor head Luc is a great guide, pointing out places only a local would know. With it, I'm getting the history of him and Tobi: where he proposed, where they first told the other they loved them, and how they first met in the famous bookshop, Shakespeare and Company, when they both reached for the same copy of *Candide* byVoltaire.

'Like *Serendipity* only with a better taste in books,' he jokes as we wander into a gorgeous sunlit park. We find a bench and sit.

'That's so romantic.'

He laughs. 'Yeah, it would have been if I hadn't been so annoyed with him for getting the book before me. I stormed out – the full flounce, you know – and that could have been that. Except that when I stopped by the Seine to catch my breath, I looked down and there was the book beside me. He'd bought it, followed me from the store and was standing there with this great big loon grin on his face.'

Instantly, I think of Sam. 'I met someone yesterday,' I say, the words dancing out before I can stop them. I hardly know Luc and I'd said I wouldn't tell anyone. But in the soothing green of the small park, overlooking a colonnade swathed with flowering blue wisteria and the white dome of Sacré-Cœur rising behind, it feels right. 'I think he could be someone really special.'

Could I have imagined myself saying this two days ago? Or a year ago? Already I feel so different and I like how the change sits in me.

Luc peers at me over his sunglasses. 'Tell me more, *mademoiselle*.'

'I met him when our trains were delayed.' I find Sam's photo on my phone and show Luc. 'That's Sam.'

'Cute. And you *left* him there?'

I laugh and hope it disguises the dip my heart just took. 'He was travelling to Scotland. For a year.'

'Okay.'

The sun sparkles on the crazy silver-glitter laces Osh gave me for my turquoise Converse. Suddenly I'm self-conscious. 'We've promised to meet up in twelve months if we still feel the same.'

He is quiet for a while and I wonder how sensible it was to share something so personal with someone I hardly know. I'm about to stuff a different, safer subject into the gap when Luc turns to face me.

'Y'know, Phoebe, a year is good. Test the theory. I'm all for spontaneity but you've got to give your head chance to catch up with your heart. I mean, I tell the story of T and me like the moment he gave me that book all my dreams came true, but it wasn't like that at all. The *moment* was spontaneous; the working out how the hell it was all going to happen took a long time. Over a year, actually.'

'It did?'

'Mm-hmm. I was a visitor here when we met, on a three-week vacation. Tobi had never been to Canada. We knew nothing about one another, other than the chemistry and the fact we both wanted to read Voltaire on the same day. We both had careers, owned property, had lives in our countries we couldn't just pack up and leave. Then there was all the legal stuff – visas, applications. Where we'd live. The boring reality that inevitably follows after your heart's run away with a notion. I don't regret a thing, but I wish I'd seen all those frustrating delays as important time for laying foundations. If we'd rushed it, who knows if we'd be together now? The details can derail you, if you're not prepared.'

We watch the world pass our bench in our tiny patch of Paris. I haven't looked beyond returning to Sam in a year's time. It seems far too early to think about that stuff, but when would the right time be? A month from now? Six months? Just before I go home?

I'm nervous about thinking too far ahead but Luc is right about making the most of our time apart to really think things through. I remember his text last night:

I miss you too.

That's what I need to focus on. Everything else is just logistics.

Luc is decidedly less delicate by 2 p.m. so we venture a little further afield and spend a few hours wandering around tiny art shops, artisan food stores and a farmers' market he tells me is Tobi's favourite. We buy bits of cheese, bread and cured meats, enjoying the samples offered by every stallholder.

One stall is covered in tiny watercolour paintings – some no bigger than a postage stamp, some two inches square and some the size of postcards. I choose a beautiful one of a Parisian street with cherry blossom trees and tiny window boxes at every window. It's the perfect first postcard to send to Sam, who emailed me the address of his friends in Glasgow earlier today.

Luc goes to buy some envelopes for me and coffee for us both.

I sit on a bench opposite the market to write my card to Sam. I don't know when he is going to be leaving his friends' house and travelling to Mull, so I hope the card will arrive in time.

Dear Sam,

Surprise! I wasn't sure how long you would be in Glasgow so I hope this reaches you before you leave for Mull.

I'm writing this by the side of a farmers' market. Luc has been giving me a personal tour of his favourite Parisian haunts and we've just eaten half our bodyweight in free food samples. The sun is shining, it's warm and it's about as perfect as days in Paris get. The artist who painted this postcard is called Mme Comtois and she started painting at night after working on the dairy farm she owns with her husband all day. She told us she paints to keep her heart smiling — how lovely is that? I think we should always do things that bring smiles to our hearts.

I miss you. I hope you're happy. And I can't wait to see you again.

All my love, Phoebe xxx

When we return from our day wandering around Montmartre, Luc shows me how to get into the tiny courtyard. There's a service staircase at the back of the building and a door at the bottom that opens into the small green space. I'm sitting there now, looking up at the square of sky framed by the ivy-covered walls of the building. It feels like a secret space and it's so quiet. It's a perfect place to read – maybe even write.

Sitting in the café made me think of the authors I love who chronicled their adventures across Europe. Maybe I can do what

Mark Twain and Johann Wolfgang von Goethe did: note down what I see, what I experience. My first full day in Paris has been so wonderful I want to remember it all. Maybe one day I can show Sam, too.

When I switch my phone on Sam is smiling at me from the screen. It's as if he knew I was thinking about him. I resist the urge to squeal as I open his message.

Hey you. My turn to break the rules. I'm leaving for Mull tomorrow, so here's the address. Just if you happened to be passing a postcard shop in Paris or anything. Email me yours and I'll send you a tartan-emblazoned one when I land on Mull (prepare yourself…) By the way, I miss you xx

Chapter Twelve

SAM

Far too many beers.

Not the most profound thought to begin the first proper day of my adventure with, but at least it's honest. Honesty is something I've promised myself for this year, too. No more stuffing the past away, no more pretending it didn't happen.

Right now, though, my head wants to leave me.

Nobody's up when I stumble into Donal and Kate's kitchen. A painful squint at my phone reveals it isn't even six yet. *Great.* Although maybe if I can neck a pint or two of water with some paracetamol I might be able to crash out for a couple more hours. That's a comforting thought.

I find a glass, fill it to the brim with cold water and am about to begin my cupboard search for painkillers when I remember Phoebe's message.

Excuse the text but it's just this once because I miss you.

I stop fighting the urge to reply and type a message, with my address in Mull. That's just important information, right? Admin, you could say. So it's *necessary.*

'So, are you going to tell me who she is?'

I jump and a slosh of water escapes my glass, splashing across the tiled floor and my bare feet.

Kate laughs and leans over the sink to tear off a strip of kitchen roll, ducking to mop my feet and the floor like I'm one of her kids. It's endearing and mortifying at once.

'Cheers, Ma,' I say.

'Oi, seven months younger than you, thank you very much.' She flicks the paper in the bin and grabs the kettle. 'You're busted though, Mr Mullins. I demand all the details.' She's annoyingly fresh, considering she matched Donal and me dram for dram last night. 'Can your poor head stand coffee yet?'

'I'll risk it,' I grin, pulling out a pine chair by the table. Sitting is definitely safer than standing this morning.

'So?'

'So what?'

'Who is she?'

I lay my phone carefully on the table. 'You should work for MI6.'

'They tried to recruit me. Too badass for them.' Her damp auburn curls dance across the collar of her towelling robe when she laughs. It's not the red it was, threaded with strands of gold now, but it's still like watching fire. 'You don't have to tell me. But whoever she is, I'm glad she makes you happy.'

This might be the only chance I get to talk to Kate about Phoebe, before the thunder of remaining Cattenachs descends upon us and the moment is lost.

'Her name is Phoebe Jones,' I say, my chest swelling as her name plays on my lips. 'You're going to think I'm nuts, but I think she's perfect for me. As in *long-term* perfect.'

Kate's mirth softens and she sits next to me, anticipating the story that will follow.

Once I begin, it all comes out. And despite the hammering in my head, I can't stop my smile. I fall over my words, somewhere between confession and breathless laughter. And the whole time, Kate watches, a strange half-grin resting on her face.

When it's all said, she sits back, the boiled kettle long forgotten between us. 'I've never seen you happy like this, Sam.'

'I don't know if I've ever been this happy before.' It's strange spoken out loud, but it's the truth.

'Do you have her picture?'

If it were anyone else in the world asking, I'd refuse. But this is Kate Cattenach, long-time confidante in matters of my heart. I find the image of Phoebe and me together by the platform barrier and slide the phone across the washed pine table for Kate to see.

'She's beautiful.'

'She is.'

'And you only met her... yesterday?'

I know where this is going. 'I did.'

'Wow.'

'I know how it sounds, but...'

'No, Sam, really, you don't have to explain. Sometimes you just know, I guess. Not that it was like that for your man and me. I reckon Donal and I have the slowest love-at-first-sight story on the planet.'

'Yeah, but *we* all knew.'

She laughs. 'So I've been told. By every single one of yous.' She hands the phone back. 'Phoebe – the radiant, shining one. Pretty apt name.'

Name meanings have always been Kate's thing. Within a day of us all meeting she'd told us what our names meant: Kate – *pure* (we always added 'alcohol' to the meaning as a nod to her incredible drinking prowess); Donal – *ruler of the world* (which, trust me, he still brags about); Niven – *saint* (jury's still out on that one); Shona – *happy* (which is what we all hope she might be one day); and Sam – *heard by God*, which I always thought was a bit odd until Kate said that being a musician made it the perfect name for me. Who wouldn't want God as an audience? God or Aly Bain in my case – I'd be happy with either. I don't know how much I believe in name meanings, but finding out Phoebe means *shining* and *radiant* makes me smile even more.

'That's how she seemed to me. Her laugh – it's like sunshine.'

Kate pulls a face. 'You've got it so bad. Bless you. She must be special.'

'I think she is.'

'But – you still came away? And let her go, too?'

Said like that, it doesn't sound good. 'We both have things to do. Promises we've made ourselves. I don't want to jump into another relationship unless I'm certain it's right. Not after Laura.'

Kate nods. 'I get that. But are you sure you're not…?' She exhales and peers through her curls at me. I know what that look means. We've been here countless times before. I can rely on her to speak her mind – even if this morning I don't want to hear it. 'Tell me where to get off if you like, but are you sure you haven't agreed to a year apart as a way of *not* committing?'

'Yes, I'm sure.'

Am I? I was yesterday…

'Because it's okay if you're scared, Sam. We all get scared. And Laura damn near destroyed you.'

I wish she didn't know that about me. And yes, I know the urge to head for the hills at the first sign of trouble is strong in my bones. But Phoebe's not like Laura. She's worth me being different for,

74

or at least trying to be. 'It's a test, being apart. We should test how we feel, if it's what we both hope it could be. Don't you think?'

'A year is one hell of a test.'

'Maybe.'

She smiles and reaches across to squeeze my hand. 'Then, good for you. She'd better be worthy of your faith, mind. Tell her if she messes you around she'll have me to contend with.'

'Okay.' I might not pass that message on *just* yet. The thought of Kate gunning for anyone is terrifying.

Within an hour everyone is up, including the family's ancient corgi 007, mostly known as Bond these days, although whenever they take him to the vet they use the former. It's a never-ending source of embarrassment to Donal when the vet calls '007 Cattenach' into the packed waiting room.

In the middle of the noisy whirr of laughter, breakfast-making and conversation, the doorbell rings. Lexie beats her brothers to answer it and I hear excited squeals from the hall. A moment later, a familiar smile moons around the kitchen door.

'Am I too early for beers?'

Niven McNish's laugh rumbles beneath the crush of hugs that follows and it's a welcome sound.

'Okay, okay, put your uncle Niven down,' Donal says, reaching in between us to rescue our friend. 'Good to see you, man. Can we get you breakfast?'

'Aye, you can. Sam! Surprise!' He holds his arms open, chuckling away.

'I didn't know the McNish-Meister was gracing us with his presence,' I say, slapping him on the back, as the family resumes their vociferous assault on toast and eggs around the table. 'I heard

75

they didn't let you leave the Island these days. Being the national treasure you are.'

My friend shrugs off his leather jacket and grabs toast from the fresh stack Donal has delivered. 'I snuck out. I'm officially a fugitive.' He downs a mug of tea as if it's the first he's had for weeks, wiping his mouth with the back of his hand. I can imagine him as a Viking invader, downing beer after a conquest. Tea isn't exactly warrior fare, but the image still suits him. Especially with that hair and wayward straggle of a beard. Has that man ever had a decent haircut? Not in all the time I've known him.

'Is there a reward for your capture?' I ask. 'I could do with some cash right now.'

'Probably not much, knowing the Island. So, how are you? And how dare you not have aged since the last time I saw you?'

'Get away. I found a grey hair the other day.'

'Yeah, *right*. It's those musician genes of yours, keeping time at bay.'

'Are they the tight ones?' Lexie asks earnestly, frowning when we all descend into giggles.

Niven ruffles her hair. 'Different kind of genes, Lex. But I reckon Sam has musician jeans, too. Probably far too tight for a man of his years.'

'Hey!'

He shrugs. 'Say it as I see it. Fiddle players – right posey bastards.' He holds up a hand in apology when Addie, Ivor and Lexie giggle and Kate shushes him. 'Kids, you didn't hear that, okay? Sorry, Kate. So, Mullins, when are you heading off?'

'Tomorrow.' I offer a sympathetic grin as the children protest. 'But you've got me all day today, guys.'

'You never stay long enough,' Ivor complains.

Donal and Kate's house is cosy, but accommodating three adults, three children and an elderly corgi is stretching its capabilities. Where they're going to put Niven tonight is anyone's guess.

'When I'm on my way back to London, I'll come and stay again for a night. How's that?' I look over to Donal and Kate, who nod happily. 'And of course you're all welcome to visit when I'm settled on Mull.'

'I've plenty of room at mine for the lot of yous.' Niven grins and instantly the kids are placated. He has that ability to be oil on troubled waters – always has. Where Kate was the mum of the group, and Donal the dreamer, Niven was our peacemaker. Maybe that's why he's been so successful as a teacher. Island kids face all kind of issues mainland children don't get and behaviour can be a problem when frustrations rear up. With Mr McNish in charge, the kids have the best chance of navigating it.

'What brings you here, anyway?' I ask, my question answered when I see Niven exchange a glance with Kate. 'Ah.'

'Now don't be mad at Kate. I've been on a residential course in Glasgow for a fortnight so I was on my way back anyway. The timing was just – *providential*.'

Providential my *ass*. Knowing this lot they will have cooked up the whole thing between them. 'Right. And I don't suppose you were planning to travel back to Mull tomorrow by any chance?'

Niven's grin could charm swallows out of the sky. Man, I've missed my friends.

I'd always envisioned making my way to Mull alone, but secretly I'm glad of my surprise travelling companion. Going home is never simple – Kate and the gang understand that. At university there were Christmases and Easter breaks and summer holidays where everyone else piled off to their families and I just *didn't*. My friends clocked this early and so I always ended up with invitations to stay from across the UK and Ireland. I'll forever be grateful that they noticed and didn't let me wallow alone.

There's so much *stuff* wrapped around the Island and me. It's where I was born, where two generations of my family lived before me, so it's in my blood. But it's complicated. My father made that happen. I'm going home because I want to understand that: who I am and where I came from, but also why Dad walked away. I have a year with no commitments, barring meeting Phoebe at the end of it. I might never have this luxury again.

We spend the day hanging out and chatting, moving between the house and Donal's studio, until the inevitable happens and Addie, Ivor and Lexie beg us to play something. Niven doesn't have his fiddle, so he borrows Lexie's while I fetch mine; Donal and Kate grab guitars from the impressive selection hanging on hooks across one wooden wall of the studio; Ivor sits at the keyboard, Lexie chooses a tin whistle and Addie produces a bodhrán drum.

I love the moment when musicians gather. The shuffle and tuning, the moving of chairs and sharing of smiles. It's all part of it, before a single note plays. There's a peace that settles between musicians before the music begins, a silence that's both comforting and energising. Because before it is preparation and after it is music – an adventure shared between likeminded souls. I remember a professor of ours saying there's no way to describe music without expressing how it makes you feel. And it's true. You can know everything about the theory and the mechanics of music, but it all means nothing without experiencing it.

When we play, it's messy and unrehearsed and we laugh as we miss chords and hit bum notes, but it's still magical. And for me, it's *family*. I've missed it. I've missed the immediacy of it: you sit down, you play. No agonising beforehand, no getting mired in plans and strategies. When I play, I'm not thinking about anything but the music.

The last time I felt like that was… with Phoebe.

When I get to Mull, I'm going to call her. Screw the rules. I reckon we'll figure it out as we go. Besides, I need to hear her voice.

Next day, I am staring at a stack of garish tourist postcards, turning the white wire carousel slowly to find one that won't make Phoebe reconsider me on the spot. I wasn't the biggest fan of her idea to send cards to one another. But receiving hers this morning as I prepared to leave for Mull was the loveliest thing. Like she'd just snuck into Kate and Donal's hall to smile at me.

So my first postcard back to her *has* to be right.

On reflection, the ferry terminal at Oban was maybe not the best place to do this. We didn't have time to buy anything at Glasgow Queen Street because Niven and I missed the first bus back to the city from Donal and Kate's, so we entered the station like a pair of crazy rucksack-toting sprinters and only just caught the train.

Ironically, I now have several hours to make my choice from the slim pickings here. The weather's closed in since we arrived and the last two ferries were cancelled. Is this entire year going to be one long delay?

'Are these supposed to make people stay away from Scotland?' Niven reaches past me and picks one with a psychedelic tartan piper on it, who appears to be striding up the middle of a B-road in the Highlands. His hair is an unnatural shade of satsuma and his swinging kilt so scarlet it practically jumps off the card and slaps your face. 'I wouldn't want to meet that fella on a deserted road. Or receive this image in the post when I've a hangover.'

He has a point. In the end I opt for a too-green Highland landscape, its tartan border only slightly less offensive than the others on offer, and take it to the gravel-faced assistant behind the counter to pay.

'Were you hoping for a crossing?' he asks.

'Yep.'

He makes a sucking sound with his teeth like the noise of water draining down an almost-blocked sink. 'You'll be lucky to get across this side of dark,' he says. Ah, the cheery banter of the ferry port. I'd forgotten the joys. 'You two lads on a jolly over there?'

'Seeing family,' I say, hiding my smile when he gawps at me. Clearly he'd pegged me as a tourist.

'Ach, well. Not a good day for that either, I reckon.'

Like I said, *cheery*.

'He thought you were English,' Niven mocks as we head for the dubious-looking snack concession at the far edge of the car park, the only food provider brave (or daft) enough to be open in this weather. The food kiosk in the ferry terminal was already locked and shuttered when we arrived.

'No he didn't.'

'Face it: you've been away too long, Mullins. Swallowed up by that great big London place. Your people have forgotten you.'

'Shut up.' I smile, but my stomach shifts.

I know Ailish will be glad to see me, but does anyone else from my early life remember me? My family didn't exactly leave with a farewell parade. I still remember the shock of being woken before the sun, Ma stuffing just what she could carry into holdalls and bin bags, dragging Callum and me away from the only other home we'd known: Grandma's house.

My maternal grandmother is long gone and I don't miss her.

She made Ma's life hell after our pre-dawn escape from her home on Mull and I don't think she ever forgave her, spitting out her bile and fury at us long distance in phone calls my mother felt obliged to endure. Grandma loved my father, you see. Thought he could do no wrong. Ma was a failure for *not being enough of a woman* to keep him.

I shouldn't be glad someone is dead, but in her case I am. I'm pretty sure Grandma's hateful attitude to Ma added to her self-loathing, hastening her own death from years of alcohol and hurt. It's part of why us returning to Mull as a family was never an option. Ailish was here, of course, Niven too – although I don't remember him much as a kid because we moved away so early. The coincidence of meeting him again over five hundred miles away at university in London felt like a gift of providence. Still does.

We brave a coffee and a bacon roll each and scurry back to the shelter of the ferry terminal.

'Don't take the lid off your coffee,' Niven says when we're squeezed onto bright-blue rigid plastic chairs in the departure lounge.

'Why?'

'It's not pretty. I didn't know coffee came in *grey*.'

'It's warm and it's wet. That's all I care about.' I roll my eyes as Niven chokes on his sub-standard coffee. 'You haven't changed.'

'Apart from being AWOL from the Island,' he says, wiping coffee from his chin.

'What's going on there?'

My friend slumps in his unforgiving seat. 'It's complicated.'

'How?'

'Can't really explain. My mates at home reckon it's a premature midlife crisis. It's just – nothing seems as fulfilling as it did before.'

'Before Ruth?' I'm careful not to look at him when I say it.

'Not just that. Lots of things, really. Ruth was the start of it, I think.'

'The teaching?'

I see his boots tapping together. A sure sign he feels uncomfortable. It isn't that he can't take confrontation, more that he'd rather work it out himself than by committee.

'I love the kids. I'll always love working with them. But since Ruth, everything's come up for renewal. When we were together I was looking to a future where a safe job on the Island was necessary. But now… now I just don't know.'

When I've pictured returning to Mull, Niven in his teaching job was as sure and immovable a feature as Duart Castle or the peak of Ben More. I hadn't realised how much the break-up could shake him. But that's the point – I haven't noticed because I haven't been involved in my friends' lives for so long.

This year, I will be a better friend to them all.

Almost two hours later, our luck takes a turn for the better. Against all odds the leaden skies break and the wind drops. The sunshine that appears is the weakest, weediest excuse for sun, but we're delighted to see it. Twenty minutes later, an announcement comes over the tannoy to inform the thirty or so of us noble pilgrims who've stuck out the wait that a ferry will be heading to the Island in an hour.

It's almost 4 p.m. when we reach Craignure. I've missed several buses and the next one won't run for another hour and a half. *More* waiting. I think of transport back in London, how I consider anything over a twenty-minute wait to be unreasonable. This year will teach me patience, if nothing else.

'Hey, don't go waiting for a ride to Fionnphort,' Niven says when I start to head for the bus stop. 'I'll drive you over.'

'I can't ask you to do that. It's miles out of your way.'

'You haven't asked. I've offered. I've a friend here who lets me park on his drive when I go to the mainland. I can't stand the bus. I always meet some ancient local who knows my mum and has embarrassing stories about me they'll happily share with every other passenger. Come on. Accept a lift from a dodgy local, eh? Start living dangerously.'

It isn't an offer I'm likely to pass up. 'Sure, why not? I'll make sure Ailish pays you in cake.'

'Deal. And you can buy the first round when we go drinking.' He grins as we set off. 'Because we *will* be drinking many times, Sam.'

Single-track roads are a feature of the Island and something I'd forgotten the thrill of navigating. I'm usually a dreadful passenger but right now I'm glad Niven's driving. To take my mind off the scarily narrow road ahead I look out at the landscape, the sight of the sea and moorland, hills and mountains summoning so many memories.

We've been driving for a while when I'm struck by the strongest need to be out in the wild, open beauty of my birthplace.

'Wait – can we stop for a second?'

'Er, sure, hang on.' Niven frowns but he doesn't question my request.

We pull into a small muddy passing place beside a hummock of wild grass, looking out across miles of empty moor. I open the door and jump out, shaking the stiffness from my legs.

Out here the wind blows unabated from sea to land, across dramatic craggy moorland peppered with pink granite, the vivid swathes of green bracken dancing with the first flush of purple heather. I plant my feet on the soft peaty earth, my body braced against the buffeting breeze.

Suddenly, everything returns. The scent of salt and heather on the air, the light from my earliest memories of life, the colours… For a moment, I can't move; scared it will all vanish if I do. I want to capture everything just as it is now. I've forgotten it once: I don't ever want to do that again.

'Are you all right, man?' Niven is standing beside me, hands shoved deep into the pockets of his jacket.

'Just – breathing it in,' I say, surprised by the emotion I hear in my own voice.

He nods but doesn't say anything. I know he understands.

No matter what your experience, where you come from is rooted deep within you. I was happy here as a child, in the way that kids always find joy in life. It was only after we left the Island that all the resulting pain and recriminations moved in which characterised the rest of my growing up. I didn't know what Ma was living through when we were here – how could I? I was 9 years old. She hid it from us because she loved her kids. Until we were old enough to hear it all.

'So, you're going home?' Phoebe had asked on the day we met. But it's only now I can truly answer.

Yes, Phoebe. I'm going home.

Beside me, Niven coughs.

'We should probably be getting on. There won't be much light left soon.'

I nod, grateful that him driving me to Ailish's house gave me this moment. The bus wouldn't have let me stop to find it.

'You know, you can stay at mine,' Niven says, as the car bumps along the rutted road. 'There's just me knocking around there. You'd be closer to things, too.'

'That's kind of you, but I promised Ailish. I think she wants me to stay because of Ma.'

'Fair enough. Then we'll do beers, soon. And *often*. And would you maybe be up for a gig or two? Plenty of room in my band if you're after a bit of cash while you're here.'

'Deal.' One of the things I'm most looking forward to this year is hanging out with this guy, and if anyone can show me the traditional songs it'll be Niven. Besides, I want to help him find something else to get his teeth into. Niven not being happy is worrying.

Ailish McRae's voice was a feature of my childhood, thanks to the weekly phone calls my brother and I fought to answer.

'Hello, petal. It's Auntie Ailish. Is your ma there?'

She is the one and only person in the world to ever have the right to call me *petal*. Even Phoebe can't use that one.

Ailish's home nestles on the side of a small hill not far from the beach, overlooking the Fionnphort ferry crossing to Iona. The house is whiter than I remember, its windows beginning to glow gold in the late-afternoon sun. As the car rumbles over the rough track from the main road towards it, I see the pale blue front door fly open and there she is. Her hair has turned from auburn to white-blonde but is still swept up on the top of her head as she's always worn it. Callum and I used to think her hair was magic – in the highest of winds and worst weather it never moved from where she'd pinned it. Ma thought she was magic, too, having turned up in her life when she most needed a friend. I feel lucky to be surrounded by friends I'm pretty certain will still be there at the end of my life.

We park on the sweep of gravel at the front of the building, Ailish grinning on her door step, her feet dancing on the slate flagstone like an excited child.

'Oh bairn! There you are!'

I'm gathered into the biggest, happiest bear hug and when Niven steps out of the car she beckons him into it, too. He squashes in beside me, turning red as we're squeezed together.

'What a happy day this is!' When she releases us, tears fill her eyes. 'I wish your ma could see this, Sam. Her poor heart…'

The last time I saw Ailish was in the grey churchyard on the outskirts of the village where Ma spent the last year of her life, on the day we said goodbye to her. Not even 60 and vanished from the earth. At the end, I hardly recognised my mother. Alcohol is brutal – Ailish understands that more than most. Both her parents died before their time, cursed by the demands of drink.

'I reckon she's watching,' I say, disguising the lump in my throat with a cough.

'If I know her, she will be.' Ailish chuckles and wipes her eyes with the edge of her sleeve. 'Now, enough of this! Come in, both of you. I've the kettle on and cake made.'

Niven tries to make his apologies but Ailish is having none of it. Not that he protests too strongly, knowing cake is imminent. I grab my rucksack and violin case from the back of Niven's car and we follow my honorary auntie inside.

Chapter Thirteen

PHOEBE

I don't want to go out today, but reading isn't occupying my mind enough. I wander around the apartment trying to find something to distract me. Tobi and Luc have left a stack of DVDs and magazines on the coffee table – I sort through them but nothing appeals. I'm restless, as though there's something I ought to be doing but I haven't worked out what yet.

Two weeks into my Grand Adventure and I'm having an off-day. I've been to all the places on my list and have found some new ones, too. I can't understand it. I have one of the most amazing cities in the world on my doorstep but today I don't feel like exploring at all.

Of course, what I *should* be doing is firming up details for the next leg of my journey. Thing is, I can't decide whether to go to Rome first or Florence. I've found Airbnbs in both and narrowed my list down to three in each city. They're all within my budget and perfectly acceptable but – I don't know – there's something missing. It's probably the idea of staying somewhere alone, or with hosts I don't know. Which is daft, considering I didn't know Luc and barely knew Tobi when I arrived in Paris. They've just become such good friends and the rhythm of life here suits me – striking out on my own during the day and returning to Tobi's cooking and Luc's funny stories about his workplace in the evening. Large parts of this year will be going from one unfamiliar place to the next and I'm okay with that but I'll miss the friendship.

Today isn't the day to decide, though. Not while I'm in this mood.

When I'd pictured this year I never expected to have boring or indecisive days. The Phoebe Jones of my imagination left all of that stuff in London and marched confidently though every one of her 365 European days. But you can't leave yourself behind. All of the doubts and insecurities and ridiculous hang-ups that characterised me at home are still with me.

And anyway, I know what the real problem is: I miss Sam.

Neither of us is sticking to the rules we agreed for communication. One of us should be sensible, but it gives me hope because he isn't in a hurry to forget me, or parcel me into neat boxes of time. The flipside of this is that every bit of communication makes me long for him more.

I jump as my mobile buzzes. It's happened a few times lately: just when my heart has been longing for him he's appeared on my phone. What was it he called it back at St Pancras? *Spooky*.

On the wide love seat by the window I sit and open the message. It's a photo of Sam on a hillside with the sea in the distance. His dark curls are being whipped up at the front by the wind and he's wearing a sweater and coat, despite it being July. I'm in a T-shirt today and although all of the windows are open, the apartment is stuffy with heat. Another reason I've chosen not to go out today.

Feeling the now familiar rush of adrenalin, I type a message back.

Where are you? xx

The dancing dots underneath the bubble of my message jig in time with my heart. And then his reply appears:

On the hill behind Ailish's house. I can see the Iona ferry from here xx

You look amazing – sorry, IT looks amazing xx

Cheeky xx

Sorry xx

I wait while he types the next message. I can't hide my smile.

Firstly, I don't believe you are sorry. Secondly, carry on xx

That laugh of his dances through his words.

You look cold xx

Probably because it's freezing here. Niven's right, too many years living in the South have made me a wuss. He's swanning around in a T-shirt today. Not even a goosebump on him. I'm a disgrace to my Caledonian race xx

He's mentioned so many names in our conversations. Kate, Donal, Ailish, Lexie, Addie, Ivor – he talked about a Niven but I can't remember the context. I can't bluff my way out of this.

Who's Niven again? (Sorry!) xx

Old university friend. Another musician. You'd like him. You'd probably fancy him. He's a proper heartbreaker xx

I only have eyes for you, Sam xx

Cute. All the same, I won't send you his photo until we're back together xx

He might not fancy me xx

He already does. He saw your picture on the Mull ferry xx

Oh, so now we discover the truth. It amuses me that Sam is nervous that I might prefer his friend. This is too good a chance not to rib him.

Oh right, so Niven gets to see me but I don't get to see him? How is that fair? xx

It's safer this way, trust me xx

I'm just thinking of what to say to that when another message arrives. Must be something about being a fiddle player – he types so quickly!

I dreamed about you last night xx

How cute is that?

Did you? Hope it wasn't a nightmare xx

Oh come on, how could it ever be bad? It was awesome. So amazing I spent an hour trying to get back to sleep so I could stay in it xx

That good? xx

THAT good xx

Wow. No pressure for the next time I see you, then xx

None at all. You're a dream lady xx

His cheekiness is endearing but I need a minute to regroup. I leave my phone on the window seat and head into the kitchen. It isn't that I don't like the flirting – I do, so much – but I want to make sure that isn't all we talk about.

It's a battle not to race back to my phone, but I take my time making coffee. Is Sam checking his phone or has he gone back to his mum's friend's house? My drink is made and I have no more reasons for delay, so I return to the window seat. The courtyard below is looking lovely today. It's tempting to go down there to message Sam again, but it was so stiflingly hot yesterday that I abandoned my attempt to write my travel journal after twenty sweaty minutes. At least here a small brave breeze is finding its way through the window.

There's a message from Sam waiting on my phone.

Did I tell you I found a guitar at Ailish's? Found it in the wardrobe in my room. It was her son Aidan's when he was a teenager. Thought he'd impress girls with it but found out having a car was more effective and far less hard work xx

So girls like guitar, do they? xx

Yup. Well-known fact. Piano and guitar are like catnip to girls xx

How about violin? xx

Worked for you xx

Ah, but I've never heard you play xx

Crap. Better brush up my guitar skills, then… xx

Our messages make me feel like the whole of Paris can hear us flirting.

So you play guitar as well? xx

I do. Haven't played for a while but I want to write some stuff while I'm on the Island. It needs new strings but I reckon I can get a decent tune out of it xx

You'll have to send me a song, Sam. I'd like that xx

I will. Anything for you xx

You're brilliant. I love you xx

I take a breath.

It's what I've wanted to say for the last two weeks and I was going to wait until I knew for certain, but who am I kidding? I knew the moment we met. I'm in love with Sam Mullins. And while I probably should have built up to it a little, or waited until we next spoke, it's said now. It's why I've been restless today, why his messages have meant so much. I *love* him. Why wait a year to say it?

I wait for his reply, for the dancing dots that mean he's composing a message. After a minute they appear on screen, then disappear. Another thirty seconds and they do the same. Why is he hesitating? How many times do you have to type *I love you, too* before you dare to send it?

The screen remains blank beneath my last message now. I stay where I am, convinced that he'll message back, or call me. Maybe he had to go to the house to use the Wi-Fi calling thing he's done before. It probably is something we should say out loud to each other. I must've taken him by surprise and now he's making sure his reply is everything he wants it to be.

But what if I scared him?

My stomach twists.

What if – oh hell – what if he doesn't feel the same?

My fingers ache and I realise I've been gripping my phone too hard. I let go, the blank screen falling to my lap.

Why did I tell Sam I love him?

An hour passes, then two. I move to my room and try to read but the lifeless screen draws my eyes back whenever I try to concentrate. The longer the silence, the more scared I become.

Reply, Sam. Or call me.

Three hours after my last message, I can't bear it any longer.

Sam, are we okay? Xx

I wait. My heart leaps when the reply dots start to dance.

We're fine x

Two words, one kiss. It feels cold. I know he probably typed it in a hurry and the lack of his usual second kiss is just a mistake, but I feel sick. I don't want to be that person but I can't let this go until I know how he feels.

I didn't mean to scare you xx

Another painfully dragging minute. I steady my breath, try to distract my attention from the clock at the top of my mobile screen that seems to have frozen.

You didn't x

This is what I hate about messages and emails – you have no idea what the other person is really feeling because you can't see it in their expression or catch subtle changes in their voice. I could call him but I am not going to make this any worse than it already is.

Are you sure? xx

His answer is almost immediate, which should ease my nerves. But when it arrives it feels dismissive. Even the return of the elusive second kiss in his reply isn't reassuring:

Yes. Stop worrying. Have to go now, Niven's coming over xx

I throw my mobile to the pillows on my bed and put my hands over my eyes. Why does it feel like the air just changed between us?

It was one impulsive comment in a thread of messages that were already careering in that direction. I feel judged. I never expected that from Sam.

If we were in a normal relationship this would probably have been our first argument. We would've sulked for a few days but then called or met to clear the air. Being so far away from him, his words are the only clues I have to go on. I can't read him because I don't know him well enough yet.

Lurching from one emotional rollercoaster to the next isn't what I came here for. I had far too much of that in London. I get up, stuff my phone in my pocket and head for the door. Paris is on my doorstep and I can lose myself in its beauty for a while. Concentrate on me.

I'll deal with everything else later.

Chapter Fourteen

SAM

Turns out my gut feeling was right: music really is the only thing I understand. Everything else confuses my brain.

So I'm writing songs on the old guitar that creaks beneath my fingers as I sit on the green bank behind Ailish's house because I don't want to think about Phoebe. About what she said…

Keeping my head busy has been my main concern for the last week. Most days I have the house to myself while Ailish is out at the many jobs she has. She bakes for the pub by the ferry crossing, volunteers at a coffee morning in nearby Bunessan for young mums and elderly ladies once a week, is a business mentor for teens up in Tobermory once a month and when she isn't doing all that, she visits friends all over the island. It's exhausting to watch, but inspiring, too. Ma was always amazed by how much of herself Ailish gave to others. I'm not sure I could do that.

A second opinion on what Phoebe said would help, but I'm not ready to share it with Ailish so early into my time here and I haven't seen much of Niven because he's overseeing exams at his school. Next week they break for the summer so that's when he's promised me 'the fun will really start'. Maybe by then I will have worked out how to respond to Phoebe.

There's nothing wrong with what she said. Given our flirting it was an obvious next step. But when I saw those words, my heart froze.

I should have said the same back, shouldn't I?

I can feel myself pulling back. I wish I didn't feel that way. I told Laura I loved her first. And regretted it immediately. She had her first affair within a month of me saying it. You don't just say *I love you* like that. I laid my heart out for Laura and she trashed it. I can't risk that again. Not until I'm certain.

The sun has managed to kick through the mist that has claimed Fionnphort for the last five days and the wind from the ocean beats against my face and chest as I sit on the lush bank, the guitar a surprisingly effective windbreak between the edge of the Island and me. The Iona ferry isn't in yet but it's due to appear within the hour. One car is waiting already, small and lonely from my vantage point. I've become accustomed to the rumble of tyres and sudden swell of noise when the ferry arrives. It's a curious break in all the natural sound here, where so little of modern life is visible. I would have loved this place as a kid, if I'd been able to see the Island this way, and not as the battleground that robbed me of my father and, years later, my ma. My heart contracts and for a moment I'm fighting tears.

Sitting here I am connected to the land in a way I didn't think possible. Physically, emotionally, historically – and as I've done countless times before, I channel the building emotion into music. The tune that emerges is a *grace* – music for an ancient Island blessing. It's half-remembered from my earliest days playing with Jonas and the lads in the Dumbiedykes pub band, half improvised.

Closing my damp eyes I give in to the flow of the tune, losing myself in the strange place between being awake and dreaming when the music catches you.

'That's it, lad. Don't let the sting stop you,' Jonas used to say. 'The sting is what reminds you you're alive.' I didn't understand then. I do now. So much of being a musician is mind over matter: playing when you ache, when you haven't slept; endlessly repeating sections until muscular memory kicks in and you can switch off your brain.

Out here, though, with no audience, nobody to see and the music I make carried away on the breeze, sore fingers aren't making me play on.

The memories are what sting.

Then the pain finds a new outlet through my voice and I start to sing – a jumble of random words that dance with the rhythm my fingers make. And I'm free, in this wilderness with its startling beauty. I'm one with it.

'We-ell, it's original, I'll give you that, but those aren't the words I remember.'

Niven is standing by the dry-stone wall that marks the boundary between Ailish's square of garden and the wild hill it nestles into. Arms folded, head on one side like a sheepdog hearing a whistle, ridiculous grin plastered all over his face.

'Cheers. I like it.'

He scrambles up the path, chuckling, and flops down onto the peat-scented ground beside me. 'I didn't think you did much with the trad tunes now. Thought it was all beardy-hipster "new-folk" and mandolin versions of Led Zep songs.'

'I've forgotten the ones I learned as a kid,' I say, not protesting when Niven liberates the guitar from my hands. My fingers were starting to complain anyway. I shove them into the pockets of my coat. 'It's one of the things I want to do while I'm on the Island.'

'Learn the old stuff? That'll be easy enough. Come and gig with me Saturday night up in Tobermory.'

'I'm not sure I'm ready for that.'

'Not on *this* pile of kindling,' he says, plucking a string and frowning at its rusted, sorry excuse for a vibration. 'On your fiddle. My lot are a good bunch of lads, reliable and fun. It'll be a blast. Come on, what do you say?'

I've never turned down a gig in my life, so the answer is academic. Playing might be what I need to take my mind off Phoebe.

Niven's bandmates are great. A real mix of ages, which is as it should be – from John-Jack Macallan in his early eighties to Gowan Burnie, barely 17 years old. There's no hierarchy like I've found in commercial bands and that's so refreshing. Egos always get in the way of the music. Here, you rock up with your instrument, take a seat, maybe buy a round of beers (Gowan excepted, naturally; he gets the crisps in) and play. There's no setlist, either, just a quick conversation of *this one, that one and then we wing it…*

At one point a lady from behind the bar comes over, hutches up between Niven and John-Jack and sings two songs with us. There was no agreement with her prior to the gig, and if someone gave a signal I missed it. But nobody protests, which makes me think this is an unspoken invitation. When you're amongst friends, everyone can pitch in for a spot of entertaining.

Unlike every other gig I've played in the last six years, every punter in the pub just listens. No phones held aloft, recording it for endless shaky playback after the event. Once our gig is over, there will be no record that we were ever here, apart from the memories in the minds of those who listened.

Too much of my life is lived through frozen images on my phone. Photos, recordings – supposedly for posterity. Even Phoebe is becoming an amalgamation of message streams, half-remembered facts and the single image I have of the day we first met. That and the three words I can't escape.

I will talk to her about it.

Soon.

Just… not yet.

'Frank's lad, yes?' I look up to see Niven gone, the rest of the band taking a break to stretch and visit the bar. There's an elderly gentleman standing next to me, his sharp blue eyes twinkling over ruddy cheeks and a snow-white beard.

'Sorry?'

He lowers himself onto Niven's stool and slaps his hands on his knees as he leans towards me. 'Frank Mullins. Fiddle player. Are you his boy?'

I'm so surprised I can't reply.

'Knew you were the moment you started playing. Only other person I ever heard play "The Rigs o' Barley" like that was Frank Mullins. Terror of the Island. But he could charm the angels out of paradise when he played that fiddle.'

'You know my father?'

'Know him? Aye, son. We all knew Frank. Notorious round here.' He sticks out a fisherman's brown hand in greeting. 'Euan McAllister. I knew your granny.'

That's less of a welcome revelation. Was this man close to Grandma? If so, was he part of the gaggle of locals who believed her lies about Ma? I stuff the thought away. What matters is that he knew my father. 'I'm Sam. Good to meet you. How long have you known Frank?'

Euan blows out his cheeks and the blue eyes roll up towards the pub's wood-clad ceiling. 'Oh, forty-odd years it must be by now. We were neighbours when he and your ma first married. Remember them pushing you around as a wee bairn. Proud as anything.'

I only ever remember the strange tension between them, the comments that made Ma crumple, her retorts that brought my father's frown. I don't remember them being happy. But then I was just a kid when Frank left us. Suddenly we were at Grandma's, definitely *not* going home again, and where my father had been was a gap that didn't make sense.

'I don't suppose you had any contact with Frank after he left the Island?'

'Sorry, lad. Last I heard he was living on the mainland driving trucks. But that was years ago.'

'Oh, okay. Thanks.'

Euan gives a gravelled cough and glances over his shoulder. 'I heard about the business with your ma. She should never have had to put up with that. Your granny was a beast of a woman. I can say that now she's gone.'

I nod back, not sure how else to react.

'Tell you what, though, I might know someone who kept in touch with Frank.'

'You might?' There's a cheer from the bar that makes me jump and the band begins to reform around us. 'Who?'

'Pal of mine: Morag Andersson. Lives not far from here. Look, best play your tunes now, son. I'll give you her address when you're done.'

As the music resumes, my heart is thudding faster than the reel we play. This is it: the first real breakthrough in my search for the truth. Maybe Morag Andersson will know what happened to Frank – and where I can find him.

Chapter Fifteen

PHOEBE

'Phoebe.'

I look up from my journal to see a large steaming cup held by a concerned Canadian. Luc is so tall he has to duck beneath the trails of ivy in the courtyard garden to stand by the bench where I'm sitting, and I have to shield my eyes from the bright lunchtime sun to see him. 'Thank you. You didn't have to bring me tea.'

'I did. Because this is the best *thé au citron* in Paris. And also because Tobi says you are sad and you won't tell him why. So I thought you might tell me.'

'I'm not sad.'

'Okay.' He sits beside me. 'Heard from Sam lately?'

Ouch. I thought I was doing a good job of playing the happy tourist around Luc and Tobi. I've been out in Paris every day and have almost finalised the next part of my European journey. Most afternoons I've returned to read in the lovely garden and most evenings I've chatted and laughed with my hosts late into the night. I didn't think my feelings about Sam were visible to anyone but me. Shows what I know.

'I get a text every few days. He's been playing gigs with his mate Niven and he's writing new songs. He's promised to send me one.'

I sound defensive but I don't mean to be. Yes, Sam has contacted me. We've even attempted to flirt a couple of times, but the great three-word elephant looms in between us, casting its shadow over everything.

'I told him I loved him,' I say, my words rising to meet the carefree clouds in the Parisian sky.

If Luc has an opinion, he's careful to hide it. 'Ah.'

'I didn't mean to. I mean, I *do* love him, but… I just said it before either of us were ready.'

'But he feels the same? You said at the station he seemed to.'

'I thought he did.' I close my book, hoping this ends the conversation, and take a deep breath. The air tastes of cool green leaves and lemon steam. 'Anyway, I'm moving on soon, so that's what I should be thinking about. If Sam and I are meant to be together, this will all work out. If we aren't…'

Luc nods and there's no need to finish my sentence. Far above our heads tiny white clouds traverse the summer blue. 'You've decided where you're headed? Is it Florence or Rome?'

'Florence first, then Rome. It makes sense to do it that way. But I won't go there straight away. I plan to visit a few places in France first.'

'Tobi and I know an artist in Rome. We met her on our honeymoon.' Luc turns to me. 'Hey, I could contact her, if you like? See if she might let you stay for a while?'

It's so out of the blue that it takes a moment to take it in. If I could save even a few days' worth of accommodation costs it would be a huge help. Not to mention staying with a friend of Tobi and Luc.

'Really? You wouldn't mind?'

He sparkles at my reaction. I love how Luc transforms into a delighted kid whenever he makes someone smile. 'It would be my pleasure! Besides, you know Tobi and I will worry about you when you're out there. Rome is crazy, especially if you visit alone. If you're with our friend it will be much better.'

It doesn't solve everything, but it is enough to take my mind off Sam – for now.

A postcard from Sam arrives the next day. It has a cartoon of the Loch Ness monster firing a cannon from Edinburgh Castle painted in colours so garish they make my eyes ache. Sam wasn't kidding when he said Scotland excels in the weird and wonderful when it comes to postcards. Each one he's sent is more bonkers than the last, whereas I've tried to find a more beautiful one each time. I wonder if this is another sign, another difference between us. Is he taking this whole thing seriously? If he isn't, no wonder he backed off when I said *I love you*.

I don't read it immediately, waiting until I'm wandering slowly around the beautiful galleries of the Louvre to pull it from my pocket and turn it over. I love this space, so much so that I've kept returning. The unrushed, unhurried air within is so markedly different from the tourist buzz outside. It's cooler and quieter and I love it.

Returning to the galleries has made me feel less like a visitor and I've been able to write in its serene stillness – perhaps the biggest surprise of my time in Paris. I've written an entry in my journal every day and when I read the pieces back at night I'm proud of what I see.

The Louvre is the perfect spot to people-watch, too. Growing up on a fruit farm in the middle of the rolling Worcestershire countryside I didn't get to observe other people much, unless you counted my teenage shifts in the farm shop, which were more a case of serving people as quickly as possible while trying to avoid eye contact.

Here, everyone exists in their own space, inviting you to watch from a distance like the artwork on display. I see friends and couples, excited school kids and elegant pensioners; brand new acquaintances and rendezvous with people hoping to be more than friends. All of them move through the space to their own rhythms at their own speed. But as I watch, it hits me: all of the people passing by *know* where they are going. Everybody here knows where their next steps will take them. I thought my next steps would bring me closer to Sam. Now I'm not so sure.

After a while, I find a quiet place and read Sam's card.

Hey you,

This is the most horrific postcard in the whole of Caledonia. You're welcome!

Things are okay here. Music and walking, hanging out with Niven and being force-fed cake by Ailish. I'm going to have to take up running or something or else I'll be rolling myself back to London like an overstuffed haggis.

Let me have your address when you know where you'll be staying. Also, can I call you? Things have been a bit weird – I've been weird, I know. I don't think I can explain on a postcard or in a message. I need to talk to you. Text me a good time to call, please.

I really do care about you, Phoebe. I want this to happen for us.

Speak soon

Sam xx

Sam wanting to talk is a step forward. So why don't I feel reassured?

After dinner I call the only person who will understand. Meg sounds tired but within seconds she's sparkling down the line, telling me about the huge events she's being hired to manage. It's so good to hear her voice and slip back into our familiar patter. But pretty soon, she susses me.

'Anyway, you didn't call to be appraised of my diary, did you? So, what's up?'

I finally admit the truth. 'I told Sam I love him.'

I can hear her slow inhale. 'That's – *fast.*'

'I know.'

'Fast for you, I mean.'

'Yep.'

'And he said…?'

'He didn't. He *hasn't…*'

'Oh, Phee…'

'I mean, he's still contacting me – more than before, actually, which is a bit strange. And then today I received a postcard that said he wants this to happen for us. Whatever that means.'

'It means he's trying to apologise.'

'You think?' I want it to be true more than anything.

'I don't know the guy but if he was trying to put you off I doubt he'd say something like that in a postcard. How long have you been worrying about this?'

I smooth down the corner of a page in my journal that's bent itself over. 'Almost a week.'

'You're such a berk, Phee. Why didn't you say anything?'

'I didn't want to admit that things weren't brilliant with Sam and me. You know, after making such a big deal about meeting him at the station.'

'What possible difference could that have made?' Meg's frustration grazes my ear.

'I know what you think about it. And the others, if they know, which I'm guessing they might.'

The pause on the other end of the line confirms my suspicions. But why shouldn't Osh and Gabe know?

'Are you having second thoughts, Phee? Because it's okay if you are. And nobody will judge you for it.'

'Gabe would love that,' I say, surprising myself. Where did that come from?

'He's a wind-up merchant. You know he is.'

'I just don't want him to know about this.'

'I won't say anything. Besides, he's still reeling from you being away…'

'What do you mean?'

'Nothing. We all want you to be happy, Phee, Gabe included. And we might be hundreds of miles from you but that doesn't mean you can't talk to us about stuff.'

I close my eyes. 'I feel a bit of an idiot.'

'No more than the rest of us. *All* the time.'

'Yeah, right.'

'I'm serious. You seem to think we've got it sorted, but the truth is we're all just blundering around from one thing to the next. Everyone is. Osh has just had a short film commissioned but I spent most of last night talking him down from a huge panic attack about it. He's chased that commission for months but yesterday he'd convinced himself he was going to stuff it up and never work again. And Gabe did the table read for his play on Monday and wouldn't speak to the rest of us for two days because he thinks it's going to make his career nosedive. None of us knows what we're doing.'

It doesn't make me feel better that my friends are having a hard time. 'I'm not sure the whole Sam thing is on a par with that.'

'It's something you care about and you're scared it won't happen. I'd say it's exactly the same. Give him time. You're both away for a year, so why does every decision need to be made in the first few weeks?'

I wish I could hug her. 'You are wise, Meggy.'

'I'm glad you noticed. Just focus on the next part of your journey and let Sam have space to work out what he wants. You have so much amazing stuff to look forward to, Phee. Don't wish it away before it happens.'

When the call is over, I grab my guidebooks and map. It's time to plan exactly where the next leg of my journey will take me.

Chapter Sixteen

SAM

Hey Sam, what's the goss from the Island? Xx

I rest the dram of whisky I've been drinking on the arm of my chair and look at my phone. Despite the ball of nerves that's just rolled into my stomach seeing Phoebe's face beaming up from the screen, it's good to hear from her. I've felt like a git since *that* text and half-wondered if the card I sent a few days ago might have shocked her.

All good here –

I lie, wanting to sound jokey and charming, not the bag of anxiety I've been all day knowing that tomorrow I'm meeting a woman who knew my father.

Niven's taking me fishing tomorrow xx

Another lie. The text glares at me accusingly. Technically it's possible – one of the many activities Niven has hinted we might do at some point this year. But it isn't happening tomorrow. There's only one thing I'll be hunting and it won't be found dangling on the end of a fly line.

I might not be able say *I love you* to Phoebe yet, but hiding this stuff from her is wrong. She's shared so much with me already. If I'm serious about having her in my life, I can't hide anything.

I stab at the touchscreen until the words are deleted. In their place I type:

> Potentially big stuff. I'm meeting someone tomorrow who knew my father.

Written down, it's scarily real.

> Crapping myself about it xx

A moment later, her reply arrives.

> You're doing the right thing xx

Am I? Talking with Euan McAllister after the gig it seemed the easiest thing to do. Just asking for stories about my father, no more than collecting anecdotes. But ever since, it's become this enormous monolith in my path. Because whatever I find out tomorrow will change the Frank Mullins in my head. I've grown accustomed to the half-finished, barely consequential ghost of my father I've carried with me most of my life. Am I ready to trade that?

Deep down I know Phoebe is right – she understands. She's my ally for tomorrow, albeit an invisible one.

> I just wish I could wait a while longer. It's a bit sudden xx

The moment I see her reply, I know it will make me get in the car tomorrow:

It isn't sudden in terms of your life, Sam. 32 years isn't
sudden. You deserve answers xx

Morag Andersson's studio is hidden from the road up a steep track. I've almost convinced myself I've taken a wrong turn, driving the car I've borrowed from Ailish, when the simple glass and wood structure comes into view. It's built into the side of the hill, so that it appears to be peering out of the earth. It's startlingly modern when I see it up close, the kind of structure I've only seen on trendy TV renovation shows.

Stepping out of the car into the strong wind, my thoughts drift to Phoebe. She told me she's started writing in her journal, and I picture her in that hidden garden she's sent me pictures of. Making her mark on the world – and thinking of me. That's pretty special. Having her thinking of me today makes this windswept hillside feel less foreboding. If I close my eyes I can almost imagine Phoebe holding my hand… But then those three words appear again and my stomach twists. I'm not ready to picture that yet.

'Sam, is it?'

I turn back to see a woman standing at the front door. She's tall and swathed in layers of knitted wool that make her look like a Celtic warrior. I can't work out how old she is. Her skin is smooth and her ash blonde hair is tied into a long braid that snakes around her shoulder. Her eyes are the kind of startling blue that you see a lot of on these islands – our Scandinavian heritage never too far away.

Pulling my thoughts together, I offer her my hand. 'Hi, Ms Andersson.'

'Morag, kid. Formality worries me.' She smiles as she shakes my hand. 'Please, come in.'

Inside, I discover Morag's studio is also her home. There's a large central space with wraparound, full-length windows that frame the wild Mull landscape like a constantly changing work of art; leading off this are rooms that go back into the hill. It's far bigger on the inside than it appears from the approach. Light floods the studio living-space, but where the light gets in the sound of the wind outside is denied access. It's as quiet as the live room in our studio, all outside noise blocked out.

'It's good for recording music, if you ever need it,' Morag grins as if reading my thoughts, motioning for me to sit on a much-loved corner sofa. 'Euan tells me you've just set up a studio in London?'

'I have. My business partner is running it for me while I'm away.'

There's a pot of fresh coffee on the low table beside her and she pours a cup for me without asking. Caffeine is definitely needed today. We take our first sips in the eerie silence of the room. My heart is hammering hard and I can delay the question no longer.

'How well did you know Frank?' It makes sense to call him by his name. Using *Dad* or *Da* or *my father* feels wrong. As far as this conversation is concerned, he's just someone we both have in common. Nothing more.

'Very well, back in the day. I sang with him in a couple of bands. My sister and me both did. She was younger – I think Frank might have dated her for a while. Before he met your ma.' She adds this caveat quickly as if I might think her sister was one of Frank's many supposed indiscretions while he was with my mother.

'How long were you in bands with him for?'

'Quite a few years. Ten maybe? And then he left the Island.' She peers at me over the rim of her cup. 'I didn't play any gigs with him after that. Although I heard he was still playing when he could.'

'But you kept in touch?'

'We did.' She shifts a little in her chair, picks at a seam in her long embroidered skirt. I notice the stacks of silver rings on each of her fingers.

'Where did he go? When he left Mull?'

'Glasgow, initially. Then he rocked up in Shetland for a time. I think he got a job with the refinery although I've no idea what he was doing there. Frank wasn't the most practical of people but he could pretty much talk his way into anything.'

I've always been able to blag my way into work and I didn't get that from my mother, who never pushed herself forward. It would have been her idea of hell, her own quietness and solitude the only place she ever felt safe. I haven't dared compare myself with my father before, and it's strange to think we might share a personality trait, aside from the music. Though the music found me, I tell everyone, the day I met Jonas and his pals. I haven't wanted to consider Frank gave me anything but half my DNA.

'Did he stay on in Shetland?'

'No. Lasted maybe eighteen months? No more than that. Next I heard he'd moved again to Edinburgh and was settling there.'

'With someone?' The question has rushed into the stillness of the studio before I can think better of it.

'If it was he never mentioned it to me.' She takes a long sip of coffee, her blue eyes tracking the fast progress of smoke grey clouds across the dirty white sky. 'But I imagine he had relationships. Frank always did.'

We lapse into silence again, me taking this in. Did he have a fling with Morag, too?

'Are you wanting to find him?' she asks suddenly.

'I'm – not sure. Ailish reckons he was driving HGVs at one point?'

She gives a small laugh. 'Wouldn't surprise me.'

There's something I can't decipher in her expression. It unnerves me. In the pause that follows I look over to the four easels over by the window. Morag works in oils, thick sweeps of vivid colour building into patchwork representations of the landscape around us. The canvases are large and I imagine not cheap, judging by her home. Something has to pay for this and to my knowledge there's no significant other to split the bills with. I assume her work will be sold at a fair profit in sleek art galleries in Edinburgh and Glasgow, maybe even London.

'Are you in touch with him now?'

She's been expecting that question. I can see it in the way she straightens her spine, sets her jaw. 'I was – until about a year ago.'

'What happened?'

'I'm not sure. I hadn't seen him in years but we'd swapped Christmas cards, had occasional phone calls, you know. But then they just – stopped. The last time I called him, the number was unobtainable. We never fell out and I hadn't offended him, as far as I'm aware. He just disappeared. I imagine there was some kind of trouble. It's usually the reason Frank Mullins runs.' Her cheeks redden a little. 'Sorry, I didn't mean… I just didn't hear from him again.'

Did Ma know this about Frank when she married him? I haven't considered it until now, but the way Morag talks it sounds as if it was common knowledge. Did Ma believe she could tame him, that she was enough to plant him firmly in one place?

Not for the first time, sadness hits me that I didn't ask enough questions, didn't try to understand what Ma had been through beyond what she told me.

Before I leave, Morag hands me a bag. Something of Frank's she'd kept for years, she says. It rests unopened on the car seat beside me as I drive back to Fionnphort. Most of the journey I ignore it, but temptation eventually wins. I pull into a patch of stone-pocked mud that passes as a parking place, kill the engine, and sit there for a while staring at the passenger seat. Sheets of rain hit the windscreen and pepper the car roof. My heartbeat joins the rhythm, pounding out a contrary beat. I take a breath and remember Phoebe's words: *32 years isn't sudden.*

Inside the cold plastic bag is what looks like a roll of checked tweed fabric, fastened with a crimson ribbon. When I untie it, the fabric unfurls to reveal a flat cap.

Frank's cap.

I turn the cap over in my hands, the thought that *he* wore this once, a sharp stab to my heart. If it were anyone else's I might be tempted to try it on. But this is *his* cap. I can't risk looking in the rear-view mirror and seeing my father staring back.

I run my hand over its crown, flipping it to reveal the lining and a large square central silk label so faded that any words once printed on it have long since disappeared. The stitching is loose on one side. There's the lightest crumpling sound, almost lost in the hammering of rain against the car. I slide my finger underneath and it touches something that feels like paper. I manage to catch the edge and pull it out.

It's a folded photograph.

I can hardly breathe.

Frank's face emerges from the cracked folds as the image is

revealed. It's a little blurry, but I can make him out, surrounded by people I don't recognise, a battered old fiddle tucked under his chin. It's dark, but the tin-topped table and collection of empty pint glasses leaves no doubt where the picture was taken. Corner of a pub, near a bar: the default location for a ceilidh band to play.

He's wearing the cap. His smile is crooked, a limp cigarette pinned between his clenched teeth. And I am overwhelmed with the strongest sensation of seeing that smile before. The fag and the gritted-teeth grin. It punches the air from me.

But a bigger kick follows when I look on the back of it.

Written in large, sloping capitals is a message:

> *MORAG MY LOVELY*
> *MORAG MY SUN*
> *OCEANS MAY PART US*
> *BUT HEARTS LINGER ON*

There's a phone number, too. A landline number. The code stops my breath. 0131. Edinburgh. That can't be right, can it?

Morag might have lied about just how close she and Frank were. But the phone number is my first real lead. Part of me doesn't want to know, the old fury at Frank resurfacing and making my hands shake where they hold his picture. But thirty-two years is long enough to know what I have to do next.

Chapter Seventeen

PHOEBE

'Phoebe, we have a confession.'

Tobi and Luc stand together by the kitchen counter and their mirrored solemnity is so comical I have to fight the urge to laugh.

'What have you done?' I ask, sounding scarily like my mother.

'We will tell you at dinner,' Luc says.

'Oh. Okay.'

'Just know that what we did came from a place of love.'

There's no sign of dinner cooking, which is unusual given Tobi is such a creature of habit about mealtimes. 'Are we eating out?' I ask.

'In a manner of speaking,' Tobi says, steering me by my shoulders out of the apartment into the stairwell and around the corridor to the service staircase door. 'Down there, *mon amie*.'

As we near the bottom of the stairs I can hear laughter and conversation drifting up towards us. And when I reach the open door to the courtyard garden, my breath leaves me completely.

The whole garden is ablaze with white lights, tumbling down from the first-, second- and third-floor balconies, draped around the walls and standing sentry around the perimeter in tiny white paper lanterns resting on the courtyard floor. At the centre a long table has been covered in white linen, a hotchpotch selection of chairs surrounding it. And standing around the table is a group of about ten smiling people, some of whom I have seen using the garden or said hello to as we've passed in the hallways of the apartment block. When we approach, they raise their glasses and cheer. I lean against Luc's arm for a moment to steady myself. It's *magical*.

In that moment, I wish Sam were next to me. Despite all the confusion over what I said to him, I believe he is a romantic at heart. He would love this.

I check myself. Thoughts of Sam don't belong here tonight. 'When did you do this?' I ask.

Tobi hands me a glass of wine. 'Earlier today, when you were out. And here is the confession: I told my friends about your *grande aventure* and they wanted to give you something to take with you. I hope you don't mind?'

Before I came to Paris I might have balked at my business being shared with relative strangers. It was always a bugbear of mine in London that my friends, lovely and caring as they are, could never understand that some things in my life weren't for sharing with everyone. But here in the City of Light I like feeling part of something bigger than I am. I smile at Tobi and give their friends a little wave.

'Sit, sit!' Luc says, guiding me to a chair near the head of the table.

And I do as I'm told because everything else fades away in the sparkling light of *this* moment. Mum says that some moments in life arrive just to be enjoyed for what they are. She talks about meeting Dad; the first time she held my brother Will and me; the first time they brought in a harvest on the farm they'd taken over from Granny and Grandpa – the big things you'd expect to be significant. But sometimes she'd get one of her smiles and stand completely still, one finger raised: 'There. You see? Just stop, kids.

Take that in…' A particular bird's song, a flower growing between the pavement slabs in our local town; a scent of something we passed as we walked down the street – tiny things we could have so easily missed.

Maybe if I can tear them away from the fruit farm for a whole weekend, I might bring Mum and Dad to Montmartre to meet Tobi and Luc and see this tiny garden where I've discovered my own words alongside those of the authors I love.

All of the guests are seated now, their glasses refilled. Their smiles beam across the table to me as Luc stands.

'So, *ma fille chérie*, our friends wanted to share their favourite places with you for your journey.' Tobi picks up a gift box covered in what looks like pages from an atlas, tied with a huge bow the colour of the summer sky. The gathered guests smile as they pass it towards me. Their collective excitement is palpable as the box reaches my hands; twelve held breaths as I untie the ribbon and lift the lid.

Inside, lying on a bed of primrose yellow tissue paper, is a leather journal embossed with a gold-leaf phoenix.

'This is *beautiful*.'

'Look inside, Miss Phee,' Luc says.

The first ten pages are covered in a patchwork of handwriting – some small and studied, some flamboyant and looped, written in a mix of blue, black, red and green inks. The rest of the book has quotes at the top of every other page, written in Luc's beautiful hand-lettering. Each one comes from a classic novel. It must have taken him hours to complete.

'The pages at the front are lists of our favourite things to see in the places you will be visiting,' Tobi smiles. 'All suggestions of course, but things your guidebooks might not tell you.'

'And the rest of the book is yours to write in,' Luc adds, his hand warm on my shoulder. 'All of your adventures, all of your thoughts.'

I am stunned by their kindness and what this gift signifies. Not only love for my journey but support for my fledgling writing. Halfway between sobs and laughter, I stare at them all. 'I – I don't know what to say…'

Tobi takes my hand. 'Say nothing. *Write* instead.'

The next day, on my way back to Tobi and Luc's, I decide to walk down a street that I've always passed by but never ventured into. It leads me to a small paved square with a little green park at one side. *Square Jehan-Rictus.* I'm surprised to find it packed with tourists. When I follow the line of their trained camera lenses, I see why.

On blue tiles mounted to one wall of the garden, the words *I love you* have been written in hundreds of languages. The effect of so many versions of the same phrase is beautiful – and utterly overwhelming.

So many words, all expressing the same thing. Crossing borders both physical and psychological, crossing the divide between languages and religions – the single unifying emotion that makes us all human. It's a powerful statement in a world more attuned to hate and suspicion. Love isn't a soppy, frivolous emotion: it's powerful, honest and potentially world changing.

I don't regret saying I loved Sam because I do – but those words have so much more power than I realised, and I understand that now. Coming at him as they did, completely unannounced, must have felt like the impact this mural has had on me. Even if he loves me – or is on the way towards it – being presented with it so suddenly must have been overwhelming. And typed, too, not said.

I take my new notebook from my bag and start to write. I

want to tell Sam immediately, call him right now and say that I understand. But that would be wrong. If he loves me, he'll tell me. I have to trust him.

Instead, I pour out my heart in the pages of the journal. Until now, everything I've written has been about what I've seen: this is the first time my heart has strayed onto the page. The words appear in my mind faster than my hand can capture them and it's almost as if they are being dictated to me from somewhere else – as if the many-accented voices of the mural tiles are calling out to me.

When I'm finished, I read it back.

It's powerful – far from perfect, but the emotion sings from the marks I've made on the page.

In that moment, I make myself a promise: in this journal I will be completely honest. I will write down everything I think and feel, alongside the places I see and the people I meet. If Sam and I make it through this year, I will let him read it. If he loves me on the day we meet again, this will be my gift to him.

'Isn't it wonderful?' A lady smiles as she stands beside me. She is tiny and has a camera around her neck with a huge lens attached that seems to be almost half her height. 'A guy in the café across the street told me about it. There are a thousand *I love you* messages, in over three hundred languages.'

'Would you take my picture in front of it?' I ask, the thought appearing as I say the words.

'Of course,' she says, accepting my camera and waiting for me to find a space in the posing tourists beside the mural.

Afterwards, I buy a coffee from the café across the street and take a seat in the garden opposite the mural. Each couple and group find their language on the wall and pose for photos. It's lovely to watch.

'*Excusez-moi, parlez-vous anglais?*' A young man is standing by me when I turn.

'Yes I do.'

'Oh great. Would you mind taking our photo? We're on our honeymoon.'

After the man and his beaming bride pose for their photograph, we get talking. Giselle and André are from Prince Edward Island in Canada. They met at high school and when they tell me *how* they met, I am stunned.

'We only met because our math teacher mixed up our assignments. I would never have had the guts to talk to her if it weren't for that mistake.'

'And I'd been in love with him since the first day of school, but he'd never even looked at me before. It was a random error but for us it was the start of everything.'

Listening to their story I'm struck by how both of our situations could have been called mistakes or bad luck in the beginning. Getting someone else's paper and having the embarrassment of asking the other person for it back; being stranded at a train station for six hours on the day your biggest adventure is due to begin, meeting someone in the middle of your panic…

My heart is warmed by the young lovers' story. Maybe one day Sam and I will be by a landmark like this, sharing our story of how we met to inspire someone else reeling from a crazy serendipity that's sent their lives spinning in a new direction.

Maybe in the end we are all just stories waiting to be shared.

Later still, on a bench in the park near Sacré-Cœur where I told Luc about what happened at St Pancras when my train was delayed, I write an email to Sam.

Hi Sam,

I'm almost ready to leave Paris and last night Tobi, Luc and their friends gave me a gorgeous travel journal with lists of all their favourite places in France and Italy. I'm heading to Troyes first – I found a great place on Airbnb that's right in the heart of the town. Probably won't be there long enough for another scary Scottish postcard (in case you have more in your arsenal) but feel free to message me if you like.

Can I just say something? I haven't wanted to address it before but today I realised how forward I was saying I loved you. It was a spur of the moment thing, not a test. I don't need to hear it back or anything. It is how I feel but I understand how it came out was probably a shock. I'm sorry for chucking that at you.

I hope things went well with the person who knew your dad. I think what you're doing is amazing, Sam. I hope you find the answers you're looking for.

I'd love to know how you're getting on. You said before you wanted to call me. If you still do, I'd love to talk.

And you promised me a song, remember?

Phoebe xx

As I send it I lean back against the sun-warmed bench, the sounds of Paris filling the space where the words have been. Now I'm ready to move on.

Chapter Eighteen

SAM

Ailish is quiet this morning, her library book open beside her plate and her reading glasses teetering on the end of her nose. We've breakfasted together almost every morning since I arrived and like every other aspect of Island life, I've settled into its easy rhythm. But today is different. It isn't the sunlight stretching across the linen tablecloth and yellow crockery, or the sparkling silver ocean beyond the window changing things this morning. I know she's waiting for something. It's been a week since I visited Morag and I haven't said much about it, just how the drive across was and what Morag's studio was like.

It's time she knew the rest.

'Morag gave me this,' I say, pulling Frank's cap from my jacket pocket where it's sat like an uncertain talisman for days.

She says nothing, inspecting the cap with a half-smile. Her eyebrows are lifted too high for her to appear disinterested, so I wait. When she still doesn't speak, I hand her the photograph of Frank.

'And that was hidden underneath the label. I think he and Morag might have been more than friends.' I hear hesitation in my voice and know Ailish will have picked it up, too.

'Mm.'

I catch the flicker of her eyes to the view beyond the window. 'What?'

'Morag Andersson, you say?'

'Yes. She's an artist…'

'She's also not an Andersson. Or she wasn't at the time your father was sniffing around her. We all knew her as Morag Ross.'

'So she married?'

Ailish purses her lips. I know a story is imminent. Cal and I loved the stories she'd tell when she visited us as kids. Ailish has the inside track on everyone. Ma loved Ailish's top-class gossip more than all of us. '*Said* she married. Disappeared to Norway for half a year, came back an Andersson. No sign of a husband.'

'Was this when she was gigging with Frank?'

'No. Later. When he'd gone.' Her frown softens and she reaches for my hand. 'I'm not saying she chased your father. She was too young to know any better.'

'She said her sister dated Frank before Ma.'

'Possible, I suppose. But he was with your ma when they were both so young. Anyway, that's ancient history. What matters is this phone number. Have you called it?'

'No.' I was so certain when I found Frank's photo that I'd call the number the next day. But by the morning I'd talked myself out of it. Since then I've just quietly shelved my plans every day. 'It isn't that I don't want to know. I just don't know if I'm ready to find him yet.'

The pearls round Ailish's neck make a light *click-click* as she nods. 'I understand. And there's no rush. You have to do this when you're ready. Nobody can tell you when that'll be. But maybe we can do a little more digging on the Island, see what others remember about Frank? They might know something that means you never have to call that number.'

I hadn't thought of that. It would certainly feel less of a direct challenge. 'Do you know anyone else we could talk to?'

My honorary auntie grins a grin no self-respecting lady of her years should unleash. 'You're with me now, bairn. I know *everyone.*'

If I let Ailish ask around first, it will buy me time before I have to act on anything and she'll also feel like she's helping me. I'll look like I'm moving forward without having to consider it yet.

I need time to work out what I want from Frank, should we find him. This is the perfect plan.

They say the weather changes when you blink on the Island and today Mull is proving its reputation. Two hours after breakfast the sparkling sun and clear skies have vanished. It's blowing a *hoolie* out there and it's definitely looking like a day for staying indoors. Rain lashes against the wide picture window and the smudge of grey sky is so low I can't even see the beach any longer, let alone the shadow of Iona across the bay.

I'm stuck in the front room of Ailish's, waiting for Niven who's insisted on driving over. We're supposed to be working on some songs to take round the Island – Niven's idea. He's started doing house gigs in the small villages so that the community can hear live music without having to travel to Tobermory. It will be just him and me, with possibly a whistle player or piper if he has a mate nearby.

By the time Niven arrives, it's early afternoon. A tree had blown down in one of the villages on the way here and was blocking the road. So Niven jumped out of his car to help a local farmer, fellow drivers and a group of locals to shift it. That's what you do here – everyone mucks in. I think about London and the chaos one fallen tree would cause there. Not for the first time lately, I'm glad I'm on Mull.

Ailish is on her way out as Niven blows in, but she fusses round him getting towels and a huge beige knitted jumper – neither of us wants to enquire who might have worn it first. Niven chuckles as he picks bits of pine branch from his hair, drowning in questionable knitwear.

'It's what all the best-dressed males on Mull are wearing this season. We're calling it Rustic Hebridean Chic.'

'Oh aye, the fresh bits of tree behind your ears really set it off,' Ailish grins back, preening Niven like a mother cat cleaning a kitten. He rolls his eyes but it's clear he's loving every minute. As long as I've known him, he's had this effect on women of a certain age. Must be his boyish good looks that make older ladies want to mother him. 'Now boys, there's gin and lemon cake in the kitchen and if it gets chilly there's blankets in the box and whisky in the sideboard.'

'Marry me, Ailish McRae!'

She raises an eyebrow at my friend. 'You'd never survive, Niven. I'd eat you for breakfast.'

She's grinning when she leaves though, the bloom of a blush dancing across her cheekbones.

'Auntie Ailish, Queen of the One-Liners,' I say as Niven feigns shock.

'And you wonder why she never remarried.'

'I don't think she's that bothered,' I grin, as he follows me through to the kitchen. 'She has a gaggle of admirers scattered across the Island.'

'Admiring her from a distance because she's too scary up close, eh?'

'Just because she spurned you, pal, doesn't mean there aren't others she'll accept.'

Half an hour later we've demolished two slices of Ailish's epic homemade cake each and the teapot is on its second filling. Niven unpacks his guitar while I tune my fiddle. Jonas's violin will always be my first love. Unfortunately its days of coping with gruelling gig schedules are at an end and it now resides in pride of place in the studio Chris and I have built. I'll still use it for recording.

My current violin is brighter sounding than Jonas's. I can't explain it other than that it *sounds* younger. Jonas's violin has lost that quality but its seasoned old body captures the sonorous lower notes with a clarity and warmth that younger instruments will never achieve. For the gigs Niven and I might play on the Island, though, my current instrument is perfect. Bright and fun, sharp and quick. Enough to invite people's feet to tap, their heads to nod and maybe even their bodies to dance.

'Do you know where we'll play yet?' I ask, as Niven perches on the far end of the sofa.

'I've a couple of venues lined up,' he grins, popping a biro behind one ear and rolling up the huge sleeves of Ailish's jumper. 'One in Bunessan, one up in Calgary. And my pal Russ says we can deck out his barn in Dervaig for a ceilidh next month sometime. Once folk hear about it I reckon we'll get more. You up for it?'

Daft question.

We start to run through reels, jigs and graces; some I've not heard since childhood, others that are new to me. And as we play my mind drifts to a tiny apartment in Montmartre, where a beautiful woman is preparing for the next stage of her Grand Adventure.

Phoebe's email arrived while I was having breakfast but I didn't open it then. When I did, it wasn't her apologies that hit me – *It was a spur of the moment thing, not a test. I don't need to hear it back or anything* – but my own pang of guilt. I went to see Morag because of what Phoebe said. Her advice meant so much to me. *You know where I am if you want to talk.* I want to tell her that, and explain that she is still important to me. I just need to find a way to say it all.

Chapter Nineteen

PHOEBE

It's time.

I'm leaving Paris today with my plans in place and a stack of suggestions from Tobi and Luc's friends. My two months here have been wonderful and I've learned so much. I wonder what awaits me on my onward journey through France?

My phone buzzes as I'm stuffing the last of my books into my luggage. I snatch it up from the bed but my finger hesitates before accepting the call. Since I emailed Sam, his little messages and texts have peppered each of my remaining days in Paris. But while we'd agreed we would call soon, we haven't spoken yet. And now I'm nervous of what he might want to say.

'Hey you.'

A rush of joy races through me when I hear the smile in his voice. Just like it was on the day we met. 'Hi, stranger.'

'I didn't know if I'd get you before your train. You're leaving today, right?'

'I am.'

'How do you feel – about moving on?' The second part is tagged on quickly as if he's scared I'll think he's talking about us.

'Good. I have everything booked and Tobi and Luc's friend in

Rome confirmed yesterday that I can stay with her for two months after I've visited Florence.'

'That's great.'

'It is. And I have all the suggestions in the journal the boys gave me between Paris and Rome.'

'I'm really excited for you.' I can hear the cry of gulls and rush of waves behind him.

'Where are you now?'

'On Calgary Beach. West coast of the Island. Niven wanted to take photos here. It's pretty spectacular. I'll send you one when you're on the train.'

I try to picture Sam sitting in grassy dunes at the edge of the beach, buffeted by the wind. 'What can you see?'

'Mostly clouds but the sun's trying to beat them. The wind's so strong it's blowing the white sand in waves across the beach. And the view across the water is incredible. Moody blue out to infinity.' His chuckle warms my ear. 'And *that's* the title of my next prog-rock album, obviously.'

'I like it.'

I *love* it – but I won't say that to Sam. The ease has returned to our conversation, and I've missed that. But what if he's relaxing because I'm about to move further away? I bundle the unwelcome thought from my mind.

'So, Troyes next, eh?'

'Yes. You've been paying attention.'

'Don't sound so surprised. Actually, I've done a bit of research.'

'Have you?'

'I have indeed. I found a really cool thing you have to check out. Make sure you visit the Quais de Seine when you're in Troyes. There's something there I think you should see.'

'What is it?'

'Ah, no, I'm not telling. It's my secret mission for you.'

I can imagine him grinning like a cheeky kid. 'Okay, boss.'

'And when you see it, you have to think of me, okay? And take a picture.'

'Anything else?' I laugh.

'Just be happy, Phoebe Jones. And have the best time.'

Now I think I will.

Troyes is only an hour and a half's train journey from Gare de l'Est, a short walk from Gare du Nord. It's a medieval city, right in the heart of Champagne country. I will be staying with Gilbert and Amelie, a retired couple who now volunteer as local guides as part of the city's Greeter scheme that pairs locals with visitors.

I had planned to say goodbye to Tobi and Luc at the apartment and get a taxi to the station, but they won't hear of it. So we walk together in solemn procession, Luc carrying my holdall and Tobi bearing the canvas bag containing homemade treats. At the station they buy coffee and fuss around me. It's an hour before my train and they won't leave until I'm on it.

'You're like our sister now,' Luc says, when I laugh at their fussiness. 'You have us until the train takes you. No arguments.'

We sit together in a small café concession, with Tobi doing his best not to show how appalled he is by the quality of the coffee, and we talk about all the plans I have for my onward journey. Luc asks for my journal and shields the page from me as he writes a message.

'Read it when you reach Troyes. Tobi will write something, too. And then all of the words must be yours.'

I try to imagine the journal filled with my words at the end of this year. What will I see? What will I learn?

And will Sam be there to read it when it's complete?

Suddenly it's time to go. I share final kisses with Tobi and Luc and wave as I hurry to my platform. Paris has warmed my heart and set me on course for my European adventure. What lies in store for me next?

Chapter Twenty

SAM

'A massive red beating heart!' Phoebe says, without even saying hello first. She sounds breathless, somewhere between laughter and tears.

Thank goodness for Google showing me the heart when I searched for Troyes. 'You like it?'

'It's gorgeous, Sam! You're gorgeous – um, I mean it was a gorgeous thought…'

My chest contracts as her voice trails away. I hate that the uncertainty is there. I'm doing my best to cancel it out, but it's not enough.

'I'll take gorgeous. You're not so bad yourself.' I wince at the cheesiness of my reply, thankful that her laugh follows on its tail.

'Well, thank you for noticing.'

There's still something that doesn't line up between us. Sending Phoebe to find the heart at the Quais de Seine was my attempt to bridge the gap. She sounds happy, which is all that matters. I just wish I wasn't questioning everything. That's how it started with Laura – I can't let that happen again.

'The heart is amazing, Sam. It's made of a lacework of steel and the red light inside beats faster the closer you get to it. I visited last night at dusk. There are jets of water that dance around it and purple floodlights. I can't believe I didn't know it was here.'

'I thought you'd like it. I expect photos, you know.'

'Already on it. I'm going back there again this evening. And you owe me a song.'

My stomach twists. Maybe I can film something at the gig tonight.

The stomp of approaching boots heralds Niven's return. When he gestures at my mobile I mouth *Phoebe* and he feigns a swoon before grabbing the gear from the open boot of his car. I watch him laughing all the way back into our gig venue.

'I hadn't forgotten,' I say. 'I have a gig tonight, actually. Aros Hall. It's right on the seafront on Tobermory's Main Street.'

'Big gig?'

'Biggest one we've played yet.'

'I should let you go then.'

'Probably. Have a great time, Phoebe.'

'You too. Let me know how the gig goes. And' – that hesitation returns –'thanks. For the heart.'

Now is my time to say something. A heart is a hell of a symbol, especially when you send someone you care about to see it. What else could it mean? *Say something, Sam.*

'You – us – it matters,' I stumble. *What?*

'To me, too.'

'Good. Just remember that, yeah?'

There's a sheen of laughter in her voice. 'Hard to forget. Speak soon.'

'You too.'

And then the call ends. I kick at a stone by my feet. What was *that*? At least she didn't sound offended. But I could have said so much more. I turn back to the sea and let the salt-tang air blast through my lungs. I am still blown away by the view from here – looking out across a pewter sea to the mountains of the mainland in the distance. Everywhere has a long vista on Mull, no matter where you go. Huge skies, wide seascapes, wild mountains and moors. And everywhere looks towards somewhere else, as if the Island is constantly inviting you to go deeper, consider more, dream wider.

I've been able to breathe again since I came here.

I just wish I could express that to Phoebe. I have to try harder, regain the ground I've lost. I want her in my life, but we have ten months before we meet again and Frank Mullins' ghost looms large between us. He needs putting to rest before I can dare to give Phoebe the room she deserves.

I rub my eyes and head back into Aros Hall.

Thirty minutes later, we've made some progress setting up, but not as much as we should. This is largely due to Niven, as usual, apparently knowing everyone here. Volunteers preparing the hall keep interrupting him to say hello and share news. If you ask me, this is a ruse of his to get me to do all the work. Guitarists are tricky like that. And people think fiddlers are the cheeky ones. I watch him laughing and shaking hands with people who have known him forever and I'm suddenly hit by a pang of envy.

While I set out microphones and stands on the stage, I wonder – if we'd never had to leave Mull, if Frank had been the husband Ma deserved and Grandma had never been given licence to get her oar in, if we'd had the childhood I knew I should have had, even as a boy of 9 being taken by night to the mainland – would the people in Tobermory and beyond be greeting me today like they do Niven?

He catches me looking over, grins and gives a shrug.

Yeah, like heck are you innocent in this, McNish.

I chuckle and go back to uncoiling microphone leads.

There's a great buzz about tonight from the people setting up the room and I have a good feeling about what might happen. It will be good to play with the other musicians. Two of them I know already from other gigs: Ally the drummer and Cara the accordionist who play together regularly in their own band. The whistle player I've not met yet and I can't recall if Niven's even mentioned their name. But I'm getting used to people just rocking up to play.

When the stage is ready and the sound as sorted as it can be before the rest of the band arrives, I join Niven in the centre of the hall on the scuffed and creaky floorboards.

'Looks good,' Niven smiles. He's on form today, that restlessness I'd seen in him when we were travelling to Mull from Glasgow is absent now. I think the gigs are helping him refocus.

'Not bad for a southerner, eh?' I say.

'You'll do.' He checks his watch. 'Ally just called. He's picking up Cara from the ferry at Craignure, then they'll head straight here.'

'Great. And the whistle player?'

There's a creak behind us and the door opens. Niven looks over his shoulder and smirks. 'Ah now, *she's* a real handful. I heard she's a terror.'

'Get stuffed, McNish,' a voice says behind me.

I would know that voice anywhere.

When I turn, I see the last of my uni clan striding across the hall towards us. The leather jacket, black T-shirt and ridiculously short mini skirt, bright red tights and heavy biker boots haven't changed, but where her hair was bottle blonde at university it's now the colour of melted dark chocolate.

'I didn't know it was you,' I laugh, as I scoop her into a hug.

Shona Delaney smiles against my cheek. 'That's because I swore Niven to secrecy. On pain of death.'

'And I wasn't likely to blab. She's bloody terrifying,' Niven says, ducking a swipe Shona makes at him before they embrace.

'Better than being a guitarist wuss. So, you happy for me to play, Sam?'

'Sure,' I grin. 'Think you can keep up with us?'

Shona dismisses this with a raise of her eyebrows as she shrugs her pipe bag off her shoulders and pulls out a penny whistle. It spins in her fingers like a majorette's baton. 'Oh, I reckon I'll manage.'

Yet another local collars Niven for a chat, so Shona and I head over to the stage.

'It's so good to see you,' I say. And it is. She's been the missing piece of my journey so far.

'You too. Enjoying your time here?'

'I am. Wasn't sure I would because – you know. But no, it's good. So, what are you doing these days?'

'Gigging, whenever I can. I lecture part-time at Strathclyde Uni and tour the rest of the year with a trad band.'

'I had no idea you were a *prof* these days.'

Shona unpacks the last of her whistles and fastens a holster to the microphone stand by her seat in the stage. 'That would be because you're useless at keeping in touch.'

'Sorry.'

'Nae bother. Just good to see you now. And hey – I'm sorry to hear about the girl.'

For a moment I'm confused. Does she mean Phoebe? And then the penny drops: Laura. 'It's okay I'm over it. And you?'

'Divorced. At long last.' She flips a handful of hair back from her face. 'So, footloose and fancy free the three of us, eh?'

I'm about to reply when Niven strides onto the stage. 'Ally's just leaving Craignure. Reckon that gives us at least forty minutes to start sound-checking, and maybe go over the set?'

Shona claps her hands and heads to her spot. I'm struck by how confident she is now. At university I always felt she wore her characteristics like the oversized biker jackets and huge army surplus shirts that formed her uniform back then. Now, everything fits.

I realise I'm staring as she arranges her pipes in the mic-stand holster and selects a low whistle to start playing. When she looks up at me, I avert my gaze.

She is *so* different from the last time I saw her. The change is remarkable: I'm a little stunned by it. Things aren't helped when Niven nudges me, mid-song, and whispers, 'Close your mouth,' nodding in Shona's direction which, thankfully, she doesn't see.

I knew she'd had a rough couple of years with the guy she's just divorced. He was a rugby player, all flash cash and model looks with an adoring Instagram army running into the hundreds of thousands. Kate reckoned Shona liked the attention after years of doubting her appearance and appeal. The guy wooed her – expensive holidays, gifts, a wedding covered by celebrity magazines and even an impressive studio in the basement of their home. But he never made her happy. Donal and Kate were worried about her for a long time. It's great to see her happy and back in control.

And she looks *amazing*.

I check myself and focus on Phoebe. I'll send her photos of this gig tonight, just to prove I don't only play in small Island front rooms. Not being a musician herself I don't think she really understands what it's like as a performer. We haven't really spoken much about my job or what she does, for that matter. I know she worked in the office for a theatre production company most recently, and that she studied part-time for a PhD. I should know this stuff. Both our lives will be different if we end up together. We'll both have to make changes.

Next time we speak I'll ask her about her dream job – or what she plans to do when she's back in London. When she's back with *me*.

Niven and Shona are pulling faces at each other across the stage like a couple of kids. It's like the six years we've spent apart just didn't happen. I can feel myself reverting to the Sam Mullins I was last time we played together – before Laura, before the studio, before I even considered coming back to Mull. I miss that version of me. He wasn't happy all the time and was broke more often than not; he went from gig to gig, working all the hours, hardly sleeping. But there was simplicity in his life that I've lost.

I don't know why I'm thinking about this now. Maybe it's the knowledge that I'm not just a visiting musician here: I'm *Frank Mullins' boy*.

Ailish is right: at some point I'm going to have to follow up the lead from the photograph. It's what I came here for. And I will do it.

But tonight, I can hang out with the other Sam Mullins and let the music take me from every concern and responsibility. Enjoying the fun, not thinking any further than the next tune. The freedom is intoxicating.

Tonight is going to be a great gig.

Chapter Twenty-One

PHOEBE

Hi, Sam,

I arrived at my Roman host's home a week ago and it's the most wonderful place. I loved Florence but visiting in the height of the tourist season wasn't the brightest idea. Both the apartments I stayed in were miles out of the city centre so I felt a bit removed there. I've seen everything I wanted to see, but I don't feel I found the heart of that city. I'll go back one day at a better time and do it properly, I think. Maybe you can come with me.

Rome is completely different. Tobi and Luc's friend Giana is the perfect host and her home is wonderful. She's already taken me to three places I didn't even know existed. It's nice to be in one place for a while, too. And it's funny, but I didn't expect to love Rome as much as I do. It's ridiculously busy and hot and never quiet, but it's wonderful.

Giana is fascinating. She's an artist, originally from America, and she always wanted to live here. I feel like I've known her for years not days and I've already heard her life story. I love how she found her perfect place in Rome. And she adores books so she's totally my kind of person!

How are the house gigs going? I bet your audiences love you. Anyone would. Have you had any more news about Frank? I hope so.

I miss you. Write soon. Or text. Or even call... You know, as we're sticking to those rules of ours so rigidly. (I'm glad both of us are rubbish at obeying rules.)

Phoebe xx

There was no point even trying to fit everything I wanted to say to Sam on a postcard this time. I fold the piece of notepaper I've written my message on around the postcard of the Piazza del Popolo that I bought at the little gift shop two doors down from my current home and smile as I fit it into the envelope. I am sitting in the small library room of Giana Moretti's apartment. She asked me to help organise her books and we struck on the idea of making rainbow shelves. As an artist it appealed to her.

Every day so far, Giana has made coffee and sweet sugary *bomboloni* doughnuts for our mid-morning snack. Espresso, sugar, book print and paper makes the most amazing perfume. She's in the kitchen preparing it now and she'll bring it to me soon. My stomach is rumbling just thinking about it.

Writing to Sam has made me realise how at home I feel here compared with Florence – and thinking of home brings thoughts of my friends back in London. I wonder how they are. I check the old wooden clock above the counter – half past ten. What will they be doing now? Meg has Thursdays off so she'll probably be pottering around the house or maybe heading to the British Library to write. Last I heard from Osh he was neck-deep in pre-production prep for the festival film he's finally secured funding for. Gabe will be appearing in it, in between rehearsals for his new play at the Almeida Theatre.

Picking up my phone I compose a group text:

Hi beauties! I'm making a book rainbow in the library of my new home in Rome. How's your Thursday going? Miss you all LOTS. Tell me all your news. P xxx

Within a minute, my phone buzzes with replies:

Phoebe bloody Jones, we miss you too. Get your butt back to London and I'll sneak you into my movie. I'm doing a movie at last! Just call me Danny Boyle! Are you going near Siena on your travels? I have 3 days filming a commercial there. Got to pay ma bills, right? Maybe we can meet up? Let me know. Big love, Osh xx

PHOEBE! You're alive! Up for a chat later? G x

Phee! Give me 5 and I'll call. Lots to tell! M xxx

I smile at the rush of love in my notifications. My friends haven't forgotten me. Not that I ever thought they would, but I've never tested our friendship before, save for the occasional week away on holiday. We're connected again, even though they are hundreds of miles from me. It feels good to be striking out on my own and still being part of a circle of friends.

I'm about to reply when another text arrives, just as Giana appears with a tray of the most delicious tiny doughnuts and a pot of espresso.

Unscheduled text (sorry) just to say I'm thinking of you.
That's all xx

Sunlight bursts through the single window in Giana's library. Books, coffee, *bomboloni*, sun, a new friend in my host and now a message from Sam. Today is going to be a great day.

When Tobi told me I'd be staying with his deaf friend in Rome, I was nervous. I don't know much sign language and I didn't want the kind lady to be offended by my lack of understanding.

But as soon as I met her, I knew my fears were unfounded. And now, two weeks into my two-month stay Giana Moretti and I are firm friends. She's an artist and translator, originally from Chicago and one of the most fascinating people I've ever met. Her lip-reading and speech are brilliant, but I've asked her to teach me some American Sign Language, too. I want to give her proper respect while I'm living under her roof.

But today I discovered something about her that inspires me even more.

It's rained solidly for the past week and I've been earning my keep by helping Giana reorganise her new artist studio. The roof space she's just started to rent from her landlord in her apartment building is quite small, but even on a dank day the light is lovely. We'd just finished shifting the last of the boxes her landlord had been keeping in the room and had taken a rest, pulling cobwebs out of our hair and drinking coffee from the flask she brought with us.

'Phoebe, how would you like an adventure?' she asked, her nut-brown eyes sparkling.

'You mean more than this?' I laughed.

'Even more than this. I have a secret I think you should know.'

And that's when I discovered just how special Giana Moretti is.

Back in her apartment, she opened a large lidded tin box in the kitchen filled with smooth pebbles small enough to sit in the palm of your hand. 'These are my secret weapons.'

'You throw these at people?' I asked.

She's still laughing about that now as we sit at her newspaper-covered dining table, a palette of paints in the centre.

'What do I paint on it?' I ask, the child in me thrilled by the prospect of painting a pebble.

'Whatever you feel,' she says. 'It could be how you feel today, or something you've seen. It could be a single word or just a picture. One thing that's important, though: it doesn't just have to be positive. I think the best way to live is to mark every moment, good or bad. In the moment when you feel it – whatever it is – that emotion is valid and has worth. If you acknowledge that, nothing has the power to silence you.'

And then she tells me how painting pebbles became part of her life.

'All my life, I was told to be quiet. My words, they didn't matter, you see. Because, in my family's opinion, if I couldn't hear them, nobody else should either. My family spoke first and always at once. Every day I would watch them fight to be the loudest. Even in the silence they were deafening. There was no room for my voice.'

'That must have been terrible,' I say, careful not to imply any judgement although I can't believe a family could be so cruel to a child they were supposed to love.

'At the age of twelve, I got new hearing aids. I hated them at first. The noise nearly drowned me. My family thought I was ungrateful and refused to listen to me when I tried to explain how disorienting I was finding the world. I struggled for a couple of years until a friend told me about a new group in my deaf community centre. Half of us had hearing aids, half didn't, but we all used sign language. It was our safe place – our sanctuary.

'One day, when I was sixteen, an artist came to visit, and he asked us to paint a pebble. That was my first. "Put something beautiful on it," he said. "Something only you can see. And write a thought on the other side." And then he said something that changed my life: "Your thoughts matter. Your views matter. For every time you've been dismissed, or felt less worthy than someone else, find a pebble and paint your beautiful thoughts. Then send it out into the world. Because kindness has power and your words have the potential to change the world. Like when you throw a pebble into the ocean and the ripples reach out, wider and wider, to infinity."' She beams. 'That's where it started for me.'

'Oh wow, I love that.'

'I've been amazed that one small pebble can make such a difference. Even if the difference is only the power it gives you to make it. If you believe your words have meaning, they will.'

Since I've been in Europe, I've wondered about the kind of impact I have. My life has. On this world. All the people I admire made a difference – or are setting about leaving their mark. I think about the novelists I studied for three years and loved for many more – did any of them realise the difference they were making while they were doing it? Do we ever really know our impact, or does it come later, when we've gone?

'What made you move to Rome?' I ask.

Giana tells me she has been in love with Rome since she was tiny, from a picture book her *nonna* sent her from Italy one Christmas, so when the opportunity to move here arose in her early twenties, she didn't hesitate. I love that she followed her heart to be here.

'Nonna was born in Rome before her family emigrated to Chicago. She died without seeing it again, so I wanted to see it for her. My parents didn't approve, of course: they said I'd be back in six months. Well, that was twelve years ago. I am grateful that life has brought me here and that I made it happen. So my gratitude is in the pebbles and I send them out into the world to make a difference. To tell the world that I am here and I matter. I think maybe you need to do the same?'

She opens a site on her computer and the screen fills with painted pebbles. We scroll through them. Alongside the photographs are details of where people have taken Giana's work home with them. Japan, Senegal, Australia, Portugal, the UK, Columbia, Latvia, Norway. On and on, country after country, visitors to Rome have taken their treasure back to their home countries all over the world and re-hidden the pebbles for others to find. It's astounding.

'Many people tell me they have started to paint their own pebbles after finding mine,' she says. She taps the screen and I see that her page has hundreds of thousands of followers – complete strangers, joined together by ripples from Giana's painted thoughts and now sending out their own into the world.

Looking at the photos of smiling people across the planet holding her artworks, I realise something: I want my life to make a difference, too.

We fill a basket with the pebbles we've decorated and head out into the city. It's still raining but I'm buzzing with anticipation.

'Where do we put them?' I ask as we walk down the rain-glossed street.

'Anywhere they can be discovered. I try to put some at head height, some at ground level where people won't trip over them, and some near places where people might sit. That way all ages can find them – and they do.'

Heading out into the great city with our stash of pebbles is the most exciting thing.

We hide a couple of pebbles at the Piazza Navona, the long square where Giana tells me chariots used to race; we cross cobbled streets that catch the golden sun to leave our treasure in terracotta planters and behind pavement café A-boards; and hide a couple on the Spanish Steps where it seems all of the beautiful people of Rome come to meet and sit and be seen.

Then we head for the Campo de' Fiori street market, with its huge stacks of every conceivable fruit and vegetable, verdant bunches of fresh herbs and whole stalls of spices and dried peppers. Giana knows everyone here, it seems. Each stallholder welcomes me to their city and insists we sample the food and drink products they sell. Within an hour I am grinning and very full. We hide pebbles there too, tucked away under the edges of tarpaulins and behind flower vases on tables in the eating area. Then we brave the crowds by the Pantheon and the Trevi Fountain, slipping stones in unseen nooks while tourists from all over the world buzz around us.

I'm going to do this wherever I go from now on, I decide, a few days later, as Giana and I stroll through the Villa Borghese Gardens with its pools, elegant statues and lots of green space, which reminds me of London's parks. A trail of my adventure through Europe.

*

That evening, when the dusk glows and the famous buildings are flooded with light, I leave a pebble with Sam's name surrounded by music notes tucked beside a riverside bookstall. I don't know if he'll understand about the pebbles but I hope he will. He's a musician – instead of decorated stones, he's hiding inspiration and magic for people to rediscover whenever they need it. In that way, we're doing the same thing.

Making our mark where we are with what we have.

Chapter Twenty-Two

SAM

'Let me get this straight: you're spending a year away from the woman you want to be with?'

Put like that, it doesn't make much sense.

Part of me wishes I'd never mentioned this to Shona, but it's too late to change it now. Besides, it's really Niven's fault. He made a joke about long-distance love and Shona was on it before I could steer the conversation away.

It's been three weeks since she surprised us at our Aros Hall gig and I've seen her most days. We've talked about all kinds of stuff, catching up on the last six years, but not, until this moment, about Phoebe. I don't know why I haven't mentioned her before.

Okay, maybe I do.

It's because of her expression right now, like she's battling saying what she really thinks. At least her attempt to combat her impulse is better than when we were at university – she was famous for having no filter when it came to her opinions. A symptom of her immense shyness, most probably, but it didn't make it any easier to be on the receiving end.

I glare at Niven, who has suddenly remembered something he really needs from the car, leaving Shona and me sitting on the silver sands of beautiful Langamull Beach in Dervaig. It's a gorgeous day, just a hint of a breeze and the sun warm on our bare feet as we relax on the sand. Shona's even deigned to lose her leather jacket, which is a minor miracle. In the sunlight her hair reveals deep red streaks nestled between the chocolate brown and her skin is more tanned than I remember.

'We both have things we want to do first,' I say, working hard to keep my tone steady.

'Is that why you're not talking to her much? Keeping the mystery alive?'

I stare at her. 'I talk to her a lot.'

'Not according to Niven, you don't.'

I look back towards the car but the sun is obscuring the windscreen so I can't see him. Good job. I can't believe he'd talk to Shona about this. 'Niven knows nothing. We send postcards, emails, texts. I sent her a song last week. "Iris" by the Goo Goo Dolls.' It felt good, filming it on my phone and seeing her delight when she video-called me the next day.

'It's amazing,' she'd said, her smile warmer than the sunshine warming my back today. 'It means so much.'

I want to make Phoebe smile. She has the loveliest smile.

'Classy,' Shona says. 'So have you told her about looking for your dad?'

I bristle at the question. 'I'm guessing Niven told you that, too.' Is nothing sacred? Next time I'm alone with him, I'll tell him exactly what I think about his public information service. I don't owe Shona any explanation, but I know the direction this conversation is headed and it needs to stop. I'm already feeling cornered. 'I have told Phoebe, actually. It was because of her that I started looking.'

'Right.'

I can't read her expression. That's probably a good thing. She picks up a small pebble and passes it across the top of her fingers by moving each one in sequence. I remember her doing that with a penny in endless bars during our student days. Manipulation. Like illusionists use. She did it as a meditation, usually several beers into a drinking session.

She catches me watching and grins. 'Still got it.'

'So I see.' I'm conscious of heat at the back of my neck.

'What are you doing to find your father, Sam?'

I stare at her. 'I met someone who knew him and she gave me Frank's cap. There was photo in it. A phone number too.'

Shona shields her eyes from the sun to look at me. 'A number? Did you call it?'

'Not yet.'

'Why?'

'Can we talk about something else?'

'I think this is more important, don't you?'

'Ailish is asking around on the Island. She reckons someone will know where Frank is. If that brings up nothing, maybe I'll call the number. And no, I haven't told Phoebe about all that because until anything comes up there's little point.'

Shona doesn't buy this. Part of me doesn't blame her.

'So she's the woman of your dreams but you won't tell her about the biggest thing in your life?'

'I will, when I have something to tell her. And she has things to do in Italy. It's good to have distance. It tests how serious we are about this. We do what we promised ourselves first and then we'll be in a good place to be together.'

'What, sexually frustrated?' She sees my expression and holds up a many-ringed hand with a laugh. 'Sorry. I would be, that's all. Willingly keeping yourself from someone who's a sure thing? I couldn't do it. Spend a year in bed with them not wasting a second, more like. If it fails at least you've had a hell of a lot of fun.'

'Yeah, well this is about more than sex.'

'More than sex?' She shifts in the sand to face me. 'Would you listen to yourself? This isn't the Sam Mullins I know.'

'So Shona, how's *your* love life?'

She pulls a face. I know I'm being defensive but I don't need challenging about Phoebe. Or Frank. Especially not by Shona Delaney.

Niven returns and the topic of conversation shifts at last, to my relief. Until this moment, everyone has accepted the decision Phoebe and I have made. Kate questioned it, but only as a concerned friend and because she wanted to understand. I can't work out what Shona's motivation is yet. Maybe I'll call Kate later when I'm back at Ailish's if it's still bothering me.

Part of the problem is that Shona no longer fits the image I've always had of her. Everything I'd learned about how to be her friend years ago – things she responded to, topics to avoid, approaches appropriate to her personality – are now like a bunch of slightly bent keys that don't fit the locks as they once did.

It doesn't help that I haven't contacted Phoebe since I sent her the song. She seems happy with the artist in Rome and the last I heard she was painting pebbles to leave across the city and rearranging a library. It sounds wildly romantic and is exactly the kind of thing I imagined her doing. It's what I want for her, as much as being here in Mull is what she wants for me. We both said there would be times this year when we wouldn't be in touch. I'm not worried there's a gap in communication right now.

Besides, I've been obsessing over an old text of Phoebe's I'd forgotten I had on my phone. She sent it to me from Carcassone, back when she was travelling through France. It's a turreted walled settlement on a huge hill and ridiculously pretty. The kind of place Peter Jackson would fall over himself to set a film in. Fairy-tale turrets, rounded towers, flowers everywhere.

> Hi Sam. I've found our house – fancy it? I reckon we'd suit a castle. Miss you, P xx

At the time I thought it was cute. When I found it again, I still loved the joke but this time it pulled me up. Was she thinking about that stuff already? I haven't even considered it. I know we were both renting in London before we left, so own no property we have to return to, but do we find a place together immediately or wait to see if Phoebe and Sam work in the real world rather than just our imaginations and the strange limbo of our year apart?

The problem is that the Island gives you too much time to think.

And Shona muddies the waters.

Danger is too strong a word, but I'm on high alert around my friend and I can't ignore it. She was always unpredictable and had the capacity to throw curveballs when you least expected them. But this is different. *She*'s different.

And, like the pebble sailing across her fingers on this beach, it's mesmerising to watch.

Niven has been dropping hints lately about a 'great idea' that are about as subtle as the huge split rock on Fionnphort beach. Now, he tells us.

'We could start a music club,' he explains. 'On the Island. Either after school or weekends, depending on what the take up is. I'm pretty sure my school would love it and there's nothing like that for the kids right now. Between us we have guitar, fiddle, whistles, flute, drums, pretty much the whole thing covered. My pal Ruari can do pipes if there's kids want to learn. Admit it, I am a genius!'

He's talking at a million miles an hour, his eyes bright above his beard.

'Hang on, slow down,' I say. 'It's a great idea, but *us* teaching *kids*?'

'I do it for a job. Shona teaches. The only reason you've not done it yet is you've not had the opportunity…'

'Or the inclination?'

Niven groans. 'Okay, fine. But think about how you started, eh? You're always talking about Jonas. Think about how he changed your life. He wasn't a music teacher, he was just a musician – but that was enough to get you playing.'

'Where would we do it?'

'I floated the idea with Archie from the Aros Hall and he's well up for it. Come on, it'll be fun.'

It's the perfect solution: I can hang out with my friends without having time alone with Shona and worrying about my obvious attraction to her; and Niven can find an endeavour to scratch the itch that's bothered him since Ruth left. Besides, it will be good to give something back, even if I'm out of my comfort zone surrounded by kids. Phoebe would tell me to go for it. And it's something I can share with her from the beginning.

This challenge will give me a focus.

More importantly, it will keep me safe.

Things happen fast – with the venue secured, the school on board and a crowd of kids eager to sign up, we're up and running in two weeks. Pretty quickly the music school becomes a regular part of my week – familiar without being overbearing and new enough to be exciting. I enjoy the comfort of the life I'm building on the Island and everything becomes calm.

Which is why, when the sea changes, it hits me head on.

The moment Ailish walks in, I sense a storm approaching.

'Tea?' I ask, as she bustles past me and dumps a shopping bag on the kitchen table.

She mutters something in reply but nods, so I take that as a *yes*. When I hand her a mug she accepts it, but her head is bowed as she walks into the living room. Should I follow? In my time here I've seen her tired, a little worse for wear after a bottle of wine occasionally, but never like this.

Simmering. Silent.

Ma called Ailish's temper a *well-caged lion*, hidden for most of the time. The trip switch that unleashes it takes far longer to flip than it would do for most people. To my knowledge Ma only experienced it once, not long after she'd left the Island, when she admitted she was drinking again. The force of Ailish's fury was enough to never invoke it again.

I steel myself for the inevitable.

'You okay?'

Rain hammers against the glass as the storm swings direction from traversing the garden to hitting the house head-on.

'No, Sam. I'm not.'

'What's up?' I keep my voice steady.

The light in the room seems to dim.

Her sigh escapes her like the sea receding across a pebble beach. 'I've said nothing, Sam. I've held my tongue because you needed time and I didn't think it was right to push you. But I'm afraid I can't do it any more.'

Whoa.

'Ailish, if you want me to go…'

She was insistent when I arrived that I was to stay with her and wouldn't hear of my suggestion that I accept Niven's offer of accommodation or look to rent something in Tobermory. Has she changed her mind?

She looks at me and I see the tiger Ma warned me about. '*No,* I don't want you to go. I want you to do what you came here for, Sam. I want you to stop hiding from it.'

'I'm not hiding…'

'Yes, you are. So you have the music lessons and the concerts with Niven and that's all well and good. But you found out about Frank when you first got here and what have you done with that? Nothing!'

'Now hang on…'

'I don't know what your ma would have said about you wanting to find him, God rest her soul, but I see that same pain in you that she could never deal with. Her whole life was wrecked by that man because she never got answers. *You* have the chance to find them. So what are you waiting for?'

How is this my fault? And whatever happened to, 'do this at your own pace, Sam'?

'You said you were going to ask around for me.'

'Aye, when you were ready. But you've not mentioned it and as far as I can tell you weren't planning to, either.'

'I just haven't had chance yet…'

'Oh *bollocks*, Samuel!'

My mouth gapes. 'What?'

'I'm sorry, but that is utter bollocks.'

'It's the truth.'

'No, it isn't. You have a whole year here to do whatever you want. You aren't working most of the time. You have entire days when you could call that phone number, find out where he is. Or ask me to start talking to people. There are more folk on the Island than Morag Ross who knew your father. Some of them will have stayed in touch with him when he went to the mainland. If nothing else your father had friends, always. Thick as thieves most of them, which is what made it so hard for your poor mother. He had allies all over Mull. Nobody believed she wasn't responsible in some way for him leaving.'

'In that case, why should I want to talk to the people who made her life hell? Why should I give them the chance to feel better about their prejudice?'

'Oh get over yourself!' She shakes her head. 'You're as stubborn as she was. Don't you think they might be useful now? It's not about absolving them of responsibility. It's about finding the truth, so Frank Mullins doesn't screw up your life like he did your ma's.'

'He didn't screw up my life! He's irrelevant to it. He means nothing to me.'

I'm furious but she's on her feet now. It's a full-throttle attack and I am not ready for what she unleashes.

'Oh really? You never stay in one place. You have a job that always gives you an excuse to not put down roots. You've met the girl of your dreams – someone who has real potential to make you happy for the rest of your life – and you get on a train in the opposite direction for a whole year!'

'Phoebe and I agreed. We said…'

'Aye, well perhaps your Phoebe is as terrified of getting hurt as you are.'

'I'm not terrified!'

'You're not? When Laura left you, you fell apart. Not just because she cheated. Because you let her close enough to hurt you. You are terrified of loving anyone because they might walk out on you, like your dad did to your poor ma. And you saw what that did to her. What it made her become. Did she survive? Yes. Was she happy? No, never. She was still breathing but her spirit broke the night that man walked out of her life. You are scared of winding up like she did. Angry at the world, thinking so little of her own worth that she drank herself into an early grave. You see your brother headed the same way and it scares you.'

How dare she? She knows nothing about me, or Callum. 'Leave Cal out of this.'

'Why? He's as scarred as you are by that man. But where he drinks, you run.'

'You don't know my brother. And you don't know me.'

'Oh don't I?'

'No. If I'm so scared, why did I come back?'

'I'm starting to wonder. Why come back and not address what started all this? You get one lead and you scurry away inside your cave.'

Is she serious?

'My *cave*?'

'Well what would you call it?'

'I'm not hiding in a cave. Maybe I'm not ready. Maybe just being here is changing how I see my childhood, how I see myself. Is that not enough?'

'I don't know, Sam, is it?'

I can't believe I'm hearing this. I'll let Ailish McRae get away with saying stuff nobody else can, but this is a line crossed. I feel like the room is crowding in on me. I have to get out.

'Look, if it bothers you this much I'll move out. Then you won't have to worry,' I say, reaching for my coat on the back of the sofa.

'Yeah, that's right, Sam. Run away. Just like your father!'

There is no coming back from that. I snatch my coat and head for the door.

'Wait – Sam – I didn't mean…' she says, hurrying after me.

But it doesn't matter what she meant: it's *said*. And now I know where I stand, there's no way I can stay here.

My head is a mess as I stalk away from the house. Rain drives at me and the wind lashes my hair around my face. But it can't push me back. Ailish's calls are stolen by the storm and I wouldn't turn around even if they reached me. I need space. I need to work out what the hell just happened.

I head for Fionnphort beach with its huge split rock, where enormous waves are beating the silver shoreline.

I tell myself that the water blurring the view and tumbling down my face is a consequence of staring into the storm. But that's a lie. Out here on the bleak, deserted beach I am 9 years old again, nursing fresh bruises from an emotional kick I never saw coming. This is no more my fault today than it was then. So why do I feel I'm to blame?

Ailish is wrong. She's wrong about Frank and she's wrong about Laura and she is so, *so* wrong about Phoebe. I am not running away from her. I am making sure we are in the best place to be together. Maybe I am protecting myself a little, but why shouldn't I? I don't want to have my heart broken and neither does Phoebe. We're both working this out. If she were with me now I could say everything I don't feel able to in texts and phone calls. Face to face I would find the words.

I close my eyes against the storm and the fury and imagine myself back in her embrace. Her lips warm and inviting. Her fingers holding my face. Her body tight against mine. I push past the pain in my chest and focus on the fierce heat generated by my heart. We might be apart, but she is as real and as present within me as if she were wrapped around me on this beach right now.

That is what matters: not some distant shadow from my past who couldn't even be bothered to be part of his son's life. I meant nothing to Frank Mullins. Why should he mean anything to me?

Chapter Twenty-Three

PHOEBE

I hate leaving Rome. Giana has become a good friend and I will miss our pebble drops around the city. As a leaving gift she presents me with a beautiful little wooden paint box and brushes, to leave my own marks wherever I go. I will treasure it.

'I'll use it as often as I can,' I promise. 'And everywhere I go I'll tell people your story.'

Giana smiles. 'That's sweet, Phoebe. You have the dearest heart. But don't share my story: you have your own story to share.'

Giana makes me promise to visit her again and bring Sam next time. I hope if I return he'll be with me, that these frustrating doubts will have been dealt with. So much of the distance between us will be solved by just being back in the same space, I think, breathing the same air.

If we make it that far.

It's strange to see Rome slipping away as my train leaves but my destination is back towards Florence – the city of Siena – so it almost feels like heading home. This is where I'll be staying with Noura and Stephan, a couple who run an organic cheese business. One of the reviews on the accommodation site caught my attention and made my choice academic. *It looks like it's been carved from the mountains and hidden in the clouds. Also, Stephan makes wine – beware!*

After the heat of Rome a mountainside retreat sounds divine, and I might even get to see Osh while I'm there because he's filming a commercial nearby for a few days. I've missed my friends so much. I still get snippets of updates from them occasionally but being able to hang out with Osh, even for a few hours, will be so good. I've missed his gossip and big loony smile.

I have a confession – one I won't even tell Osh: I looked at Gabe's Instagram last night. Instantly hated myself for doing it, of course, and I still don't really know why. I saw the images of him, always smiling or laughing, in faraway places or hanging out with beautiful friends on beaches during rare summer weekends when nobody was busy. It looks like another world, one that revolves around him and his perennial smile.

I even found myself in one of the group shots – me and Osh, Meg and the gang with Gabe at our centre, a sentinel. We're all laughing; we all look like life is a blast. What did Tobi call it? *The beautiful ones in the beautiful life.* Except I know Gabe was out of work then, had just had the biggest fall-out with his agent and had spent a whole week convinced his career was sinking. In desperation Osh dragged us all out to Brighton (he'd threatened to chuck Gabe off Brighton Pier if he didn't smile). He'd filmed us that day and I remember the unreal feeling of us all watching it back in London, seeing filtered versions of ourselves dancing around in a parallel universe.

Funny how you forget the boredom, the frustration, the wishing to be somewhere else, when you're outside looking in.

The Instagram Gabe is in final rehearsals for his play. He's grinning for the camera, mucking about with daft videos, star-jumping off chairs in the rehearsal room, smouldering beneath street lights with a pint during Pride, posing shirtless and sweaty on his early morning run. Every image has four thousand likes, with hundreds of adoring comments, hopeful questions about his sexuality, proposals of marriage and desperate begging for him to notice them or follow them back. I don't know if he ever even reads them. But he needs it: the reassurance of seeing the red hearts in his notifications. He'll be in a panic right now, as he always is just before a production opens, convinced it's a wrong move that will side-track his career. He'll be seeking the affirmation from his followers more than ever, all the while playing the cool, fun-loving actor at the top of his game.

Is any of it real?

My own images tell of a carefree traveller, exploring Europe and following her heart. My few hundred followers post occasional messages of encouragement, a little shower of hearts and smiley faces dancing down the comments. But do they think I've got it all sorted, like they believe Gabe has the perfect life? Do they think I'm happy?

Has Gabe seen my squares while I've been away?

Has Sam?

I didn't ask if Sam was on Instagram. I didn't get his Twitter handle or FB profile. When I was with him what mattered was *being* with him. Not viewing him through a lens or trying to filter him into a perfect image of the moment. What mattered was his touch, his breath against my face, the way he'd held me.

I wish Sam were here. Maybe then we could sort everything. Perhaps it's the niggling uncertainty that arrives whenever I think of Sam, but on the train I find myself composing a text to Gabe.

Hey G. I figured you'd be panicking about opening night. DON'T. You'll be amazing. You always are. Sorry I won't be there to see it, but I'll raise a glass to you from the cheese farm (!) where I'm staying. Break a leg (please don't really) P xx

I don't expect him to see it – the last few weeks before a theatre production are fraught to say the least. It just feels good to know my message will be waiting on his phone.

I reach Siena with an hour to kill. Noura and Stephan's farm is near Montalcino, so they are going to meet me here and drive me up. Finding a café I order coffee and crisp pistachio *cannoli* and settle in to watch the world go by.

The café has free WiFi so I log in and check my email inbox. I've learned to do this when I find signal and not worry about it when there's none. I have the best excuse to miss messages this year so I intend to use it whenever I can. And I mostly haven't missed being contactable.

That's odd. Three emails from the accommodation website, the most recent flagged with an urgent sticker. I open it – and my heart sinks:

Due to personal issues your booking has been cancelled. Your deposit has been refunded. STAYHERE.com apologises for any inconvenience.

There's a personal note from Noura and Stephan added beneath the standard message:

Miss Jones, we are sorry to cancel at short notice. My mother was taken ill last night. She has been released from

the hospital but will be staying in the guest accommodation
so that we can care for her.

We offer our sincere apologies and hope you will visit us
in future.

My heart hits the floor. What am I supposed to do now?

I can't be angry with them for cancelling, but it leaves me in a city I hadn't planned to stay in, with no idea of alternate accommodation. Even if I find somewhere to stay tonight, I'd planned to spend four weeks in Montalcino. How likely is it I'll find accommodation for that amount of time at short notice?

Think, Phoebe!

I've become so used to all my accommodation bookings going without a hitch. It never occurred to me that they might fall through and I would need a contingency.

A year ago, a problem like this would have terrified me. Even six months ago I would have been thrown into panic. And while this is a mess for sure, I'm not the scared Phoebe Jones who almost didn't wait for her train at St Pancras when the delay was announced.

I make myself breathe. I can sort this.

A waiter in the café directs me to the local tourist information centre, a short walk from the square. I just need to find a room for tonight and then I can work out where to head next.

The woman at the desk smells of expensive perfume and wears the kind of flawless make-up that looks as if it's been airbrushed on. She speaks perfect English and has an economic smile that appears for exactly two seconds at a time.

'It is a busy time,' she says. 'We have a festival.'

'But there must be rooms in Siena for tonight? I'll take anything.'

166

She wrinkles her nose and taps at her keyboard. 'I am sorry. No vacancies.' She twists the computer monitor to face me and grants me a two-second smile for solidarity. 'Perhaps next week? It will be quieter then.'

The sun stings my eyes as I emerge from the building. The street hums with the beat of hundreds of feet. I'd seen the crowds but not registered how busy Siena is. Being in Rome for the last eight weeks must have desensitised me to waves of tightly packed tourists. I wander the streets for a while. I don't know if I'm hoping to magically spot a hotel with vacancies or if it is just that physically moving feels less like defeat.

I spot a tiny cobbled square where an artist has set up a table of her ceramics, a sunny yellow canopy shielding them from the midday sun. It's hopeful, in the chaos of everything else. I take a photo with my phone and it's only when I check the image that I see the notification from Osh. A message to say they've arrived at their location.

Osh – of course!

I hit 'call', praying he's somewhere with enough signal. On the fifth ring, he answers.

'Phee! *Ciao*!'

'Hi,' I manage, before bursting into tears.

Two hours later, I am waiting in the car park Osh told me to head to, when a dirty white crew van swings into view, honking its horn madly. I ignore the disgruntled stares of people around me as I wave back. When it pulls alongside me, Osh jumps out. His bear hug is the loveliest embrace I've had since I said goodbye to Sam.

'We've got you,' he murmurs into my hair.

'Thank you,' I say, hugging him back.

When we pull apart, Osh grabs the handle of the side door. 'Got a surprise for you.' He slides it open.

And Gabe is there.

Arms flung wide as a magician revealing his greatest trick, dark eyes sparkling with mischief, utterly proud of himself.

Behind him, Osh's crewmates cheer.

He jumps from the van like a Shakespearean player leaping from the stage. Not the highly filtered Instagram imposter *@MisterGMarley*, but the real, living, breathing Gabriel Marley.

Our Gabe.

'Phoebs! *Wassaap*?'

He gathers me into a hug. He smells of vanilla and spice. I let myself rest for a breath, feeling the ground firm again beneath my feet.

'What are you doing here?' I ask, breaking free and holding him at arm's length to check he really is here and not just a mirage caused by the Tuscan sun.

'Had a couple of days off before previews so I thought I'd cadge a lift with our esteemed director.'

'He's wangled a starring role in the commercial,' Osh says as Gabe slaps an arm around his shoulders. 'Bloody thesp.'

Their twin goofy grins are the best slice of home I could have wished for.

'Part for you too, Phoebs, if you fancy it?'

'Not likely!' I smile at my utterly wonderful friends, who have appeared at the moment I needed them most. 'It's so good to see you.'

The road to Montalcino takes us high up into the mountains, weaving through an impossibly beautiful landscape. Osh winds down the window, the hire van's air-con being less than effective, and as we ascend the breeze becomes cooler, bursts of green herbs and lemons scenting the air.

'We had the same problem as you with accommodation,' Osh says. 'Finding rooms for the five of us was impossible.'

'Where are you staying now?'

'On the vineyard where we're shooting the commercial. We're pretty much just camping in one of the barns and stashing our stuff in the tour van. But there's plenty of room and the chap who owns the vineyard has given us a ton of food.'

'And *beer*,' Gabe adds, his head appearing in the gap between the driver's seat and front passenger bench. 'Which is the most important thing.'

I pat his cheek, his skin cool beneath my palm. 'I thought you were meant to be working.'

'It's a beer commercial. I'm a method guy, what can I tell you?'

The vineyard is stunning. Nestled into the gentle slope of a hillside, its lines of perfect green vines run up from a beautiful stone villa that glows in the afternoon sun. Marco, the owner, is a crinkly-eyed, white-toothed wonder, welcoming us like long-lost family and insisting on bringing us plates of fresh mozzarella with thick slices of beef tomato drizzled with olive oil, and loaves of fresh bread his wife baked that morning. He is instantly in a bromance with Gabe, who laughs and jokes and entertains like Gabe always does, to the delight of our host and his three enraptured kids.

Gabe was born to do this. No matter what the size of his audience is, he has the ability to command everyone's attention and make each person believe the show is purely for them. He knows I'm in on his game, too, which makes it all the more delicious. His eyes slide to me after each beat of his performance, that smile of his impossibly audacious.

That night, we drink beer under the stars around a fire pit and even though we're surrounded by the summer sounds of a Tuscan hillside, it feels like home.

'Thanks for rescuing me,' I say to Osh, as we watch Gabe entertaining the film crew with his on-set tales.

'My pleasure. Not so much a knight in shining armour as a knight in a dusty hire van, but I reckon I did a good job.'

'You did a *great* job.' I lean my head against his shoulder. Sparks from the fire dance up into the starlit night. 'It's so lovely here.'

'It is.' He takes a swig of beer. 'So what are your plans now? Stay in Tuscany?'

It's beautiful here but I thought I would be learning to make cheese and experiencing life on a real working farm. 'I was wondering about maybe finding a job somewhere. Stay put in one place for a bit.'

'Money getting tight?' Osh asks.

There is that. My savings and the money Mum and Dad gave me for the trip are definitely dwindling, even considering what I saved by staying with Giana. 'Always. But I want to do more than just be a tourist, you know?'

'Sure.' He chuckles as Gabe launches into an energetic retelling of his one-time attempt to break into action films. 'Marley is such a tart. I wonder how many bones he'll break this time.'

'... *three* ribs cracked and my leg in plaster for eight weeks,' Gabe declares. 'The Rock I'm *not*...'

'Three ribs,' Osh says, raising an eyebrow. 'Last time it was only one and a sprained ankle.'

'Bless him.'

'You're welcome to hang with us for a couple of days, Phee. We're filming in the vineyard and might do a bit around here if Marco fancies it. The guys wouldn't mind.'

'It's a kind offer – I'll stay tomorrow but then I need to move on,' I say, my resolve strengthening as I speak the words.

When the dancing flames in the fire pit have settled to a molten red-orange glow and Osh and the others are asleep in the barn, I sit with Gabe. I'll probably regret all the beer in the morning but the buzz is as welcome as the company tonight.

'Thanks for your text, Phoebs. Earlier. It meant a lot.'

'My pleasure. Was I right?'

His dark eyes reflect the fire's glow. 'Of course you were. You always are.'

'You'll be great in the play. Sorry I won't be there.'

'It's okay. I'm sure Meg will regale you with the gory details.' His gaze slides to me. 'I've missed you.'

A log in the fire pit splits, sending a shower of sparks up into the night.

'I've missed you too. And Osh and Meg.'

He's quiet for a while. I look up at the night sky studded with thousands of stars. They glow here like they're never allowed to in London. A shooting star dances across the midnight blue.

'So tell me about the guy.'

Of course he knows. Meg and Osh do so I couldn't expect them to keep it from Gabe. And anyway, why shouldn't he know? When Sam and I are together next year he'll see him all the time.

I can't read his expression when I look back at him. 'His name is Sam. He's a musician, he's Scottish, he's completely gorgeous...'

'And you're in love with him?'

'I am.'

The fire glow dances along the brown glass of his beer bottle as he lifts it to his lips. 'But he's in Mull and you're in Tuscany.'

I don't know why, but I feel I've just been accused. 'We text and email most weeks. Call each other, too.'

'But you *love* him. He's burst into your life and stolen your heart and you aren't with him?'

'We're both away for a year. When we get back—'

'How do you know, though? That it's the real deal? That's what I don't get, Phoebs. I mean, it could just have been a great snog when you needed it.'

I sit up a little, pulling my jacket around me. 'What are you saying?'

'I'm *saying* if he's the love of your life why would you want to be anywhere else?'

'We have things to do first.' I don't want to have to justify myself to Gabe and I don't want to fight with him, either. 'It works for us. Anyway, it's late. I should get some sleep.'

'I wouldn't leave you for a year,' he says – and suddenly I can't move.

'What?'

'If you were the love of my life and I knew it like you say you do, I couldn't walk away. I'd do anything to be with you.'

There's something in his gaze that I'm not ready to see. I stare at the fire. 'Yeah, well, you're not Sam.'

'Evidently.'

'What is that supposed to mean?'

'Nothing.'

What is he trying to say? I should push him for more but we're treading on dangerous ground. 'I'm going to bed.'

'Phoebs – wait.' His hand catches mine as I move to stand. 'I'm sorry, okay? Stay a bit longer. Please?'

I don't want to but I don't want an unresolved row to keep me awake tonight. So even though I'm tired, I sink back into my seat. 'You don't know Sam. And you don't know how I feel about him.'

'Sure. Sorry. It's just I…' His sentence remains frustratingly unfinished.

'I don't expect you to understand.'

'It's the beer making me talk bollocks. Ignore me.' He takes another long swig. 'I just think you're worth more.'

'Can we change the subject, please?'

'Okay. No, actually, one more thing…'

'Oh *come on*…'

'I think you're amazing. I think whoever you choose to give your heart to should count himself the luckiest guy on the planet. You give so much and you don't think people notice, but they do, Phoebs. *I* do. I should have said it before you went, but I'm saying it now and hoping it still counts. If you're sure of Sam, if you know you can be everything you want to be to each other, go for it. Just – make sure you're certain, okay?'

'I am certain,' I say, but my voice isn't as strong as I expect.

'Well, good.' He opens his arms. 'Bring it in.'

I let him hug me because I want him to see I'm settled in my decision. I'm irritated that he even thinks I want his opinion, but I can't deny how uncomfortable his question has made me.

His hand cradles my head against his chest and I feel the brush of his lips on my crown.

'Sorry for being a jerk.'

'A drunk jerk,' I say against his chest.

'The *drunkest* jerk in Tuscany.'

'Drunkiest isn't a word.'

'Everyone's a critic.'

It's almost 2 a.m. when I finally crawl into my sleeping bag on the bed of hay bales Marco made for me. I keep thinking about what Gabe said. I want to call Sam and talk to him, but things have been on a more even keel with us lately and I don't want to spoil that. Besides, he'll probably have been asleep for hours.

Next morning, I pick my way around the sleeping bodies of my friends, open the barn door a little and slip outside. Stillness surrounds me, a prickle of moisture in the air before the heat of the day. In the light pink dawn, the hills roll endlessly like blue-grey waves. I hug my arms around myself and take it all in. Another view I hadn't planned. Another gem I might have missed. This year is becoming a year of serendipities and I'm determined not to repeat the stress and concern of yesterday. For this moment, I don't have anywhere else to be.

I don't grab my phone to take a photo. I don't swipe to any social media app to frame this moment in a tiny square most will miss.

I keep my eyes open – and I breathe it in.

The serendipities keep coming.

Osh finds a website that lists volunteer jobs across Europe and when I scroll through the opportunities a position in Italy catches my eye. It's in Puglia – not a place I'd originally planned to visit, but I know from travellers I've met that it's a gorgeous region. There's a villa that's being restored to host weddings and events but the scheme has run out of money in its final stages. They are offering bed and board in exchange for a range of tasks: painting, re-establishing a terrace garden and creating a library. It's the final task that wins it for me. I send an email, which is followed by a phone call with the owner, Lisabeta, and a day later I'm catching a train from Siena to Lecce.

Osh and Gabe drive me to the train station. I savour our final hugs and don't mind that Gabe's is longer than it should be.

'Call me whenever you want,' he says, his breath warm against my ear.

'You'll be busy with your play.'

'Never too busy to talk to you.' His eyes are wide and still when we break apart. 'Remember that, okay?'

It's hard to let my friends go. I wave from the moving train until they become two tiny figures on the platform, a tunnel finally stealing them from my view.

It turns out Villa Speranza is the most perfect place. Or it has the potential to be.

The moment Lisabeta Sjöberg shows me the bare bones of what will be the library, I'm in love. A large double-height room lined with empty mahogany bookcases draped with dusty white sheets. The floor might once have hosted dances, its intricate inlays and faded gold leaf still beautiful despite the neglect. It's a huge project, but the end result would transform the room.

'I want to offer weddings here,' Lisabeta tells me, gazing out through the tall glass doors towards the Puglian landscape that sweeps away down the hillside. 'And host writers, artists, maybe even orchestras on summer breaks. The main villa has huge rooms that aren't being used. The library is the biggest challenge inside – we have boxes of books that the previous owner put in storage when there was a flood. The old shelves look solid enough but I've no idea if the books are in any condition to be saved. If we can restore this room, and open these doors onto the replanted terraces teaming with flowers and grasses, I think this will be heaven.'

Sadness clings to her words. It's profound and out of place in such unkempt beauty.

'It's beautiful.'

'Thank you. I hated it at first.'

'What – *how*?'

'My husband fell head over heels for her at an auction when we first came here from Sweden. All our savings are sunk into this project. I felt like she was his mistress for a while. And then, just when Karl had persuaded me I could love her too, he passed away.'

I feel the thud of my heart, the sadness startling. 'I am so sorry. I didn't know…'

Lisabeta smiles beneath the loss. 'Partly I want to restore her so the world can see what Karl saw. And I want people to be happy here.'

That's my heart gone. 'I would love to help you do that, Lisabeta. If you'll have me?'

Her smile is instantaneous. 'Phoebe, I would love your help. Welcome to Villa Speranza!'

It isn't just me working on this project, thank goodness. The garden is being tackled by a team of volunteers from a college in Lecce who are here for meals but go home at dusk. In the library I'm working with Amanda, an English professor on sabbatical from Plymouth University. She knew Lisabeta at university and loved the challenge of reinstating the library at Villa Speranza. But there's so much to do that everyone pitches in wherever we're needed.

Before long I am completely in love with this place. Puglia is gorgeous, quieter than Tuscany but breathtaking everywhere you look. Working is good for my head, too. I keep thinking about Sam and what Gabe said about him that night in Marco's vineyard.

If you're sure of Sam, if you know you can be everything you want to be to each other…

I am sure of Sam. I *am*. So why do Gabe's words keep returning?

Chapter Twenty-Four

SAM

Ailish and I didn't speak for a week.

Well, we spoke, but only in self-conscious bursts of politeness as we navigated uneasy paths around one another. In all honesty, that was worse than total silence. In the end we broke the stalemate one evening with a large bottle of whisky and tears from my honorary auntie. Ailish apologised for our row and I admitted she had a point.

A few days later, with no more reason to delay, I bit the bullet.

I called the number on the photograph.

I wasn't going to. But I was out walking over the hill behind her house this morning and found myself dialling it.

Unobtainable.

I wish I hadn't called it now. Because the one scrap of a lead I'd had has proved useless, right when I'd decided to push on with my search. I haven't told Ailish yet. I will – and when I do I know she'll offer to help. But the sting is too great right now to share it. Frank has eluded me once more and all the old pain has rocked back up uninvited. I don't know if I want to risk its kick again.

It's late afternoon now and I'm in the community room at Aros Hall in Tobermory where we hold the music club. About twenty kids ranging between the ages of seven and fourteen are scattered around the room clutching instruments. Some are their own, some have been donated by parents, grandparents and Niven's school. I wonder how many attics have been plundered to find these ancient treasures.

I have two fiddle players sitting beside me today – Molly, 10, and Bailey, 11. Both have a basic understanding of how to make a sound from their instruments, but beyond that they have little experience. I'm not bothered, though – this is exactly where I was when Jonas started to teach me. Molly and Bailey are both keen, which is more important than anything. I can work with keen.

Over in the far corner, Shona is teaching three small girls to play their tin whistles, stifling her giggles when the squeaks of the new players inevitably sound. I know she loves it from the way she flits between her students, correcting finger positions and demonstrating proper technique with her own whistle. Her enthusiasm is infectious and I see the way her students' eyes light up whenever she compliments them. They want to try for her, like I wanted to try for Jonas.

Niven is in the middle of the room with nine guitarists, all of whom are swamped by their enormous guitars, little legs and feet swinging from beneath their instruments, none quite meeting the floor. He's grinning at them as they master single finger G chords. Their excitement is palpable from here.

The noise in the room is something else, but it's exciting and fun, and there are shimmers of laughter and whoops of encouragement peppered through the discordant fug of sound. I love the positivity of it; the potential for igniting life-long passions for music just by sharing our own. These kids know Mull as home, most of them having been born here, and music plays such a huge part of the Island's heritage.

Around the room parents are sitting, watching the semi-organised chaos with a mixture of amusement and horror. I *think* they like what's happening. At least they're *here* to witness it. Frank never knew I played. Ma was often too drunk to notice. My earliest concerts at school more often than not had no seat in the audience filled by a member of my family. I don't blame Ma for not being there – where her head was at that time didn't allow her to think of anyone else because taking care of herself demanded all her efforts. I played for her a few times before she died, when she was pretty far gone, the nurse coming in to see her three times a day. Shortly after that she was moved to a hospice – no chance of playing any music for her there – and then, a week later, she was gone.

I wonder if she knew. If somewhere, way down beneath the layers of self-hate and hurt and the relentless demands of her body for the thing that was slowly killing her, she was proud of her eldest boy and his fiddle that he stuck with, even though she'd told Jonas I'd soon tire of playing.

Seeing the photograph of Frank playing his fiddle and knowing what I do now, Ma's horror at me choosing the same instrument makes more sense. I remember the fear in her eyes as she yelled at me for accepting Jonas's gift. Did she think I'd turn out like Frank?

Our session ends and I congratulate my happy students before joining the small group of parents helping to clear everything away. Niven nudges me as we carry chairs across the room.

'You okay, pal?'

'I'm fine.'

'Right. It's just you're a bit – far away today.'

We hand our chairs to Tattooed Joe, the barman from the pub we often play in, and walk back to fetch more.

'I called the number,' I say. 'From the picture.'

'Frank's number?'

'Mm-hmm.'

His eyes are saucer-wide. 'And?'

'It was unobtainable.'

'No! Mate…'

I shrug but the reality is heavy on me. It really is a dead end.

Niven puts a hand on my shoulder, his brow furrowed. 'There must be another way to find him. He can't just disappear, not in this day and age. There has to be a way to… hang on – Julie!'

He calls across the room, where a woman looks up and heads over to us. I recognise her from the first time I visited Niven's school, surrounded by a gaggle of adoring 4-year-olds. Her daughter is one of Shona's whistle-players.

'Julie's husband is a sergeant with Mull Police. He works out of the station in Tobermory.'

I didn't expect to get the police involved. I'm about to stop Niven but Julie has already reached us.

'Hey. What's up?'

'Bit of a random question, Ju: how easy would it be for your Doug to find a missing person?'

Julie laughs. 'You been a bit careless with your pals again, Niven?'

'Not for me. For Sam.'

She grins up at me. 'Depends. Who've you lost?'

'My father.'

Instantly, her smile fades.

Of course she knows about Frank. Everyone knows. Even people who weren't born when my father left the Island. It's become as familiar a whispered tale here as the ancient legends that seem to be attached to every stone of Mull.

In that moment, I think twice about asking for her husband's help. It won't be a casual enquiry if the police take it on. It will be official – a missing person's report, a public search. I'm not ready for that. But my friend thinks he's helping and it's too late to take back the suggestion.

'Sure he could help. I'll ask him.'

'I don't want to put him to any trouble…' I begin, hating the weakness of my protest.

'Ach, it's nae bother. He'll be glad of the work. Mull's hardly the crime capital of the Hebrides right now.' She pats my arm, which just makes me feel worse. 'Don't you worry, Sam. We'll find your da.'

We're at Niven's place, later that evening, eating frozen pizza and drinking beer. He's been casting glances in my direction when he thinks I'm not looking for the best part of an hour now and he blushes when I turn to catch him.

'What? Do I have pizza cheese on my chin?'

'Nah, but you have a big loony face.'

'Be serious.'

'It's nothing. Go back to your beer.'

'Don't give me that. What's with the staring?'

He groans. 'Okay. I have a question. If Doug can find Frank, will you go to see him?'

'I don't know.' It's the truth. 'He's probably dead, for all I know.'

'But if he isn't?'

'I guess I'll find out. They might not locate him, anyway. From what I've heard, Frank was always good at evading people.'

His question begs another one: do I *want* to know what happened to my father? What he did with his life once he'd cut us out of it? I'm not sure. But what if the police *don't* find him? Will it hurt more than the unobtainable tone I heard this morning when I called the number on the photo? These questions won't be answered unless Doug and his colleagues look for Frank. Wheels are in motion. Now I have to wait.

Chapter Twenty-Five

PHOEBE

The days become colder; the light more reluctant to arrive in the morning and stay in the late afternoons.

By November the library is repainted, the bookcases varnished and the floor brought back to life. Lisabeta has the glass doors replaced and crates of books begin to arrive from the storage unit. Amanda and I set up a table and carefully clean each book, checking the pages for signs of damp or water damage before stacking them in alphabetical piles around the edges of the room.

I send Sam a few postcards. He responds with emails and the occasional call. He laughs when I accuse him of getting off lightly. I'm only half-joking, but if he realises this he doesn't let on. I've felt him pulling away lately and I've battled fear that he's having second thoughts.

'I told you, my handwriting is shocking,' he says and I can hear the winter wind buffeting the island around him. Here it's colder than when I arrived but still warm enough at midday to work in T-shirts and jeans. When Sam video calls me from the arts centre where the music club is taking place, I'm surprised to see he's grown a beard. It suits him, but I'm still taken aback by how the seasons are changing us. My skin is the most tanned it has ever been. Streaks of gold run through my hair. And I am content.

And then, before I know it, Christmas arrives.

It's funny, but I hadn't thought much about where I would spend Christmas this year, or how it might feel to be away from my friends and family for the first time in years.

Fog cloaks the garden and all our talk around the knotted wooden table is of plans and dates, hopes for the coming year and dreams yet to happen. We are lying in wait like the dormant terrace flowerbeds and the half-finished library, all our bright hope and potential hidden for now.

'Next year, I want to have our first weddings in the diary,' Lisabeta says, passing a plate of *amaretti* biscuits around. We're drinking hot milk spiced with cinnamon and nutmeg, sharing our dreams for the year to come.

'That's totally possible,' Amanda says, dunking her biscuit in the warm white froth. 'I want to be doing a new project at work. Something that celebrates the great literary heritage we have in Devon and Cornwall. No idea how yet, but I'll work it out.'

They turn expectantly to me. What do I tell them? 'I hope I'll be doing something my heart loves,' I say. It's hopelessly vague but true. I don't know what I want to do this time next year. Part of my year away is to give myself the chance to think about stuff like that. I do know I don't want to settle for any old job like I did before. Maybe that's enough of a step forward for now.

And Sam. I want to be with Sam.

Where will we be this time next year?

Together, I hope.

*

Just before Christmas, a rare gift arrives at the villa, addressed to me – a handwritten Christmas card from Sam. Inside the appropriately Scottish-shortbread-tin design is a message. I can almost hear his voice speaking:

To

Phoebe,

Just think,

this time next year we'll be

arguing where to put the Christmas tree.

Or we'll be

hogging the mistletoe. Just us.

In a log cabin. Miles away from anywhere. For

weeks…

Okay, I'll stop now.

Seriously, with all my heart,

all I want for Christmas is 14th June. And you.

Me and you.

Sam xx

P.S. Can you see the Christmas tree? ☺

A message written in the shape of a fir tree. It must have taken him hours to work that out – but I love that he did. This little message means the world. He wants to be with me. He still believes it's possible.

It isn't *I love you* yet. But *I want to be with you* is pretty close.

If you were the love of my life and I knew it…

Gabe's words from the night in the vineyard return without

invitation. No, I tell myself, forcing my focus back to the precious Christmas note from Sam. This is enough for now. Sam wrote this message to let me know he's still mine. He took the time to say it. If he wanted to push me away he wouldn't have bothered.

I couldn't walk away. I'd do anything to be with you.

Would Gabe really? It's very easy to say the right thing when you're not the one in the situation. It could have been a line from one of his acting jobs for all I know. But I don't like that I'm still thinking about what Gabe said. My lovely Sam wanting to be with me, and the promise of celebrating Christmas soon in my Puglian home with Amanda and Lisabeta are all I want to think about.

We string up paper chains across the rooms in the villa, made from the packing paper used to keep the books safe in their storage cases. On Christmas Eve, the celebrations begin. Lisabeta's neighbour Aña brings us a feast of traditional Puglian Christmas treats: *frittelle* – little fried dumplings stuffed with tomatoes and mozzarella, sautéed onions and pungent ricotta cheese – all served with *cime di rapa* – boiled turnip leaves scattered with fried pancetta cubes; tiny *pettole* doughnuts dredged in sugar; and the centrepiece *cartellate* – long strips of fried dough rolled into roses and dipped into spicy mulled wine. Neighbours and friends, the college students from Lecce, and Lisabeta's sister Gudrun over from Sweden all gather around the old table in Villa Speranza's large kitchen. Aña jokes that Lisabeta has become a true Italian because her table can expand to accommodate whoever shows up for food. It's a family gathering like none I've experienced before and it's wonderful.

On Christmas Day, another feast takes place – this time Swedish delights prepared by Lisabeta and Gudrun. That evening, after we've all rolled ourselves away from the table, I sneak to my room on the first floor overlooking the terrace garden and call home.

Mum answers immediately and I wonder how long she might have been carrying her mobile with her, waiting for my call. I can hear the hum of conversation in their farmhouse, peppered occasionally by barks of laughter from Dad and Will.

'Tell me everything,' she says, and I imagine her settling into the old velvet armchair in the snug behind the kitchen, Gran's crocheted blanket over her knees and probably a glass of sherry warming on the old milking stool by the fire. The thought makes me miss her, as I always do when we talk. I don't think I could live at home again, but that rush of nostalgia never changes.

'The library is really coming on. Half of the shelves are complete and the new floor looks amazing. I reckon it'll be done before I head back to Paris.'

'You're staying on till then? Not tempted to squeeze in some more travelling?'

'It's been nice to stay in one place, feel part of something more than tourist lines. And the villa is gorgeous, Mum. You and Dad would love it here.'

'And you get on well with everyone?'

'They're all great. Amanda is hilarious – she's invited me to visit her in Plymouth when we're back in the UK. We've been joking that we're the Two Doctors because of our PhDs – she's Tom Baker and I'm Jodie Whittaker.'

'I'll tell your father that, he'll be over the moon you're staying true to your Whovian roots.'

'Always.'

'And – Sam?' I can't miss her hesitation.

'We're good. He has things to do – so do I – but yeah, it's okay.'

I glance at Sam's Christmas tree message on the table by my bed and smile. I haven't heard from him today – I half expected I might, it being Christmas Day. I shake the thought from my mind. *This* is enough.

'Just make sure you're doing what makes *you* happy. The rest will sort itself out. And remember, men are a strange breed. I love your dad with all my heart but some things he does are still a mystery to me after all these years. Be happy, Phoebe. That's all that matters to us.'

I love that Mum supports me, even across the miles. I love her more for not telling me what she really thinks about what Sam and I are doing. I suspect I know, but her faith that I will find my way through it all means the world. I will find a way to make this work. I have to believe Sam will, too.

We settle into an easy rhythm after Christmas. Winter nights are simple affairs at the villa – we sit together and chat, listen to music, or read. Occasionally we check our phones but in such lovely surroundings with such fascinating people conversation usually wins our attention.

'What did you do in Rome, Phoebe?' Lisabeta asks one evening, when we're relaxing after dinner.

'Pretty much everything,' I laugh. 'I was there for a while.'

'I'm definitely visiting Rome before I go back,' Amanda says. 'Even if I can only squeeze a weekend in. What was your favourite thing?'

I don't even have to think about it. 'It wasn't in any of the guidebooks, but I think it might change the way I live.'

'Great pizza?' Lisabeta asks.

'No, although the food in Rome was as epic as you imagine. Hang on, I'll show you.'

Leaving my bemused companions I race up to my room. Tucked in the inside zipped pocket of my bag is a pebble I painted before I left Rome. I painted a snowglobe on one side and *Carried in my heart* on the reverse. I fetch the paint box Giana gave me, too and head back to my friends.

They love the idea. I knew they would.

'Why the snowglobe?' Lisabeta asks.

'I have a snowglobe at home – back in London. My friends bought it for me the week I moved in.' I point to the building within the glass dome. 'That's Shakespeare's Globe theatre. It was the first place we visited together because my friend Gabe was playing Orlando in *As You Like It*. After the performance we went out for food and that's when they asked me if I'd like to move in with them. So they bought me the snowglobe to remember where it all started – and it's a play on the name of the theatre, which I think William Shakespeare would have approved of. I was going to bring it with me but it wouldn't fit in my luggage.'

'And the words?'

'It was a day I was really missing my friends. I wanted to mark that, so the snowglobe was the perfect emblem for the love I've left behind.' I stroke the pebble and tell them Giana's story. 'The best part of being in Rome was sneaking around the city leaving painted pebbles for people to find. Tiny bits of our lives scattered for strangers to find.'

Lisabeta beams. 'We could do that here. In the garden. Paint our hopes and dreams for the years to come and leave them there for our future guests to find. And then when people stay, we'll encourage them to paint a pebble, too and leave it here. It can be like coins in the Trevi Fountain – leave it in our garden to make sure you return.'

So, that's what we spend our evenings doing. We paint pebbles to nestle between the plants and flowers that will appear in the terrace garden. Each one will have a date painted as part of the design – either a date we want to remember or a date we're looking forward to.

I love how one simple idea Giana was given in a community group has grown to become something personal to everyone it has touched.

In the middle of all the dates passed around Villa Speranza's table during the long winter nights, there is one I can't wait to arrive:

14th June 2018.

The day Sam and I have promised we'll meet again.

Chapter Twenty-Six

SAM

I'm sitting with a bunch of musicians in a Tobermory pub, my head a little woozy from festive drinking and my stomach blessedly full of the landlady's famous beef and ale pie. I'm a Mull lad but this is the first Hogmanay I've spent on the Island as a man. That seems wrong somehow. But it's changed. I've changed. And not just the beard, which is Niven's favourite thing to mock and the cause of Phoebe's double-take when she saw it in our last video call.

I hope she liked the Christmas tree note. I planned it as a surprise to bridge the gap that's opened between us. My attempt to step up where I could. She has to know nothing's changed about wanting her in my life, despite the dreadful way I've handled things. I hate not sharing news of my search. Not that there's been any news – but that's beside the point. I want to talk to her about it. I hate that I can't. But until Doug finds anything – *if* there's anything to find – there's nothing I can say.

We finish the song to cheers and promise to be back in twenty minutes. Tattooed Joe the barman declares Happy Hour and a swell of bodies presses to the bar. I reach for a glass of whisky as a hand pats mine. Julie Pritchard smiles and I move to let her squeeze onto the bench seat beside me.

'Love your playing, Sam,' she says, her voice several tones higher than usual, no doubt due to New Year whisky, the same as the rest of us. 'Like an angel you are.'

'Pleasure.' I clink my glass against hers. 'You having fun?'

'As ever. I love Hogmanay.'

I smile. 'Me too.' I see her smile flicker and take the cue. 'I'm guessing Doug's heard nothing?'

She pushes her lips together and pats my knee. 'I'm sorry. He's not giving up, though.'

We've had the same awkward exchange every week since Julie asked her husband to look for Frank. But at the turn of the year, knowing I'm halfway through my time here and aware of how fast the first six months have passed, it's a blow. Worse, because I haven't just been waiting for the police to uncover information. I've tried doing my own searches in Tobermory's library, too, trawling old internet sites that list former bars and music venues and the musicians who played there, searching for death notices in newspaper archives. No mention, not even a passing reference. For someone regarded as such a legend here he's startlingly absent from any kind of online record.

Ailish catches my eye from the other side of the pub and raises her glass. I do the same. I won't tell her yet what Julie said, although I reckon she's already guessed. Since our row about Frank she's made a determined effort to be on my side. I think she shocked herself with what she said to me. And she knows I'm trying to find Frank now.

'Looks like we might be stuck here,' Niven says as Julie leaves. 'The snow's coming down fast.'

'I can think of worse places to be stranded.'

'There is that. Everything okay?' He nods at the seat beside me where Julie was sitting.

'No news.'

'Ah. Maybe they'll get lucky soon?'

Do I want them to? I'm getting used to *not* knowing. And what do I hope they'll find out, anyway? That Frank's dead? Or that he's still around, causing trouble for someone else?

I don't have any answers to that. Like a lot in my life right now, I just have to trust that I'll know what to do when the time comes. Overthinking achieves nothing for me. It makes me more likely to run, and I don't want to run this time. I'm better when I play by heart.

Niven's right: we are snowed in. Those who live near enough struggle through heavy snow back to their beds. But for those of us left behind, Tattooed Joe offers accommodation in the pub. He declares a free bar and we help him fetch pillows, cushions and blankets from upstairs to make the pub comfortable for an overnight stay.

When Niven is chatting to Joe over a triple dram, I find a corner away from the bar. It's late and I don't know if I've sufficient signal, but there's someone I want to talk to. I don't know if it's the unusual place where I'll be sleeping out Hogmanay, or the effects of Tattooed Joe's hospitality, but I'm suddenly brave. I don't want Phoebe to be in any doubt of what she means to me.

'Sam?' Any remorse I might feel for waking Phoebe up is lost in the joy of hearing her delightfully sleepy voice.

'Hey, sorry to wake you.'

'You didn't... Well, you did, but it's okay. How are you?'

'Good. Missing you.'

She makes a happy murmur. 'Miss you, too.'

'I'm snowed in.'

'In Fionnphort?'

'No, a pub in Tobermory. With Niven and Ailish. And a free bar.'

'Sounds like heaven.'

'It is. It would be – if you were here.'

'I wish I could be.' There's a pause and I wonder if she's drifted to sleep again. Then: 'Sam, are you sure you still want this? I know you have stuff going on…'

'Yes, I want this. Things might be complicated now and I can't say why. Just believe me that it doesn't change how I feel.'

'That's hard when you don't talk to me.'

That cuts deep. 'I know. I'm sorry.'

I hear her slow exhale. 'It's really late…'

'Yeah. Go back to sleep.'

'Thank you. For calling me.' I hear the smile return to her voice. 'I miss you.'

I close my eyes, the first dull ache of the night creeping across my brow. Sleep won't be far from me either. 'I miss you too. Happy New Year, beautiful.'

Over the next eight weeks the music club restarts and so do our house gigs, when the weather permits. Shona rents a house not far from Niven. One silver lining to divorcing a high-profile rugby player who isn't keen on details of his private life leaking to the press is that their out-of-court settlement has provided Shona with a valuable nest-egg. She plans to invest money in the music school, too. It's good to see her putting down roots, even if part of me is nervous about her becoming a permanent feature of life on the Island.

Phoebe and I resume our regular texts and emails, a little of the earlier ease we enjoyed returning. Thinking of her makes me *not* think about Shona and that works for me. At New Year I promised myself I would be better for Phoebe and I'm determined to step it up. Shona is a complication I don't need.

I settle into a good rhythm – until a phone call at the start of March blows everything out of the water. Doug Pritchard calls and asks me to meet him at Tobermory Police Station. Suddenly, all my carefully laid foundations are shaken. But I need to know what he's found.

Ailish insists on making biscuits 'for the boys'. It's a little strange to walk into a police station with a flowered tin, even if the police station in question looks more like somebody's bungalow than the crime-fighting hub of the island. But hardly anything on Mull works the way it would on the mainland, so I just go with the flow. Besides, this is Ailish's way of showing her support and I appreciate it.

Sergeant Doug Pritchard greets me at the front desk, his eyes sparkling over his impressive red beard when he sees the gift from Ailish.

'She's a star,' he grins, opening a hatch in the counter that would be better suited to a pub bar than a police station reception. 'Ailish used to babysit my sister and me when we were bairns. Her shortbread biscuits are the stuff of legend. Come on through, Sam. Can I get you a tea? I'd offer you coffee but the stuff PC McNulty makes is thicker than peat.'

A middle-aged female officer reading a newspaper at the front desk tuts and turns the page.

'Tea would be good, thanks.'

'Great. Do the honours, Dora, would you?'

'After that glowing endorsement how can I refuse?' she mutters after us.

I suppress my smile and follow Doug through to a glass-partitioned office with just enough room for one desk and a chair on each side.

'Take a seat. Biscuit?'

I decline. My stomach has been in knots since he called me this morning and tea is about the only thing I dare ingest.

Five minutes later, Dora arrives with two incredibly strong mugs of tea, not stopping to accept my thanks when I offer it.

Doug pops a shortbread biscuit in his mouth and places another on the desk as he closes the tin. 'Cheery, she is. Good in a chase, though.'

The mind boggles.

'My kids love your music club, by the way,' he continues, dunking a biscuit into his tea. 'It's all the wee one talks about. Shona's great with them.'

'Thanks. It's been fun to set it up.' Small talk is great, but waiting to discuss what I came here for is threatening to make me sick. 'You said on the phone you have some news?'

'I do. Tricky bastard to find, your da, so it's a bit of a result, if I say so myself.'

This is it.

I take a breath and settle myself.

'What have you found?'

Doug's smile softens for just a moment. 'I'm guessing this hasn't been easy for you. What with him high-tailing it when you were a bairn.'

'I'd just like to know what happened to him,' I say, the chair suddenly granite-hard beneath me. 'It's taken me a long time to come to that.'

'I'm not surprised. Pardon my saying so, but what kind of a callous bastard walks out on his family like that, eh? I couldn't imagine breaking contact with mine. Even if Julie turfed me out – which she may well do one day – I'd have to stay close so I could see our girls.' Checking himself, he raises a hand in apology. 'Forgive me. So, I contacted my superior at Oban and called in a favour. Unless we have reason to believe the missing person is either suspected of a crime or in personal danger, we don't usually authorise searches. But Caroline is an old friend and she'd heard the stories of your father, too, growing up here. So, she pulled some strings.'

At least Frank's mythology has proved useful for once. It doesn't make me feel any more comfortable, though. 'I appreciate it, thanks.'

'Pleasure.' Doug takes a stapled set of A4 sheets from the tray on his desk. 'Now before we start, I have to say we don't know whether your father is still alive. Having said that, there's no death certificate registered in his name that we could find. We didn't manage to locate him in person, but we have good reason to believe that we've found his most recent address.'

'Where?'

'Edinburgh. The phone number you gave us was that area, so we worked on the assumption that while the number was no longer operational, Frank might still be in the city. Eventually, after more than a few blind alleys, we got lucky.' He slides one of the sheets across the desk to me. 'The address for the number you had was in Leith. Now, we think he left the city for a while because at that point the trail goes cold. But then, he suddenly turns up again. We believe Frank's most recent accommodation is in Abbeyhill.'

I scan the typed search information, taking time to absorb it all. I'd recognised the code in the number on the photograph but had no idea when my father had given that to Morag. 'Do you have any idea how long Frank was living in Edinburgh?'

'Aye, we looked into that, too. With the exception of a few months in Glasgow and almost a year on Shetland, we think he pretty much remained in and around Edinburgh until, as I say, his brief disappearance between his Leith and Abbeyhill residences.'

The news hits me like a rock. Was Frank close to us when we were in Dumbiedykes all those years? Was he no more than a bus ride away from the family he'd abandoned? Thank heaven Ma never knew. It might have killed her sooner than the drink.

'This new address – in Abbeyhill – how recently was he living there?'

'Well, there was no answer when my colleagues visited, but a neighbour confirmed Frank lived there with a woman. The last time she'd seen him at the house was about six months ago, she reckoned. We placed several calls to the property but none were answered. The line is connected, which suggests someone is living there, but we checked with the council and it's listed as a rental property – private landlord. So there's every chance he's moved on.' He sits back and takes a slurp of tea. 'It's a lot to take in, I know. And I'm sorry we couldn't find the man himself. But maybe you'll have better luck if you decide to visit?'

I don't return immediately to Ailish's car when I leave the police station. My head is ablaze with questions and I need to walk while I try to untangle them. Had I known my father was in the city would I have tried to find him? When I was a kid, long before I had WiFi or my family had access to a computer, I'm not sure I would have known where to look. And back then all I could see were the effects of Frank's disappearance on Ma and Cal – the toll on our lives.

The Dumbiedykes flat wasn't an easy place to live. The landlord scared the bejeebies out of us kids and Ma was forever complaining to him about the damp and the smattering of black mould rising up the walls from its festering carpets. I'm convinced Ma's drink problem was hastened by the place we ran to. She blamed herself for trusting Frank, for not being the woman her own mother told her she should have been. She *hated her own bones*, as our neighbour used to say, a face full of pity over the cigarette slouching from her lips when we met her on the concrete walkway leading to our flats. *It's no wonder she drinks, your poor ma. If you blame your own skin for holding you together, what hope is there?*

I walk into Tobermory and skirt the multicoloured houses of the seafront, the smell of salt from the ocean strong and the gulls screeching overhead. Compared to where my mother eked out an existence for us, this place is a dream. How bad must life have been with my grandmother to make her prefer our grim, damp-ridden flat to this?

I'm about to leave the seafront and climb the road up the hill out of Tobermory when my phone buzzes. I check the screen and double take.

PHOEBE – VIDEO CALL. ACCEPT?

I know she's been working long hours at the villa lately, cataloguing books and restocking the library, so I'd told myself not to expect much contact for a while. But this is the sweetest gift anyone could have offered me today.

'Surprise!' she grins. My life, she's beautiful. Her skin has caught the sun even more than in the last photograph she sent me. Gold streaks dance in her hair, which is wavier than I remember. Behind her the sky is a deep blue and she's shielding her eyes from the sun. In the shadow cast by her hand, they look enormous, slate-green against her skin.

'You look amazing,' I breathe.

'Sorry, you might have to speak up. It's not the best connection.' There's a moment's delay between sound and picture, which makes her look as if she's talking in a dream. She *is* a dream – a vision on my phone.

'I said you look amazing,' I repeat, my heart swelling when I see her laugh.

'Okay, I heard you the first time. I just wanted you to say it again.'

'Shameless!'

She shrugs. 'Not sorry, either.'

'It is so good to see you.'

'You too. Amanda and I came into town to get some supplies and I just found a pavement café with WiFi. I thought I'd give this a go.'

'I'm so glad you did.'

'Sam, I just wanted to…'

'I've had some news.' I can't hold it in any longer. 'It might mean I have to go to Edinburgh.'

'News about your dad? Oh Sam, is he still alive?'

I want to tell her everything but she looks so happy and I just can't hit her with it. I haven't told her about the police search, or my row with Ailish. She knows nothing except my gigs and the music school. I want to tell her, but all I manage is a nod.

'If you want to talk…'

'It's okay. It might be nothing. I'll sort it.'

It's too late, her smile is gone. Why did I even mention it?

'I'd like to help.'

I want her to help. I do. But there's so much crap in my head – about Frank, about where he was during my lonely childhood years and, worse, about why he ran from us. I haven't forgotten Ailish's words about my urge to run like my father did and it scares me. Doug's revelations and this curveball when I felt I'd found an even keel – it's a juggernaut thundering towards me. And it's too much to land on Phoebe. 'I know. Forget I mentioned it. How's the library?'

'It's good.' She runs a hand through her hair but it isn't to move it out of her eyes. I see what I didn't want to: her frustration with me. 'Sam, tell me to shut up if you like, but just let me say this? If you find your dad, if you have the chance to see him, I think you should go.'

Her image freezes – a frown I wish I hadn't caused.

'Phoebe? Are you still there?'

It's a while before she answers and the picture begins to pixelate.

'Yes…' Burrs and clicks steal her voice.

'Phoebe? I think I'm losing you…'

'You're breaking up, too. Can you still hear me?'

'I can.'

'Sam, if it was me, I'd want to know.' Her image is almost unrecognisable now and panic rises in my gut.

The screen goes blank.

PHOEBE – VIDEO CALL. CONNECTION LOST

I walk to my car, Phoebe's words fresh in my memory.

If it was me, I'd want to know.

I'm scared and I still don't know if I'm ready. But Phoebe's right. There's only one way to resolve this.

I'm going to Edinburgh.

Chapter Twenty-Seven

PHOEBE

The sun is so bright today.

Amanda and I slip on sunglasses as we sit on the terrace with mugs of strong Swedish coffee from Lisabeta's stovetop pot. It's good to be in the fresh air after the dust and heavy scent of ancient print in the library. The last of the students from Lecce are finishing off the terrace and although many of the plants will mature over the coming year, it looks incredible. Swathes of lavender and rosemary line the gently curling path like scented clouds. Butterflies dance and bees hum around the blooms.

'Can you believe how good the library looks?' Amanda asks. 'Almost finished after all those hours of unpacking. The completed shelves look like rows of jewels.'

'That'll be the guidance of a great literature professor.'

'That'll be a bloody hardworking Doctor of Literature.'

We share grins. The library is perfect. And we made it happen.

'Lis says she has a couple interested in saying their vows here already.'

'I'm single but I'd consider marriage if I could do it surrounded by those beautiful books.' Amanda nudges my elbow. 'Maybe you and Sam might do your vows here?'

My smile vanishes once it's inside my mug. Marriage might as well be the moon. I know Sam is going to look for his father. And I think he heard me tell him to go for it before our video call gave up the ghost. But if he's serious about being with me, why cut me off like he did? I've told him everything, in calls and messages and texts and emails.

A bee passes inches from my mug, bumbling along to the lavender at the edge of the terrace.

Okay, I haven't told him *everything*.

I said Osh and his film crew came to my rescue in Tuscany. I may have mentioned Gabe in the list of crew names. But I didn't say it was *Gabe* Gabe. And I didn't tell Sam what we spoke about that night.

I didn't write it in my journal, either. That's what concerns me most. I've documented every detail of my time at Villa Speranza, good and bad. The days we've seen real progress, like when we shelved the last book in the first section. And the days when nothing has gone to plan: like the time when the pipes burst in the hallway next to the library and we spent three days bailing the water, building dams of sacking to save the floor. Or when I've felt alone here, in the quiet dark before sunrise, when communication with Sam was thin on the ground and doubt raised its head.

But I didn't write about the night at the vineyard.

When Amanda goes inside, I check the signal and call Meg. It's a long shot, but I need to talk to someone. I wait while it rings and when Meg's voice dances onto the line it's the loveliest sound.

'I'm not disturbing you, am I?'

Her laugh is as warm as the Puglian sun today. 'Not at all. I'm working in the members' lounge at the Royal Festival Hall. It's full of TV writers having loud conversations about how successful they want everyone to think they are. Trust me, your call is making me look important.'

'How does Lady Thames look today?'

'Beautiful, in a brooding fog-covered way. How is gorgeous Italy?'

'*Gorgeous*. Warm and sunny and the lavender smells incredible.'

'I'll bet, you jammy git. Next time you head off on your travels I'm packing myself in your rucksack, okay? I'd kill for some Italian sun today. So what's happening?'

I might have known Meg would clock my mood. 'Sam.'

'Good or bad?'

'I don't know. He's gone to look for his dad – I think. He knows where he might be at least.'

'But he hasn't told you what he's doing?'

'Not really. No, he hasn't. And I know I shouldn't feel left out but I do.'

I hear the *click-click-click* of her ballpoint pen, a thing Meg does when she's debating what to say. 'Phee, he's doing a huge thing…'

'I know. He probably can't think of anything but that.'

'But it makes you feel like you aren't enough?'

I rub my forehead. Spoken aloud it sounds worse. 'Yeah.'

'Mm. Are you having second thoughts, hun?'

'No!'

'Because it's okay if you are. You've championed it for nine months. That might make you think you can't change your mind because you've been so sure, but you can.'

'I haven't changed my mind.'

'But it hurts that he's shutting you out.'

Meg knows she's hit the nail on the head by my silence.

'Phee, give him space. Give yourself some space, too.'

'I know you're right.'

'Hey, I'm a hugely important person trying to pretend I'm an important TV writer. Of course I'm right.'

Talking to Meg soothes some of my concerns, but I still wonder what Sam's doing. Is he in Edinburgh already? I don't know whether to wish he finds his father or not. It's another reminder that I don't know him as well as my heart thinks it does.

My mobile rings later that evening. I grab it, pausing when I see the caller's name.

'Phoebs! How are you? Where are you?'

'Hello, Gabe. I'm good and I'm writing my journal in my room. How are you? And why are you calling?'

I hear his laugh and instantly feel mean. 'Oh well, *that's* charming.'

'Sorry, what I meant was—'

'Relax, it's fine. Meg mentioned she spoke to you today so I thought I'd give you a call. Also, I have a question: when are you heading back to Paris?'

'In a few weeks. I'm coming back to London on 14th June.'

'Right. Now the play is over I'm taking a couple of months off. We're still waiting for the damn release date on the feature film so I don't want to commit to anything else until it comes through. And I'm knackered. I fancy a break. So, how about I pop over to Paris when you're there?'

Even though he can't see me, I freeze. 'I—'

'You know, we could spend a couple of days wafting around, walking pink poodles, reading Proust?'

'I'm… not sure when I'm likely to be there. And there's Tobi and Luc: they want me to stay with them before I come home and they've been so good to me sorting out all the places to stay.'

I don't want Gabe to be in Paris. When I return to Tobi and Luc's I only want to be thinking about Sam. About what he means to me. About everything we could be.

'You hate the idea.'

'I don't hate it. I just – er…'

Have I offended him? I hear his chuckle and imagine the half-frown he has when someone mocks him. 'No problem. Just thought I'd ask. Are you still loving villa life?'

'Yes, it's going to be a wrench to leave it,' I reply, relieved the conversation has veered off its worrying course.

'I think what you've done there is wonderful. Saving a library? I can't imagine a more perfect job for you. Send me photos when it's done, yeah? I want to see your handiwork.'

'I will. Sorry, Gabe. About the Paris thing.'

'Hey, don't sweat it. Your loss! Anyway, it will be good to have you back in June.'

'Thank you.'

'You're welcome. Go back to your scribbling.'

I stare at my darkened phone when his image fades to black. I'm not sure how to feel. The Gabe I left in London had been doing his best to tell me I wouldn't be able to manage a year away. The Gabe I met in Tuscany could see the change in me. And the Gabe who just called acknowledged I'd found my calling in Puglia.

The change is remarkable. And it's raised a question I never thought I'd have to consider: if Gabe had been like this the day before I left, would I have gone?

Chapter Twenty-Eight

SAM

Abbeyhill has changed from the place in my memory. It helps that it's a sunny day today. Everything looks brighter, more hopeful with a wash of sunlight.

Or maybe that's wishful thinking.

In my hotel room last night I lay awake going over everything. I wish I could say that when I planned to find out about Frank I actually imagined meeting the guy. I just expected to find out more than I'd known before, like learning the history of an ancient monument you'd grown up by.

If he's there, what will I say to him?

What do you say to the guy who cared so little about his son that he removed himself from his life? To him I'm as good as dead, anyway.

If it was me, I'd want to know.

I remember the stillness of Phoebe's eyes when she said that to me, how it contrasted with the wild dance of her hair as the breeze whipped it around her face. Until she said it, I don't think I would have considered doing anything with the information Doug had given me.

But I'm here because of her words.

I don't know what time Frank's likely to be at home – if it's even still his home – so I opt for mid-morning first. If there's no answer, I'll try again around 6 p.m. and again at 9 p.m. In between I'll head back to the hotel and try my hardest not to get drunk. I haven't had any alcohol since I arrived yesterday but I can't guarantee what happens today won't send me seeking solace in a bottle.

I've told Ailish I'll ring her as soon as I find anything. She knows to respect that and won't try to call me before. She still feels bad about our fight but no matter how in control of your life you are, sometimes you just need someone who loves you enough to give you a great big push.

What would Ma have made of me being here? Never mind the irony that her absent husband was likely living in the same city as us for at least some of our time in Edinburgh. Would she be angry with me? The kid in me who never wanted to make his mother cry worries a little now. I hope she'd understand, even if I suspect she wouldn't.

The taxi drops me off a few streets away, a deliberate move on my part to give me a chance to get myself together. I walk past houses in various states of repair, most of them proudly cared for but the odd one here and there with broken fences and cars parked across gardens, as if they've been dumped in a hurry. Most are semi-detached houses now; back in the day they would all have been council flats. Some of the buildings still have the flight of concrete steps outside rising to the first floor from the driveway. There are lines of spring flowers standing sentry-like along some of the garden paths. Black wheelie bins, pink plastic bottle boxes and green and blue recycling bags edge the pavement. Each one is a glimpse into the lives of the residents – beer bottles and folded pizza boxes in one set, bags of brightly coloured wrapping paper and children's toy packaging in the next.

I don't get stage fright before a gig but right now every nerve within me is on high alert.

The streets are empty, but I feel as if the world is watching.

It strikes me that this is one of those moments in life that can't be anything but monumental. My story as Frank's son will be forever altered the moment that door opens. Even if he's long gone, or dead after all, my life has already changed just by being here.

There it is: the junction with Airdrie Road and the small sign that marks its beginning. He's already closer than he has been for twenty-three years.

I follow the houses on the odd-numbered side of the road. Each one is divided into two flats. Which would Frank choose, ground floor or first? Head in the clouds or best placed for a speedy exit? I wonder...

151... 153... 157... 159...

I slow beside the house next door to the address I'm looking for and glance away from the well-kept garden to the edge of the pavement. There are two black bins and four recycling bags outside 161. And painted in hasty white strokes on the bins: 161A and 161B.

My heart skids to a halt. I wrench breath into my body.

Doug said his colleagues had tried to get an answer from 161B on four occasions but failed. It was a neighbour who'd confirmed Frank lived there, although they hadn't seen him for a while. But he has to be here now because the bin and recycling bags have been put out. By Frank, or someone who knows him.

The latch on the gate opens with a creak and flakes of old green paint stick to my hands when I push it open. Brushing them away, I walk up the path to 161B. Ground floor: ready to run. Figures. My fist shakes as I raise it to the dirty white uPVC door and knock.

Please be in. Please be home.

I wait, listening to my breath and the distant hum of traffic. The *whoosh* of a bicycle passes on the pavement beyond the gate and somewhere a woman laughs.

Nothing.

My heart sinks. I knock again, louder this time, staring at the closed door for longer than is comfortable. Nobody's home. I knew this was a possibility and there are still two more opportunities to visit before I have to return to Mull.

It isn't over, I tell myself. *It's just the first strike.*

So I'll come back at teatime – and, if necessary, at 9 p.m. as well.

I retrace my steps down the cracked flagstone path and reach for the gate.

'Can I help you?'

The door has opened and a young woman is standing on the step, a baby wriggling against her shoulder. She has dark hair pulled back into a straggly ponytail and looks as if she hasn't slept for weeks.

'I'm sorry to disturb you. I'm looking for Frank Mullins?'

'Who?'

I approach her carefully, pulling the crumpled photograph of my father from my back pocket and holding it out. 'Frank Mullins. Originally from the Isle of Mull? I was told he lived here?'

She glances at the photo but hardly long enough to make out Frank's blurry image. 'No, sorry.'

'Oh.'

They got it wrong. Or maybe he did live here, defaulted on the rent and the landlord moved this lady in instead. I can better believe that of Frank from what I've discovered about him.

'Can I ask how long you've lived here?'

She doesn't return my smile. 'Three years.'

How can the police have made such a mistake? There must have been an error with the council tax record. Maybe they wrote the number down wrong? A hundred possibilities race through my mind. But the bottom line remains: this isn't where Frank lives now. My search is over.

'I see. Sorry. I'm his son, by the way. Not that it matters to you, or should matter to you. I haven't seen him since I was nine. And – I just wanted to see if I could talk to him.' I realise I'm rambling to a complete stranger who doesn't know or care about Frank Mullins. I raise my hand in apology. 'Anyway, sorry to disturb you. Have a nice day.'

A flush of indignation and embarrassment claims my face as I hurry back to the gate. I need to get out of here now. The last thing this poor woman needs is a nutter sobbing in her garden.

'You have his eyes.'

I daren't turn back. My feet are frozen to the spot, my hand resting on the green gate, my heart in my mouth.

'What?'

'And the colour of his hair. He frowns like you do, too.'

I look at her, not quite believing I heard her speak at all.

'What did you say your name was?' she asks.

'I didn't. It's Sam.'

'I'm Elspeth. Ellie, to everyone' – the baby gurgles loudly and she gives a nervous laugh – 'except this one. This is Barney, my son.'

Is Frank the kid's father? My stomach twists as I walk back to the young woman. There's nothing to stop him fathering more children, I guess. He'd be – what – in his sixties now? It's biologically possible; even if morally, practically and emotionally inadvisable, given his past record.

'Is Frank…?' I nod at the baby.

Ellie's eyes widen and her hand flies to her mouth. 'Hell, no! Oh my gosh.'

'I'm sorry. I just… I didn't know…'

When she takes her hand away, she's laughing. 'You're fine. Wow. That would be something. No, Sam, Frank's not my partner.'

'Right.'

Her smile softens. 'He's my dad.'

Chapter Twenty-Nine

PHOEBE

'Hi, this is Sam. I can't come to the phone right now so please leave a message and I'll get back to you.'

I end the call and kick the ground, a shower of pebbles marking my frustration.

'Phoebe? Everything okay?' Lisabeta looks over the terrace wall and instantly I feel ridiculous. I didn't even know she was there. My face flushes as she navigates her way over the flowerbed and hops down onto the path.

'Sorry, Lis.'

She nods at my phone. 'Bad news?'

'No. It might be.'

'Like that, huh?' My host takes off her work gloves and claps them together. A cloud of terracotta dust swirls into the air. 'I'm popping to town to run some errands. You want to come? Coffee's on me.'

'You don't like the coffee in town.'

Lis laughs. 'I'll risk it if cheers you up.'

When she puts it that way, how can I refuse?

The market is in full swing when we arrive, a giddying rush of colour, sound and aroma. I've seen so many markets this year but each one has had its own personality. Here the stallholders know

Lisabeta so we are greeted like long-lost friends. It takes an hour to buy all the things she needs because each purchase comes with a slice of the latest gossip.

In a café at the edge of the market square we flop down at a table and order coffee and cinnamon sugar-dredged twists of fried dough that look like Mexican *churros*.

'How are you now?' Lis asks.

'Better,' I smile. 'Thanks for bringing me.'

'My pleasure. So, what happened earlier?'

'I tried to call someone but they weren't answering.'

Lis dunks a strip of doughnut in her espresso cup. 'Your Scotsman?'

It always amuses me when she uses that name. 'Sam, yes.'

'Let me guess: you fell out.'

My expression must be easier to read than I thought. 'Good guess.'

She laughs. 'Let's just say I recognised the signs. You know, Karl and I had to spend a year apart, not long after we met. He was two years older than me, so he went to study at Uppsala University. I was still at high school. And crazy though it sounds, twenty-five years ago not everybody had a mobile phone. I certainly didn't.'

'How often did you see him?'

'During holidays. Never at weekends like my friends did with their boyfriends. In the meantime we kept in contact with letters and the occasional phone call.'

'How did you cope?'

Her laugh garners smiles from customers gathered at a nearby table. 'With a lot of misunderstanding and pointless arguments. I lost count of the number of times we'd run out of change for the payphone mid-conversation, or misread something in a letter.

Everything took so much longer to resolve. And even your phone now, with all its clever technology, is really little better for showing you someone's true reactions. Texts are misread, calls are cut off. It's all the same.'

'I spoke to Sam a week ago. I said something important and I don't know if he heard me because our video call broke down. And now he isn't answering his phone.'

She considers my predicament as she portions out the remainder of the doughnut sticks. The calls of the market float across to us on the warm breeze. 'The only way you can ever know what someone's true feelings are is to stand next to them and watch. It's all the tiny little movements, the non-verbal communication our brain sees but our eyes don't. The whole picture is what counts here. Text messages will never convey it fully. Calls can be misconstrued. Even video calls can be unreliable – as you've discovered.'

It should give me hope, but instead the distance between Sam and me stretches even further away. 'So when will I know where he is on all of this?'

Lisabeta's smile is sad. 'When you breathe the same air and can see every flicker in each other's expressions. In person. Not via a satellite or a screen. Until then, you just have to trust.'

It's not what I wanted to hear. Do I trust Sam? And can I wait until he contacts me again to make sure he heard what I said about Frank?

Chapter Thirty

SAM

I have a half-sister.

And a three-month-old nephew, who is currently chewing my jumper.

I have a sister and a nephew and a very wet shoulder and right now I can't tell how much of this is real.

I knew today was going to change my life. But I could never have predicted how. It's like I've been dropped in a different universe.

'Are you sure you're okay?' Ellie asks, putting a mug of tea on the low table between us.

'I'm fine. Just – taking it all in, you know?'

She sits on the chair opposite, hands clasped between her knees as if without a child to hold she doesn't know what else to do with them.

'I think Barney likes you.'

'I think he likes my sweater.'

'Counts as the same as far as he's concerned. You've won him over. Usually he screams the place down if anyone else holds him.' She smiles again. 'I'm sorry I said no earlier. I wasn't expecting anyone to come for my da – for Frank.'

'I'm guessing you didn't know about me? Or Callum, my – our brother?'

A wrinkle folds above her nose. 'Two brothers? Wow.'

That's answered my question. 'Right. So, I'm thirty-three. Cal will be twenty-nine in July. We don't talk at the moment. Haven't for a while, actually. Long story.'

'Well, you – *we* – have another brother, too. Matthew. He's in the States, so I don't talk much to him, either. I'm twenty, Matt's twenty-two.'

'Welcome to the family,' I joke, hoping my nervous laugh conceals the stab of pain in my chest. So Frank would have fathered a new family less than two years after leaving us. Did he abandon them, too?

'I was told council records had Frank registered here,' I begin, careful to keep any hint of emotion from my voice.

'That's right. He was here until late February.' Her head drops and she gives a long breath. 'He hadn't been in my life for a long time. Just walked out one night when I was fourteen and Matt was sixteen. Mum never knew where he'd gone. And so, you know, we grew up thinking he'd left us and didn't matter to him.'

I nod, not trusting myself to reply.

'And then he turned up, out of the blue, a year and a half ago. I was working at a garage just up the road and he strolled in. Brought his car in for a new exhaust. I saw him through the workshop window and I just knew.' She shrugs, her eyes meeting mine. I notice they are a slightly paler shade of my own. *Frank's* eyes. Did our poor mothers get a look in when it came to our genetic characteristics? 'He didn't know what to do. I don't know if he was more surprised to see his daughter again or that I was elbow deep in oil fixing cars. Bit of a traditionalist, our father. Anyway, I agreed to meet him for a drink and over the next few weeks we talked. I called him a bastard for leaving; he accepted it. Russ and I – my fiancé – were buying this place and Frank had just been chucked out of his own, so he moved in with us. He helped me around the house when I was expecting Barney and we thought he'd just be part of the family. Mum wouldn't see him, of course, but she has her new fella now so I think we decided we could work round each other for the little one's sake.'

I sense something coming. Ellie isn't speaking of Frank in the present tense and there's no sign of him in the neat interior of her home.

'What happened?'

'He left. Right before I was due to have Barney. No note, no explanation. I was sick with worry, furious with him for leaving me again, you know? And then the police came.'

No...

'Was he—?'

'He'd been hit by a car. A glancing blow, they told us, but he was pretty drunk and walking down the central reservation of a dual carriageway. Hadn't a clue where he was. They took him to hospital, patched him up, did some tests.' She rubs her knees, suddenly looking more like a child than a mother. 'I am so sorry to hit you with all this, Sam. It must be so much to take in.'

'It is. But please, go on.'

'He'd had a stroke. A mini one they reckon when he fell in the road and a much larger one when he reached hospital. He lost his speech, didn't recognise any of us. At this time I went into labour and had Barney so Russ visited Dad in between visiting us. By the time we were ready to come home, he'd been moved into a hospice. They reckoned he had cancers, too, that had never been diagnosed. It's possible they caused the strokes, but nobody's been able to tell us for certain.'

I think of the capable, mischievous man in the photo, the one who'd jump on tables to play his fiddle, the one who slept his way around the Island before proposing to Ma. All that *life*, all that energy, reduced to a hospice bed and bewilderment. Some would say that was a fair end for the way he'd paralysed not just one but two families with his leaving.

But holding my half-nephew and staring at the sister I never knew I had, I can't feel like that. I thought I'd be angry, jealous of the time Ellie and her brother had with Frank when he should have spent it with us. But all I feel is a deep sadness.

What a waste.

At least he'd tried to make things right with his daughter, even if he'd been caught on the back foot by meeting her again. He rebuilt their relationship to the point where she was happy to have him under the same roof. And although she's not said it specifically, it sounds like he was excited by the prospect of getting to know his first grandchild.

What made him walk out when he'd repaired so much in his life?

I have another question. I don't want to ask. But I can't escape it.

'When did he die?'

Ellie blinks at me. I hope she doesn't cry. I might be holding her baby but I have no idea of the protocol of hugging your half-sister when you've only just discovered she exists. The gap before she speaks is excruciating, so much so that I wish I could grab the question and stuff it back inside my gullet. I watch the rise and fall of her chest, the first glimpse of tears glisten in her eyes.

'Oh Sam...'

'I'm sorry, Ellie. I—'

She reaches her hand across the table and I grasp it, holding on as if an earthquake is about to rip a chasm in the ground between us.

'Frank's not dead.'

'What?' My question is a whisper in the cacophony of my brain.

'He's still in the hospice. Over in Trinity? St Columba's.'

Barney stirs against my shoulder where he's napping, as a sob escapes me.

'How long…?'

'Last we were told, about four weeks. It's hard to tell. He's stabilised for now although he was poorly last week. Pneumonia, they said.' She gives my hand a gentle squeeze. 'I'm going to see him later. Do you want to come?'

I don't know what to say.

The hospice is brighter than I expected. I'd imagined dark, grey rooms with dim light painting everything sombre monochrome. This place is light and airy and ironically full of life. There's soothing music and colour and it's not at all a place of grief.

I don't know if I should be grieving for Frank. I'm not sure what to feel.

He's dying, of course. He wouldn't be in this place if he weren't. But the man I have only the vaguest recollection of died twenty-three years ago, so will I even recognise the person I'm about to meet?

I feel like a vagabond, schlepping in with my holdall and the fiddle on my back. I'll be catching a taxi from here to the station after this. I'm still not sure why I brought my violin, only that it goes everywhere with me. It felt right that it accompanied me back to the city where I first fell in love with music.

Ellie thought there might be somewhere we could leave my stuff, but all the nurses were busy elsewhere when we arrived. They have far more important demands on their time than my luggage. So,

Ellie, my bag, my violin and me make the journey towards the man who connects us. As we walk, I'm suddenly struck by the thought that I'm carrying similar things to those Frank must have taken the day he left us: his bag and his fiddle.

Am I like him? Ailish said I was running away before.

And I can't deny it: I have packed a bag, picked up my fiddle and run away, many times.

But I'm not running today.

The corridor seems to stretch for miles and though we move quickly, our destination at the end of it – the final room on the left – takes forever to reach.

His room.

All the miles that have separated us, all the years he remained out of my life, out of reach, are now being closed. Distance has caught up with Frank, just as time has. He can no longer run, but now I'm moving towards him.

And then, we arrive. The door is already open, the air from the open window at the end of the corridor fresh as it moves in. Ellie smiles at me, risks a squeeze of my arm. Then she enters. Cautiously, I let the breeze blow me in too.

I don't know the man in the bed. He looks old, although I'm guessing the strokes have aged him. He seems sunken beneath the white bed sheets. His hands rest, palms up, on the green wool blanket draped over his body. It might be many years since he last played, but the callouses on the tips of his fingers are unmistakable. A fiddle-player's hands. Long slender fingers, toughened at the ends, the muscles taut from years of moving over a fingerboard.

He's sleeping. That's a relief. A sleeping old man I can deal with. Perhaps he won't wake at all while I'm here. Ellie prepared me for this in the taxi over. The meds he's on make him sleepy, apparently, a deliberate act to ease his suffering and confusion. I think they hope if they steadily increase the morphine he'll gently slip away when he's ready. It seems altogether more humane than forcing him to stay awake in a world he no longer recognises.

I drop my stuff in the corner by the window and we fetch a dull green plastic chair each from the stack by the wall. Ellie plants a kiss on Frank's forehead. I look away.

'They've given him a shave since yesterday,' Ellie says as she sits. 'He won't be happy about that.'

'Likes the haggard look, does he?'

'Dad's no hipster but he never likes to look too tidy,' she laughs, her smile fading as soon as she looks at me. 'Oh – Sam – I'm sorry.'

'No. It's okay. It's good you know stuff like that about him.'

'Did your mum never tell you what he was like?'

I shake my head. 'She was too angry. Hard to talk about the amusing quirks of the person who destroyed your life.'

'Sure.'

I can't expect Ellie to understand this. Her good memories are as valid and valuable as my bad ones. Neither of us shares one clear image of who Frank Mullins was.

He stirs and my heart leaps to my mouth.

Ellie leans close to his ear. 'Hey, Pa. It's Ellie.'

Frank mumbles something. I can't hear the words.

'Barney's at Mum's. I have someone else to visit you today.'

I watch Frank's sleep-crusted eyelids split open and eyes the colour of mine are revealed.

Twenty-three years since they last focused on me.

I hold my breath. I don't know why. My chest aches from the effort.

My father is staring at me – the son he abandoned a lifetime ago.

And there is nothing there. No flicker of recognition. No glimpse of remorse, or shock, or… anything.

The 9-year-old me wants to run out of the room, out of the too-bright corridor with its soothing pictures and hopeful sunlight, out of the building into the real world. This *isn't* real, is it? It's a place of soon-to-be loss; heavy sadness and fear carefully tucked out of view in the colourful interior. The man lying in this bed might as well be a mirage.

I feel like I should cry, or yell, or say something that could make him remember me – because he *should* remember me. He shouldn't be allowed to forget – *again*.

A hand gently rests on my knee. I look up and see Ellie's concern. 'Talk to him.'

The eyes-like-mine stare back from the bed.

What do I say?

'Um… Hey… Hello, Frank. I'm Sam.'

The eyelids flicker, don't quite close.

'I'm your son. Jean's boy? Jean from Mull?'

Nothing.

'Go on, Sam.' Ellie's voice is soft and low, the voice Ma used when Cal and I woke with nightmares in the Dumbiedykes flat, months after leaving Grandma's. 'He can hear you.'

'Can he?'

She nods. I'm not certain I believe her.

'I live in London now. I'm a musician. Er – I play the fiddle, funnily enough. I've played all over the world and made records, too. And I've a studio – I own it with a friend…'

Not even a blink.

'When we… when Ma took us to Edinburgh – Cal and me – I met a fiddle player called Jonas. He taught me how to play.' My voice cracks and I can't tell if it's because I've mentioned Jonas, who was everything Frank Mullins *should* have been, or because I'm finally sharing the details of my fatherless childhood with the man who abandoned us. I swallow hard. I won't grant him the privilege of seeing my tears. 'I just wanted you to know. I understand. The music. What it means.'

Frank stares ahead.

His face reveals no emotion, no cognition, no *life* at all.

But his left hand twitches.

I look down. His fingers are beginning to curl over. Their progress is so slow it's painful to watch every muscle's laboured move. Is he making a fist?

No – his wrist is curling, too.

And I see it. Playing position. Fingers bowed ready to dance across strings, thumb ready to support the fiddle's neck, wrist held low beneath.

'Wait,' I say, jumping to my feet. I grab my violin case and unzip it. The instrument glows, its conker-brown varnished body warm and reassuring as ever. Always there. Always the same. The single steady constant in my chaotic life. And at that moment, I understand. Music saved me because it was there when I needed it. The way Frank chose *not* to be.

With no hesitation, I lay my fiddle across his palm, slotting it with care between his curled finger and thumb. A sob sounds from Ellie beside me but I keep my eyes on the fiddle and Frank's hand.

His fingers find the strings, the neck strong and sure beneath. I watch them flex across the four strings and I wonder which tune is playing in his mind right now.

A knock at the open door makes me jump.

'Hi, Ellie, just need to do Frank's obs. Won't take a – *oh*.' The nurse stops halfway between the doorway and Frank's bed. Her mouth forms a perfect 'O'. 'Is he *holding* that violin?'

Ellie wipes her eyes. 'Yes. Sam gave it to him – this is Sam, Frank's son.'

The nurse rushes over and pats my shoulder. 'I'm so sorry, forgive me. I'm Sheila Martin, the ward sister. I didn't know Frank had another son.'

'There's two of us,' I say, shaken by the suddenness of everything. 'From his first marriage.'

'Right. Wow. You're a lucky man, Frank. All these people who love you. Would you look at that grip! Good position you've got there!' Sheila smiles at me. 'Is this yours?'

'Yes.'

'We've been hearing about Frank and his playing. Do you play, too?'

I nod, but Ellie interrupts. 'He's a professional violinist. Played all over the world.'

Sheila's eyes widen. 'Wow. I don't think we've ever had a professional visit us here. You should play something.'

I stare at her. 'I don't think so…'

'Go on! I love a bit of fiddle. My grandad used to play. Hang on – I'll fetch the girls.'

She hurries out. Panic rising, I turn to Ellie. 'I can't do this – not here.'

Not for him.

'Why not?'

'It's a *hospice*,' I hiss back. 'It's not… appropriate.'

Ellie shrugs. 'Sheila thinks it's okay. And trust me, that lady is scary. She'd be the first to tell you if she didn't want something on her ward.'

How can I explain?

Just being in the same room as my father has taken every ounce of courage I have. I handed him the fiddle without thinking – it just seemed the right thing to do. But *play* for him? That's like giving him something from my soul and I'm just not ready to do that. Why should he be able to have such a precious gift when he never afforded me the right to have him in my life?

I want to think about it, go away and consider it all. I want to talk to Phoebe – she's the reason I'm even in this room.

And then I remember what Phoebe's host in Rome told her, the lady with the painted pebbles. It made such an impression that she's mentioned it many times when we've texted or spoken since. *Mark the moment.* Good or bad. Acknowledge it. No judgement, no pressure to feel it about or act upon it in any way. Just mark it.

This is happening, right now. I don't have time to work out how I feel. When I walk from this room, my chance will be over.

I remember being 9 years old, sitting up every night for a year then, wanting to be awake in case *Da* came home. Because he *would* come home – I was certain of it. To keep myself from falling asleep, I would imagine the conversation we would have, the things I would tell him that only Da would understand. That I'd been out on the beach the morning of the day he left, early before school, and found a starfish washed up on the shore. It was little, no bigger than a fifty pence piece, and it made my palm look like a giant's hand when I held it. I'd left it behind the rocks at the edge of the beach, carefully wrapped in strands of oily black and green seaweed, so that when Da got home I could drag him down there to see it.

I never returned to that beach until a few weeks ago. I walked alone along the shoreline, finally allowing myself to remember. I couldn't even locate where I'd hidden my beach find, but it didn't matter. Ghosts were laid to rest as the sun began to slink down to the horizon. They had been my companions for too long. I left them at the edge of the ocean and walked back to the road. Mull might call me back in the future, but I won't return to those sands.

I don't have a starfish to show my Da. But I do have *this*...

I wait until Sheila returns with three giggling colleagues, all in matching pastel coloured scrubs, before I gently retrieve my fiddle from Frank's hand. I remember the tunes I have learned again on Mull, the traditional songs and laments I avoided for so many years because Ma remembered how *he* played them. And then I play a song that used to make her cry – a lament of unrequited love, written by Robert Burns:

> 'Ae fond kiss, and then we sever;
> Ae fareweel, alas, for ever!
> Deep in heart-wrung tears I'll pledge thee,
> Warring sighs and groans I'll wage thee!'

The pastel-clad nurses fall silent. Ellie closes her eyes. Frank's eyes remain open and expressionless, but then I notice the fingers on his left hand are flexing in time with mine. Muscular-memory: the body internalising each move from years of constant repetition. Frank would have heard the song sung by his grandparents, his own mother, his neighbours at gatherings. I would catch Ma humming it when she was drunk, pausing to sob. It was one of the first songs Jonas taught me, making me laugh with his Polish-infused rendition of Burns' words as he sang in that shaky voice of his. I'd abandoned it for most of my life, but during the first gig in Tobermory it was one of the songs Niven's band chose to play.

And now it is the song I'm playing in the bright hospice room, with an audience of quietly sniffing nurses, my half-sister and an old, frail man in a bed with not many days left on this earth.

My *da*.

I can't stop my tears as I play the final verse, knowing that my time here is at an end. In a few weeks I will return to London, to my real life – and to the woman I know will play a huge part of it. Because now I'm ready to be all I can be for her. I'll tell Phoebe everything because I can now. Every step that led me here. I'm not afraid any more – and I won't need to run away ever again.

In the final bars of the song, Frank's eyelids flicker and a silver streak of saltwater runs down his face.

It's enough.

Chapter Thirty-One

PHOEBE

'*Phoebe Jones!*'

I laugh as Tobi and Luc pull me into a huge group hug. '*Bonjour, mes amours!*'

'Welcome home! Come in! We have wine!'

It's so good to be back in Paris.

The last week has been a whirlwind completing the library at Villa Speranza and we were so busy I thought we might never finish. But the heart-stopping moment arrived where I stood arm in arm with Lis and Amanda, unable to hold back our tears as we took it all in. Hundreds of books edging the walls, their gentle colours and gold-edged spines the most beautiful faded kaleidoscope surrounding us as sunlight danced on the polished swirls of the mahogany floor.

Just like that, it was done. And then I was hugging Lis and Amanda goodbye and catching a train back to Paris.

I can't believe I've lived in Europe for a year, and tomorrow is the day everything has been leading towards: 14th June 2018. I honestly don't know how I feel, less than twenty-four hours away from seeing Sam again.

I want to see him. We need to talk – a lot. He has to let me in more. I can blame the distance, the patchy communication, the year we've had apart for it, but ultimately we have to be in this as a team from tomorrow on.

Tomorrow. The day we meet again.

But first, I will spend the last night of my grand tour in the place where it began. Beautiful Montmartre. With two people I will count as friends for life.

It's impossible to be back here without comparing how I found it when I first arrived – shaken by meeting Sam, questioning everything, surprised that I even caught the train.

I still have questions, but Paris makes me feel the pull of possibility once more. Being here makes me remember how sure I was of Sam last year. The way I felt when I was with him – that I have lost sight of in recent months – returns. Because tomorrow I get to hold him again. In his arms I believe I will find the answers to the frustrating gaps our time apart has revealed.

Tobi and Luc show me the garden, which has been decked out for a summer party. They've made entertaining here a regular thing since I was last with them and it's the talk of the neighbourhood, apparently. Tonight, I am guest of honour and Luc wants me to share stories of my travels.

It's lovely to be back in the courtyard. Tobi and Luc leave me to sit here for a while before all of the festivities begin. I've brought my journal and Luc made me a large cup of fresh lemon tea.

My notebook is almost full. I've written for an entire year and now I can't imagine my day without being able to record it. Flicking though the pages I see my adventure pass at high speed – France and Italy blurring through my fingers like the countryside past the window of the train that brought me back. And as the train home to London will do tomorrow. Now I'm back in my small green square of sanctuary the time away feels as fast moving as the pages in my book.

I pick up my pen and am about to write the penultimate entry when my mobile rings.

SAM – MOBILE

I take a breath. He's been quiet since our broken video call.

'Phoebe, I caught you.' He sounds short of breath, like he's been running.

'Are you okay? Is everything—?'

'I'm fine. I just ran up the hill to call. I didn't know if you'd still be on the train.'

'I'm in Paris. In the garden at Tobi and Luc's place.'

'Great. Phoebe, there's something I need to say.'

I try to push the rising panic back but it won't budge.

'Are you still there?'

'I'm here, Sam.'

The pause before he speaks again hurts. I close my eyes, wait for whatever is coming.

'I want to say this, in case you're doubting getting on the train tomorrow.'

Does Sam have doubts?

'Just say it.'

'I found Frank. My father. I wanted to tell you but it all happened so fast and I—' I hear a rush of breath against the phone. 'I was scared. I'm not used to having anyone who is able to share that with me, let alone who wants to. You offered your help and I just couldn't deal with that…'

'I'm sorry…'

'No! No, don't apologise, Phoebe. This is all on me. I found Frank because *you* told me to. You said if it were you, you'd want to know. You have no idea what that did for me. And I realised, way, way too late, that you're incredible. And that – I love you.'

The birdsong ceases. Beyond the building's walls the low note of traffic dims. I open my eyes and stare at the swirls of lemon steam rising from my cup. And I have no words.

'Phoebe, I was scared when you said it. I should have said it back.'

'Not if you didn't feel the same.'

'I feel it now. I've felt it for a long time but this stuff with Frank just messed with my head. I want you to know I love you. If you get on that train tomorrow, I'll be waiting, Phoebe. I will. If you want me, I'm yours.'

And there it is: the one thing missing from our story.

I'm dazed when I return to Tobi and Luc's apartment, the page I'd intended to fill with my thoughts today left blank.

He told me he loves me. It's what I've longed to hear him say all year. It's just the timing that worries me. Has he rushed to say it before we meet again? Have I pulled back from him, too?

This is pointless. I'm clearly overthinking, letting nerves get the better of me. Sitting on Tobi and Luc's comfortable low couch I remember the trembling thrill of being there having just left Sam in London. I knew then that I loved him and I know it now. It's okay to be nervous: tomorrow, everything changes.

It's my final night in Paris and I'm determined to enjoy it. Mark the end of the most extraordinary year of my life, as Giana would say. Some good, some bad, but mostly wonderful. I've learned so much about my own resilience and creativity, my resourcefulness and my capacity to embrace new experiences. I haven't just survived. I've left my mark on Europe with the library in Puglia and the pebbles I painted in Rome and every conversation I've had as I've travelled. I believe in myself more than I ever have. Gabe saw it in Montalcino; Meg commented on it last time we spoke. Even Dr Amanda said how much she'd seen me bloom during the time we spent at Villa Speranza. The Phoebe Jones returning to St Pancras station tomorrow is the best she's ever been.

And she is in love with Sam Mullins.

That evening, we gather in the courtyard garden, the June air as warm and lovely as the conversation around the dinner table. I am able to thank everyone who wrote suggestions in the front of the notebook that's become my companion. I tell each of them what I've seen and the places I've discovered, the stories I've learned along the way, even daring to read out a few extracts from my journal. The laughter and hearty applause that greet my words mean the world.

Now it's time for one more step.

Chapter Thirty-Two

SAM

When I returned to Mull, Ailish and I talked more than we ever had. She told me things about Ma I never knew – that she'd refused to believe the rumours around Frank's infidelities before they married and long after Cal and I came along. How her hope was ultimately what killed her. I think I saw that as a kid and was determined it wouldn't happen to me. But Ma chose to put her faith in things that could never be and when they failed she had nothing left to cling to.

Phoebe is still there, after everything.

'She put her faith in you, despite your best attempts to push her away,' Ailish said.

'But what if she makes the same mistake Ma did?'

My almost-auntie took my hand, the glint of tears in her eyes. 'Then be the man she deserves. You're not Frank Mullins, bairn. You never were. This is your chance to prove it.'

When my bags are packed in the hall waiting for Niven to arrive to drive me to the ferry port at Craignure, I duck out of the back door and scramble up the bank at the back of Ailish's house. It's as green and wild as it was a year ago, the wind casting verdant ripples across it as I climb. I reach the large rock – where I've come most days to play my guitar or just take in the view – and take my seat on it for the last time. Out on the water the Iona ferry is preparing to leave Fionnphort dock. I'll be on the next one. I'm sad that my year is over, but so much awaits me back in London. It's time to go home.

But first, I need to call Phoebe.

She sounds surprised when I blurt out the speech I've rehearsed since returning from Edinburgh. It's not perfect – too rushed, far later in our year apart than it should have been and nowhere near as eloquent as I'd imagined. But I hope she hears me.

'…I love you. If you get on that train tomorrow, I'll be waiting, Phoebe. I will. If you want me, I'm yours.'

'I love you too, Sam.' Her voice sounds far away.

After the call, I watch the ferry edge slowly from the shore. Ahead of it the green shadow of Iona waits, ancient and familiar. A promise at its journey's end.

My heart is hammering by the time I return to the house and Niven's car pulls into view.

I stand on the doorstep by the wonderful Ailish McRae, fierce advocate, honorary auntie and the brightest soul I've ever had the privilege to spend time with. Niven is sitting in the car, waiting respectfully for our goodbyes to take place.

'I'm not going to cry.'

'I never said you were.'

Ailish dabs her nose with a tissue, pretending she isn't wiping her eyes. It's fooling nobody. 'You just mind you take care, okay?'

'I will.'

'And you will not, under any circumstances, leave it years before you come back, do you understand me?'

I wrap my arms around her and hug her tight. 'Loud and clear. Thanks for looking after me, Auntie Ailish.'

'My pleasure, bairn.' *Now* she's crying.

She pulls back and laughs at her streaming tears. 'Look at me, I'm a wreck. What time is your ferry?'

'It leaves in an hour.'

'Aye. Well. Quite a year, Samuel.' She reaches up to my cheek and pats it. Her skin smells like icing sugar and freshly baked shortbread, a scent I've become used to in her kitchen.

'Quite a year.'

'And you'll be okay? After – *that man.*'

I smile and hug her again. I don't think Ailish will ever fully understand why I went to see Frank, but she knows it was what I wanted. The more I've thought about finding him when I did, and discovering his second family, the more convinced I am that I made the right decision. 'Don't worry about me.'

'Easier said than done. You're not *him*, remember? You don't have to repeat Frank's mistakes.'

'I won't. Thanks – for what you said.'

'For kicking you up the bum?'

I laugh. 'Aye, that. I needed it. And you were right.'

She nods but I can tell she still isn't happy about what she said. 'And what about Phoebe?'

'Well, I just told her I loved her, so…'

Her eyes sparkle in the June sun. 'I am so proud of you! Be happy. Be the man you know you can be. That will be all she wants.'

And now my journey back to the best decision begins. Thirteenth of June. The day before we meet again. Now our meeting is almost here I can hardly believe a year has happened. Tomorrow I will, at last, be in the same space as Phoebe.

I will miss the Island, though. Staying with Ailish and becoming involved in the community has made it more of a home than I've had for years and I know I'll return. Last night the kids in the music club surprised me with a concert in my honour. It was amazing to see what I'd helped create and very emotional to hear from parents about the difference music is making in their children's lives. Next time, Phoebe will be with me to see it.

Niven walks with me to the ferry terminal.

'Are you sure I can't tempt you back to Donal and Kate's for tonight?' I ask.

'Better not. Work and that.'

We trade suitably blokey back-slaps and then Niven gives me a bear hug that squeezes the air out of me. 'Hey. Come and see me in London, yeah?'

'I want to do the music thing more,' he says. 'Not give up teaching, but, you know, maybe take a bit of time over the summer, play some live stuff. I've loved playing with you and the lads. Donal mentioned he had some gigs coming up in August so I might tag onto those.'

'That's great, Niv. And if you want some summer stuff in London, give us a shout, okay?'

He grins. 'You might regret offering that. But aye, that'd be good.'

On the bus to Port Glasgow, I think about Phoebe. I am so close to seeing her again and I just want the journey to be over. I hope I didn't shock her with my phone call. I had to say it before tomorrow, so she is in no doubt about how I feel. There's one last night with Donal, Kate and the kids and then it will be the day we've promised each other. There are so many things in my life I have little clarity on, but I know that I love her. She isn't Laura. She won't bail on me or break my heart. She gave me the push I needed to find Frank.

THE DAY

14th June 2018

Chapter Thirty-Three

PHOEBE

Gare du Nord is packed, the early morning commuters as crammed into the space and impatient as they are in Euston or St Pancras or Victoria. Except that they still manage to look French and unhurried, effortlessly elegant and nonplussed, all at the same time.

My heart is so full of everything. Leaving Paris, saying goodbye to Tobi and Luc and the knowledge that Sam loves me and will be waiting at the end of my journey. At least, I hope he will be.

I have some time before my train is called, so I manage to find an empty seat and sip the coffee I picked up from Luc's favourite neighbourhood café. Around me people buzz about their day, sure of their destinations. How many of them are on their way to fulfil a promise, I wonder? There's no way to tell. If I've learned one thing this year it's that you never know what anyone else is facing.

I'm excited, but I have so many questions. Where will I live? Where will I work? What do I want my life to look like with Sam in it? From the moment we meet again by Sir John Betjeman's statue, our lives will change. They'll have to. Two complete lives dovetailing together. Even when it's what we want, it's going to require work and compromises. He didn't share all of his journey to find Frank with me. That still stings. If we have a hope of lasting, he has to trust me more than he has this year. I have to trust myself, too. But I should have prepared more for when I get home. Why am I only considering this now?

I make myself inhale long and slow.

Calm down, Phoebe.

He loves me and I love him. We can work out the rest.

I have imagined this moment so many times and now it's racing towards me instead of me heading towards it. In less than five hours, Sam and I will be in the same space. The distance closed. The decision made.

A couple pass by, their arms linked together as if some force will imminently pull them apart. I remember that feeling as we waited by the barrier for Sam's platform, that urgency and the bittersweet rush of love and longing as time slipped away. We're doing this in reverse now. Apart for not much longer, then nothing left to separate us again.

I close my eyes and mark the moment. Like Giana would do. 'Good or bad, mark it in your mind. It's a touch point for the future. One day you might need to remember how this was for you.'

Nearly there, Sam. So nearly there…

Chapter Thirty-Four

SAM

Eight rainbows. That's broken the journey up. In the brave early light they are magical. It *has* to be a sign.

I never looked for signs before I met her.

This year has changed how I see myself so much. Where I'm from. Who I am. What drives me. What scares me. I'm from Mull and Frank Mullins is my father, but I am not Frank Mullins. Or Jean Mullins, who he left behind. I'm Sam Mullins, musician, studio co-owner, son, brother and soon to be lover of the most wonderful woman in the world.

There was one more missing piece to fit. Something I never thought I'd do. Last night, in the stillness of Donal's garden studio, I called my brother.

'Sam?'

'Hey, Cal.'

'What is it?'

'I found Da.'

I don't know if Cal expected this call to happen one day, but his response was immediate and shocking. I haven't heard my brother cry for twenty years.

When he was able to speak again, we talked for an hour. He's not in a good place – off sick again from his job with anxiety and

243

stress, still reeling from his second divorce. The more we spoke, the more I could see the damage done to his self-esteem, the little boy who never recovered from losing his father. I thought he didn't care. I was wrong.

'I can't believe he was living so close to us all that time.'

'I know.'

'I thought – I always thought I wasn't enough to make him stay.'

'Me too. But the truth is, *he* wasn't enough. Deep down he couldn't be the man we needed. He wasn't running from us, Cal, he was running from himself.'

'I run. That's my problem. I run and hide in a bottle. I'm the worst bits of Ma and Da.'

It broke my heart to hear it, but given what I now know, it wasn't a surprise. 'You don't have to any more. You're not Frank Mullins, kid. Neither am I. He ruined the best part of our lives: let's not let him take any more. Leave Frank to his own demons and deal with your own.'

I never thought I'd say that to him, but I could feel walls being chipped away as we spoke. I offered to send him details of the hospice, but Cal refused. I hope he'll contact Ellie when he's ready.

'Let's chat more, yeah?' he said, before he hung up. 'Soon. I'd like that, Sam. You're all I have.'

It wasn't an easy truce, but it was a start.

I follow the rainbow until it slips from view. New beginnings. Putting right the past. That's what I'll take from this year. Discovering I can be whoever I want to be. Finding my feet.

And at the heart of it all is Phoebe Jones.

I love her. And in a few hours, I will be back with her.

I haven't a clue what happens next. How we will actually *do* this. Should I be concerned? Who knows? None of it scares me, though.

Not like it used to. It's the sweetest freefall from the highest altitude and every atom of me hums with the audacity of it.

We did it, Phoebe: we tested this thing for a year and it's real. The closer I travel to my destination, the more I feel it. I've never been in love like this.

I just hope she can forgive me for not sharing stuff when I should have.

After my call with Cal, Kate and Donal joined me. Their excitement for me – and for the woman they've never met who stole my heart – meant the world. Still does.

'I'll admit, I was worried in the beginning,' Kate said, handing out another round of beers. 'But she's proved herself this year. And you're happier than I've ever seen. So, I take back what I said: a year away has been good for you.'

'Thanks.'

'Oh look, he's blushing!'

'Ach Kate, leave the poor beggar alone! Ignore my wife, Sam. We couldn't be happier for you. As soon as you can, get both your backsides up here to see us, okay?' Donal said.

And of course I agreed, because I can't think of any better place to bring Phoebe. All these things we've talked about – my friends, her friends, her family, the studio – we're finally going to be able to share it all with each other.

I can't wait.

My life will start over when we meet today. Everything will now include Phoebe. It's going to take some getting used to, but I am up for the challenge.

I'm counting the hours…

Chapter Thirty-Five

PHOEBE

It's almost time.

My train is minutes away from St Pancras. I don't know if it will be busy, but it doesn't matter. None of my questions do. The only thing I care about is that Sam will be waiting for me.

My Sam.

I've thought about what I'll say when I see him. Like the postcards we sent, I feel like the words I greet him with should be memorable. I want him to remember me as the person he fell in love with and then spent a year getting to know. I hope it will always be a memory that warms his heart.

My heart feels like it might not last the journey. What will Sam think? What will his reaction be?

I hope his journey back to London is a good one. I know he's changing trains twice on the way and praying he makes both connections. Between us I think we've had enough delays to last us a lifetime. Although maybe we should be grateful: a delay is responsible for us even having this date to meet.

Will he be tired from his journey? Does Sam get grumpy when he's tired? Or is he like Osh, who just becomes cute and sleepy? Or Meg, who suddenly disappears to bed without saying a word? I know Sam isn't an early bird, but is he bright when he does wake?

Gabe isn't the best at getting up, but once he decides to face the day he's completely committed to it. The full megawatt smile and one hundred per cent energy switches on and that's him for the rest of the day. All of these tiny, everyday details I don't know about Sam yet. A million and one unknown things that make up the man I'm in love with. What does his face look like when he's sleeping? When the first rays of daylight pass over his skin? What would it feel like to wake beside him? What would I see if Sam were my first sight in the morning?

I know that I love him. But in so many ways he's still a stranger. He's made decisions I didn't understand and I've said things he couldn't deal with. All the certainties wait by the Betjeman statue. Nothing will be the same after today.

I glance at my watch.

10.50 a.m.

By the time the train halts it will be 10.55 a.m. Five minutes till the time we agreed to meet.

And then…?

Chapter Thirty-Six

SAM

'We are now arriving at London King's Cross, where this service terminates. Please ensure you take all your personal belongings with you. Thank you for travelling with us today.'

This is it.

It's almost 11 a.m. I have a dash across the road from here to St Pancras where Phoebe will be waiting. My hands are shaking as I stuff my book, water bottle and jumper into my rucksack. I'm suddenly aware of the staleness of the air in this carriage that we've all been breathing for the past five hours. My stomach swims with nerves and anticipation, the same kind of knotted tension that appears in the minutes before I take the stage. Only today my audience is just one person.

I can't wait to hold her. Kiss her. Replace the dimming memories I have of those sensations with the real thing. Suddenly the twelve months since I left become no more than a single thought: the past. All that matters now is getting to the Betjeman statue and beginning my life with Phoebe Jones.

I join the line of shuffling, impatient passengers moving down the carriage and time seems to stretch for an eternity until the *beep-beep-beep* of the opening door locks makes my heartbeat spike.

Get me off this train now. She's waiting for me.

And then my feet step down onto station platform concrete and adrenalin powers through my body. I don't even try to play it cool: the moment I leave the train, I'm running…

Chapter Thirty-Seven

PHOEBE

The air is still beside the Betjeman statue.

Sir John's tilted face catches the mid-morning sunlight beaming down on him through the glass roof high above his head, pooling around his feet. I don't see the commuters hurrying past, or the pockets of tourists posing with the famous poet's memorial. Here the station noise is muted: I can hear my breath, feel the urgent pulse of blood at my wrists and hear the quickening thrum of my heart louder than any other sound.

11 a.m., 14th June.

One year exactly from the day we met.

Where I promised I'd be.

Sam's train was due in before mine, but it will take him a while to get across from King's Cross and up to the first floor of St Pancras. He'll come running up the stairs any moment now, the distance between us finally closed like two hands meeting, two halves of a heart joining.

What will he do when he gets here?

What will he say?

I close my eyes. Mark the moment before everything changes forever.

Chapter Thirty-Eight

SAM

I pass the concourse where we first kissed, the coffee concession where I fell in love with her, and approach the staircase we walked down together to begin this whole crazy journey. And as I take the stairs two at a time, the hands of the huge station clock above the first floor moving just past the hour, I see the Betjeman statue rising into view. His hat first, then the billowing mackintosh and, as I reach the top step, the bag he carries, the smart shoes and his words etched in slate that loop around his feet.

A group of tourists pose awkwardly in front of the statue, all forced-smiles and puffed-out chests. I wait until they are done and smile at them as they start to leave.

One minute past eleven. Not bad timekeeping considering my dash across the station. And hey, one thing Phoebe needs to know about me is that musicians and time management are not natural bedfellows.

One by one, the tourists mill away, until just Sir John and I remain.

Just me and the statue.

Just *me*.

… What?

Where is she?

I check my watch – is it fast? Its face matches the giant station clock.

I make a slow, 360-degree turn in case she's heading over from the Eurostar platform and I just haven't spotted her yet. I know her train has arrived: I saw it listed on the arrivals board as I ran here.

Sir John's half-smile and upward-turned chin assures me all is well.

But if her train has arrived and it's just turned 11 a.m., she should be here.

I look at my phone. No messages. When I call her number, it directs straight to voicemail. Perhaps it's in her bag for when she got off the train, or still on silent from the journey?

Nerves building, I leave a message.

'Hey, it's me. I'm here. You know, just hanging out with sweet Johnny B…' My laugh sounds forced. I swallow hard against a dry throat. 'Are you…? Are you on your way? I can't see you.'

Over by the top of the stairs a woman watches me. She has blue streaks in her pale blonde hair. Something about her expression unnerves me. I end the call and turn my back on her as I face the statue again.

And then, I see it.

Tucked between Betjeman's shoulder and his neck is a single yellow rose. And from it, a brown luggage label hangs. I'm drawn to it even though it has nothing to do with me. People leave floral memorials all over this city – their own grief, their own reasons to commemorate someone. It's fascinating, but none of my business.

It's only when my fingers halt the slowly spinning label that I see my name:

My wonderful Sam –
I am so sorry.
It isn't that I don't love you. I do love you.
I hope one day you'll forgive me.
All my love, Phoebe xx

I can't breathe.

I can't think.

This isn't happening. It *can't* be. She said she'd be here. She said she loved me.

I've been punched so hard in my core that my feet won't hold me. I make it as far as the glass barrier at the edge of the walkway before I slump to the ground.

In my hands the rose is too yellow, too bright. Through aching eyes I scan the message again, looking for something, *anything* that I might have missed. The smallest detail on which I can hang my hope and prevent my heart shattering. But it's too late. All of my hope for us, all of our promises, every word we've shared for twelve long months apart, broken irrevocably. Gone.

It isn't even her handwriting. I know it from the letters and post-cards she sent me. The messages I've carried like jewels everywhere I've travelled. I would know her writing in a heartbeat. Every loop, every flourish. This is like an ugly scar scratched carelessly over stone. This is nothing like Phoebe's hand.

It isn't the Phoebe I know. But then it hits me: I don't know Phoebe Jones. I thought I did. I thought my heart did. But I never knew her at all.

I ran all the way home for this. She was supposed to be in my arms, right now, her kisses on my lips. All our promises fulfilled.

Did she ever intend to meet me again? Was any of it real? And if she isn't by the Betjeman statue – where she'd promised she'd be – then where is she?

Phoebe lied.

Worse than her absence is that she couldn't even be bothered to tell me in person. If she loved me, she'd be here.

I was a fool to believe she would be. She's no better than Laura.

Why couldn't she tell me and save me this pain? And where is she now?

Chapter Thirty-Nine

PHOEBE

I open my eyes.

Around me the station noise continues its clamour while faceless commuters hurry to their destinations. Except that it's wrong. It's *all* wrong. Wrong decision, wrong country, wrong station. Paris Gare du Nord isn't where I should still be.

My hand aches from gripping my phone. When I release my fingers there's an ugly red line carved into my palm where the edge of it has bitten into the skin. The screen is filled with notifications that accuse me:

MEG – 3 MISSED CALLS
MEG – 1 NEW MESSAGE
SAM – 4 MISSED CALLS
SAM – 3 NEW VOICEMAILS
TOBI – 1 MISSED CALL

But it's the time displayed on the screen that delivers the biggest blow:

1.39 p.m.

What have I done?

I daren't listen to the voicemails from Sam. I know what I'll hear and it might end me. I know what the message from Meg will be, too. She's disgusted with me. I could tell by the tone of her voice when I called her in tears and asked her to leave a rose on the statue for Sam. It's testament to the wonderful person she is that she even agreed to do it. But will she ever forgive me?

Can I ever forgive myself?

I hug my arms around my body, trying to soothe the ache in my chest. But I can't even feel solidarity with myself. I can't believe I got as far as this seat in the station and missed the train I'd dreamed of boarding. The train taking me back to Sam.

I don't know what happened.

I heard the call for my train. My hand reached for the ticket in my pocket, the other taking the handles of my bag. Ready to lift. Ready to leave. And then... I couldn't move.

I just *couldn't* stand or leave my seat. I remained where I was as a flood of people raged past. Like I was half-buried in sand watching waves sweep away across a bay. For twenty minutes I fought with myself, hearing the continued calls for passengers and the final boarding announcement as loud and as close as if they were screams directly in my face.

What are you doing?
Get on the train! It's about to leave!
Get up! Sam is waiting!
RUN!

But I couldn't do it.

Fear won. And I let it happen.

So instead of running for my train, I sat firm in the prison of my seat, and played out the whole journey in my mind. My penance for utterly failing the man I'm supposed to love. I made myself relive every stage in real time; every moment – the Eurostar journey, St Pancras Station and Betjeman statue of my imagination identical to the ones I'd experienced when Sam and I parted last year. Except that when 11 a.m. arrived there was no Sam Mullins grinning by the statue. No hope for us. My mind's facsimile of where we should have met was revealed for what it truly was: a cold and empty wasteland where love couldn't survive.

I am furious. Why fall at the final hurdle? I love Sam. I've spent all year waiting to see him again. And last night he told me he loved me. What did everything I've learned this year mean if it didn't change me at the very moment it mattered?

I just kept thinking about what Gabe said, that night in Tuscany: *If you're sure of Sam, if you know you can be everything you want to be to each other…* And the time he called me at the villa – his inference that Sam wasn't as serious as I was, the implication that I might be fooling myself, too. That I should be with someone who didn't wait almost a year to say he loves me. That I deserved to be certain. I remembered what Mum said about being happy, and what Meg had said about taking space to make sure we both made the right decision. I laid them all out like fragments of a puzzle that didn't quite fit – Sam's eleventh-hour declaration of love only confusing the picture more.

But I know I love him. And, as of yesterday, I know he loves me too.

So why did I hesitate?

I should have been on that train. Or the next. I could still find one today, scrape the money together, risk it on my credit card – *anything* to get me back to London. Perhaps if I call Sam, explain the reason for my panic and promise him I'm on my way right now I can still save this? Us?

He was alone by the statue. I abandoned him. What must he think of me?

My phone rings and I see my best friend's smiling face on the caller ID. At least it isn't Sam. Tears flood my eyes as I accept the call.

'Phoebe, where are you?'

I open my mouth to reply but a loud sob shoulders into the space where words should be.

'Phee. Are you safe? Tell me where you are.'

'I-I'm…' The words won't come. A loud French station announcement echoes around the space, interrupting my attempt.

'Are you still at the station?'

'Yes.'

She swears. There's a pause and I think she might slam the phone down. Then: 'Right. Stay where you are, okay? Tobi and Luc will come and get you.'

'No, I—'

'Shut up. They're on their way.'

'I'm sorry,' I rush, slapping tears away from my cheeks. 'I panicked…'

'Just don't – I don't need to hear it now. You've been there for hours, Phee, you need to be somewhere safe. Stay there. Don't move. We will – I don't know what we'll do, but we'll find a way to get you home.'

She doesn't yell, when she has every right to tear strips off me. But her weariness and disappointment stings more. Meg's always told me I can achieve more than I think I'm capable of. Well, I've blown that belief to the sky, haven't I? I wouldn't blame her if she wanted rid of our friendship altogether after this.

I throw my phone in my bag and cover my eyes. I want to hide but I can't run from what I've done. I've failed Sam. I've failed my friends. Worst of all, I've failed myself. And my life will never be the same.

Chapter Forty

SAM

It's getting dark when I leave St Pancras.

Don't ask me why I stayed so long. It's a mystery to me. I just had to make sure she wasn't coming, that she hadn't thought better of her mistake and caught a later train. So I watched every arrival from Paris like a half-crazed train spotter.

She has to come back some time, right?

I'm assuming she's still with her friends in Paris, although of course she could be anywhere. She could have flown home, or headed back into Europe. Is she hiding somewhere? Does she even care about where I am?

I've left voicemail messages and will email her eventually, but not tonight. I need to let my friends know I'm okay – and that I'm back in town. I can't face finding words for Phoebe Jones yet.

Outside, London is the same as always, carrying on regardless of whatever's happening in your life. I've always been comforted by that in the past – that London doesn't indulge your celebrations or your pain. But this evening it feels like the capital is dismissing me. To this city I'm no different than I was a year ago. But everything has changed.

The lights of the British Library shine out as I pass but this time I won't enter the courtyard where in the past I've busked or met mates for coffee. I don't want to be soothed yet. The pain is necessary. I hid from it after Laura and clearly didn't learn what I needed to. I won't make the same mistake with Phoebe.

I can't believe she wasn't there. I don't know if it will ever make sense.

I'm passing Euston Station when the call comes.

It's her.

I stare at the picture of us smiling up from the screen. I should decline the call, block her number. But she owes me an explanation. On what might be the last ring before voicemail claims her call, I answer.

'Phoebe.'

I can hear her breath, shaky and uneven, and a sound that might be a cough or the beginnings of a sob. My heart is torn between elation that I can hear her and fury that she's calling me now. I *want* her to be upset. I want her to feel terrible.

'I… so sorry…'

'Where are you?'

'In Paris. Still.'

My words fail. I nod at the pavement, trying to keep control.

'Sam, are you still there?'

'Still here.'

Where else would I be? I kept *my* promise.

'I just – I don't know what happened…'

'Well, you weren't here. That's what happened.'

'I know. I can't believe I let you down. I was on my way – I mean, I was at Gare du Nord, and…'

'Phoebe, don't.'

'But I need to explain…'

'There's nothing to say. We said at the beginning we might

260

change our minds. So, you changed your mind. You could have changed it yesterday, or last week, or any time before I set off to meet you, of course. But that's immaterial. It happened. You did what you had to.'

'I never wanted this... I didn't want to hurt you...'

I can hear tears in her voice. This is worse than if she'd remained silent.

'Listen, I don't think I can do this now. Talk about it, I mean. I have to work it out. Alone.'

'But there's so much I need to say to you, Sam.'

'No. No, you really don't. It's very simple – you lied to me and you don't love me. That's why you weren't there. I love *you*, which is why I was.'

'No, you're wrong. I never lied to you. I just panicked.'

'Phoebe, it is what it is.' My words crash across the end of hers. 'It's not what I wanted. Not what I thought we both wanted. But I'll get over it.'

'No, listen to me. I just need some more time. To get my head around it.'

You've had a year, Phoebe. You either want to be with me or you don't. You shouldn't have to convince yourself. I don't want to be the guy you talked yourself into being with. I deserve better than that.

But I don't have the strength to say that to her tonight.

Instead, I say: 'Yeah, me too. Look, just be happy, okay? Find something you know you want. And – don't call me again.'

'*No*, Sam...' This hurts too much. Hearing her voice is a knife to my chest. It has to end, now.

'I've got to go.'

'*Please...*'

'What more do you want from me? You weren't there. That's

all I needed to know. So thanks for a great year and all the good stuff. But we need to move on. If you ever cared about me at all, please leave it now. Goodbye, Phoebe.'

So, that's it. Doors closed and bolted. No way back.

As soon as I hang up, I find DeeDee's number and call it. My eyes sting and I know I won't be able to hide the tears from her. But I don't want to be alone. Tonight, I need my friends.

Chapter Forty-One

PHOEBE

He hangs up. And the world is suddenly an echoing, lonely chamber.

I've lost him.

All because I was too scared to get on that train.

Luc holds my hand and Tobi watches, concerned, from the kitchen where he's making more tea. For a Frenchman he has an excellent understanding of English crisis management. I love that they are here, but I wish they didn't have to see this.

'That sounded brutal,' Luc says, his voice low.

I blink at him. I can't even find words to say how I feel. I knew it would be bad – part of me even hoped Sam might let my call go to his voicemail so I could blurt it all out and not have to hear him. I wish I hadn't heard him. The hurt in his voice almost destroyed me. I put it there – I caused that in the man I've been in love with for an entire year.

If you're sure of Sam…

Why won't those words leave me alone? I am sure of Sam. I *was*… Why did I listen to the doubts?

'I am the worst person.'

'No, you're not.'

'Why didn't I go through with it? If I loved him, I should have been there.'

263

'Phoebe, if he loved you he should have given you the chance to explain.'

'He was there. I wasn't. It was academic.'

'*Mon amie*, you are torturing yourself. Whatever happened, it happened for a reason. You won't know what that is yet. But equally, there is nothing to be done about it now. So. We have spoken to Meg and she agrees it is better for you to stay in Paris with us for a while.'

'No, Tobi, I need to get back. I have to make this right with Sam.'

'And you will. But not immediately. He is hurt and angry. You are hurt, too, and confused. What good can you do until you understand yourself?'

I don't want Tobi and Luc to be right, but I can't escape the truth. However much I want it to be different, the damage done today just isn't fixable yet. But I don't want to outstay my welcome here. Tobi and Luc have been incredible hosts, friends and confidants. They've done so much for me already and I can't take advantage of their kindness. Besides, I need to get back to London to work out what to do next.

I accept a strong hug from Tobi who has just brought us another pot of tea. 'What would I do without you, my gallant knights?'

'It's our pleasure, fair Lady Phee,' Tobi smiles. 'So, you'll stay?'

'For a few days. But then I need to go home.'

My whole body feels beaten and bruised. But my heart is just numb. Tomorrow it will hit me fully, I think. Tomorrow I will wake to my first day without Sam Mullins. *Then* it will feel real.

I wasn't sure if I was going to be able to rest tonight, but as soon as I get into bed weariness slams down on my body. The last thing

I see before I fall asleep is the rainbow of book spines, their quiet order on the bookshelves above me reassuring and familiar. At least I still have this, I think. I may have thrown away my future plans with Sam, but I still have my year. I still did it. On a day when positives have become scarce, this is one I will cling to.

Chapter Forty-Two

SAM

It's almost 11 a.m. when I wake. For one blissful moment I am lying in sunlight, comfortable and warm, breathing in the morning.

And then, I remember.

Why does life do that to you? Whack you with reality just as you're enjoying your dream? A few minutes longer and I could have imagined her beside me.

If only.

I choke back the pain, stuff my face into the pillow and wait until it subsides. I never thought I'd cry as much as I have in the last eighteen months. First Laura. Now Phoebe. Except with Phoebe it's worse. I don't know why that should be – maybe I'd spent so long vilifying Laura that I held Phoebe up on a pedestal she didn't deserve. Perhaps I expected too much of her.

I don't do complications. I should never have let my heart run away with itself. So I'm as much to blame as Phoebe. I asked her for the impossible without realising what I was doing.

Maybe that's why she missed the train.

When I get up and wander into DeeDee and Kim's kitchen to find coffee, I dare to switch on my phone. While Kim's beloved but battered Nespresso machine does its thing, I scan my inbox. Nothing from her. I don't know why I expected there would be, only that just before I ended the call last night Phoebe was asking for more time to explain. I thought she might have composed an email last night, while I was confessing everything to DeeDee and Kim and sobbing like a child. I'm not proud of that, but by the time I reached their flat in Battersea, I had nothing left to fight it with.

I was pretty clear when I spoke to Phoebe that it would be the last time we'd speak. Clearly she took me at my word. I don't want it to be over, but it is, and yet I can't bring myself to delete her number.

'Hey, you.'

I look up to see DeeDee strolling into the kitchen. She looks tired, but then consoling your heartbroken friend till well past 4 a.m. will have that effect on you. We lost Kim almost two hours before we called it a night, when she yawned her apologies and headed for her bed.

'Morning.'

She glances over my shoulder at the kitchen clock and chuckles. 'Just. How you feeling?'

'Like I just did ten rounds with Anthony Joshua.'

'Nice.'

I hand her a mug of coffee. 'I'll live.'

'Yes, you will. I told you that last night. Things will work out, babe, if you stick around long enough. I know you don't want to hear that now, but they will. You need time. You both do.' DeeDee lowers her gaze and I brace myself. 'Are you going to see Phoebe when she comes home?'

'I don't think so.'

My friend nods but I know she's not done with me on this. 'Whatever feels right, babe. Don't rush anything. Might be helpful later on, though. Words said in person are always better.'

I hope my brief smile is enough of a reply. I don't know how

I'd feel if I saw Phoebe again with us *not* being together. I don't think I could bear that.

'So, what's the plan?'

'I have no idea. Get back into the studio, I guess. And sort out somewhere to live.'

'Does Chris know you're back? Or Syd?'

'Not yet. I'll go and see Chris today and then catch Syd if I can. Any idea if the guy who took my room is still there?'

DeeDee shrugs behind her coffee mug as she takes a sip. 'Dunno. Last I heard he was thinking of selling.'

That's a blow. Not that I'd assumed I could move back into my old place, but Syd's talked about moving out of the city for a while now. I have money to find somewhere else, but a year on Mull has seriously depleted my savings. Until the studio starts turning a profit, I need to take any work going.

'Right. I'll sort it. I always do.'

'Well, Kim's off on a European tour next week for two months, so there's room here if you need to stay a while.'

I appreciate the offer, but I'm back now so I need to get sorted. Besides, while I love DeeDee and Kim and they love me, staying under their roof for any extended period of time would not be healthy for our friendship.

Today is the start of the next chapter of my life. I'm determined to make it count.

I promised Niven I'd call him today and while the news I'll have for him won't be what he's expecting, I have no intention of reneging on that promise. We've become so much closer while I've been on Mull and I don't want to let that slide now I'm back in London.

All of that can wait for an hour, though. I need to get my bearings back and eat, even though my stomach is stubbornly twisted against that idea. I think of Ailish and how she kept going for Ma when everything fell apart. Ma crumbled, Ailish built scaffolding around her to keep her breathing. I know who I want to be like. I don't want to go under like Ma did.

An hour and a half later, I'm at the studio. I reckon Chris must have worked a late one, judging by the teetering tower of takeaway containers spilling out of the bin in the kitchen. He's by the control desk, lost in the depths of a drum mix, when I clamp a hand on his shoulder and almost give him heart failure.

'Bloody hell, Sam, where did you spring from?' He laughs and gives me a heavy back-slap that passes for a hug.

'I got back yesterday. I brought you brunch.'

'Legend!' Chris accepts the large takeaway coffee and bag of doughnuts from me like I've just given him a sack of gold. 'I was here till three a.m. and ended up kipping in the live room.'

I peer through the glass and see the pile of floor cushions and an old travel rug. 'Cosy.'

'It wasn't bad. Stays warm in there. I'll spray the air freshener around a bit before the string section comes in later this afternoon, though. Not sure my overnight odour will enhance their performance.'

'How's it going?' I ask. 'We busy?'

'Manic, dude. Glad you're back. We're going to be under it for a few weeks. Three of the big labels have blocked out time for albums. We even had a waiting list last month.'

That's the best news. To be busy is a blessing. And creating music is the best way to claw back some power when everything else is uncertain. In the studio I can lose myself. I'm going to be spending a lot of time doing that, I think.

When I call Syd a few hours later, he mentions his brother has a flat I can rent for what I paid on our place, in pretty much the same area. Tomorrow I'll go and have a look at it, then arrange to bring my stuff out of storage and move in next weekend, if it all goes to plan.

Practical stuff is no compensation for a broken heart, but at least it will keep me busy and make me feel not so out of control. I put off calling Niven until I've seen Syd's brother's place. He won't mind. As far as he knows, I'm too busy being reunited with the love of my life.

I swallow the ball of emotion the thought raises and move into the live room to help the newly arrived string quintet set up.

This is what matters now. This is my life.

Chapter Forty-Three

PHOEBE

Luc insists we go for a last walk around Montmartre before I pack to come home. I don't want to say yes, but staring at four walls going over and over what happened is less appealing.

I think we're just wandering as we did the first day Luc showed me around, until we turn a corner and it all becomes horribly clear.

The Wall of Love mural. The one I'd sent a photo of to Sam. One thousand *I love you* messages, each one mocking the words I'd said to him. Because how could I have told him I loved him and then broken his heart?

'I don't want to see this,' I say, making to leave. But Luc catches my arm.

'No Phoebe, there is something you haven't seen yet.'

'One thousand *I love you* messages? Yes, I see them. And I don't want to.'

He puts his hands on my shoulders and turns me back to face the wall. 'Look harder. Between the words.'

I can't see anything else, just the dark blue tiles and the white writing. 'There isn't anything else to see. Please, let's go.'

'*Non, mon amie.* Look at *these…*'

I follow the jut of his index finger to the corner of one of the tiles. A red blob. When I step back, they are everywhere, right across the mural. 'What are they for?'

His fingers squeeze my shoulders. 'They are pieces. Broken pieces of a heart. And if you were to collect them all and fit them together, you would fix that heart.'

Tears well up in my eyes, the letters and the red heart shards dancing in my view. 'I don't understand.'

'All you see is love. You don't notice these small pieces. I know your heart is broken, but there is enough love surrounding you to fix it. Because where love is, hope is there, too.'

Maybe when it doesn't hurt so much, when I've forgiven my mistake, I'll start to search for the pieces of my heart. But I'm not ready yet.

Arriving back in London is a bittersweet event.

I'm here. But the time is wrong.

It's too late.

Too late to keep a promise I should have kept.

Meg and Osh had offered to meet me but I just want to get off the train and leave St Pancras as quickly as I can, alone. Head down, not looking at the giant lovers or the huge station-clock confirming my lateness. And *definitely* not passing the Betjeman statue: where Sam was waiting for me, but not any more.

After a year away, doing what I'd promised myself I'd do – and so much more besides – returning to St Pancras should be a celebration. I *did it*. Followed my heart for twelve months, all by myself. Except that, when it mattered most, I failed to listen to what it told me.

Around me my fellow passengers are already on their feet, collecting coats and cases, bags and belongings before the train has even begun to enter the station. A queue is forming by the doors, mobile phones pressed to ears as we pass railway sidings and the red and yellow brick signal box that mirrors St Pancras' design in miniature. The passengers know where they're going. Nobody else will doubt their place in the capital when they leave this train.

Except me.

When I step onto the platform, I will have no job, no plan, no onward journey. And no Sam.

My heart drags as the train brakes engage. The glow of late-afternoon sun paints the famous brick building red-gold as we enter the station, the blue girders cool against the famous walls. At the end of this line the bright pink neon Tracey Emin sign hangs: I WANT MY TIME WITH YOU.

I've loved it since it was unveiled but I don't want to see it today. It's my deepest, most painful thought suspended from the roof for the world to see. And the only person I'd want to see it isn't here.

Where is Sam now? Is he still in London, in the studio he owns with his friend? If it didn't hurt so much, I'd consider looking him up. He never told me the name of his studio but it can't be hard to find. I could Google the address and just go. I could do it tomorrow. But what do you say to someone whose heart you've broken?

In the shadow of the station I catch sight of my eyes reflected in the train window. They're swollen and soulless. I am so tired of hurting. But at least I'm home. I might have nothing, but I can build from here. Staring into a face I hardly recognise I make another promise – this time just to myself:

When I leave this train, I'm only looking forward.

I have cried enough. What matters now are the first steps I take from this train. I allow myself one moment in my seat to steady my breath. Then I rise, collect my luggage and join the end of the line waiting to leave.

Warm London air fills the carriage as the door opens and we shuffle out. Long shadows stretch beneath the blue girders and red brick as the sun continues its dip. It feels like home, my feet on the platform making the past twelve months concertina together, almost as if I'd never left. It's strange how quickly you slot back into life after a journey. It's the longest one I've ever made, so I'd wondered if it might take more time to readjust, but instantly everything is familiar and as I left it. Everything physical, at least.

I don't want to linger on this level, with Sir John and the lovers and every thought of what might have been. So I duck my head and follow the stream of passengers down the stairwell to the lower concourse. From there I can head straight for the anonymity of the tube and decide where to go next.

Meg called this morning as I was saying goodbye to Tobi and Luc, and told me their lodger moved out, so my room is free if I want it. I have enough for two months' rent, thanks to the little gift Lisabeta insisted I take for my work in the villa's library – and the thought of being back in my room, surrounded by my friends who I've missed so much, is instantly appealing.

That's where I'm going, although I need to decompress first. It's getting late but there'll be somewhere I can grab a drink, maybe even something to eat, and be quiet for a while before Meg, Gabe and Osh descend on me. Tomorrow I'll start looking for work – or maybe the day after. Wait and see how I am once I'm home and this journey is finally over.

We emerge from the corridor through large stainless-steel doors into the lower concourse and instantly my heart contracts. I might have avoided the Betjeman statue and the neon pink words, but I'd forgotten where I'd end up – just metres away from where Sam and I took refuge together, where we kissed for the first time, where everything began. And worse still, hugging, kissing couples and families suddenly surround me, reunited from their journeys. I breathe hard against the pain as I slowly weave my way around them, utterly alone in a space filled with love and joy. There are so many and it seems to take a lifetime to navigate a safe path between them. Every step hurts. I'm such an idiot. So much for *only looking forwards*. Not even five minutes since I arrived and that promise is already broken.

I don't want to cry here. I *won't* cry here.

'Phoebe.'

At first I ignore it, assuming the voice is aimed at someone else. I'm pretty certain I am not the only Phoebe in St Pancras station.

'Hey, Phoebe.'

And then I see him.

I can't believe it. He wasn't supposed to be here.

But he *is* – and the sight of him is so impossibly lovely I drop my bags, run into his arms, and cling to him like a lifebuoy in a storm.

'I can't believe you're here,' I sob against his shoulder. I can't bottle my tears any longer. From the way he holds me I don't think he minds. He smells of warm spice and welcome, and I just want to stay there.

'Of course I am. I wouldn't be anywhere else.'

Around us people hurry and meet and chatter but I don't move, the safety and warmth of being held by him too wonderful to let go. I spent the entire journey from Paris braced for a lonely return, imagining nothing but coldness and anonymity awaiting my arrival. For the first time since the day I was meant to meet Sam again, I feel safe. And completely *not* alone.

Chapter Forty-Four

SAM

I thought I'd be prepared for the phone call from Ellie about Frank. I knew his death was imminent, but the shock of recent weeks distracted me.

'He went in his sleep,' Ellie tells me. It's little comfort. I can hear she's in tears and they mirror my own.

'Were you there?'

'We'd just left. I missed him by five minutes.'

'I'm so sorry.'

'But actually, Sam, I think he knew. He wouldn't have wanted a fuss. I reckon he waited till we'd gone and then gave himself permission to go. I mean, that was Pa all over, wasn't it? Running away on his own terms, not minding anyone else. Except, I think he knew what he was doing this time. I think knowing we had met and you'd sought him out was a load off his mind. He must have lived most of his life scared we'd all find out about each other.'

It will only be a brief funeral and I am invited. But I won't go. I'd rather draw a line under it all. I'm staying in touch with Ellie, of course. But my story as far as Frank Mullins is concerned is done.

Besides, life is a bit tough right now. I'm beginning to struggle, and I never struggle where music is concerned. Work is long and hard at the studio and I just can't seem to find my excitement for it. Every day drags. Chris is at his wits' end with me, I know. I feel bad for not pulling my weight.

And then, my friends step in.

I thought we were just going out for dinner but as soon as DeeDee, Kim, Chris, Syd and me are seated at the table it's clear they have an agenda.

'Sam. You're miserable,' DeeDee says.

'A nightmare, let's be honest,' Kim agrees. 'You need to snap out of it.'

'Pardon me for having a crisis,' I begin, but one look from the girls silences me.

Chris leans in. 'Mate, it's good having you at the studio, but you're doing my head in. Everyone's noticed. I don't want us to lose business because you're depressing our clients.'

I stare at him. He's never the sort to voice his opinions unless you're debating the merits of microphones and compressors. 'What do you want me to do?'

'Find a tour,' Syd says. 'Any tour. Get yourself on it, get out of London for a while, clear your head. You ain't no use to us here, right now.'

'But the studio…?'

'We'll manage. We're good, Sam, just take some time for yourself, yeah?'

'Maybe call Phoebe and sort that out,' Kim begins but DeeDee shushes her. Unrepentant, she shrugs.

DeeDee reaches her hand across the table to me. 'You need to find your happy, babe. It ain't here.'

I'm furious they dragged me out to stage a public intervention, but more annoyed that I know they're right.

I need to get out for a while.

It isn't running away. Is it?

So when Niven contacts me a few days later to say he's taken a six-week sabbatical from his job at the school and is putting a band together for a month-long tour, it's the break I'm looking for. He's asked Shona, too, so it will be like old times. It's exactly what I need. Everyone around me breathes a collective sigh of relief. And as we prepare for the tour that will take me away from London and thoughts of Phoebe, I begin to feel happier. It's only a temporary fix, but it will buy me time to work out what I really want.

I travel to Leeds to meet Niven and the guys to rehearse for a few days. His pal is managing the whole thing while Niv's in charge of the band. If our rehearsals are anything to go by, this tour is going to be a corker.

Shona is there, with two lads from the pub sessions in Tobermory who are taking a year out from university to play music. It's a good set-up: the calibre of band where you aren't fretting over charts because everyone's played the songs a hundred times before.

Then our tour begins – and what a tour crammed into four weeks. Leeds, Sheffield, Manchester, Cheshire, North Wales, Lincolnshire, Bristol, Coventry before heading to Bromsgrove, Stratford-upon-Avon and ending up at the Eden Music and Arts Festival for the big finale.

It's the freedom I want at the time I need it most. Great to be with Niven again and Shona, too, who is still the most outrageous flirt on the planet. Secretly, I like it. If Shona knows she doesn't care. Her humour and sense of fun is infectious. Niven has to take us aside at one of the earlier gigs because we give each other raucous giggles during what should be a heartfelt ballad.

The rhythm of touring again draws me in – load the van, on to the next venue, unload, play, load again, drive… From one county to the next, one set of toe-tapping, approval-nodding audience members to the next. People are great and I'm impressed by the renewed enthusiasm for live folk-music I see. Even five years ago these venues we're playing would be half full. I keep thinking of the Mull music club's young musicians and how much brighter their prospects for live gigs are now compared with when I started out.

With every song played, every set completed and every bow taken, I feel I'm coming back from wherever I'd let myself disappear to.

Music takes me by the hand and gently saves me again. And the future doesn't look as cold or empty.

Chapter Forty-Five

PHOEBE

I'm not really aware of the days passing. They all seem to merge into one. I tried phoning Sam a few times, but each attempt went straight to voicemail. I haven't left any messages. He'll see that I've called. The longer it goes without him responding, the stronger his silent answer. And I'm starting to wonder if Gabe saw something in Sam's behaviour that I didn't. How serious could he have been if he wouldn't even give me a chance to put things right?

In the end, I have to move on.

Gabe has been amazing. I couldn't have got through it all without him. I've never seen him step up like this before, and neither have our friends. Meg told me she'd seen the change long before he rescued me from St Pancras.

'As soon as he came back from the commercial shoot with Osh he was different. I thought he'd met someone out there, it was such a change. But Osh said the only person he met out there was you.'

I like this Gabe. Since he met me at the station he's been there for me every day. Not fussing, just there. That means more than anything. It helps that he's in between jobs and still waiting for his feature film to get a definite release date. We've talked about anything and everything, like we did in the beginning when we became housemates. If I've wanted to talk about Sam, he's listened without judgement; if I haven't, he hasn't tried to address it. Lately I've noticed I've talked about Sam less and less.

Summer has mostly consisted of rain but then the sun remembers the season and for a week it bathes the city in gorgeous light. I love London at this time of year. Most summers here I've been stuck in an office working, but as I'm still figuring out what to do for a job, I hang out with Gabe instead. We go sightseeing, merging with the tourist blur around London's famous landmarks. It's almost like being back on my Grand Tour, except that this time I have a friend beside me to share it with. A friend whose current calmness is startling.

I tell him this when we're stretched out on a picnic blanket on Primrose Hill. The city seems to rise from a haze, making it appear like a mythical kingdom stretched out in the distance. All around us people are enjoying the day, the usual conventions of London life discarded in favour of relaxing in the sun.

'I *am* calmer,' he says, the gentle breeze ruffling his hair as he gazes at the city. 'I don't know, Phoebs, it just doesn't seem as important as it used to. I mean, I know there's work coming and when the film gets its release date the craziness will start again. And Eric, my new agent, is great, you know. I don't ever have to chase him. I don't feel I'm having to manage my career as well as working. That's such a load off my mind.'

He downs the last of his beer and pulls another two bottles from the bag we brought with us. I accept it because today feels close to perfect and I'm in the mood to celebrate. We bought bits at Borough Market, laughed and joked as we caught buses and hopped on and off tube trains. Gabe decided we should have an epic dessert for our picnic so we made a ridiculous detour across town to Peggy Porschen for cakes. And finally – *finally* – I feel like I'm coming back to myself. The Phoebe I was when I hid pebbles around the streets of Rome with Giana, or restoring the library with Amanda in Lisabeta's villa. I should have been able to celebrate my amazing year in Europe instead of feeling like what happened with Sam rendered it all void. Now I feel I can make a start.

I write this in my journal as the London sun gilds its pages. At first, I didn't bring it anywhere with me but a few days ago I dared to read some to Gabe and he insisted I write while we're out, capturing the moments when they happen.

'Make sure you mention me,' Gabe says beside me, tapping my notebook with the neck of his beer bottle. '*Magnificent* would probably work well in that context.'

'Good idea. Not sure magnificent is the right word, though. How do you spell *knob*?'

'Ha ha. You're hilarious.'

I nudge his leg with my knee. 'Thank you for this,' I say.

Gabe looks at me. 'For what?'

'Being here, now.'

He laughs. 'Slouching around on Primrose Hill, eating all the food? My pleasure.'

'Not just the picnic. Since I got back from Paris you've been amazing.'

'Well, you're pretty amazing. So that makes two of us.' He winks and it makes me laugh. He's cheeky as anything and knows it, but I love his confidence.

'We should get matching capes or something,' I say. 'Own our *amazingness*.'

'Good plan. You'd look good in spandex.'

'Cheers. Although I reckon your Instagram posse would go off the chart if they saw you in a superhero costume.'

He admonishes me with a grin. 'Don't pretend you aren't one of them, Phoebs.'

'Busted. I'm a fully paid-up member of – what is it they call themselves?'

Gabe rubs the bridge of his nose. 'Marley's Army.'

'Brilliant.' Gabriel Marley doesn't embarrass easily but when he does it's one of the greatest sights on earth. I give his cheek a playful pat. 'Aw, Mr Marley, you go so red.'

'Get off!' He wraps his fingers over my hand and pulls it away from his face. And he doesn't let go. He's smiling when he looks at me, but in that moment I'm aware of the warm breeze, the sun on my skin, the distant dance of laughter on the afternoon air. 'I do think you're amazing.'

'That's because I am.'

'You are. And my life has been so much brighter since you came home.'

Nerves skip through my voice when I laugh. 'You are joking? All I've done is cry all over you and talk your ears off.'

'And I love it.' The pulse of his fingers pads through mine where they meet. 'I was a dick before you left last year. No, I was. It wasn't because I didn't think you'd go through with it; I was scared you would. And then you left and I missed you. Every day.'

'You don't have to say that. It's okay.'

'And then when I saw you in Tuscany, you were – radiant. Don't pull a face, you were. You are. Even after all the Sam stuff.'

I don't know what to say.

'Phoebs, I like this. Being with you.'

'I like being with you, too.'

And just like that, the air changes.

It's subtle and sweet and the sun has warmed Gabe's skin when I touch it, and the birds are singing.

And then we're kissing. And it's good.

So I don't pull away because why would I? We melt into each other with the city at our feet and I realise I'm not scared. I'm not debating or obsessing. And I'm not thinking of Sam.

I'm just here, with Gabe. And I don't want to think any more.

'You need a celeb couple name now,' Osh quips as he hands me a fresh bottle of cider. 'Especially when Mr Marley's film gets its release date. What shall we call you? GabePhee? Gabee? PhoeGab?'

'Stick to directing, Osh,' Gabe says, flopping down on the grass. 'You and words were never meant to be.'

'Unlike our resident Couple of the Month,' Meg grins.

The sun catches the dome of Brighton Pavilion and the sky is the kind of impossible blue you only get in summer. It's so good to be here. I watch my friends larking around and lean into Gabe's warm chest.

'Happy?' he murmurs, stroking my hair.

I nod and lift my lips to meet his.

'Ugh! Get a room!' Osh protests.

Meg chuckles. 'They have a room. Problem is, we have to share it with them.'

I offer an apologetic smile. 'Sorry.'

She shrugs. 'No skin off my nose. I have noise-cancelling headphones.' She ducks as Gabe chucks a paper cup at her.

'Smile for Marley's Army,' Osh says, grabbing his camera.

'You'd better be joking.'

'Why? They have a right to know.'

'They do not!'

He shakes his head, laughing. 'Relax, Phee, your secret's safe with me.'

'Your poetry's improving, at least.' Gabe scrambles to his feet, brandishing a tennis ball and a cricket bat he bought from the beach stall on Brighton Pier. 'Let's see how your bowling reflexes are.'

I watch them dash off to play like the big kids they are. It's so long since we all came out to Brighton on an away day. It's just like old times: chilly dashes into the sea, ice cream from the crazy Fifties'-themed ice cream parlour on Gardner Street, relaxing in the Pavilion Gardens. I've been nervous about how things would be in our gang now Gabe and I are together, but I needn't have been. This is as close to perfect as it can be.

'Look at them. Children.' Meg smiles as she sits next to me. 'So, how are you?'

The cider is sweet on my tongue as I drink. 'Good. You?'

'Same as always. Has Gabe had any word on the release of his film?'

'Not yet.' I watch him mocking Osh as they take it in turns to bat and bowl. I know this calm can't last forever. 'His agent is talking to the film distributor today. Hopefully we'll have some news soon.'

Meg's eyes narrow. 'Hopefully?'

She knows me too well. 'Okay, maybe not hopefully for me. I like him not being busy. Having him to myself.'

'Because the moment that film comes out, he's everybody's again?'

I nod. I've tried not to think too far ahead, but I'm not looking forward to his schedule filling up again. I like him just being mine, as he is today.

'Don't worry. He'll be going into it as your boyfriend this time, not a singleton the film company can work to death. It'll be fine.'

'Hope so.'

'I know so. It's taken you two long enough to get together – he isn't going to do anything to spoil that. He's in for the long haul.'

I wrap my arms round my best friend. I know she wasn't sure when Gabe and I got together, so it means a lot that she supports us now. 'Thank you.'

'You're welcome. Stop worrying and enjoy your whirlwind romance.'

Can you call it a whirlwind if you've known each other forever? The next few weeks feel like a whirlwind, as if we've just discovered each other and the Phoebe-Gabe script is being hastily rewritten. He's tender and attentive, loving and fun to be with. He makes me feel good. Our friends give knowing nods because of course this was always going to happen eventually. I feel part of London again, but this time its heart beats through Gabe and me.

And then, it begins to change.

The date for Gabe's feature film release is finally revealed and suddenly we're caught up in a hurricane of organisation, press junkets and a planned European press-tour. We don't have time to catch breath, let alone spend time together. We both knew this was coming, but it arrives jealous and rude, dragging us both into its flow.

A date is set for the London premiere and publicity is hastily arranged in the week leading up to it. Gabe has a flurry of TV and radio interviews, magazine and press features and random Skype interviews with US media outlets, meaning he's often getting ready to talk to people in the early hours of the morning when the rest of us are going to bed.

I accompany him for some of the interviews – he's keen for me to see this part of what he does and I'm proud of him. But I'm starting to feel uncomfortable.

The people we meet are lovely and very pleasant but it's the way they look at me. The comments that feel too intrusive; the PR lady – who seems to bleed energy – just a little too keen to get me in front of the cameras. I hang back, but I see her watching me. Planning me into her next headline.

And then the invitation to the premiere arrives and with it the briefing. It's a transatlantic celebration of culture so the dress code is designer eveningwear exclusively from British or US fashion designers. I'd assumed it only applied to the actors, director and producers of the film, but with a week to go I discover they expect it from everyone.

'I don't have any designer clothes,' I protest, bristling when I see the look Gabe gives me. Until now we've been a united front and I don't like how this feels.

'We can sort it.'

'And I can't afford to buy anything.'

'I'll pay for it.'

'I can't ask you to do that.'

'You didn't. I offered.' I see the knots of tension in his shoulders as he turns away. 'It will be fine. You'll look amazing. Don't worry.'

Did he just patronise me? 'I haven't done this before, Gabe, I'm going to worry.'

'Whatever. You do you.'

Now I'm annoyed. How can he not see how out of my depth I am? Doesn't he care? 'Maybe it's better if I don't go.'

It's out before I can think better of it. And I wish I couldn't see the hurt in his expression when he rounds on me. 'You *have* to go,

Phoebs! It's a huge deal and the biggest event of my career. I want you by my side.'

'I'll go,' Osh offers, munching toast at the kitchen breakfast bar as we argue around him. It's classic Oisin timing and makes me laugh despite the building storm.

'See? Osh wants to go. Take him.'

'I don't want to take Osh because I want to take my *girlfriend*,' Gabe returns, holding a hand up to our housemate. 'No offence, mate.'

'None taken,' he sniffs. 'I'd only outshine you.'

'Besides, I can't turn up with a guy. Not this time. Eric wants to play down the gay angle since that Insta pic went viral.' He says it like it's absolutely fine and that infuriates me more. I should let it go like I have in the past but I don't feel like giving him a free pass on this today.

'The posed photo you did on purpose to promote your last play?'

'Hey, you have to play to the crowd.'

'By deliberately being vague about your sexuality, like it's something you just pop on to get an audience?'

He groans. 'Everyone does it, Phoebs.'

'I don't care. You should be better. It's dishonest and misleading to your fans.'

'Firstly, it's none of their business what I do in my personal life. And secondly, what's the difference between a fake homosexual relationship and a fake heterosexual one?'

I cannot believe I'm hearing this. 'There's no difference. They're both wrong!'

'Are you sure you guys are in love?' Osh asks, squeezing between us to get to the sink. 'Because right now I feel like a spectator at a grudge match.'

That pulls us up. I shove my hands in my pockets and Gabe stares at the ceiling.

It isn't about finding a dress or being in front of the cameras, although neither fills me with much excitement. This has been building for a while. I care about Gabe, so much. I can't say *love* yet, but neither of us is ready to approach that territory. When we're together – when it's just him and me, when it's our sole focus – it's good. But we pull in opposite directions when a schedule appears. This is his job and I'm proud of him, but the Gabe I love being with is retreating. The age-old frustrations I used to feel before I left for Europe flood back.

What's worse is that I suspect it has nothing to do with who Gabriel Marley is. I think all of this is because of who Gabe is *not*.

I have to turn it around. I can't risk losing him or alienating my friends just because I have doubts. *Stupid* doubts: doubts I don't need to harbour.

'Where would I get a dress?' I ask, offering a smile as Gabe looks at me.

'I don't know. But if you're serious about coming with me we will figure it out together.'

'I might know someone,' Osh says, without looking up from his phone screen.

We stare at him.

'Oh, just casually chuck that in,' Gabe says. 'Phoebs and I have been arguing for ages about this, didn't you hear?'

'Half of the city heard. And for the record, nobody asked me.' He pockets his phone and heads for the door. 'Let me make a call.'

Alone in the kitchen, Gabe and I look at each other. This is ridiculous. We're meant to be in the first flush of a new relationship, not arguing like we've been married for twenty years.

'I'm sorry,' I say, walking into his outstretched arms.

I feel the weight of his sigh as he holds me. 'No, I am. It's my job, not yours. This is a lot to put on you.'

'I'll be there. And I'll be proud of you.'

'Thank you.' He kisses me but it doesn't seem convincing somehow.

Chapter Forty-Six

SAM

I have never been more grateful for a band's acrimonious split than I am for the poor guys who left Niven's mate in the lurch and led to us getting this tour. It's fantastic. The gigs we play most nights are in excellent venues and while each has been small the reaction of the crowds is disproportionately loud. Slowly, we are traversing the country, moving from town to city to rural working-men's clubs and pubs.

The days become weeks and we slip into our sets easier and faster each time. Our playing becomes tighter, the little bits of jamming we muck about with during sound checks cheekily sneak into the gigs as polished little gems. We're having fun instead of ploughing through not-yet-familiar songs, and the magic I felt I'd lost returns.

As often happens with tours, the venues don't follow a lineal geographical pattern, so we'll play a gig in Bristol then be up in Sunderland next day. Consequently there's a lot of time spent on the road between gigs. We take it in turns to drive the hire van with the equipment and the hired minibus with the rest of us. When I have to drive, my thoughts increasingly turn to Phoebe. I wish I'd tried to contact her when the dust settled. Moving around has made me remember our year of journeys.

Nobody knows this, but tucked away in the zipped pocket of

my violin case I have a stack of the postcards Phoebe sent me. They represent the unfinished business between us. She made mistakes, I made them too, but it should never have ended the way it did. The more I think about that and about what Phoebe meant to me, the more convinced I become that I should seek her out when this tour is over.

I ended up talking to Shona about her last night. I didn't intend it to happen, but she asked me and I didn't have a good enough reason not to reply.

'What happened, Sam? You were so sure of her before.'

'That kind of ended when she didn't show.'

Shona nodded, playing with the silver necklaces at her throat. I watched her fingers looping in and out of the delicate links, lifting the chains from the soft skin of her neck. 'And she never explained why she didn't meet you?'

'She tried to. I mean, she called but…'

'You were hurt.'

'Yeah.'

'And angry, too.'

'I couldn't see past what she'd done. She had her reasons, but I wasn't ready to hear them.'

'I'm not surprised. Leading you on for a year then kicking you in the nuts.'

I wouldn't have termed it like that, but Shona's description tempted a naughty smile from my lips. 'Anyway, it's ancient history.'

And that's when she hit me with it.

'I wouldn't lead you on, Sam. If you wanted me I'd be there like a shot. And I'd flag down a train to get to you.'

Just like that. She dropped it like a grenade in the middle of our innocent friend-chat and then just walked away.

BOOM.

I still have no idea how it happened. Or what to do next.

I'm thinking about it as I drive the equipment van behind the band minibus on our four-hour journey along the M6. I can see Shona on the back seat, her arms folded behind her head, trusty leather jacket giving her shoulders a familiar silhouette. I used to sit behind her in lectures and I remember thinking how slender her neck was, with its line of tiny curls along the nape beneath the bob of her hastily tied ponytail. Her hair is loose today, but every now and again she scoops it up as if she's considering tying it.

'Blink, pal.'

'What?'

'You haven't blinked for a minute. I timed you.'

'You're strange, Niv.'

Niven crosses his feet on the dashboard. 'Aye. But at least I'm not perving over my friend.'

I glance at him. 'Who's perving?'

'Right. Well, either you have a particularly odd fascination with the rear of Volkswagen Transporter minibuses or just the occupant of the back seat of *that* one.' He gives a snort and shakes his head. 'You're rubbish, Mullins. I see you staring at her.'

'Would you prefer I didn't look at the road ahead?'

'I would prefer you didn't drive quite so close to the minibus. Stopping distance, Sam. Did you skive your theory test? If they brake, Shona Delaney will be in your lap.' He folds his arms. 'Or maybe that's what you're after.'

'Get stuffed.'

'I saw the two of yous all cosy after the gig last night.'

'We were just talking.'

'Oh, talking is it? Hard to do I would think when your tongue's hanging out.'

'Niv. Leave it.'

He holds up his hands. 'None of my business, pal. But if you wanted to move on, that's your golden opportunity right there.'

'What? No.'

'Look, after Ruth I couldn't imagine being with anyone else, but I knew that if I didn't get back in the saddle I'd talk myself out of it altogether. So I had a two-week thing with a teaching assistant at school. She'd just split from her fella and wanted a bit of fun. So did I. We're still mates. But it helped.'

Does he know what Shona said to me last night? I daren't ask. 'I couldn't. She's a friend. I couldn't do that to her.'

'Didn't look like she was about to complain last night. Shona doesn't want a big relationship, not yet. The dust is still settling from her last one. Maybe you'd be good for each other.' He shrugs. 'None of my business, mind.'

Could I go there? I'm not sure.

Either way, it's spiced up the four-hour M6 journey nicely.

Chapter Forty-Seven

PHOEBE

Thank goodness for my friends.

It turns out that Olivia, the person Osh called about my dress, is a costume supervisor he worked with on an advert a few years ago. As well as designing clothes for film and TV productions she also makes a few of her own pieces that she sells privately. When I meet her in the Aladdin's cave of fabric she calls her workshop near Elstree studios, she tells me she has the perfect dress.

It's a repurposed garment: the original a part of a set of gowns she'd made for a magazine photo-shoot that was supposed to be a modern reimagining of Versailles. When I first try it on it's covered with drapes of pearls and has extra material wrapped in heavy folds around the hips to mimic the opulent wide dresses popular in King Louis XVI's court.

'Don't worry about this stuff, I'll whip it all off,' she says with a mouthful of pins as she circles me, pinning parts of the dress in place. 'As long as the basic garment fits, I can sort the rest.'

'Thank you so much for doing this,' I say, a little dizzy from watching her.

'Total pleasure. Always wanted to loan a film premiere dress.' Olivia pauses as she's pinning the top of the bodice. 'I take it this is your first? Premiere, I mean.'

'First one I've had to walk a red carpet for,' I say, my stomach somersaulting at the prospect.

'Bit scary, huh?'

'Terrifying.'

She smiles and resumes her alterations. 'It's a load of bollocks, that's what you have to tell yourself. Lots of people trying to get a picture and lots of people trying to get *in* one. Don't worry. This dress will do all the hard work for you. Just enjoy wearing it.'

When Olivia's completed creation arrives at our house three days later I can't believe the transformation. The peacock-blue velvet has been gently draped where the extra pieces once were and wearing it feels like being held in the gentlest embrace. It makes the most amazing sound when I walk, too. I'm still terrified of being in the spotlight but being able to wear this dress will be a great compensation.

Gabe is preoccupied all day. By the time we're getting ready we're snapping at each other. We hardly talk in the car over to the cinema where the film is premiering. I glance at him, feeling exposed with my off-the-shoulder dress and borrowed heels. Meg did my make-up and hair and Osh found another friend to lend me some costume jewellery. When I peered in the mirror before we left the house, I didn't recognise the woman looking back. Despite her beautiful dress she didn't seem happy. She didn't look like she was living the dream.

Tomorrow Gabe flies to New York for the US premiere, then on to LA to spend time with his American agent and meet people. The machine has cranked into gear around him and he's being swept up in a rush of schedules, meetings and opportunities. I'm thrilled for him, of course. But I feel like he's pulling away from me.

Or maybe I'm pulling away from him.

'Relax, you look fine,' he says, but he sounds irritated and instantly I am, too.

'I know I do.'

He stares at me. 'Phoebs, I didn't mean… You look stunning, obviously.'

Obviously?

I watch London moving at dreamlike pace past the passenger door window. Gabe glares at his phone.

This is horrible. How did we get here? Until the film job kicked in we were so happy. I'm shocked by how quickly it all changed. It's like I don't know where we fit into this new world of flashbulbs and interviews.

I want to drag it back, find a sliver of *us* before the pantomime cranks into action again. I return to him, my heart hammering hard.

'Gabe, I think we—'

'Here we are,' the driver chirps, swinging into line behind a queue of identical people-carriers. 'Just need to wait our turn, but you'll be good to go in a few moments.'

I grip my bag and the wrap that weighs uncomfortably around my arms and wait. Gabe is adjusting his suit, checking his reflection in the rear-view mirror. He doesn't look like my Gabe at all.

The door is being opened and he's out as flashbulbs fire like angry lightning. For a moment I think he might have abandoned me, but then his hand reaches back into the car. It's warm when I take it, one tiny scrap of reassurance I cling to.

The flashes of light imprint on my eyes and I can't see where I'm walking. Disoriented, I find myself being pulled from one place to the next; a few steps and then a pose; a few more and a smile. At every stop, Gabe's hand rests at the small of my back and sometimes he pulls me into him. I look up and there's Gabriel Marley, the performer, the consummate professional, working every angle and lapping up the adulation. This is his world and he is as at home here as I am surrounded by books.

But this isn't my world.

I do everything I am expected to do, reminding myself that I'm here for him not me. I'm smiling but I'm drowning in a sea of dread, gasping for air and terrified I'm going under. It isn't a panic attack: it's a portent. If this film takes off as the buzz around it suggests, this will be the first of many premieres. The higher Gabe's star rises, the more scrutiny anyone in his world will face.

If I want to be with him, this becomes my life, too.

It's far more terrifying than facing a sea of yelling photographers on a red carpet in London, wearing a dress that isn't mine and a smile that doesn't fit.

By the time we reach the entrance and hurry inside, I know what I have to do.

Chapter Forty-Eight

SAM

In Bristol, we get early access to the venue so we're all set up by midday. Blessed with an afternoon to kill before we play we predictably end up in a pub. We haven't had a decent blowout for a week and as we're staying locally tonight we can drink a little more than usual and enjoy ourselves.

Since her bombshell Shona hasn't said any more, but I watch her all the same. I can't quite believe she meant what she said although I can find no other, safer explanation for it. This afternoon she is mocking Niven for his near encyclopaedic celebrity knowledge – admittedly not the most obvious skill you would expect Mr McNish to possess – and for a film he wants to see that she thinks is lame. Their banter is endlessly entertaining as they check a film news website. Then Shona snatches Niven's iPad from his hands and scrolls down the movie-news page he's been reading.

'Now, this will definitely be worth your time. Everyone is talking about this one.'

'*Volozhin 82*? What do you care about Russian spy thrillers?' Niven asks.

'I care a lot when Gabriel Marley's in it,' she says.

My smile freezes. I haven't heard that name for a while.

Gabriel Marley.

Gabe.

'I mean, look at the man. Sex on a *stick*. They just had the film premiere in London and it was all over Twitter and Instagram. Full-on Hollywood glam – the works. And Gabriel looks divine. Let me find the photo gallery...'

'Give us a look,' I say, hoping they won't question my sudden interest in film gossip.

Shona leaves her seat, gazing happily at the screen, as she makes her way to me.

'I wouldn't kick him out of bed in the morning. *Beautiful* man. And look – check out *that* lucky hen on his arm. Looks like the cat that got the entire Sainsbury's cream fridge. And who can blame her?'

Niven's face falls and he makes a bid for the iPad, but Shona's already handed it to me.

Gabriel Marley is smouldering for the cameras, all dark eyes and perfectly styled hair. And pulled tight against his designer suit is a woman in a stunning blue-green velvet dress.

Not just any woman.

'He doesn't want to see that,' Niven says, trying to take it from me.

But it's too late. I see Phoebe's bright smile, her hair tumbling in glossy waves over her naked shoulders – and everything makes sense.

She isn't waiting for me to contact her again.

She's having the time of her life with the guy she couldn't stop talking about since we met.

So *that's* why she missed the train.

I don't know whether to feel angry, devastated or just really stupid for not seeing what was happening. Was she using me – and the year away – to make Gabe miss her? If she was, it clearly worked. One thing I do know is that I am going to start drinking now and carry on back at the motel when the gig is over. Getting drunk is the absolute best option because it turns out I never knew Phoebe Jones and I don't want to *feel* anything about her ever again.

I almost called her today. I've had a lucky escape.

Chapter Forty-Nine

PHOEBE

We hardly talk after the premiere. Gabe tells Meg and Osh it's because he's been so busy with the never-ending promotion for his film. I've said the same. But we're both lying.

The day it happens, we've managed to grab an hour to have breakfast in the little Italian deli down the street from home. A car is due to collect him soon to take him to the BBC for an interview with film critic James King and then I'm unlikely to see him until the weekend. We're both pretending this is a normal breakfast meeting, like we do this every day. In reality, it's the first time since the film promotion began.

Across the table, between the basket of *bomboloni* doughnuts, cafétières of coffee and crockery, Gabe's spread the newspaper and magazine press clippings of the premiere. He's giving them to his agent when they meet at White City. I'm fiddling with my phone to avoid looking at them. My finger slips against the screen, the photo app opening instead of the Instagram button. Suddenly, I'm face to face with a version of myself I hardly recognise. Standing beside Amanda surrounded by stacks of old books in Villa Speranza's library. The Phoebe Jones in the photograph is tanned and happy, grinning wide for the camera, her hair threaded with gold from the Puglian sun.

My heart aches.

Gabe is talking on his phone, eyes roving the press clippings as they pass beneath his fingers.

I can't stop myself looking for another version of Phoebe Jones. The one standing by a train barrier on 14th June last year, her head pressed against the chest of a smiling man with a violin case slung on one shoulder. I can see the Phoebe Jones of the premiere over the top of the screen – and while she wears an incredible gown and jewels sparkle at her wrist, her smile is empty.

'I can't do this,' I say.

Gabe stares at me. But I already see it in his eyes.

He's been waiting for me to say it.

He ends the call and places his phone beside the press clippings. A slow, deliberate move that makes my insides contract.

'Breakfast, or us?'

He isn't smiling. I wish he were.

'It isn't you...'

'*Please*. Don't roll that one out. Just say it, Phoebe.'

And then I have no choice. 'I can't be with you. We're so different and I feel like I'm losing myself... I don't want to make you unhappy and if we stay together that's what will happen.'

'What about what I want?'

'Gabe – can you be there for me if I need you? Would you drop everything and race back to be with me?'

'That's unfair. This is my job...'

'It is. And it should be your main concern.'

'This is about Sam, isn't it?'

The punch knocks the air from me. 'No. This is about me calling this off before we lose every scrap of love we have for each other.'

His eyes are still when they meet mine. 'Phoebe. It's about Sam. He can't make you happy, but it appears neither can I.'

'We'd end up hating each other. I don't want that. Do you?'

He's angry. He's hurt. But he honestly doesn't look heartbroken. And that's my answer.

Gabe leaves early for New York next morning after a night of brutal truths and confessions and a few hours' sleep in separate beds. I'm bruised and aching but I've done the right thing.

So when Meg and Osh wake to find me red-eyed and exhausted in the living room nursing a mug of tea that lost its heat hours before, I'm able to assure them that I'm okay. And the telling thing is that neither of them looks completely surprised. I think they've known longer than I have – or longer than I was ready to admit I knew.

For a few days I drift from one thing to the next, aware that I need to sort out permanent work and start to set down roots in London again. The temp agency has been great, but it's time to find what I want to do. What will happen when Gabe returns from the States? Right now we aren't speaking and if that continues, sharing a home with him will be unimaginably difficult.

And then, life hands me a stroke of serendipity.

Out of the blue, Amanda calls. I haven't spoken to her since we said goodbye at Lisabeta's farm, although we've chatted occasionally on social media.

'This might not be what you're looking for, so feel free to say no, but I'm leading a literature-in-the-community initiative with a team of my students. We've been asked to build a Story Garden at the Eden Project. They've had storytelling and theatre groups there for years, but this will create a permanent space where Cornish novels and poetry can be celebrated in an environment accessible to everyone. It's only a six-week project, but I wondered if I could tempt you down here to help me? It would be so good to hang out again and the students would love to meet you.'

It was serendipity that brought me to Villa Speranza, where I found a friend in Amanda. This is too good an opportunity to miss. And so I'm on another train today, this time heading south-west to Cornwall.

Working with my library-rebuilding cohort again appeals to me. Many times as we catalogued and shelved vintage volumes together we talked about the magic of books and how often people miss it because they don't realise they can access them. Had it not been for the customer at my parents' farm shop leaving *Jane Eyre* I might never have read it. Some of the pebbles we painted for Villa Speranza's terrace garden carried quotes from our favourite books – tiny treasures for strangers to find. The project in Cornwall sounds perfect.

When I told Mum and Dad about Amanda's project, they were thrilled.

'You have to do it,' Dad said and I could hear his broad grin as he spoke. 'We'll come down and ask you awkward questions on a tour.'

I smile as I watch the lush countryside of the West Country flood the train with colour and light. I only half-believe Dad was joking. It's the kind of thing he'd love to do, revealing to everyone around him that I was *his Phoebe*.

I wish his Phoebe believed in herself as much as her father does.

It doesn't help that my best friend doesn't agree with me taking this job. She refused to say goodbye this morning as I dragged my rucksack out of the house. I'm *not* running away, whatever Meg thinks.

She took me to task about it last night. We were both packing – she's off to Coventry for a week for her cousin's wedding and meeting up with old school friends. With our cases side by side on the sofa it began as a nice evening, talking about our plans. But I could tell she was carefully sidestepping what she really wanted to say. And then, when the cases were packed, out it came.

'It's a great opportunity. I just think you could have waited till Gabe got home.'

'Why?'

'Because it's another situation where you haven't tied the loose ends up before moving on. First Sam, now Gabe.'

I couldn't believe what I was hearing. 'That's unfair. I tried to address things with Sam. He didn't want to talk to me.'

'Once. You tried *once*, Phoebs. Then you came home and suddenly you were with Gabe, so you didn't try to contact Sam again. Which is why things didn't work with Gabe, because Sam was still *here*.' She tapped her temple with her finger.

'This isn't about Sam. Gabe was there for me when I needed him. And yes, it didn't work out, but I didn't know that was going to happen.'

'Osh and I did. Anyone could have told you that relationship was never going to work.'

That was the fuse lit. 'Well if it was so bloody obvious, thanks for telling me, *best friend*. Because it wasn't obvious to me.'

'Don't turn this on me. You're the one skipping away from relationships when you get scared, leaving all of us to clean up the mess.'

'I am not listening to this,' I said, yanking my suitcase off the sofa. 'And nobody asked you to have to deal with my *mess*, Meg. You chose to get involved.'

'You were going to leave Sam alone at the station with no explanation. What else was I going to do?'

'I would have called him. I would have tried to explain.'

'What, like you've done since you got back?'

'Get stuffed!'

'And there she goes again, scurrying away when she can't handle things.'

'*She*? Who's *she*? Tomorrow I'll be out of your hair and you won't have to bail me out again. I'm sorry I've been such a burden, Meg.'

I intended to slam my bedroom door but she had already followed me into my room. 'I have never said that, Phoebe. But do you seriously expect me to believe that if Sam had wanted to talk you would have heard what he had to say?'

A rush of icy water doused my fury then. 'If he'd given me the chance to see him again, I would have jumped at it. But he never did. If we'd been in the same room again, I would have tried to explain.'

The memory of that moment sits uncomfortably with me now. I wish Meg and I hadn't parted on bad terms. I don't know what I would say to Sam if I ever saw him again. Not that he was going to give me the chance. He drew a line under us the day I failed to meet him and I was powerless to do anything about it.

Wasn't I?

Chapter Fifty

SAM

I'm still reeling from seeing the photos of Phoebe and her actor boyfriend days later, when we're loading gear in the warm September sun into Coventry's Big Comfy Bookshop. I have to pull myself together. This gig is important.

The independent bookshop in Fargo Village is the coolest venue with an enviable reputation for hosting the best artists and bands on the folk circuit. Michael, the owner, has hinted that if he likes our set this evening he'll invite us back, possibly to feature in his famous acoustic sessions that have a huge following on YouTube. I would love that.

Several people have arrived already, enjoying cake and coffee and browsing the shelves. It doesn't bother me to have an audience as we set up our gear.

I've almost finished running mic leads when I see her.

At first, it's just one of those feelings that a person is vaguely familiar but you probably don't know them. I get that a lot, largely because I see a lot of people in my line of work. And I'm often useless with names, so chances are if I have met you I won't remember what you're called until you remind me.

But it's more than a déjà vu with this woman – because I'm quite certain there aren't many people I've encountered who look like *her*.

Blonde hair streaked with dark blue. Eyes that seem to peel away the layers of your skin until she can see your soul.

I would know her anywhere.

She waits until the end of the first set before she approaches, but my discomfort has been steadily building all evening and my eyes have kept being drawn to her, trying to gauge her emotions and decipher her motive.

'Sam,' she says, her voice betraying the slightest quiver of nerves.

'You were at the station. St Pancras. 14th June.'

She nods, the soul-stripping gaze lowered for now. 'I left the rose. For my best friend.'

'Phoebe.'

'Yes. I'm Meg.' She withdraws her hand when I don't accept it. 'I didn't know you were playing tonight. I'm visiting old university mates.' She looks over to the table where two women smile and nod back. 'Sam, Phoebe made a mistake...'

'You're telling me.'

'She missed the train and she knew you'd be waiting. But she was a mess, Sam, truly a wreck. I don't think she could have phoned you then, even if she'd been brave enough. The rose was the next best thing.'

'So, what, she asked you to buy that rose and write the label and leave it?'

She nods. 'If it helps, I was furious with her. I thought she should have followed her heart. Because she loves you, Sam.'

'Why didn't you talk to me? Tell me what the hell was happening? Because I was completely alone there. And I expected to see your friend – the woman I was in love with? Not some poxy rose and cryptic message.'

'If you still wanted to talk to her, she'd listen.' Meg apologises as Shona shoulders her way to the stage a little too firmly. 'She's devastated.'

'Now she knows how I feel. I'm sorry, I have a set to play.'

'I have a New Year event I want to book you for,' she blurts, shoving a thick, glossy business card at me.

MEG GÓRECKA

– SENIOR EVENT MANAGER

LONDINIUM EVENTS

AWARD-WINNING CORPORATE AND
MEDIA EVENT COMPANY

'Where?' I ask slowly.

'Central London location, two-day load-in, load-out. Corporate gig at New Year, so name your price and they'll go for it.'

'We're in,' Niven grins, coming in on the last part of the conversation, oblivious to the rest. 'Is your number on there, Meg? I'm Niven McNish and this is my band.'

'Right, call me on that mobile number.' Her gaze flicks to me. 'It would be good to *talk*.'

The set passes in an autopilot blur. Too much to consider, too many questions, too much emotion. I can't process it yet.

Hours later we're at the hotel and whisky is my best friend. Whisky and Shona. She's matching me drink for drink and has gradually moved from the seats across the table to perch on the arm of my chair, her body just close enough to be within touching distance of mine. She smells amazing and I can feel the heat from her skin.

When our bandmates call it quits and head for their rooms she drops into my lap, her arms finding my neck. It's too easy to meet her kiss; too easy to accept the invitation to her room.

I don't want to think about anything but finding her in the dark, giving in to the impulse that's been building since she arrived on Mull last year.

She isn't Phoebe. But she's willing to take her place.

She isn't Phoebe. But she wants me.

She isn't…

Wait.

'No,' I say, hating that I'm pushing her away. But this is no better than refusing to talk to the woman I thought I loved for a year.

'You're joking?' Shona says, struggling upright and snapping on the light. 'I want you, Sam. It's blatantly obvious you feel the same about me. So what's the problem?'

'I'm sorry,' I say, picking up my jacket and making for the door. 'I can't do this, Shona.'

'Why?'

I shake my head and slip out into the hideously striped hotel corridor, powering away from the mistake I almost made.

Because you aren't Phoebe, I reply in my mind.

I hate that I love her. But I have to be honest with myself.

And this is the right thing to do.

Chapter Fifty-One

PHOEBE

Phoebe, call Sam. Just do it. Mx

I was angry when Meg's text arrived. How dare she tell me what to do? No apology for what she said before I left London, not even a hint of remorse. But the worst of it is, I know Meg is right.

The bones of the garden at the Eden Project are in place now and the storytelling spaces are rising up from the earth. At the moment, there is little for me to do except paint pebbles with book quotes. Nothing to sufficiently occupy my mind.

Meg's text won't go away.

Sam.

Maybe I should try…

I find his entry on my phone contacts list but hesitate. What will I say? Will he even answer when he sees who's calling? I'm freefalling: only he will determine where I land.

I hit 'call'. It rings twice, connects.

'Sam?'

'Hello?'

A woman's voice. Why is a woman answering Sam's phone? I make to speak but the words vanish.

'Hello… *Hello?*'

'Sam…' I manage. 'Can I speak to Sam, please?'

'Who wants to know?'

'It's Phoebe.' When silence greets my name, I press on. 'He'll know who I am.'

'Will he?'

'Yes.'

'He's busy.'

'I think he'll want to talk to me.'

'He's setting up the stage right now.'

'Can I talk to him, please?'

'I don't think that's a good idea, hen, do you?'

'Sorry, who is this?'

'Shona,' she says. 'And Sam's busy.'

The line dies.

Shona. I don't remember him mentioning her. She's Scottish – could he have met her while he was on Mull? My breath is ragged when I inhale the September air. It doesn't matter where he met her. She answered his phone. There is only one reason she would do that: he has someone else. I'm too late.

Great timing, Phoebe.

As the weeks pass, I throw myself into the project. It's good to reconnect with Amanda again and we're just as we were at Villa Speranza. The Eden Project is an amazing place to be and it feels like an oasis in every sense. The team of students are wonderful and I've discovered I enjoy discussing my doctorate studies with them. Amanda reckons with my PhD I should consider a career in academia. I've never thought of that as an option. But if Professor Amanda thinks I have something to offer that's a considerable endorsement.

I find time to write every day, making myself go out after work and at weekends, exploring this lovely part of the world. Everywhere I go I try to capture the experience with my words – and like I first found in Paris, I'm proud of what appears on the pages of my journal. I spend weekends on the beach in Padstow and Sennen, or staying nearer home by exploring the beautiful Lost Gardens of Heligan. Amanda and I sometimes take boat trips on the Helford River, enjoying the gentler pace of life. I know this can't last, but it's a lovely time and I feel like I'm healing. Time to breathe after too long without air.

As summer draws to a close, the highlight of our calendar arrives: the Eden Arts and Music Festival – the official launch of the Storytelling Garden. It's a work in progress and there will be more to do afterwards, but the first section is ready with magical woven withy bothies and a Cornish literature trail inspired by the novels of Daphne du Maurier.

Around the festival site the team and I leave special painted story pebbles for festivalgoers to find: pictures on one side and invitations to the Story Garden on the reverse. Management loves the idea and is making a big deal of the hidden pebbles on Eden's website and media channels. While my colleagues set to work decorating and hiding stones, I sneak Giana's paint box from my rented car and paint a special pebble, hiding it in the maze of canvas tents that have sprung up behind the stage. I have to let everything with Sam go and this is my way of saying goodbye to a chapter of my life I wish had ended better. Sam's moved on. It's time I did the same.

The heavens open the weekend of the festival. After a long, dry summer it's a shock, not least to those who had planned the festival in the hope of good weather. Chaos ensues. Bands and artists turn up with equipment and do their best to unload in torrential rain, queues of vehicles backing up across the site. Pretty soon all the available roads resemble mudslides. It's all hands to the pump to get everything safely unpacked and taken into the canvas tent village for shelter. The Story Garden team and I dash to help along with everyone else at Eden, grabbing whatever box or case is shoved into our hands from the unloading vans.

The caterer's lorry is stranded by the entrance to the backstage area so we empty it first. The priority is to get the perishable food-stuffs safe and dry and then, when everyone has unloaded, all of us will attempt to push the vehicle out of the quagmire.

We're soaked and covered in mud, but it's become hilarious due to the sheer grimness of our situation.

'Non-stop glamour, this,' Amanda yells at me over the hammering of rain and the constant burr of van engines ticking over.

'I can't handle the pressure,' I laugh back, taking another box of food from the stranded caterer lorry.

As I turn to trudge through the mud, I freeze.

Sam Mullins is waiting by a hire van, jacket hood pulled up to fend off the rain. He doesn't see me. But it's unmistakably him.

Dark hair plastered to his cheeks, the beard he grew over the winter gone.

He's here.

As fast as I can, I turn and hurry back the way I've come.

Chapter Fifty-Two

SAM

We arrived at the Eden Project early for our last gig of the tour. I've been looking forward to this for weeks.

It's filthy weather and there's a huge queue of vans, cars and minibuses stranded in the quagmire of the festival site, but it feels like a celebration. Tomorrow Niven and I will drive the hire van back to London, returning our borrowed sound gear to the studio, while the rest of the band heads home. Niven is going to stay at mine for a few days, so at least it doesn't just end after this evening.

Shona is hardly talking to me. I can't blame her. She made some cryptic comment last week about the ghost of Phoebe Jones haunting me but apart from that she's just got on with the job. I'll be relieved when she goes home, to be honest. Our friendship will survive this, but distance will definitely help.

'Oi, Mullins! Stop looking pretty and grab the amps from the van!'

'Yes, sir, Mr McNish, sir!' I throw Niven a mock salute, unlock the van and start unloading. I'm dragging out a foldback speaker when a flash of vivid colour on the ground catches my attention. Sliding the speaker back into the van, I crouch down to investigate.

It's tucked under the edge of the marquee currently serving as an artist registration tent. If I hadn't glanced down I wouldn't have seen it. I reach beneath the canvas and lift it out.

It's a small pebble, its smooth surface painted with a rainbow. When I look closer, the rainbow arcs between two blue painted mountains that could be a Scottish glen, framed by a square. It could be the view from a train window passing through sunshine and shadows. But when I turn the pebble over in my palm, the artist mark almost makes me drop it:

~ Phoebe ~

No. That's a coincidence, I tell myself. It has to be. And anyway, there could be any number of Phoebes painting pebbles and dropping them for other people to find. Since my Phoebe mentioned it, I've seen countless stone-painting groups popping up on Facebook.

My Phoebe. Like she was ever mine.

'Sam, there's a tree down over the route to the stage,' Niven yells, coming out of artist registration where he's just been receiving alternate directions for navigating the festival site. 'We've got to go via the Story Garden.'

'Where?' I ask, pocketing the pebble and lifting the speaker fully out of the van.

'Follow me.'

We follow a narrow path made to look like a mountain pass and negotiate the narrow natural corridor of shrubs towards a bank of garden terraces filled with scented Alpines and herbs. Tiny white lights in the bushes do battle with the relentless rain and structures made of woven willow branches hide at each twist and turn of the path. Lovely to look at but a pain to steer very square, very heavy bits of kit around. My foot slips and hits something hard – and when I look down, I stop walking. Marking the edge of the path is line after line of painted pebbles – each about the same size but every one unique in its decoration.

And then, hurrying the other way and stopping dead when they see me – the very last person I expected to see today. She's carrying a caterer's box and is soaked with rain and mud.

Phoebe stares at me and I can't move. The person I wanted to see more than any living soul back in June – horribly late, but *here*.

'Phoebe…' I begin, not knowing which words will appear; scared I'll say the wrong thing.

But then she slowly turns and runs from me.

Chapter Fifty-Three

PHOEBE

He's here, at Eden. And now he knows I'm here, too.

I don't know how to handle this.

Added to the problems mounting today, it's taken so long to dislodge the truck that the gig has begun, so my way around the front of the stage is fenced off. To get back to my hire car there's only one option: skirt the backstage area.

The festival is in full swing, so perhaps now is the time to risk it. Sam will be busy with his band and I can dash through unnoticed. Running as fast as I can in my mud-caked, rain-drenched jeans, I hurry around the perimeter fence, my heart in my mouth. The rain has stopped at least but anyone with any sense will be in the tents and dressing areas where warm fan heaters have been blasting all afternoon.

There's nobody here. Sam isn't here.

I have almost reached the gate that leads to the staff car park when the last tent flips open. And Sam walks out. He's standing by the line of large black flight cases behind the stage, hands by his side. Waiting.

I could run. But he's seen me and I owe him an explanation. So I force myself forwards, pulling the sleeves of my crew hoodie over my hands. I feel cold, but it's not because of the weather.

'I didn't think you'd still be here,' he says. He isn't smiling.

My heart might as well have lead weights tied to it. I feel it drop to my boots. 'We all volunteered to help free the catering truck.' The thick splatters of mud are slowly drying on my jeans, but I'm suddenly embarrassed by the state of me. I must look like I've been dragged through a peat bog.

'I guess it worked, huh?'

'Hope so. I'm not intending to add, "truck rescue" to my CV any time soon.'

He doesn't laugh, or smile, or do anything that resembles the Sam I've carried in my head and my heart this year. He could be anyone tonight. I don't know him. I swallow hard, emotion gagging my throat.

'Sam, I want to explain.'

He looks away, raising a hand to rub the back of his neck. 'There's nothing to say, Phoebe.'

'Maybe. But I didn't think I'd ever see you again and now I have. So if I don't say this now, I never will. And I'll always wonder.'

Sam glances behind at the line of flight cases. 'Then let's sit down.'

At least it's an invitation.

Words twist and fly in my mind. Trying to tether them is like attempting to catch the tail of a hurricane. *I made a huge mistake. I threw away my chance to be with you…*

'I'm sorry.' The words don't even come close to what I want to say. I take a breath, try again. 'I'm *so* sorry – for abandoning you, for not being brave enough to own my mistake.'

'And not contacting me since.'

I hang my head. 'I tried…'

'Did you? When?'

Countless times. Except he doesn't have a record of the aborted calls or the abandoned text and email drafts that litter my phone. And then, when I did finally call, *Shona* answered.

'I – *wanted* to…'

'Well. Thanks.' He picks at a thread at the edge of one of the rips in his jeans where his knee juts through. 'I'd say it's the thought that counts but I wasn't looking for thoughts. I needed you.'

I needed you, too, I want to yell. But it sounds like an excuse. 'Sam – I…'

'You weren't there.'

I make myself look at him. 'I know.'

'But I was. For a long time, actually. I waited for three trains to come in. Even when I found your note.'

'I'm sorry.'

'It doesn't…' He groans and twists to face me. 'Okay, you know what? It *does* matter. It matters that in all the time we've spoken and written postcards and done every other dumb thing to keep in touch this year, you never told me you weren't going to be there. Never once.'

'Because I didn't know.'

'We said we'd be honest, Phoebe. However shitty it might have been to break the news you could have told me. You could have saved me from… *not* finding you.'

Meg had watched him. She wasn't going to tell me what she saw, but I insisted. I had to know the full extent of my mistake. She said she'd watched his heart break. He'd sat down between the statue and the glass wall, staring at my message. And he hadn't moved for a long time. That's the image that's haunted me for months.

'He looked – more than defeated. *Broken*. I've never seen anyone visibly shatter like that. Like I could see the pieces of him falling away. It was awful… I'm sorry, Phee. You asked.'

I want to tell him why I didn't get on the train and how much I regret *not* being at St Pancras on the day we were supposed to meet again. But how can I, when I still don't understand it?

'I made a mistake,' I say, watching the stillness of his eyes as he listens. 'I just – couldn't get on the train. You'd only just said you loved me. It made me wonder how strong your feelings really were, that it had taken you a year to work out what I knew immediately. I should have talked to you. I should have asked the question. But by then it was too late: I knew I'd failed. I panicked, Sam. And I've been trying to work out why ever since.'

'It's simple, isn't it? You don't love me. That's okay. It was always going to be a possibility. I had the *opportunity* to be with someone else, too. I had to make a choice.'

I stare at him. 'It wasn't because of someone else.'

'No, I think it was. I saw the photos of your big celebrity premiere, Phoebe. Peacock-blue dress, diamonds – you looked stunning, by the way. Like you were made to be on that red carpet. Gabe's a good-looking guy.'

How had he seen that? I'm ashamed that I wasn't going to tell him. Since Gabe and I broke up I haven't thought of what happened much, only that I'm glad I realised it wasn't going to work. But Sam *knows* and now I look like a liar – again. 'We got together when I came back. Briefly. But it was a mistake. We broke up just after that photo was taken, believe it or not. I didn't miss the train because of Gabe. I missed it—'

'Because of me?' His laugh is bitter, his eyes unsmiling. 'Is that supposed to make me feel better? Because it really doesn't.'

'No.' I drop my head to my hands. It's all coming out wrong

and I hate the pain I see when he looks at me. I hate that I put it there. 'I missed the train because of *me*.'

My last word carries all the air out of my lungs and for a moment I can't speak again. There isn't an echo out here in the coolness of the night, but my confession reverberates around my mind.

Sam blinks. I can't claim to know what he's thinking, but I don't think he was expecting that. I wonder if he's about to say something – there's a held breath between us and I'm not sure if I should wait for his reply. But he doesn't move.

I think he's waiting for more.

What more can I say?

'You didn't tell me about Frank…'

He swears and looks away.

'You didn't, Sam. I wanted to be there for you. Not to pry into your business, but to support you. I kept waiting for you to be ready. But every time you just pushed me further away.'

'I had stuff to work out. You have no idea.'

'No, I didn't. And that was the point.'

His voice is low and controlled when he speaks. 'I told you I'd found him.'

'The night before we were supposed to meet. But you *didn't tell* me all the rest of the time we were talking. And okay, it was your prerogative to deal with it alone, but we were supposed to be in love and heading back to start a life together.'

'So what happened, Phoebe?'

'I had been so sure – of you, of us. All year. It was set to happen exactly as we'd promised but then… Then I was too scared to get on the train. I thought I knew myself after everything I've experienced this year, but in that moment it all left me.' My hands are damp and I hug them to me so he can't see them shaking. 'I can't ask you to believe me. But it was clear in my mind: *Sam doesn't deserve someone who has doubts.*'

'Maybe you should have let me be the judge of that.' His voice is so low I can barely hear it over the hum of music from the stage. But it hits me like a kick.

'I'm sorry.'

'Yeah, you said.' Sam lifts his head back and closes his eyes. I'm scared to watch, but I have to see what I've done. 'It's just words, Phoebe. You feel bad: I get it. You weren't expecting me to rock up here today and you're embarrassed. We're both adults. We can make up our own minds.'

'I should have caught the train.' It bursts out of me and I can't halt it.

He shakes his head but I have to say it now. Even though this will be the last time I see him.

'No – just listen. I'm not saying this to change your mind. I want you to know. Every second since I missed the train, I've wished I could have been brave. Been standing by the statue when you arrived, like I'd promised. I should have been waiting for you. I should have believed you when you said you loved me, no matter when you'd said it. I should have loved you enough to not feel aggrieved when you chose to look for Frank alone. I know it changes nothing. I'm not asking for forgiveness, either. I don't want to feel better about what happened. I hate that I hurt you, Sam. But I *should* have been there—'

'Phoebe—'

I don't want to cry here, or prolong our last goodbye, so I scramble to my feet, shoving my hands into the pockets of my hoodie. 'If I had been waiting by Betjeman, I would have told you I was yours. Completely.'

'I don't think…'

'I would have told you that I wanted to be in your life, that no doubt could stop me wanting to be with you…'

'Stop. You don't have to say this…'

'Yes, I do.' My breath shudders. 'I can't get away from it. Even with the mess of Gabe and coming here, I still wanted *you*.'

The moon is passing behind clouds when I seek help from the sky, its light diffusing into a halo. I try to hold in my tears, but it's pointless. One star pulses bravely, refusing to disappear.

Say something, Sam.

Anything.

He doesn't. Just breathes out one long breath. As if he's trying to expel everything he ever held inside for me.

I've just told him I am his. If that's not enough, no other words will be.

He doesn't stand, but he will soon. I don't want to be the one watching him walk away.

'Anyway, I need to go,' I say. Emotion strangles every word. 'I'm glad I got to see you. Safe journey home.' It's all so ridiculously formal, but how else do you escape a conversation when you've offered yourself to someone who doesn't want you? In another time, had I been the person I wanted so much to be, I would be in his arms. That hurts more than not seeing him. A few steps and I could be there. But there's a line between us I can no longer cross.

The gravel of the path crunches under my boots as I walk back to my car, the first chill of the night catching me. I pull up my hood to keep the breeze out and my tears in.

Sam doesn't follow me. He doesn't call my name.

I don't look back.

Whatever I'd hoped might happen, hasn't. I'm still alone. But I *have* been brave. Now everything's out there, perhaps I can move on.

And when I sit, in tears, behind the wheel of my car in the staff car park, I realise something else.

I can't stay at Eden.

Chapter Fifty-Four

SAM

I'm yours, Sam.

No, you aren't, Phoebe.

I should have been waiting for you.

Yes, you should. But you weren't. And that was my answer. That and the note Sir John had for me. Time enough to arrange someone to get to the station, buy a rose, attach a note and leave it – but not time to call me? Even just to say goodbye?

I thought I'd put this behind me. I was so close to forgetting Phoebe Jones ever existed.

So why can't I get her voice out of my head?

I haul another speaker up the ramp to the studio's equipment lock-up. Niven passes me on his way back to the van and smiles like he knows. Probably because he does.

'Stop moping and step it up, you great soft Southerner.'

'I'm getting old, Niv. My strength isn't what it was.'

'Bollocks to that. You'll still be skipping round like a goat when I'm crumbling to dust in a care home.'

I didn't talk to anyone about seeing Phoebe at the festival as we drove back to London where the rest of band were catching their trains. Shona picked up on my mood, but I managed to evade her questions. Niven, however, knows me too well to be fobbed off.

He's like an annoying terrier biting your heel – you can tell him to sod off but he'll keep doing it until you give him what he wants. I finally told him yesterday after his questions damn near drove me to distraction.

I didn't want to talk about her. But I'm glad it was Niven who heard it.

'You didn't think you'd see her again,' he'd offered, as we'd hunched over beers in the darkened hotel bar. 'Must have been some consolation to be able to say all the stuff you wanted to?'

'I wish I hadn't seen her. It would have been easier to forget.'

'I know, man. But life has a way of crapping all over your plans.'

'Don't ever try to write fridge magnet mottos for a living. You'll starve.'

'... From which beautiful roses can grow. See?' He'd held out his hands like a court jester expecting applause and I had to laugh because Niven trying to be sincere is hilarious.

'Can you not mention roses? I've developed a dislike for them lately.'

He'd rolled his eyes at that. 'Russian things, roses – promise me you'll never get romantically entangled with a lady brewer or whisky distiller. I am *not* avoiding alcohol if it all goes tits up for you.'

'Noted.'

'Listen, mate, you think you're over her. But in my experience, it takes longer than you've had. I *saw* how you were about Phoebe. You don't love someone for an entire year and then forget her in eight weeks. It just doesn't happen like that.'

'Make me feel better, why don't you?'

'Thing is, Sam, you come alive when you talk about Phoebe. Even now when it hurts. That isn't going to go away overnight.'

I wish he hadn't said that. And I wish I didn't know he was right.

See, I've tried to be angry with her and tell myself she was never going to be there. And that we didn't have a hope. Twelve months apart was too long to really know what we wanted. I thought I was okay with that.

I just didn't expect her to be so… *beautiful*.

Covered in mud, her hair half out of its band and her face flushed from the shock of meeting me again, she was still as stunning as the day I first saw her. And that's what kills me. Because I know I'm not over this.

'Can I say something?' Niven is waiting by the equipment store.

'Be my guest.'

'Right. Tell me where to get off if you like and please, don't hit me – but I don't think you can blame Phoebe entirely for what happened.'

I can't believe I'm hearing this. 'How do you work that out?'

He sighs. 'All that time you were searching for Frank, she kept asking how you were. She offered to help.'

'She did help. I went to Edinburgh because she told me to.'

'And did you tell her that, eh? Did you say, *Phoebe, the whole reason I found my father is because of you*?'

'Yes.' I'm sure I did…

'Okay. But did you tell her what you were going through before that happened? Did you share the journey? And yes, you may roll your eyes because I sound like a life coach. But the fact remains, Sam, there was a hell of a lot you didn't tell her.'

I dig my hands in my pockets. It's exactly what Phoebe told me. I don't want to hear it, but it's not a coincidence they both said the same. 'That was my prerogative.'

'Aye, it was. Also your prerogative to tell her you loved her. Which you did – at the last possible moment.'

I glare at him, but I don't have an answer.

'Pal. Does it not strike you as odd that the instant she returns from Paris, Mr Handsome-Ass Actor is straight on the scene?'

'She wanted him.'

'Not enough to make it work.' He lowers his voice, clapping a hand on my shoulder. 'Or maybe he was in the right place at the right time to catch the fallout.'

'What are you saying?'

'Well, it's easy to look like a hero when the one she really loves doesn't let her in. I mean, all he had to do was show up and open up. Perhaps she wasn't running into his arms. Perhaps she was *pushed* there.'

That can't be right. I did tell her what was going on – once I understood it. But then I remember her expression when the video call froze. Frustration with me. Hurt. I tried to dismiss it then, but what if Niven is right? Could I have made her run to Gabe?

I slump against the equipment-store door as the realisation hits.

'There it is.' Niven's smile is scant comfort. 'Hey, you know what we need? A bit of time off. Just a couple of days to blow away the cobwebs.'

A little time somewhere else would be good. All the stuff with Phoebe has exhausted my head.

'What did you have in mind?'

Niven chuckles as we walk back to the van. 'Ah now, you just leave that to me.'

Chapter Fifty-Five

PHOEBE

Amanda understood. Her team, too. And the project was almost at an end anyway.

So why do I feel like it's another failure?

Two weeks after the festival, I slink home, avoiding eye contact with everyone in the train, in case they see me and judge me for running away. As I hide from my imagined accusers, I make a promise to myself: the next time I leave home it will be for something I really want to do.

I call Meg from the train and ask her to meet me at a bar near Victoria station. I've let things slide between us for too long and it's time to put that right.

She is red-faced when she appears and I wonder if she has run from the tube to be here. I don't even have time to say I'm sorry before she hugs me.

'I'm so glad you're back,' she rushes. 'I'm sorry for what I said.'

'Me too. It's been a mess.'

We order food and I'm aware of Meg watching me. 'How are you?' she asks when the waiter leaves us.

'I don't really know. I said what I had to, so that's something. I just have to work out where to go from here.'

'Will you stay in London?'

'Who knows? Although I can't imagine going away again yet.'

'How was Sam when you saw him?'

Reliving it is painful, but I want Meg to know what happened. 'He could hardly look at me. And he didn't try to stop me when I left.'

'Did you hope he would?'

'I hoped he might fight for me, just a little.' Like I hoped he would listen to me when I called him from Paris, or later when I returned home. I shake my head. 'I made one mistake in an entire year. One. And it was game over for him. But I was there for him that whole year. Waiting for him. Until I saw him at Eden, I think I still was.'

'And now?'

'It's over. I just want to get on with my life.'

Meg picks up a beer mat from the table and spins it between her fingers. 'Did you say everything you wanted to Sam? I mean, if you'd made a list of what you wanted to say before you saw him again, could you have crossed off every one?'

'I said all that he'd let me.'

'That's not what I asked.'

'I don't think I could have said any more.'

She holds up the mat. 'Fine, fine. It's just that you were both in shock about seeing each other and he was understandably hurt – could he have had more to say?'

'If he did he wasn't saying it.' I can tell she isn't buying my explanation, but it's all I have. 'There was just a long silence. I said goodbye and left.'

'So, he might have had more to say.'

'He didn't say anything. And he didn't stop me leaving. What else could I have done?'

I'm glad when our food arrives to break the tension. And it seems Meg is, too, although I sense she isn't finished with this.

It's good to have her back in my life, but so many other loose ends remain. I'm rudderless again, trying to work out what to do next.

Gabe is home and while we're being civil to one another, it isn't an easy place to be. Increasingly I'm finding excuses to be out of the house during the day.

Today I'm at the British Library. I became a member when I returned from Cornwall, needing a safe place to be. Books, as always, are my salvation. And it's while I'm there that I see the job advert.

It's in a newspaper somebody left in the Members' Room. I was between books and picked it up while deciding what to read next. I'm so glad I did. The job on offer is a one-year research fellowship in the oldest English Literature department in the world. Edinburgh University is undertaking a transatlantic project studying the impact of Scottish literature in the UK and USA, working with the Edinburgh Book Festival to promote Scottish writing around the world. There's also the chance to be involved with the famous literature festival itself. I would adore that.

In the little café just outside the library, I huddle in a corner and call home. Dad answers and within a minute the warmth of his enthusiasm is making me grin like a kid.

'What's the money like?'

'Not bad. I mean, it's not a fortune, certainly not by London standards, but I could make it work.'

'Would they offer you board at the university?'

'I don't think so.'

'Hang on a mo.' I hear the rustle of paper and imagine Dad

334

sitting at my brother's old pine desk which my father pilfered for his own office when Will went to university. 'Where is it?… There's so much *crap* in these drawers… You didn't hear me say that, okay?'

'Your secret swearing is safe with me.'

'Good girl. Right, here we are. Now, how serious are you about applying for this job?'

'Very. If I can make it work.'

'Excellent. I'm going to call Alan and Sandra, see if we can sort you out some accommodation. Hang tight, sweetheart.'

An hour later, Mum and Dad's friends offer me accommodation at their holiday barns and B&B an hour outside the city for a much-reduced rent. In return, I would help them with the writing weekends they host there and the general running of the holiday business. I don't mind hard work and if it means I get to do something I really love, I'd be up for the challenge.

With everything in place, I apply for the job, cross everything and wait.

Chapter Fifty-Six

SAM

It turns out Niven McNish's idea of a great weekend away is in a spa hotel near Abergavenny.

I do *not* know my friend as well as I thought...

Sitting with him in matching towelling robes beside a pool mostly populated by hen-weekend parties is hilarious, though, so maybe that's the best therapy I could have asked for. It's exactly what I need after seeing Phoebe again. I still don't know what to do with that. I'd told myself I was over her; that I didn't need to know why she never met me. But now that I have answers – and an apology, even if I don't completely believe it – I don't know how I feel. Although admittedly, it's hard to think about that when I'm beside an aqua-therapy pool wearing very little and covering what dignity I still possess with a magazine the woman on reception gave me because 'you look like you need to read'.

All the same, the sight of my friend in white spa slippers skipping off for his treatments every hour is taking some getting used to.

'What?' Niven asks, when he returns from something called a Body Buff, which is what I imagine mechanics perform on cars before they are re-sprayed.

'You are such a knob.'

He flops down on the slatted beech lounger beside me and gives a satisfied stretch. 'Aye, but it's taken your mind off *her*, hasn't it?'

It's certainly helped. 'Please tell me this place has a bar. I'm going to need alcohol after staring at you in *that* all day.'

'Are you referring to my gorgeous complimentary robe or my rather fetching budgie smugglers?' he asks with a suggestive little wiggle that garners laughter from a group of passing hens. 'Ladies, you're welcome.'

I shake my head but my smile feels good. 'It's a shocker you're still single.'

'Can't handle the McNish magic, that's the problem.' He grins back, clearly proud of himself for making me smile. 'And anyway if we'd gone for the obvious and been holed up in some cruddy caravan in the middle of nowhere getting blind drunk and maudlin, how would that have helped?'

'Good point. Thanks. I think.'

'My pleasure. I could get used to this, you know.'

'Is this what you did after Ruth left?'

He shoots me a look like I've just asked him if the pool is filled with treacle. 'Come somewhere like this on my own? How sad would that have made me look?'

I glance down at our matching towelling robes and we both laugh.

'Fair enough. No, I opted for full on maudlin. It wasn't pretty. And it didn't help.'

'I wish I'd known,' I say, something I wanted to tell him all last year but never quite managed to. 'I wish I could have been there for you. Like you've been for me with Phoebe.'

'Hey, don't sweat it. I didn't tell anyone for a long time. Not even Kate, and she's like the bloody mafia for finding out stuff like that. I think…' He stares out across the blue and purple spotlit pool. 'I just needed to sort my head out first, you know? Just me and the crap. So much of Ruth and me was lived out in full view of everyone – well, you know the Island. You fart in Dervaig and people on the Ross know about it by teatime. I just couldn't deal with that straight away.'

That makes sense. It was a little like that when Laura and I split. Not because London is like Mull for gossip, but the music scene is similar. Everyone knows everyone else. I remember not wanting to leave Syd's flat because it felt like the moment I set foot outside I'd see someone who knew, someone I'd have to pick over the details of it with. It was too much.

Later, we are nursing beers after dinner in the surprisingly well-stocked bar and are, unsurprisingly, the only men here. If there are other guys they are all hiding in their rooms, which is understand-able. We've had to run the gauntlet of drunken hens although they're harmless really. All happy enough and having fun with their celebrations.

'Are you ready to go back to teaching now the tour's over?' I ask.

Niven exhales a long breath. 'Yeah. For the time being. But I've loved this, Sam. I'd all but given up on the dream of being a gigging musician. It's made me wonder what else I could do.'

'Could you do supply teaching, maybe? Fit it in around the gig work?'

'There's not much call for supply teachers on Mull, not enough to make it regularly viable at any rate. Which means I'd be looking at the mainland and then you have to factor in ferry crossings, accommodation and the rest. I just don't think that would work, not if I stay living where I am. Might look to doing some recording, though. I've added some great kit to my home studio. With everything digitised these days you can work remotely from pretty much anywhere. I need to think about it. Figure out what I really want.' He narrows his eyes at me. 'As do you.'

Smooth move, McNish.

'I'm going back to the studio,' I say. 'There's more than enough work there. And we have the corporate gig on New Year's Eve that will give me a fair chunk of cash to see me over the winter.'

He sniffs. 'I'm not talking about that.'

The muscles across my back tense. I wasn't paying enough attention to see that ambush coming. 'We said all we had to.'

'Yeah, I don't think you did. I mean you heard her say sorry, which you needed to hear. And you saw her again, which you wanted to do. But it isn't over, Sam.' He pokes his chest with his finger. 'In here.'

'Right, so what do I do, hmm? Meet up with her again? Go over all the same ground?'

'You might learn something if you did.'

I shake my head and down the rest of my beer. 'And on that note, I'm off to bed.'

'No – dude – just hang on. I meant she still cares about you. Otherwise why would she still be beating herself up about missing the train?'

'I don't think…'

But he's like a dog with a slipper and isn't letting up yet. 'And what about the woman we met at the bookshop gig, eh? Phoebe's friend.'

'Meg.'

'Yeah, Meg. She told you how gutted the girl was. I suppose she was lying, too?'

I don't want to be challenged on this. Of course Meg had no need to lie – she could have attended that gig and never tried to speak to me. And it's her we have to thank for the New Year's gig. Her events company, that is. And yes, maybe part of me wants to believe that Phoebe and I could have another chance, but the way it went at the Eden gig gave me no hope. I was defensive and both of us were unprepared to meet there, but we didn't have a great reunion or declare undying love. A door slammed when Phoebe wasn't by the Betjeman statue in June.

'Niven, just leave it, yeah? I don't have any answers.'

He rolls his eyes. 'Fine. Burn your bridges. But next round of beers is on you and tomorrow you're having one of those Swedish massages. Maybe the therapist can pummel some sense into you.'

I grin at him as I head to the bar but I'm annoyed. I spoke to Phoebe. I heard what she said. And it made no difference. What more could I have done?

Chapter Fifty-Seven

PHOEBE

'A weekend away?' Meg glances at Osh as they watch me from the sofa.

I'm packing my overnight bag in the living room, pretending that the letter inviting me for an interview at Edinburgh University isn't folded up in the pocket of my holdall.

I'm nervous and excited and I swear they can see my hands shaking. I didn't think I'd hear back so soon, let alone get an interview. I printed my CV yesterday while they were all out, feeling like I was engaging in illegal espionage.

'Bit sudden, isn't it?'

'I just fancied a change of scene,' I say, careful not to meet Osh's stare. 'It's only a weekend.'

'Where are you going?'

'Lake District.' I could just tell them the truth but the moment I say Edinburgh they'll think this is about Sam. This is absolutely not about Sam.

'Send us a postcard,' Meg says.

'No point, it's only a weekend, right, Phee?'

'Exactly.' I give Osh a hug,

'You off, Phoebs?' Gabe appears in the doorway, an expensive suitcase beside him. He's going to LA to start work on a new film and will be there for the next three months. It feels wrong to admit, but it will be a relief when he's gone.

'Just leaving now.'

'Great. I'll walk with you.'

It's only when we've turned the corner from our street and we're walking awkwardly side by side towards the tube station that he steps in front of me and we stop.

'You're not going to the Lakes, are you?'

There's no point arguing. 'No.'

'Hm. I thought so. That would be because you're really going to…?'

'Edinburgh.'

He nods. 'For Sam?'

I groan and look up. A bright mackerel sky arcs over the city. 'No, for me. I have a job interview at the university.'

'I get it. You've got to go where the work is, Phoebs. I just hope you're not leaving because of me.'

'No. This is my gig.'

'Good. So, Edinburgh,' he says, as if tasting the word for the first time. 'It's a long way from London.'

'Not as far as LA.'

'True,' he concedes. 'I take it you aren't catching a train, then?'

'No. I'm going to Heathrow.'

The beginnings of a smile dance across his lips. 'Which is, coincidentally, where I am heading.' He offers me his arm. 'Shall we?'

I think the interview went well. Certainly the Head of English was impressed with my PhD and I answered every question she asked. I don't know if I'll be successful, but even securing an interview is a significant step. And if nothing else, I've been able to enjoy this wonderful city. Edinburgh is breathtaking.

Of course, I've thought about Sam. Coming here to search for his father and finding not just Frank Mullins but a whole new family, too. He said he went because of what I'd said. I wonder if he still thinks that now?

Walking Edinburgh's streets today, I wonder if I'm crossing any steps made by Sam. It's a ridiculous thought, but he lived in the city as a child and now he has family here. What would he think if he knew where I was considering living? Would he be threatened? Or would he support the idea? Either way if I'm here he can't bump into me like he could do in London. His business is there, and his friends, so even now he has family in Edinburgh, it's unlikely he'd be tempted to move here.

If I get the job, this won't be about Sam Mullins. It will be completely mine: a new start, a new challenge and a new era. And if I don't get this job there are plenty of similar opportunities at other universities across the UK I could apply for. This one is a test. Regardless of the outcome, it feels like a success.

A fortnight later, I receive a job offer. I'm amazed and terrified and more than a little stunned. But I accept immediately. I've been treading water since I came back from Europe. It's time to change that.

Chapter Fifty-Eight

SAM

I throw myself back into work at the studio. It's nice to be in one place for a while but I'm starting to think that I might always fluctuate between wanting to stay put and needing to be out on the road. Maybe that is inherited from Frank.

For a long time I'd had him painted as a laughing cavalier – only caring about his own needs and everyone else be damned. But I think he wound up in impossible situations and ran away from the messes he created because he just didn't know how to make them right. That urge to run when stuff gets complicated is deep within me, too. But I hope I'm more aware of the devastation listening to that impulse can cause.

London begins to get colder as we head into November, its streets warmed by the Christmas lights that always bring back a sense of childish glee in me. And then December blows in and Christmas approaches.

I call Niven on Christmas Eve, even though I will be seeing him in a couple of days when he comes down for our New Year gig. I've roped in DeeDee and Kim on vocal duties, Chris is playing drums and Niven's persuaded Shona to play, too. That's going to be awkward, but my New Year's resolution is to face the problems

I've created head-on. We haven't spoken since the end of our tour in September, but I'm taking the fact she's agreed to the gig as a good sign.

'Actually, I have a bit of news,' Niven says, 'About my job.'

My instant reaction is to worry. 'What's happening?'

'Donal and me are starting a label.'

'How did that happen?'

'Donal has several bands who've paid, up front, for whole album recording sessions. And he's about to sign development deals with three more. Some big producers in London have heard some of the stuff he's engineered and one of them has put up money to invest in the label. The plan is to get a music publishing deal with one of the big names, which will then bring in more work.'

'Wow.'

'I know. Anyway, my school has been told to reduce the staff by one teacher. The Head didn't want to make anyone redundant but Julie Pritchard is starting a print business on the Island and was wanting to cut her hours. Long story short, Julie and I spoke to the Head and we're going to job-share. So, three days a week I'll be at the school, the other two plus weekends I'll be producing stuff for Donal. I'm expanding the studio at my place and turning one of the outbuildings into a live room with accommodation above it, so we can offer bands and artists the chance to record on Mull.'

'That is brilliant! You might tempt me up there.'

'I was wondering if we could do a collaboration thing with you and Chris? Might be good for all of us.'

I love that idea. More than that, I'm glad Niven has found something to get his teeth into. 'So what's your label called?'

'*GloamingSound*. Not my idea and yes, it's incredibly lame. We probably need to get whoever makes those dreadful tourist postcard monstrosities to design our logo. I reckon your man dragging his bagpipes up the middle of the mountain road would be perfect.'

'I'm betting Donal isn't shifting on the name?'

'You know Donal. It doesn't matter. Just be great to work with him. So, have you heard from Meg about the gig?'

'It's all sorted. It sounds amazing. She's put all the stuff together in an email so I'll send that over to everyone today.'

'And have you asked her about Phoebe? How she is? If she might be at the party?'

I roll my eyes, even though Niven's too far away to see it. 'We've talked about the gig.'

'But not about the love of your life who *happens* to be Meg's best friend?'

'Funnily enough, no.'

'You *dunderheid*. It's a golden opportunity to find out how the girl's doing and you just run away?'

'It's too late,' I say because I can't disagree with him, can I? Every time I've spoken to Meg the question has danced on my tongue. But I just don't think I can go there again.

'It's never too late, Sam,' Niven says.

I wish I could believe him.

Chapter Fifty-Nine

PHOEBE

'Come to the party tonight,' Meg says again.

She's standing in the doorway to my room, putting on her earrings and looping a long string of smoky glass beads around her neck. I remember so many Saturday nights like this when I moved in with her, Gabe and Osh. Meg is the only person I know who can conduct a full conversation while getting dressed and never miss a beat. She takes a pair of ballerina flats from under one arm and balances one-legged to slip them on her feet.

'I don't think so. I still have stuff to pack and…'

'It's New Year's Eve, for crying out loud! Nobody packs on New Year's Eve.'

I look around at the barely organised chaos of my room. I'm sure I didn't have this much stuff when I left for Europe. I still have three days to get everything together for my move to Edinburgh but the need to do it now is strong. And yes, I'm completely using it as an excuse.

This year began with the greatest intentions in the most beautiful place, but I don't like how it's ended. The only reason for raising a glass tonight is to wish the year good riddance.

'It's a lovely offer but I'm not in a party mood.'

She groans and strides into my room, stepping over the piles of books and clothes covering the floor. Kneeling beside me, she pulls her mobile from the pocket of her little black dress – because *of course* her event outfit must have pockets – and taps the screen.

'Right. I wasn't going to do this but you leave me no choice.' She holds the phone like a mirror and waits until a tone sounds. 'Hey. She doesn't want to go to the party.'

'Phoebe Jones missing a party? Put her on.'

Meg twists the screen towards me but I already know who will be there before I see his face.

Gabe is tanned and appears to be sitting on a golf buggy by a huge warehouse. 'Phoebs. What is wrong with you?'

Despite everything, he can still drag a smile from me. 'Hey you. How's Hollywood?'

'Amazing! Wonderful!' He rolls his eyes. 'I am surrounded by Botox and *loons*.'

'Living the dream, then?'

The twinkle in his eyes travels right the way across the Atlantic. 'Always. So, why is my gorgeous Phoebe not going to the party?'

'She needs to pack, apparently,' Meg says, leaning in so she appears in the inset box on screen.

'*Pack*? Pathetic, Phoebs. Path-et-*ic*.'

'I just don't feel like it. I wish everyone would respect that.'

I see his expression become still. 'Okay. Meggie, would you give us a mo?'

'Be my guest. Happy New Year, stud muffin.' Grinning, Meg hands the phone to me, her work clearly done. Then she heads out to attack the million-and-one things on her to-do list before her important event can take place. I'm in awe of her composure this close to the party. I'd be a wreck of nerves.

I *am* a wreck. But nerves aren't responsible.

'Okay, what's this really about?'

'I don't want to go.'

'To the party or to celebrate?'

He's got me. 'Both.'

I see him take a breath. 'Go to commemorate, then.'

'What do you mean?'

'Go to mark the year. Good and bad. You achieved so much – Europe, Eden, this new job. Mark that stuff. And the bad – the mistakes, the train, Sam,' he lowers his head, '*me...* Commemorate that it happened. Celebrate that it's over.'

'Gabe, you weren't a—'

'No. It's a mistake we both made. I'm not sorry, though, and neither should you be. It was fun – for a while – wasn't it?'

My smile feels weighed with sadness. 'For a while.'

'And we're still here, darling. We survived. Most friendships wouldn't. I wasn't ready. You're still in love with Sam.'

'I'm not...'

'*Phoebe...*' He leans closer, the Californian sun a halo-like blur around his hair. 'At least be honest with yourself. You never stopped loving the guy. Why else are you heading north?'

'Because I have a job,' I say, my indignation tempered by a heavy awareness that Gabe might be onto something. How can he still do that after everything that happened with us?

'Yeah, I know. But also because Edinburgh was a connection you felt with *him*. Him finding his father there – and doing it because of you.'

'That's not why I want to live there.'

'Maybe not. But of all the universities where you could have done that job, you chose Edinburgh. Where Sam *still has* family. Where he last needed you.' He raises a tanned hand to rub his forehead, the way he does when he feels embarrassed or vulnerable. 'Someone has to say it to you, Phoebs. And I'm too far away for you to hit me.'

And then, I understand. 'You've all been talking about this, haven't you?'

'Of course we have. Did you think we hadn't noticed? We love you, Phoebe. We want you to be happy. *I* want you to be happy.'

'Gabe, I'm so sorry we…'

'We were stepping-stones, kid. You as much for me as I was for you. I will always be proud that you were mine for that time, okay? But I'm prouder that you're my friend. And I want that beautiful, fearful, wonderful heart of yours to find what it really wants.'

Tears sting my eyes and I can't reply. I thought the damage between us was irrevocable and I've blamed myself for using him when all I'd really wanted was to be with Sam. This means everything.

'Go to the party. Celebrate. Been a hell of a year, Phoebs.'

Chapter Sixty

SAM

Niven and the others have started early. Good thing we don't have to load everything out tonight when our set ends. One advantage of huge corporate gigs like this is they are set up for two days at a time and nobody bats an eyelid if you leave all your gig gear till the morning. The last event I did like this, party stragglers were still dancing at 9 a.m. when we returned to collect our equipment.

Meg has done an amazing job. If she'd have us again for one of her events, I'd accept like a shot. Everything has been considered and having played so many gigs where you feel like an afterthought, I appreciate the effort. Not often the band gets a whole Portakabin with free chilled beer and food laid on before a gig. I've changed into my gig clothes in stinking toilets and broom cupboards more often than not. Having a pre-gig room like this is better than playing the O2.

'To Meg and her huge corporate-client expense account!' Niven declares, raising his bottle to the cheers of our bandmates.

Shona joins in but doesn't make eye contact with me. I've burned my bridges there, I think. Kate reckons she'll forgive me eventually. I'm not so sure. I don't know if I've altogether forgiven myself yet. Whatever happens, this will be our last gig together for a long time.

I'm sad that I won't get to play with Niven for the foreseeable, though. Before I went back to Mull I wouldn't have counted him as my closest friend but now I think he's equal to DeeDee and Kim. I love that man. I just hope when he returns to the school on Mull for his job-share post it will make him happy. He deserves a break. Good that Donal and he are working on projects for the fledgling label already. If anyone can make *GloamingSound* a success, they can.

When we were loading in this morning Meg took me on a tour of the facilities and something she said when she unlocked our dressing room has stayed with me.

'We're going for magical. Because magical things can happen at New Year.'

'Usually involving alcohol,' I'd returned – a lame joke that received a polite smile, but it was a shield because I felt cornered.

'*All* kinds of magic,' she'd said firmly.

Has Meg invited Phoebe to the party?

If she is here, I don't want to talk to her.

I've decided. It's for the best.

We had the chance to say all we wanted at the Eden Festival. She hasn't tried to contact me since and I haven't either, so it makes me think too much time has passed. I need to focus on *me* next year. Not chasing an adventure. Not searching for answers. Just discovering how the man I've found myself to be will move forward. I'll leave my heart out of it for a while, that's for sure. Laura, Shona, Phoebe – none of them shining successes and all of them shouldn't have happened. Until I understand my heart, I can't risk giving it to anyone else.

So I'll do the gig tonight and then I'll leave. It's good that we're returning for our gear tomorrow – there's no reason to hang around. London is still my home, but I feel the need to get away for a while.

So, in two days I'll be back in Edinburgh for a belated Hogmanay and to celebrate Barney's birthday with Ellie and Russ.

Family time.

Better late than never.

My brother calls me most weeks. He's not ready to meet Ellie yet – and he turned down my offer of visiting him when I head back north – but regular phone contact is a good start. The rest will follow when he's ready. I never understood how anyone could walk out of someone's life and not look back, until I found my father again. But now I get it. Frank couldn't be what we needed. He had too many demons of his own to fight. Cal needs time to come to terms with that.

You can only walk through a door: if the person on the other side chooses not to open it, what can you do? In the end, I think it's better to seek the open doors and accept those that stay closed. Life, I'm learning, is holding everything lightly; being prepared to let it go. You can't control how anyone else lives. You can love them, but that's the only power you have. You can't make somebody love you.

That's why I'm heading off as soon as our last set ends.

It's why I'm not holding out hope that Phoebe will be here.

And why I won't be seeking her out.

I'm closing a door.

Chapter Sixty-One

PHOEBE

I was beginning to feel a bit of a spare part in the main party space, so when Meg dashes over and tells me Osh is in the lighting control booth on the mezzanine level of the venue, I hurry to see him.

'You scrub up well,' he grins, planting a kiss on my cheek.

'Why thank you. Quite shocked you're not in jeans tonight.'

'You and me both.' He laughs as he brushes the jacket of his midnight-blue suit. 'One of my mates working the cameras asked me if I was going to a wedding later. Cheek.'

'Well, I think you look good.'

'Which is why I'm glad you're here, Phee. Welcome to my kingdom. Bit hot and stuffy but I think you'll agree the view is the best in the house.'

I've seen Meg's work before but this is a step above. Turquoise and blue lights bathe the vaulted glass space; on every table clusters of white pillar candles burn. Silver foliage entwines around each pillar and frames the giant steel staircase leading to the mezzanine. It's as if the entire room has been transported beneath the clearest waters of the Indian Ocean and it feels as if everything ebbs and flows with a tide.

From here I can see the main stage, the spread of banquet-style tables and chairs and the three smaller stages dotted around them where magicians, dancers and acrobats will perform as the guests enjoy a five-course dinner. No matter where guests sit, they will see things happen. Everything has been tied into the theme with all the performers dressed in a similar colour palette.

'It's amazing. Meg is so good.'

'She is. I'm trying to persuade her to work for me as a production designer, but she said she likes knowing exactly when she'll be paid too much to leave. Security is for wimps, I say.'

He picks up the lighting sheet and studies it, although I know he's already spent hours programming the light and effects sequences to run to the last millisecond. The paper undulates a little in his hand.

'Relax, Osh. This is going to be brilliant.'

'Hope so. Also hope this is the last lighting gig I have to do for a while.'

'Have you heard about the commission?'

'I'll get confirmation on the sixth, but I'm optimistic. Everything's ready. We just need that little green light and that hefty cheque from Warner Bros.'

'It'll come.' I sit in the chair next to his and look at the control desk. It's a complete mystery to me – countless flashing lights, sliders and buttons, all linked to a screen filled with rainbow coloured squares. I could imagine a *Star Trek* captain sending their ship into hyperspace at a control unit like this.

Osh discards the sheet and picks up a tablet with an identical configuration on its screen to the one above the control desk. When he taps a square several sliders move by themselves on the desk and the colour in the event space morphs from turquoise blue to silver-green, a projector sending waves of pale gold light dancing across the room like sunlight viewed beneath the ocean.

A rush of emotion takes me by surprise. Osh catches sight of my reaction from the corner of his eye and smiles.

Magic.

'Cool, huh?'

'It's beautiful.'

'That feeling? The one you have right now? That's why I do what I do. For *those* moments. It's smoke and mirrors and I know how it all works. But the moment you see the effect, *that's* the magic.' He gives a self-conscious smile. 'Sorry.'

I reach over and squeeze his hand. 'I'm so proud of you.'

'Ugh, give over. You sound like my mum. But thank you.' A light flashes on the tablet and the large screen, drawing his attention back to the desk. 'Hang on, I just have to sort this. Do you have your mobile on you?'

'Yes.'

'Would you be okay to stay here and move things if I call you? Won't be long – I don't want to keep you from the party.'

Right now the opportunity to be present at the party without actually being *in* it is very appealing. 'No problem.'

He beams at me. 'Great. You're a star!'

When he dashes out I allow myself to relax. This might just be the perfect solution. All my friends think I'm at the party, so they won't bug me. I've done enough adventuring this year. Tonight I'm happy to be an observer of other people's stories.

I've thought a lot about what Gabe said earlier. Have I accepted the Edinburgh job because of the link with Sam? Why *did* I choose Edinburgh?

The job, for sure, but I saw similar roles at Cardiff, Warwick and the University of Gloucester in Cheltenham. I can't in all honesty claim to have considered any of those.

Maybe it was because of the way Sam always talked about Scotland. Edinburgh helped make him who he is. He discovered music there and a man who looked out for him like his own father should have done. It isn't Mull. But it might be close enough to visit if I ever decided to go. I fell in love with the Island through Sam's eyes.

Gabe's right, isn't he?

I'm going to Edinburgh because the heart of the man I fell in love with beats there.

Why couldn't I see my choice for what it was?

I look down over the fast-filling room, its beautifully dressed guests bathed in sea-coloured light. And I remember Sam's descriptions of silver-sand beaches, of the ocean that changes every hour, of vast sweeping hills and mountains, and the shock of *machair* peppering the moorlands. Colour and drama and *life*. More than I've ever found in London. And suddenly, he is everywhere – in my memories, in this place, in my future that calls me into next year and beyond.

I can't escape him, even though I wanted to.

Sam Mullins is as much a part of me now as he was last New Year's Eve. And I have no idea how to move on.

My phone rings and as I answer I see Osh wave from the stage.

'Hey, can you find the third set of sliders from the left? There should be a bit of blue tape on the desk beneath them.'

'Got them.'

'Great. Move the middle two in that set up to the next mark.'

I do as he says and a warm golden light floods the front of the stage.

'Perfect. You're hired. On my way back up, dude.'

I smile and stand up to look at the new wash of light.

And that's when I see the tall figure moving across the stage, violin in hand.

And I lose my breath.

Chapter Sixty-Two

SAM

I shouldn't be on the stage yet, but my A string was dodgy so I've restrung it. Not the best time to make a change, but it's preferable to losing the string mid-gig. Plus, I need to keep busy.

A guy in a blue velvet suit that looks like it's been nicked from a 1980s lounge singer is pacing the stage, a tablet in one hand and the other pressed to a hands-free earpiece. He backs towards me as he talks and I have to put my hand out to block him from the line of instruments behind me. At the last minute he looks over his shoulder and stops, raising the tablet as a sign of apology. I sincerely hope he's working here. The last thing I need is a stage invasion from random drunks before the gig even begins.

I watch him give a thumbs up to the glass control-booth on the mezzanine floor above us, then hop down from the stage and make his away towards the steel and glass staircase. I look up at the booth, curious to see if his co-workers have been forced into the same woeful velvet monstrosity – because I can't believe anybody would wear a suit like that out of choice. But the darkened glass just reflects the lights from the room. Even when I shield my eyes and focus harder I can only make out shadows inside it. At least our only request regarding dress code was to wear all black. Judging by that poor bloke, we got off lightly.

When I return to the dressing room my friends have been enjoying the free hospitality a little too much and have started singing. I'd better keep an eye on them or else the guests may well get a show they aren't prepared for.

'Hey, hold off the beers a bit now.'

'Aw, Sam Mullins, Party Pooper!' Niven yells.

'Whatever. Just think of how much you're being paid for this gig. If you drink too much you can kiss that goodbye.'

That works more effectively than a vat of coffee.

The first set runs like a dream. DeeDee receives a warm round of applause for her Ella Fitzgerald medley and turns back to us all wearing a look of pure shock. It hardly ever happens at events like these, especially not during the opening set. To quote Niven, the crowd aren't usually *reekin'* enough to enter into the spirit at that point but by the time the third set begins just after Big Ben's chimes (always with 'Auld Lang Syne', of course), the crowd are normally so inebriated that they'll dance to pretty much anything.

When I'm playing, I can forget everything else. This is what I know: it never lets me down or abandons me. I'm not usually one for sentimentality at New Year (usually because I'm too busy with a gig) but this one is significant. This year began with so much hope and promise but now I feel its weight dragging me down. I'm determined to mark what I have achieved, though. I've learned things about myself this year that I never expected to. Even the lessons that bruised me – Frank, Phoebe – have been important. I won't be looking to repeat that kind of lesson next year, mind. I have learned more than enough about Sam Mullins.

Tonight we're playing two sets with the DJ taking the stage in between, so we have two and a half hours to kill until our next. I suggest to the others that now might be a good time to enjoy the complimentary food rather than the beer. They head back to the dressing room yelling, 'Yes, Dad!' and I smile as I watch them go. DeeDee hangs back and when I finish checking my fiddle she's waiting for me.

'Samuel. Walk with me.'

She loops her arm through mine and we follow our designated route out of the building, skirting the catering area behind an enormous star curtain and passing stacks of boxes and flight cases on our way to the warehouse doors.

'I'm worried about you,' she says.

'Don't be. I'm good.'

'So you say. So you've *kept* saying ever since we loaded in this morning. I didn't believe you then and I don't believe you now.'

I stop walking and look at her. She's wearing that expression she always adopts when a lecture is imminent – where she manages to raise her eyebrows and frown at the same time.

'Whatever you've got to say, I don't need to hear it, Dee.'

'Babe, you do. Why didn't you ask Meg about your girl?'

It's a kick I wasn't braced for. 'Phoebe is not my girl.'

'Maybe not now but she was. No way that woman hired you out of all the bands she could've had for this gig unless she had a plan. No offence, but you don't even have an events band. I mean, we're here and we're rocking it, but this isn't what we do. We're tours and studio sessions and live sets, and if we're not doing our own stuff we're doing someone else's. We ain't weddings, New Years and Bar Mitzvahs, babe.'

I have to laugh at that. 'Okay, fair enough. Meg didn't have the chance to chat, even if I'd wanted to. I mean look at this gig – you reckon she even has time to think, keeping all this going?'

'I think that woman could do this, conduct four conversations and juggle all at once and never even break a sweat,' DeeDee grins. 'We need her as road manager on the next big tour – she'd be awesome. So nice try, Samuel.'

It's a clear night as we walk outside. A few brave stars are breaking through London's light pollution and I can see our breath. Another reason to be thankful we're packing down in the morning – trying to negotiate frosted ground with heavy cases and speakers after a long gig is never fun.

'I hope Niven's laying off the booze,' I say, keen to change the subject.

But my friend isn't done with me yet. 'Let me tell you what I think.'

'Can we just not do this now, please?'

'Too late. I'm speaking. This is what I think: you accepted this gig because you thought Meg would invite Phoebe. It was a link. You two haven't spoken since you saw her in Cornwall; you've made no attempt to talk to her since. Then you get this gig and it's the chance you wanted.'

'I haven't…' I begin, but I am silenced by the look DeeDee gives me.

'What? You haven't known what to say to her? Haven't wanted to try? Haven't been *in the same room* as her maybe? Look where we are, Sam. Look who invited you.'

'Meg just wanted a band. We're both professionals just doing our jobs.'

'So, you get here and you have the chance to at least ask about the girl, but you bottle it. Why? Because you're scared, honey.'

'Enough, okay? I love you, but you're wrong. So wrong. And anyway, Phoebe isn't here, is she?'

'How do you know? Have you looked?'

I jab a thumb over my shoulder in the direction of the venue. 'I've been kinda busy in there.'

'You ain't now.' She punches her hands on her hips. *Now* I'm in for it. 'Two hours at least to kill. Go. Walk the room. Prove she's not there.'

'And what if I just want to rest before the next set? What if the last thing I want to do is skulk around someone else's party looking for somebody I have nothing to say to any more?'

My sharp intake of breath hides the unexpected kick of pain in my chest.

DeeDee gives a loud tut and shakes her head. 'I don't want to upset you, babe. You just have to be honest with yourself. Stop running from this. Because at some point you have to listen to your heart.' She pats my chest. 'Even if your heart is a bolshie bastard.'

I watch her walk across the car park to the artist cabins that line its perimeter. And suddenly, I'm afraid.

Chapter Sixty-Three

PHOEBE

'Are you staying here all night?' Osh asks, glancing at me. 'I mean, it's cool with me but it's a lot more interesting down there.'

'I'm fine,' I say. But I'm not. I haven't been fine since Sam Mullins took to the stage. He's gone now, the band's first set over and the DJ now performing. But I'm still shaking.

He played so beautifully – the first time I've really heard him. At Eden I'd long since fled by the time he was on the stage, but tonight I couldn't move. I'm not sure my legs are ready to carry me yet. Before the rest of the band joined him – when Osh was down there and I was in the lighting booth – Sam looked directly up here. Did he see me?

My phone buzzes for the third time.

'You going to answer that?'

'It'll just be people getting their Happy New Year texts in before the networks get too busy,' I say, hoping it covers my nerves. Wishing I believed it.

It's probably Meg, trying to find me. But what if it's Sam?

'That violinist is a bit handy, isn't he?' When I stare at Osh, he's still looking out at the venue.

'Meg's told you, hasn't she?'

He pulls a face. 'Yeah. Sorry, Phee.'

'Does everyone at this party know about us?'

'Pretty sure the DJ's none the wiser. Look, you still care about him. And he accepted the gig, knowing you're Meg's friend. It's at least two hours till he has to play again. And while I love seeing you, I don't think you really want to be here.' He nods at the window. 'And there's your chance.'

I look down at the stage and see Sam, hands in pockets, looking over the heads of the dancing guests, as if he's trying to locate someone.

It isn't me, I tell myself. *He isn't looking for me.*

But my heart is slamming against my ribcage.

'Phoebe. Go down there.'

I meet his kind gaze. 'If this was in a script you'd cut it for being cheesy.'

His eyes roll. 'If this was in a script Warner Bros would have paid me already. *Go.* Before Meg comes up here and drags you out.'

I don't know what I'm doing. Or what I'll say. I think of the last time we spoke and imagine this could go the same way. But he's here. And so am I. And maybe at New Year you allow yourself to act differently. Or dare to dream of better. Even if it's just a gesture as the old year dies and another begins.

Nobody else knows this, but I painted a pebble this morning. Before Meg invited me to the party or I'd spoken to Gabe in Hollywood. I slipped out of the house just after six a.m. and headed to the little park nearby. It's only a small place, with a duck pond in the middle and a kids' playground on one side, but I've always loved the light there. In summers past it was where I'd escape with a book, dreaming of all the places I might one day visit. Places I can now say I lived in for a while.

On one side of the pond, there's a bench that is different from all the others dotted across the park. It's painted in rainbow stripes, faded now but still lovely. At weekends I see people hurrying to claim it and children running right across the park to touch its colours. It bears a plaque I think must have been in place years before it received its multi-hued makeover:

For the wanderers and the dreamers,
The weary and the worried.
Rest a while here, friend.

Unlike the other bench dedications in the park there is no name, no commemoration of a life lived. But the sentiment has always struck me. It's a tiny bit of welcome in a city whose people are used to being ignored.

That's where I left my pebble – my way of marking the year. This morning I didn't think I'd be at the party, so this was going to be my goodbye – to the year, to the city I'll soon be leaving and to the life I've known before.

I painted a scene from a photo Sam sent me of Calgary Bay on the Isle of Mull – a wild mountainside overlooking the sea, the low-lying plain between land and shore peppered with tiny dots of colour in every shade in my paint box. The *machair* Sam told me about. And in the centre of the carpet of flowers, one phrase in sweeps of silver paint:

gu bràth
Forever.

I looked it up online. I wanted to honour the language of the land that birthed Sam.

When I start to descend the stairs I look out over the party. I can't see Sam. He was by the stage a moment ago, so he must be close by. But where?

The dance floor is packed with enthusiastic bodies, drinks held aloft, jostling for space as they dance and yell at each other. Trying to move through them is like navigating a crushing, sharp-edged tide. I lose count of the elbows that jab into me, the feet stamping too close to my own. The ground shakes with an insistent beat and booms with sub-bass notes that reverberate through my body. It's dizzying, making thought difficult and movement almost impossible.

I finally emerge at the edge of the stage where I last saw him, but he isn't there. Looking out over the bobbing sea of green, silver and black-clad people I scan across for a glimpse of dark curls. For what feels like an age I search until I think I see him, over by the bar that looks like it's been carved from ice. Bracing myself, I push, squeeze and weave my way through the mass of guests until I reach the other side of the dance floor. Out of breath, I emerge into a small pocket of air between the dancers and the banqueting table.

It *is* Sam.

At that moment, he turns towards me.

My heart constricts. My breath becomes shallow. And all I can see is him.

Like it did when we kissed in the packed concourse of St Pancras station eighteen months ago, the sound around us dims. The movement and the noise, the light and the activity become secondary as my feet take me shakily to him. It's not the day we were supposed to meet again. It's not the moment we met again by chance in a Cornish late summer festival. Yet here we are.

I raise my hand.

He does the same.

Neither of us are smiling. Not yet.

We begin to close the gap between us, oblivious to the guests jostling past. I don't know what I'll say; only that this is my very last chance to tell Sam I love him. That I never stopped loving him. And to thank him for changing me – for changing how I see myself. Through his eyes I saw what I never realised I could be. I think he felt the same.

We've almost reached each other now. I can see his chest rising, his hand reaching out. My hand reaches, too. I don't care if it will end with a hug or a handshake. I just want us to touch.

And then a body steps between us. A woman. Her long blonde hair trails down her bare back, an emerald green silk dress draped around the rest of her body. I move to the side, but she isn't walking past us. She's going up to Sam.

Numb, I watch as her arms slide up around his neck and her lips close on his. His hands lift to frame her waist and… I don't want to see any more.

The noise of the party crashes back around me. The room is too hot, too loud, too short of air. I have to get out.

He wasn't looking at me. His hand wasn't reaching for mine. I am an idiot. Of course he didn't see me. I became invisible to him the moment I missed the train to London.

I hurry to the cloakroom, the assistant taking too long to find my coat. And then I throw it on, turn my back on the party and my friends and the woman in the green dress and Sam bloody Mullins.

And I run.

Chapter Sixty-Four

SAM

It was only a moment. It happened so fast. By the time I've pushed Laura away, Phoebe has gone.

I was going to tell her I love her.

'I can't do this now. I have to go.'

Laura is all coy smiles and flicking hair, her body dancing a little in green silk that is somehow managing to cling to her skin. She's working through every move that once caught my attention, confident that one of them still has power. But she's wasting her time. I'm not the man I was when we were together. I can't ever be that person again.

'Aw, Sam, don't be like that. It's New Year's Eve. One little kiss is allowed.'

'Please, just let me go.'

'Thing is, I came with a date. But he's boring the hell out of me.' The same choreographed emotion, the slight pout and downturn of the lips. Head bowed a little, eyes peering up at me. 'And then *you* took the stage. I think that's what they call *fate*, Sam.'

I look over her head. Phoebe's gone. And Laura won't move out of my way. I don't want to shove past her but if she doesn't take the hint soon... 'There's someone I have to see.'

Her hand is back on my arm, her fingernails painted bright

369

green. I hate that colour. 'So speak to them later. They'll still be here. Nobody worth bothering with leaves a New Year's party early.'

I shrug her hand off me. 'They've gone now. Cheers.'

She pops out her bottom lip in an infantile attempt to pacify me. 'Problem solved, then. Now we have time to talk.'

It's like I'm back where I started. I remember Laura's feeble attempt to get back in my life the night before I left. I didn't want her then; I sure as hell don't want her now. She's made me miss the one person I really wanted to see. Because DeeDee is right. And Niven. And Ailish. I've tried running from this, but I can't escape Phoebe.

'No, Laura, I don't want to talk to you. Ever. I need you to understand, I am not interested. I won't ever be interested. So you can take your act and go and find some other poor sap who'll fall for it. We are done.'

She laughs but tears well in her eyes. 'We will always have this, Sam. You're in love with me.'

'Not any more. I'm in love with someone else.'

But I've lost my chance to tell her.

It's almost time for our second set. The DJ is building up to playing Big Ben's chimes that he's cued up on the decks and I have to be on stage, ready to play, by the twelfth chime. There's no time to go after Phoebe.

Laura lifts her head, her tears on show for everyone close enough to see. Then she slaps her palm across my cheek, the sound so loud it summons an audience. I say nothing. As the room begins to buzz with anticipation of the New Year, I leave my ex sobbing by the bar and hurry back to the stage.

'Okay people, it's almost time. Let's have a countdown. Ten… nine… eight…'

Out of time. Out of chances...

'Seven... six...'

My cheek stings. I deserved that, but not for Laura's sake...

'Five... four... three...'

Phoebe could be anywhere now. And she thinks I have someone else...

'Two...'

I hop onto the stage to the collected glares of my friends and pick up my fiddle. *Idiot!* Stupid pride, stupid fear!

'One...'

There's no going back now.

'Happy New Year!'

The cheer makes my ears ring as the venue bursts into celebration. Confetti cannon explosions, streamers and balloons dropping from the net suspended over the dance floor, whooping and hugs and kisses, yells and tears.

Niven nods and we begin to play 'Auld Lang Syne'. But every note drops on me like another nail driven into the coffin.

It's too late. A New Year has begun. A year Phoebe won't be part of.

The set passes by in a blur. I can hardly feel my fingers on the strings. At least our audience are happy.

We take our final bows and leave the stage. As we pass through the star curtain the first crashes of dance music begin.

I wonder if she went home? Maybe I should stay till the end of the party, find Meg and ask for her help. She might be able to get Phoebe somewhere I can talk to her before I go up to see Ellie, Russ and Barney. I want to explain. I know exactly what she thought when Laura kissed me.

Bloody Laura.

I saw her as we were playing the last song, snogging the face off some guy. She'd recovered remarkably well considering how heartbroken she'd looked forty-five minutes ago. I hope the bloke thinks better of it when the hangover wears off. Poor git.

Back in the dressing room there are fresh beers and a round of bacon sandwiches from the caterers. That settles it: Meg is officially our best booker. I wonder if she brought them over while our set was coming to an end. Is she anywhere near?

'Well, personally I reckon we rocked,' Niven says, swaying a little. I'd better make sure I get him in a cab soon. He's on the sofa bed at DeeDee and Kim's tonight then catching the train back up to Oban tomorrow.

'We did,' I smile. 'Great to gig with you.'

The rounds of New Year hugs ensue until Niven swipes a fresh bottle from the cooler, holding it high. 'A toast!'

Kim rolls her eyes and Chris chuckles.

'Not another one, dude. We need to get you back.'

'Ach, away with you, Mullins! It's New Year. Lighten up!'

Outnumbered I open a bottle too and we toast a great gig. Then Chris and Niven sneak back to the stage to pack down what they can, and I pack my fiddle away, my heart heavy despite the party raging around me.

'Will you be okay getting Niven back?' I ask DeeDee, who is pulling jeans on under her black sequinned gig dress. 'I'm worried he might wander into the city and get himself lost.'

'Leave him to me. You're welcome to crash at ours too, if you like? We're closer than your place.'

I should wait for Meg.

But I'll still see her in the morning when we come to load our gear out. With a little sleep I might know what to say to her – and she might be in a better place to hear it. Meg is my last link to Phoebe. I need to get her on my side. I owe it to myself to do it at the best time.

'Cheers, Dee. But I need my own bed tonight.'

'Old man! Go on, go home to your Horlicks and your pipe and slippers, eh? Leave us kids partying.' She gives me a kiss on my bruised cheek, then apologises when I wince.

I grab my things and head out – just as the Goo Goo Dolls' 'Iris' booms back from the venue.

Her song.

I remember Phoebe's surprise when she received the video of me and Niven playing it, the joy in her smile in the photo she sent me of the moment I surprised her. I'll talk to Meg in the morning, when I've worked out how to ask for her help.

But now I need to get home.

Chapter Sixty-Five

PHOEBE

I run until my feet hurt. Then I walk.

The streets aren't empty because London never is. Every bar and restaurant is packed. We must be getting close to midnight, judging by the level of expectation that radiates from every place I pass.

I couldn't have stayed there. Not knowing Sam has somebody for the coming year and seeing him on stage with everyone celebrating. I don't feel like I'm on the cusp of a new beginning. I feel like I'm commemorating a death.

When I'm in my new home, with my new job, things will be brighter. Maybe even in a few hours when the year has turned and I can breathe again, it won't all look so bad. But in the dying moments of this year, it's okay to feel sad. I don't need anyone's permission and I won't be spoiling the moment for anybody around me. I just need to acknowledge how I feel.

Mark it, Giana would say. I had an email from her yesterday, wishing me a bright new year. And I think her approach to everything is what inspired me the most on my European adventure. Acknowledge everything you think and feel because then fear can't squeeze in. If you believe being angry or scared or hurt is something to hide, you give fear the right to own it, to remind you of it when you're trying to move forward. I'm sad now – devastated, actually

– but that's okay. I'll learn something from this if I acknowledge that's how I feel.

For the next few hours, when the only person to notice is me, I'm going to be sad that I missed Sam: sad that we had chances to move forward that we didn't take; sad that we didn't get to talk this evening. There is so much else I can celebrate about the time he was part of my life, so it isn't the defeat it might have been. All the same, once this moment is over, I'll be glad to leave for my new life.

A yell from an open doorway makes me turn and I see a crowd of people on their feet, looking towards a TV over the bar. The camera is zooming in on the famous clock. One bloke raises his hand and the people yell a countdown.

'Ten… nine… eight…'

Sam will be on stage now.

'Seven… six…'

The band will be standing in their positions, too.

'Five… four… three…'

Up in his lighting booth, Osh will be ready to tap the switch that releases streamers and balloons over the partygoers and fires three huge confetti cannons from the edges of the stage.

'Two…'

I couldn't have stayed at the party. To be so close to Sam knowing we couldn't be together would rip me to shreds.

'One…'

I hurry away, not wanting to see the moment the year turns. But all around me the sound of cheers and 'Happy New Year's and the crack and thud of distant fireworks fill the air.

It's over. The year is done. And I'm completely alone.

*

It must have rained while we were in the party. Puddles pepper the dark pavement and roads, the late-night lights dancing in them as I pass. It's beautiful. I am going to miss this city. Just when you think you know everything about London, it surprises you. Part of my heart will always be here.

Happy New Year.

I think it will be.

Now *that moment* is over, it's better. Before Big Ben's chimes I couldn't see anything but what was passing, but now that's just part of history.

I could go straight home, but it's nice out tonight. There's only a hint of chill in the air. I'll have a better chance of being positive while I'm walking, too; ruminating in a cab or on a night bus won't do me any good. This is okay – this walk can be my goodbye to London. One last night spent hanging out with an old friend I love.

I've just let myself wander, like I did in Paris, Florence and Rome, so it's not until I look up that I suddenly realise where I am.

No.

I didn't even think I was anywhere near here.

I gaze up at the red brick magnificence of the St Pancras Renaissance Hotel. Light glows from its windows, the damp January air making it look like each one has been smudged around the edges. It's still a magical building. It still means something to me.

There's one place that was part of my adventure I haven't returned to: one friend I've yet to see again. I avoided him when I came back from Paris. I haven't dared visit since. But as tonight is supposed to be my goodbye walk in London, this feels like the right time.

I climb the stone steps from the street, remembering the butterflies I'd battled when I came to the station eighteen months ago.

Back on that morning the staircase and the building rising from it were washed in the first, brave, pink-gold light of dawn. Everything sparkled. And despite my nerves, I was excited. I'd *made it* – I hadn't given in to the fear that might have cancelled my trip. I'd walked through the arched entrance into the station, reaching the giant statue of the lovers first, skirting their feet and heading for the Eurostar entrance with its champagne bar, where the barman was already setting up. On my way, I must have passed the Betjeman statue, but my head had been filled with a rush of plans, questions, expectations and contingencies so I don't remember seeing him. Not until the delay – and the crowd – and the dark-haired man with the smile in his eyes, who met me by the unassuming iron statue.

It's a very different place now – too early for the dawn, the first day of the brand-new year barely an hour old. The orange flood-lights on the fairy-tale building give it an otherworldly glow, casting deep shadows across the steps as I climb. And yet its familiar face welcomes me, as it must have countless weary travellers over the years.

Rest a while here, friend.

The rainbow bench dedication returns to my mind as I reach the top step, gazing up at the building that rises reassuringly tall above me. I imagine its carved arches and square tower reaching out to receive me. I've avoided even passing this place but now I'm not scared of the weight it will lay on my heart. I'm just saying hello to another old London friend. One that shared a moment in my life I will never forget.

Because that's the thing, isn't it? What happened here on 14th June 2017 was a lovely serendipity. At the point when I'd been so terrified of losing the adventure I'd set my heart on, I met a friend. A wonderful friend. More than a friend – a man who decided, having known me for hardly any time, that I was the love of his life.

Sam didn't see all the frustrations I've wrung my hands over, the countless times I feel I've fallen short. He didn't see the physical attributes I wish were different, or the parts of my character I'm not proud of. He just saw *me*. And I was enough to make him fall in love.

Even Gabe can't say that. I don't think he even believes in love at first sight. I didn't think I did, until Sam Mullins grinned around the shoulder of a kind-faced iron gentleman in St Pancras station – and my world changed.

I don't think I'll ever experience that again.

What happened here was magical. Having Sam in my life for a year was even more so. Regardless of how it ended, it will always be ours. That part of him will always be mine. I should celebrate that.

And maybe, believe I was worthy of his belief in me.

I *am* enough. No matter what anyone thinks. It's taken too long for me to understand that, but I'm going to let it guide me from now on. I'm going to trust my heart.

I take one last look at the building's grand façade and turn to walk down the pillared walkway through into the station.

There's someone I have to see.

Chapter Sixty-Six

SAM

There are no cabs. And I've drunk too much to take the van. I'm stuck.

I glance back at the venue and briefly consider going in again. But if I do that I'll end up trapped, facing conversations I don't want to have. I'm tired and I need to rest so I can think clearly tomorrow.

Stuff it. I'll just walk and hope I can hail a taxi on the way.

It's a decent night, at least. Last year on Mull the snow fell so thickly while we were playing the Hogmanay ceilidh that we all ended up sleeping in the bar, with blankets and pillows. That seems like an age away now. I smile when I remember it, and decide I'll call Ailish tomorrow. Perhaps I'll make it a tradition to visit her and Niven at New Year. Maybe I can persuade Donal, Kate and the kids to join us, or we'll meet somewhere in the middle. And with Barney's birthday so close to Hogmanay, I can come home via Ellie's, doing my uncle bit. I'm going to like being an uncle. And having a sister.

It's a good night for a walk. Not too cold, with a fine mist that's a pleasant balm against my skin. I drank more than I'd planned and the fresh air is a medicinal boost. Hopefully it'll mean I've a clearer head in the morning.

Would Phoebe see me again? She'd be completely within her

rights to refuse. I was a git. Twice. I can see that now, months too late. I mean, she called me on the day she missed the train – admittedly far later than I thought we'd be speaking – but she didn't hide away from what had happened. I didn't understand then because I was angry and hurt and I felt like I'd been lied to. All of which were legitimate. I'm still not completely sure I understand, but if she panicked and realised too late that she couldn't go back, what choice did she have? Even if she'd braved a later train, I might have been long gone and still not willing to listen.

What would I have done in her situation? Would I have called immediately, tried to own my mistake? I know the answer to that, and it isn't pretty. I would have run away, like I've spent most of my life doing.

Too late, I see a black cab speed past me. Damn it. *Keep your eyes on the road, Sam.* Next one I see, I'll make sure I flag it down. I have no intention of walking all the way home.

Why am I only thinking about Phoebe's side now?

Perhaps enough time has passed for me to stand back and see it. Or perhaps it's because the tables have been turned tonight. Phoebe believes I don't care about her because she thinks she saw me choosing Laura instead. And I didn't go after her, knowing my mistake, knowing how hurt she'd be. The band could have played *Auld Lang Syne* without me. I had enough time to find her. But I panicked. Like *she'd* panicked last year. It's a total mess.

A large group of very happy revellers cheer as they approach me. 'Give us a tune, mate!' one of them yells, raising a two-thirds-empty bottle of Jack Daniels.

'"Amarillo"!' another shouts.

'You can't play "Amarillo" on a violin!' their friend chimes in but it's too late. The group are already singing it at the top of their lungs and they continue happily until they are out of sight.

Who said there was no joy left in this world?

I like that people are happy – even if it's only on a drunken night out they won't remember most of in the morning. It's too easy to think the world is ending and everyone is angry. There's a lot to be scared about, but more *not* to. It's where you decide to look, I think. Being on Mull reminded me of that. People just get on with their lives there, so I did the same. And there was more to enjoy and experience than obsess over.

Since I came back all I've done is be angry. Picking at it over and over again so it keeps bleeding. That's not me.

So if – *if* – I get to see Phoebe again, I'm going to apologise for not appreciating her bravery in calling me the day we were supposed to meet.

And if she won't see me?

I stop walking.

If she won't see me, I'll be better. I won't make that mistake again.

'Excuse me,' a woman says, stepping out in front of me.

Crap, she's seen the cab before I have. Where did she come from, anyway? The street was deserted a moment ago.

I must have said something out loud because she turns to face me, arm still outstretched.

'I'm sorry, were you wanting a taxi?'

'I was. But I wasn't fast enough. Next time, eh?'

The black cab swings to a halt beside us, the driver lowering the passenger side window.

'Evening. Where to?'

The woman gives me a brief smile. 'Would you like to share? I wouldn't normally offer but it's New Year and these things are like gold dust. I've walked a mile already to find this one.'

See? Life can still surprise you. One less thing to be angry about. 'Would you mind? That would be great.'

She beams. 'Fantastic. Where are you going?'

I lean in and give the driver my address, then climb into the cab.

'Thank you,' I remember to say, when I am in my seat.

'My pleasure.' She turns to the driver. 'And St Pancras Renaissance Hotel for me, please.'

All around me, the city swims.

Chapter Sixty-Seven

PHOEBE

I'm the only person here.

But it doesn't matter.

I've just come to mark the moment with an old friend.

He's still gazing up. His trilby is still tilted on his head, the breeze from the platform still billowing out the hem of his mackintosh. Of course he hasn't changed. But in the early hours of a new year, it's comforting. It would be easy to think everything is different. Perhaps I should notice what's remained.

My friends. My love of books. Mum and Dad.

And London – even though the city is constantly on the move. In my heart it will always be home.

It isn't the day I said I'd be here. But now that I'm standing by Sir John, I have the strongest feeling it's the day I was *meant* to be here. If he knows, he isn't saying. I wonder how many other secrets he's tucked away beneath that trilby.

It's done. I've finally come full circle on my Grand Adventure. I could never have guessed how it would pan out or what I would experience.

How do I feel now it's ended?

I touch the nook between Sir John's neck and shoulder, where Meg hid the rose for Sam when I couldn't be there.

Gratitude. That's the overriding emotion. Even though there are moments and actions and decisions I might want to change, I'm grateful I had the chance to experience them at all. In the end, maybe that's all that's important.

I wasn't here for Sam that day. But I didn't leave him completely alone. Meg was here, and my message. If I'd never cared about him, I wouldn't have given a second's thought to what he was going to find by the statue. I did what I could where I was. That's all I can ever do.

I'm still sad that we didn't make it. I have to acknowledge that so it isn't a shadow hanging over the next part of my life. Being in a different city will help – lots of new things to demand my attention. But I won't ever wish it hadn't happened.

'Thank you, sir,' I say to the statue in the empty station. I don't care that I'm talking to an inanimate object. I'm pretty sure I'm not the only person to sneak a chat with the great man. He's just a modest public artwork in a place that belongs to everybody – but Betjeman's statue is now part of my life. We've shared a unique moment in time. That's a beautiful thing. I stroke his cool face, surprised by a sudden welling of tears. 'I'm sorry you got caught up in it. But thanks for passing the message on.'

'I don't think he minds.'

I close my eyes. The memory of Sam's voice is so vivid, so real, that it shocks me. It's warm and close and I can hear that smile of his dancing through each word. He had a wonderful voice. I still remember the thrill of hearing it, hundreds of miles from home; how it seemed to resonate deep in my soul. Like I'd known it for a lifetime already.

'I hear he's good at meeting people.'

No, that's wrong. That isn't what Sam said. Am I forgetting him already?

'Even people who make total idiots of themselves.'

Light floods back in to my eyes. And there he is.

'I was just saying goodbye,' I manage – not the words I expected to say.

'To Sir John or me?'

Looking at Sam feels like the biggest step of faith. 'Both.'

'Why?'

'I have a new job. New home, too. I leave in two days.'

'Oh. Congratulations.'

'In Edinburgh,' I rush, because if I don't say it all now there won't be another opportunity. 'And I know you have somebody else now but I wanted to tell you that I think I chose Edinburgh because it would remind me of you. Of what you've meant to me.'

'Phoebe, it's not—'

'And I think that, finally, I'm doing this because it's what I want to do. I have you to thank for that. For believing in me, in the beginning. And keeping that faith in me all the time I was away.'

Holding my nerve is a battle. *Sam is here.* How could he possibly have known this is where I would be? He's here and he's looking like he doesn't know whether to laugh or run away.

'You left me a rose.'

'I know, and it was nowhere near enough. But it was all I could do.'

'No, listen. I understand. I didn't for a long time – until tonight, in fact. I thought you abandoned me, but you didn't. You left the rose and then later you spoke to me. You didn't run away, Phoebe: I did.'

'I wasn't there…'

'And I hadn't been there for you while I was looking for Frank. I am so sorry I didn't let you in.'

'Finding him was important to you.'

'It is – it was – but it would have been far easier if I'd had somebody to share it with. I didn't see the mistake until Niven pointed it out. I never meant to hurt you.'

'The last thing I wanted was to hurt you. I didn't think I'd see you again.'

'Me either. But here we are.' His brow creases. 'Sorry, did you say you're going to Edinburgh?'

'Yes.'

'Where?'

'At the university. That's where I'll be working.'

'In *Edinburgh*?'

'Yes.' How many times do I have to say it?

And then he laughs, his head thrown back and the sound filling the empty concourse. It's unexpected and beautiful and a precious gift I've been lost without.

'You're going to Edinburgh because of me and I'm staying in London because of *you*.' He shakes his head. 'What is it with us and trains in opposite directions?'

Is he laughing at me? Or should I get the joke? Either way I'm confused. I don't know why Sam's here or what I'm supposed to say to him and we're the only two people in the station with an old iron statue between us. I have no script for this. My words are useless.

Sam's smile softens. 'I love you.'

Why say that? When he's not free and I'm going to live four hundred miles from him? 'I don't think…'

'I love you. I wish I didn't – that is, I wished I didn't until right now. But we met here by chance *again* tonight. I'm not big on the whole destiny thing, but even I can see that's one hell of a coincidence.'

'I love you, too. But you have someone else…'

'No, I don't. That's what I wanted to tell you earlier, at the party. That's my ex – Laura. I told you about her. And ten minutes after she kissed me she slapped my face in front of the whole room and then found a complete stranger to snog. So no, I don't have anyone else.'

Tonight feels endless. It was supposed to be my goodbye to London, to everything Sam had meant to me. 'I don't know what to say.'

'Me either.' He pats the Betjeman statue. 'Look at us, eh Johnny? What have you done to us?'

I still can't tell what Sam is thinking. His words whirl round me like the curling script carved in stone around the statue's feet. High in the iron-and-glass roof, there's a sudden beating of wings.

'I'm going, too. To Edinburgh. Tomorrow, actually. I'm spending a few days with Ellie and my nephew. So, I don't know, if you were free to meet…? Maybe we could find a coffee shop, or a bar or a random statue on a train platform?'

That smile could end any argument, I think.

'I'd like that.'

'So would I.' He moves from Betjeman's side, less than a step away from me. 'There are a million and one things I want to ask you. To say to you. But I don't even know where to begin.'

There are times in life when you should step back, consider and be level-headed before making a decision. And then there are moments when you just need to believe your heart has everything covered.

I reach out and flatten my hand against Sam's chest, feeling his heartbeat beneath my palm, as strong and sure as I remember. Has it really been beating for me all this time? In spite of everything?

My breath stalls. I dare to look into his eyes again.

'Then let's begin here.'

This time, Sam kisses me first.

Questions wait, our lives meet again. The meeting is what matters; we'll work out the rest when we leave St Pancras. For now, we are just Phoebe Jones and Sam Mullins, two wandering souls reunited by the Betjeman statue, where so many travellers have met before.

And anything can happen on our next journey.

Sir John keeps his attention on the arcing glass roof, his bag of books in his hand and his coat whipped up by the wind of an unseen passing train. One shoelace is untied, his collar unbuttoned, too. But he doesn't mind. His work here is done.

Acknowledgements

Lovely reader, welcome to my tenth novel.

Ten years. Blimey!

I am so proud that my dream continues, ten years after my very first novel flew out into the world. I have *you* to thank for it, first and foremost. Thank you for reading my books and coming back for more. You make this dream happen.

Huge thanks to my lovely new publisher HQ – and the phenomenal team who have welcomed me so warmly and whooped and cheered *The Day We Meet Again* onto the page. My brilliant editor, Manpreet Grewal, who is, quite simply, awesome; Cara Chimirri, Lily Capewell, and Lisa Milton and Kate Mills, for their faith in me. Thanks also to Jon Appleton for wise copy edits and Sara Kinsella.

Thank you to my agent, Hannah Ferguson, for her continuing faith in me and for finding Phoebe and Sam their perfect home.

I've sneaked some lovelies into this story:

Amanda Moran appears as Dr Amanda, Phoebe's friend in Italy.

Michael McEntee and his fabulous Big Comfy Bookshop in Coventry appears as himself! Osh and his film crew are inspired by Teddy Powell and his production company Weekend.

Thank you to #TeamSparkly for being superstars and my brilliant supporters on Twitter, Instagram and Facebook, for your excitement and brilliant suggestions in my annual #getinvolved challenges. Special thanks to @lizwm for suggesting the painted pebbles which became so important to the story; to Nina Pottell aka @Matineegirl for suggesting the snowglobe for Phoebe; and to @michellejenkinstropic for suggesting the flat cap.

Huge love to my writer friends who have cheered, consoled, provided giggles and spurred me on: Louise Beech, Cathy Bramley, Jo Quinn, Julie Cohen, Rowan Coleman, Kim Curran, Liz Fenwick, Kate Harrison, Fionnuala Kearney, Rachael Lucas, Tamsyn Murray, A.G. Smith, Cally Taylor and the ace Dreamers. Thanks to my family and the Peppermint Massive, too.

And last but never least, my gorgeous Bob and fantastic Flo. You rock! xx

This book is about taking chances, celebrating everything and allowing life to surprise you. I hope it inspires *grandes aventures* of your own!

Miranda xx

A few things that inspired Miranda when writing *The Day We Meet Again*

Sam's Journey

If you've loved discovering Mull, Edinburgh and Port Glasgow with Sam, here are some links for further adventures:

www.visitmullandiona.co.uk
www.visitscotland.com
www.edinburgh.org
www.peoplemakeglasgow.com

Phoebe's Journey

When researching Phoebe's journey I found the Travel Guide vlogs by Samuel and Audrey about Paris, Rome and Florence really helpful. Check out their YouTube channel and their blog at **www.backpacking-travel-blog.com**

These websites are also great for planning your own visit:

www.roughguides.com
www.ee.france.fr
www.en.parisinfo.com
www.italia.it
www.lonelyplanet.com/italy

The Books that Inspired Phoebe
A Room with a View by E. M. Forster (1908)
A Tramp Abroad by Mark Twain (1880)
Italian Journey 1786-1788 by Johann Wolfgang Von Goethe (1816-17)

Frankenstein (*The Modern Prometheus*) by Mary Shelley (1816) – the story goes that Mary Shelley created her famous novel to win a bet while on a grand tour across Europe with Percy Shelley and Lord Byron!

The Music that Inspired Sam
Sam's musical journey to Mull was inspired by the wonderful Scottish and Irish folk music produced by a host of musicians, including: Julie Fowlis, Aly Bain, Phil Cunningham, Kris Drever, John McCusker, Heidi Talbot, Ross & Ali, Duncan Lyall, LAU, the cast of the Transatlantic Sessions (including Jerry Douglas and John Doyle), Cara Dillon, Michael McGoldrick, Eddi Reader, Donald Shaw, Karen Matheson and RANT.
Thank you to these fabulous musicians for the huge inspiration they have given me and for shaping Sam's journey back to his roots.

The Day We Meet Again Playlist

This is the music I listened to while writing Phoebe and Sam's story:

- 'The Beast' – Duncan Lyall – (*Infinite Reflections*)
- 'With Fingers Entwined' – Rael Jones – (*Emotional Cinema*)
- 'Back In The Water' – HAEVN – (*Eyes Closed*)
- 'All We Do' – Oh Wonder – (*Oh Wonder*)
- 'The Right Track' – Mary Bragg – (*Violets as Camouflage*)
- 'Place from Where I Fell' – Elenowen – (*For the Taking*)
- 'Someone You Loved' – Lewis Capaldi – (*Breach* – EP)
- 'I Don't Want to Know' – Sigrid – (*Raw* – EP)
- 'Wonderful' – Gary Go – (*Wonderful* – EP)
- 'Running Home' – Reuben Halsey feat. Miranda Dickinson – (*Eucalyptus Tree*)

ONE PLACE. MANY STORIES

Bold, innovative and
empowering publishing.

FOLLOW US ON:

@HQStories